Alan Jones read English and French at university, going on to complete a Masters and a Doctorate in Education. He has extensive experience of teaching creative writing and literature. He is also an enthusiastic jazz drummer. He lives in Canterbury and is married to that precious thing, a Librarian.

Also by Alan Jones

Surrogate (Matador, 2020)

BLOOD
and
STONE

ALAN JONES

Copyright © 2021 Alan Jones

The moral right of the author has been asserted.

Apart from any fair dealing for the purposes of research or private study, or criticism or review, as permitted under the Copyright, Designs and Patents Act 1988, this publication may only be reproduced, stored or transmitted, in any form or by any means, with the prior permission in writing of the publishers, or in the case of reprographic reproduction in accordance with the terms of licences issued by the Copyright Licensing Agency. Enquiries concerning reproduction outside those terms should be sent to the publishers.

This is a work of fiction. Names, characters, businesses, places, events and incidents are either the products of the author's imagination or used in a fictitious manner. Any resemblance to actual persons, living or dead, or actual events is purely coincidental.

Matador
9 Priory Business Park,
Wistow Road, Kibworth Beauchamp,
Leicestershire. LE8 0RX
Tel: 0116 279 2299
Email: books@troubador.co.uk
Web: www.troubador.co.uk/matador
Twitter: @matadorbooks

ISBN 978 1 8004 6553 4

British Library Cataloguing in Publication Data.
A catalogue record for this book is available from the British Library.

Printed and bound in Great Britain by 4edge Limited
Typeset in 11pt Baskerville by Troubador Publishing Ltd, Leicester, UK

Matador is an imprint of Troubador Publishing Ltd

No need to panic, Molly Harrington told herself.

Actually, as she well knew, there was every need to panic.

Jennifer Ormiston, host of the morning show on Digital City Radio and part of the station's DNA, hadn't shown up this morning. There'd been no call, no text or email, nothing on social media. She'd cut it a bit fine before but never failed to show. Deborah, the morning show's producer, had suggested re-running the previous Tuesday's programme, but pointed out to Molly that Jennifer was also down to carry out an interview at 11.15 with Councillor Stella Delaney about the widely criticised plans for a new multi-storey car park. They both knew that only Jenny could carry that off.

Hence the panic, and hence Molly's decision to drive out to Jennifer's place of residence to see what the hell was going on.

As she got out of the car, Molly looked up at the block. Nice flats but, from what she'd heard, a bit overpriced, especially out here, way beyond the city limits. Since taking on the stewardship of Digital City, she couldn't remember having to drive to the home of any presenter to drag her out to work, yet here she was. Of course, managing Jenny Ormiston had never been easy; she'd had to speak to her more than once about the odd colourful phrase, the odd inappropriate come-on to a guest. If it weren't for that interview with Delaney…

She got out of the car and looked around the car park. Four other cars, all neatly parked in their bays, and that one there, next to the wall… She walked over to the red Mini

Clubman she recognised as Jennifer's car. As she approached, the alarm went off at a startlingly loud volume. Inside, the glovebox was open, and a pair of leather gloves had been left on the flap. In the back seat, Jenny's famous bright yellow jacket had been thrown hastily down.

She walked over to the entrance to the block and pressed on the button next to Flat 41. Nothing. Pressed again. Still nothing. She heard a car draw up behind her. The sound of a rapid exit and clattering heels as a woman in her mid-thirties approached the main entrance.

'Excuse me, I'm looking for Jennifer… Jennifer Ormiston. Flat 41.'

The woman looked her up and down.

'You police? You don't look like police.'

'No, not police. I'm the station manager at Digital City – you know, the radio station.'

'Oh, right.'

'Can you let me in? I need to contact Jennifer urgently. She should be conducting an interview in…' She looked at her watch. 'In something like twenty minutes.'

'So that's what that bitch up in the top flat does, is it? I'm more Classic FM myself. I've tried passing the time of day with her, but all she ever does is brush past with a tired smile on her face.' She paused, as if weighing up what she should do. 'You got a business card?'

'Oh, yes, of course.' She fished out a card from her shoulder bag. 'Here.'

'Thanks; just in case, you know…'

'Of course, that's fine.'

Inside the building, she took the lift, just catching the

'Good luck' from the echoing stairwell. Emerging at the fourth floor, she pressed the bell of Flat 41, heart pounding as though she'd climbed the stairs. It emitted a tinny version of Jennifer's breakfast show jingle. She pressed again but, as she did so, noticed the narrow gap between the door and the jamb. It was obviously on the latch. She pushed the door open and took a single step inside. Keys on the hall table to the left.

'Jenny?' Nothing. 'Jennifer?'

As she moved further into the hall, a strong feeling that she really shouldn't be doing this came over her, but a glance at her watch told her there were only seventeen minutes to the interview. She could detect no noise from anywhere in the flat, no streamed music, no radio or TV on in the background. She walked through into the lounge, a spacious, sparsely but tastefully furnished room with panoramic views but no evidence of Jenny's recent presence. The kitchen opposite was scrupulously clean and surprisingly large, its central island perched on expensive wood flooring, its units blindingly white and glossy, with dark red wall tiles behind. It could have been installed yesterday, ready for the first to view.

At the end of the hall, the door to the main bedroom was open. Inside, the sliding doors of the fitted wardrobe gaped wide, something like twenty pairs of shoes neatly stacked under an array of colourful dresses and tops and a rack of blue jeans. The quilt had been turned back neatly on the bed. As she approached the door to the second bedroom, down a corridor to the left, she saw it was closed.

Jenny was clearly not in the flat, and Molly's visit was

turning from the professional to the purely inquisitive. Time to go and, reluctantly, cancel the meeting with Stella Delaney at the last minute and think of some way to fill the air-time. Then, later, she would have to consider the matter of where Jenny actually was. She'd done a bunk, but why?

Molly wondered if she had time to use the loo before she left. Surely, thirty seconds wouldn't hurt, would it? A short way further along the corridor, she could see the open door of what she took to be the bathroom, the frosted glass of the window above the basin clearly visible. As she approached, she could hear for the first time a noise, the drip-drip of water from a half-closed tap. This merely intensified her need to pee, and she entered the bathroom with both hands already reaching up under her skirt.

She was thus completely unprepared for what she saw. To her left, in a curvilinear white bath tub entirely detached from the wall and raised from the floor on Queen Anne legs was Jennifer Ormiston. Her face was turned towards the door, as if in challenge, the eyes staring. Her right arm was hanging loosely over the side and a pool of water had accumulated on the floor.

Molly was drawn, despite herself, towards the bath. Three or four feet from it, she stopped, no longer needing to come any closer. Frozen where she stood, she took in the odd pinkness of the water, the mess of Jennifer's left wrist, the sheer bulk of her naked body, half-submerged. Then she felt the wetness between her own legs and the room circling and growing dim. As she dropped, her head struck hard wood and one of her arms sent something scuttering across the floor.

An antique bath tap continued to sound in the echoing, abundantly tiled space – drip, drip, drip. But now there was no-one at all who could hear it.

Part One

Aftermath

Three weeks earlier

One

It's all over now, she thought. Finished. In the past.

Louise Bryant was sitting in the café opposite the church, her church, the church where that man had had control of her life for so long. As she looked across at the forbidding darkness of the building, now seeming squeezed in amongst retail units and town centre flats, she wondered whether, now he was gone, she would be able to return to the church itself and resume her active faith with the new, younger priest. He would surely reach out positively to her, wouldn't he?

The café itself brought back memories of another time, a time before the whole of her life had turned inside-out, before the idea she had been thinking about in this very place, at this very table, had turned sour. Of course, it was not the same in here now, she thought; there were new owners and they had brought with them a new look, a new splash of bright blue paint, work by local artists on the walls, better coffee and pastries, and, needless to say, higher prices. All the same…

Since the court case, she had been very careful about leaving the house. Her husband had told her not to be so paranoid, but her natural caution took control. She went to the supermarket very early in the morning and avoided local shops altogether. She immersed herself in housework and persuaded Edward to cancel the newspaper. She kept her contacts online to a minimum, deliberately avoiding social media. Today was really the first day she had ventured out into the town and sat in a public space like this, open to the looks and nudges of other pedestrians and customers. She had taken the safer route through the park, and the few people she had come across had seemed oblivious to her identity. Thus far, no-one in the café, which was in any case mostly full of tourists, had looked meaningfully or judgementally at her. She could feel her body and mind very slowly begin to relax.

Nevertheless, she remained painfully aware of who she was and what had happened to her. She was the woman who had had a child with her husband's brother, who had shamed herself in the eyes of her church and allowed her child to be snatched from her. The miracle was, though, that the child had survived, traumatised and broken but still alive, and that it was her God, the God with whom she had been told she needed to make her peace, who had allowed in his mercy for this to happen.

Except, of course, that it hadn't been God alone who had brought back little Sammy to her. It had been Sergeant Timothy Laughland. It had been the sergeant who had fought against the idea that her child had been taken by a paedophile, who had persisted to the very end and saved her child from the wreckage of an old Ford in a country lane.

Now, they had been told, Sammy might soon be returning home from the residential paediatric hospital in which he had been cared for by specialist child psychologists. Naturally Edward would deal with the situation in his usual way, with a kind of cool practicality and efficiency. But would she be able to cope as easily? And that question, of course was the real reason she was here in the café; without realising it, she had come to prepare herself for the short walk across to the church, for a meeting with the new priest, for the comfort that only her church could give her.

She looked at her watch: almost twelve, the time of her appointment with Father Davidson. It would take her only a matter of seconds to cross the pedestrianised street, enter the church and walk past the confessional to the priest's office, the room where she'd had those difficult, distressing meetings with Father Christian. She was determined not to be late, but felt suddenly overwhelmed by doubt. Perhaps it was time for a clean break with her faith and her church, and anyway she had not discussed this meeting with Edward. There would have been no point in any such discussion, of course, Edward's tolerance of her religious belief having been stretched to the limit and beyond by Father Christian's part in the abduction of Sammy.

She raised herself from the table and went to pay at the counter. She recognised the woman who took her money; she had worked in the café for years and had been re-employed by the new owners. The woman smiled at her as she gave her her change, a smile that was full of sympathy and discomfort in equal measure. Somehow, it was this smile that saw off any doubts she might have. As she went through the door of the café, the bell rang loudly as it had always done and she headed across the street with renewed purpose.

She entered the church through the dark wooden door to the right; there was a door on the other side for those leaving the church, as though those coming and going might rise to an unfeasibly large number. It creaked in the way that was still so familiar to her, but it was, she reflected, not a sound she had heard recently. As she made her way in and walked down the right-hand side of the pews, the dark, aromatic interior of the church momentarily struck her blind. Her sight readjusted itself as she reached the confessional and made her way past the altar to Father Davidson's office. The door was slightly ajar; this would never have happened in Father Christian's day. She came forward and tapped lightly to announce her presence.

There was a shuffling inside before a head poked itself around the edge of the door. It was a youngish head, and its eyes communicated a mixture of emotions, delight and warmth, but also alarm and trepidation. Louise was shocked by her own reaction. She had known the new priest would be in his late thirties, but the face that was framed in the elongated space between the door and its frame looked much younger.

'Ah, Mrs Bryant, is it? Do come in. Have a seat…'

He opened the door wider and spread out his right palm suddenly and awkwardly, stepping back as she entered. And now, as she lowered herself on to exactly the same chair she had sat in when Father Christian had breathed foully at her and accused her of being sinful in her pursuit of IVF, she felt the full weight of what she was about to do. Who would begin the conversation, and what could she possibly say? The fresh face in front of her seemed suddenly aware of her discomfort and gave a short nod, accompanied by a relaxed smile. It was a round, pleasant face, below rather a close-cropped, receding hairline, a face that seemed to tell her he would take charge of this conversation, if that's what she would prefer.

'Mrs Bryant…' He looked down at an opened file on his desk. 'Louise…shall we begin by saying a prayer?'

This was exactly the right thing to do, thought Louise, impressed by the way her new priest had understood the delicacy of the situation. And so they spent a minute in prayer. It was not a prayer she had heard before; it was slowly delivered and contained words like 'forgiveness' and 'recommitment'. She assumed by the end of it that it was a form of words made up by Father Davidson himself, a feat which also impressed her, as perhaps it was meant to.

'I sense, Louise…is it OK to call you Louise?' She nodded. 'I sense this meeting between us would be easier if I were to, as it were, kick us off?'

'Yes, thank you, Father.'

He leaned forward on to his elbows, so that his face was a foot closer to hers, clasping his fingers together and leaning his chin on them.

'So we should begin, perhaps, with the whole matter of Father Christian's role in the misuse of Church funds, and subsequently in the abduction of your child.' He had become suddenly a little more business-like, as though it helped him to breach the awkwardness between them.

'I can't…I can't…I'm ashamed to say I can't find it in my heart to forgive him for what he did.' This came unbidden from Louise. She had heard him say 'abduction' and 'child' and a dry, tense fury forced her to speak.

'That's completely understandable, Louise. It would be asking a lot of you to forgive him under the circumstances.'

'And the courts, what the courts decided…'

'Yes. The verdicts must have surprised, even shocked you.'

'That's putting it mildly.'

'Yes.' Father Gregor Davidson leant back again on the hard wooden chair, which creaked underneath him, as though assaulted by her vehemence. He tapped his thumbs together, contemplating what to say next. Instead of kicking things off, he had somehow ended up defenceless in front of an open goal. 'Yes, well, indeed…'

'What seems so unforgiveable to me is that he is to be punished more harshly for embezzlement than for his part in Sammy's disappearance. Surely, that's all wrong, isn't it?'

They had come to the heart of things much more quickly than Father Davidson had anticipated. He remembered the long meeting he'd had with the Dean before he'd taken up his position. It was important, according to His Excellency, to take a properly balanced approach when speaking or writing about the events surrounding the removal from office of Father Theodore Christian. Father Christian had been a long-serving minister in his community of souls, and one venerated by both those within the Church and those outside it. His errors of judgement on two occasions should not detract from the essential spiritual strength he had shown in his pastoral role over many years, yet the Church had taken the right course of action in asking him to step away from his role and had co-operated fully with the police in achieving the most appropriate outcomes.

'From your perspective, Mrs Bryant, Louise, I can see how wrong it must seem, and I share your pain with regard to Samuel and what he was forced to go through. A truly terrible series of events that will, I know, be with you for the rest of your life.'

'But…?' The fire of Louise's anger had subsided a little, but at a breath might be rekindled.

'There's no but, Louise, only the plain fact that, unlike his role in the appropriation of Church funds, where there were clearly no mitigating factors, his actions in removing your child to a safe environment, albeit one a long way from his home, could be said to have been motivated by a desire to protect Samuel.'

'Protect him?' The anger had flared up again. 'That's ridiculous, utterly ridiculous. If he'd wanted to protect Sammy, the best thing he could have done would be to contact the police or return him to me, not drag him off to some place in Cambridgeshire to be imprisoned by that equally corrupt brother of his.'

Father Davidson looked at the woman across the table; she was bent forwards, gripping the seat on either side of her thighs and breathing heavily. Nothing in the seminary prepared you for this, he thought. He allowed ten seconds or so to pass, waiting for the Lord's voice to guide him. There was nothing, only the bleak silence punctuated by the ticking of the mantelpiece clock and Louise's tremulous breathing.

He did, of course, agree with her, that was the main problem. It should be possible to be honest in the expression of one's thoughts and feelings whilst remaining true to one's Church and one's Faith. It did not feel possible at this moment, however, and when he spoke it was from his own personal shame.

'It's hard to disagree with you, Louise, hard indeed. I can see there is still a lot of passion, distress, anger in you, and that's entirely to be expected. I have prayed myself many times to the Lord to ask for his guidance with regard to what happened here and how this church should move forwards.'

'And what guidance did you receive, Father?'

'Well, that's perhaps between me and my God.' He was prevaricating, and he could see she was aware of the fact by the slight smile on her lips and the sad fall of her eyes from him. How had this become about him, about his own doubts and discomfort? He needed to get back to where he'd thought the prayer was taking them, to the possibility of Mrs Louise Bryant returning to the fold. Apart from anything else, he agreed with the Dean that the only way to restore the congregation to the healthy numbers it had enjoyed before the events surrounding Samuel Bryant's disappearance was to let everyone see that Louise herself had made peace with her God and returned to the Church.

'I think I need to go now, Father.' Louise had suddenly raised herself up and was looking full into his face again.

'No, no, please.' He stood himself, spreading out his hands and motioning her to take her seat. 'Please sit down again, Mrs Bryant. I promise…I promise to be honest with you. I think honesty was probably what you came here today for, and I'm very sorry not to have been honest with you just now. Please…'

Louise looked at the eager, distressed face in front of her, so unlike the image of a priest she habitually conjured in her mind. Its expression had changed; there was a desperate pain behind the eyes that made her feel sorry for him, despite his equivocations and evasions. She gave two short nods and slowly lowered herself on to the hard plastic chair again.

'Thank you, Louise.' He too resumed his seat in front of her. 'The answer to your question about God's guidance is that I received only silence. It appeared that God had nothing to say to me, that I would have to deal with the situation alone.'

'Thank you for being honest about that, Father.' His frankness gave her the confidence to continue their conversation. 'During the time when Sammy was taken from me, us, I felt, I still feel, that God had abandoned me. For a long while, when I thought of the Church, that part of my life seemed utterly bleak and meaningless. At least you appear still to have your faith, if only because you're sitting opposite me now, here…'

'Yes, you're right, but it's perhaps a rather different faith now, one chastened by the situation we are all in. One in which God is perhaps telling me to sort the mess out by myself. You will understand, Louise, that there are three things at work here – God, the Catholic Church and this particular place, its priestly leadership and much diminished congregation. Though He has chosen not to speak to me, I still hold on to my faith in God. As for the Catholic Church, my faith has been, shall we say, shaken somewhat. But it's here, in this place, that the hard work must be done to restore a shattered community.'

Father Davidson had become slowly more passionate as he spoke, leaning forwards and gesticulating, his eyes turned towards her, but not fixed on her, as though focused on some spiritual middle-distance. Nevertheless, it was clearly up to her to respond.

'And does that hard work start right here and now, with me?'

'Yes, yes, in some ways it does.' His eyes had refocused on her. It was obvious he had decided that all evasions were pointless now. 'Of those three things I mentioned just now, I imagine you feel betrayed by both the Catholic Church and this particular place, this…' He looked up and swept an arm around in front of him, '…this manifestation of the Church's power.'

'Yes, that's it exactly, a sense of the deepest betrayal.' She was warming to him now, his words showing her that he understood.

'Yes, so what I'm suggesting you need to do is, well, turn your faith off and turn it on again.'

'Like a computer?' Louise's face betrayed an odd mixture of surprise, amusement and dismissiveness.

'Yes, exactly.' The Father's short laugh quickly turned to seriousness. 'I'm sorry if that sounds facetious. Of course, you've already, in a sense, turned off your faith; turning it back on would mean plugging yourself back into God himself, ignoring the Church and your feelings about this place and committing yourself to intimate worship all over again.'

'But surely that intimacy with God would have to happen here, at least some of the time?'

'Yes, of course. But two things would be different. First, you would be filling this space with your humility, your reaching out to God, rather than allowing it to fill you. Second, you have me, that is, you have someone who understands the terrible things that happened here and in Father Christian's house and who can, well, guide you through to a re-affirmation of your faith, should you choose to accept my guidance.'

He had spoken well, saying things that seemed to cut though her pain and offer hope for the future, for a rejuvenated, personal route to God. Yet she could also hear the voice of her husband, Edward, saying emphatically that she should not be taken in once more by all this mumbo-jumbo. But that was Edward, and Edward would never be persuaded by the emotional and spiritual nourishment of faith.

'Thank you, Father. I need to think about what you've said and come back to speak to you again.'

'Yes, of course. But may I hope to see you on Sunday? It would be such a pleasure personally to see your face in the congregation…'

'Well, perhaps, I'll see.' She saw Edward's dark looks and heard his bitter words again.

'Good. And before we meet for a second time, I think we should both reflect on what we've talked about today, and pray once again for God's guidance, even if it appears there is only silence.'

They rose to their feet simultaneously, Louise taking the Father's outstretched hand. It felt clammy to the touch, and she realised just how difficult this meeting had been for him also. For Father Davidson, the touch of her soft hand and the warm smile that faced him across the table triggered for a painful instant the pangs of his commitment to celibacy.

'Yes,' said Louise. 'Yes, Father. Reflection and prayer; in the end, that's all we have, isn't it?'

Two

In a residential hospital deep in the Sussex countryside, very different from the one in which Samuel Bryant was being nursed back to health, Ben, Edward's younger brother, sat at the bedside of the slender figure of his wife, who was, as was often the case during one of his visits, sound asleep. Even when she was awake, Leticia seemed to have very little to say to him and each visit produced a different response. At her most lucid, she would smile weakly at him, allowing him to place his left hand gently over her right, though it felt cold and lifeless as though she had not, after all, been rescued from her botched suicide attempt and died in the water where she was found. At other times, however, she would simply stare at him and shake her head from side to side as though she didn't recognise him at all.

How did he feel about it all now? When he had married her, she had saved him from his obsessive affair with Louise, his sister-in-law, and he had adored her gentle, aristocratic loveliness. But later, when it was finally revealed to him that she had abducted little Sammy, the child he had given to Louise, something disappeared from this adoration. This was, perhaps, inevitable, he told himself, but it did not affect the powerful sense of duty he felt, a sense of duty that kept him coming back to her bedside in the hospital as often as he could.

The police were waiting to interview her, but everything would depend on her recovery from the physical and psychological trauma she had suffered. They had been refused permission to see her, despite protestations from on high, and so two officers had come to Ben's office at Thurgood and Thurgood Solicitors in the city to question him further about the abduction and try to ascertain from him what state his wife was in and whether she would be likely to recover any time soon.

He had been able to give them very little extra information about the abduction, since he'd been pretty much in the dark about Leticia's movements and motives himself at the time. As for his wife's condition and likely recovery, he could say even less, over and above what the doctors were saying. The two officers had been very supportive, but he was sure they felt Leticia was exaggerating her condition and deliberately slowing down her recovery in order to avoid the police and judicial process. This was not something they said, it was more the looks they exchanged, the silences that fell at some points in the conversation. It was a thought that had occurred to him, too, if he was honest, especially after one of those visits in which she'd remained asleep throughout, or virtually wordless and vacant.

This had been his world during the sad, dark days of December and early January, his work at the office and this sour feeling of duty. Except, of course, that wasn't quite the truth. There had also been someone else in his life.

There had also been Jennifer Ormiston.

She had come to his office late one afternoon in the very early days of his wife's confinement in the hospital, having somehow got past reception. She did not expect him to forgive her for what had happened, she said, she was simply getting it off her chest; if he hated her forever as a consequence, she would quite understand...

Ben opened his mouth as if to speak, then realised that these tersely articulated words had struck him wholly dumb; he had had absolutely no idea what to say to this extraordinary woman who had taken a seat before he could begin to invite her to. Her presence, he remembered, had seemed to fill the room like a scent. Before he could find any word to say to her, she had spoken again, this time in a very different, low-ish, melodious voice.

Listen, she said, this will probably be the last thing you'll want to do, but...could they have a drink together so that she could explain what had happened in more congenial surroundings? Would early evening at the Spanish tapas bar in town be good for him? Say, Friday at six? She had allowed the briefest of smiles to play across her mouth and tilted her head very slightly to one side. Then she raised herself from her seat, leant over his desk, turned a notepad around and used his heavy silver biro to jot down her mobile number. She presented her breasts to his gaze and he followed them as she straightened herself in front of him. Send me a text, she said, let me know how you're fixed, and with that she had moved languidly to the door, turning with a rather fuller smile as she slipped out of his office and simultaneously into his life.

Jennifer had chosen the tapas bar with care, secreted as it was down a chic side street that insinuated its way artfully around the perimeter wall of the cathedral. She had turned up fifteen minutes late – media stuff, too boring to explain, apparently. She'd worn very tight jeans that delineated the shape of her lower body to perfection, though he wondered how she could possibly breathe or move freely in them, and above, by contrast, a loose, apricot-coloured silk blouse that allowed the weight of her breasts to fall untrammelled beneath.

'So, Benjamin, have you ordered?'

'Er, no.'

'Then let's have some white wine and a couple of plates of something tasty, yes?'

Without waiting for his reply, she raised herself from the chair and moved across to the bar, returning a few minutes later with a full bottle of Valencian white in an ice bucket.

'No sense in fiddling about with glassfuls of this stuff. Salud!'

'Yes, salud. Jennifer, I...'

'Don't talk, drink.' Raising her glass to her lips but holding it there for a moment, she looked intently over the rim at him. 'You know, you're really very different from your brother, don't you think?'

'Different in what way?'

'Well, everything's a bit more fleshed out with you, I'd say. And you're much more relaxed, more at ease with the world.'

'You shouldn't underestimate Edward.'

'Oh, no, I don't, of course not...so, your wife, your wife and poor Sammy.'

'What about them?' He put his glass down on the table in front of him, wondering all over again why he was here, where this assignation, if that's what it was, could possibly lead.

'It must have been so difficult for you, the father and yet not the father, all that. And then that stupid fucking priest.'

'You're overlooking the fact that it was you who started the whole thing off by going out of your way to tell Leticia I was Sammy's biological father – I thought that was why you wanted to meet this evening, to tell me how sorry you were.' He'd begun by raising his voice angrily, but then dropped it almost to a whisper, realising where they were and what he was saying.

'Did she tell you I came right out with it, deliberately told her about Sammy?'

'Yes.'

'And you believed her?'

'Why wouldn't I? Leticia and I were…are very close. I love her and trust her.'

'You don't think she would have done what she did anyway? It might have been a different child, of course, but still. It all came from her, anyway. She asked me outright. What was I to say? Did I think Sammy was your child? I said I really had no idea. She persisted; I was Louise's best friend… surely as a journalist I had an eye, an ear for such things, I must have heard something on the grapevine, all that. And so I told her what I thought. That, yes, there was a resemblance between Sammy and you and that the whole thing would have been an easy way out for Lou. Trust me, I had no idea what it would lead to, no idea at all, how could I?'

He remembered looking at her across the low table. Her eyes had been fully on his, open, unblinking and with a practised warmth, the whole effect completed by that tilt of the head again, the suggestion of a smile, redolent of heartfelt empathy and suppressed desire in equal measure. He hadn't believed what she'd said to him, though it came across with an apparently unforced sincerity. As to why, that wasn't easy to say. He'd known there must have been something else to make her tell Leticia about his surrogacy, there being otherwise no real connection between them.

'And where did this conversation between you and Leticia take place?'

'It was some presentation about that new supermarket; there were plans on display. I was there as a journalist, she was with that old fart of a boss of yours, part of the legal team. I'm not sure where you were. Anyhow, as I say, she sought me out in a corner and pressed me to say what I thought.'

It had all seemed so plausible, yet he couldn't remember any papers relating to the supermarket site application being mentioned in the offices of Thurgood and Thurgood. Not that he was involved in every case, despite being a partner; some things Bill liked to keep for himself, particularly if they involved someone in his Lodge, or some old Oxbridge chum. Nevertheless...

'And it didn't occur to you at all that your suggestion I might be Sammy's real father would be a pretty life-changing thing for Leticia?'

At this, Jennifer's expression had changed, the slight smile with its touch of warmth vanishing, to be replaced by her serious journalist's face. She leaned back and looked at him with arms folded, as though sizing him up, deciding no doubt how to deal with this version of him that was very far from the broad-shouldered, fleshy, fanciable puppy of a man she'd hoped to go some way towards seducing over a heady Spanish white. He'd been aware then that the seduction had probably come into her head, fully formed, out of nowhere, an impulse she'd found it difficult to resist. She would have her way with him; it would be fun.

'Well, yes, of course it occurred to me. But it was your wife's reaction that led me to believe that what I'd said would be very unlikely to change her life. Just the opposite, in fact…'

'Just the opposite?'

'Yes. I'd have said, if you'd asked me at the time, that she'd already had strong suspicions that what I'd said to her might be true.'

'That's ridiculous. She said nothing to me, nothing that would have suggested even the vaguest suspicion.'

'Well, she wouldn't, would she?'

In the ensuing silence, two tapas plates arrived, Jennifer leaning forward immediately and filling her mouth with food. He looked at her in wonder; this was a woman of strong appetites, that much was clear. As she raised a piece of chicken towards her mouth, a drop of salsa sauce had fallen on her blouse. She looked down at it, then at Ben, biting her lower lip like a naughty child and moving the middle finger of her right hand up the material of her top over the curve of her left breast to remove it.

'Oops.' In an instant, the mock-childish tone had changed with a long exhalation of breath. 'You know, Benjy, you're wasted.'

'Wasted?'

'Wasted on that dry office you work in, wasted on that flaky wife of yours, wasted on this clapped-out, bourgeois city.'

'Says the provincial local radio host.'

'Ah, but some of us are looking at the stars, as someone said.'

His words had momentarily hurt, yet she'd seemed excited by the flare of passion they'd betrayed, raising herself from her chair and moving behind him, pulling a card from the hip pocket of her jeans. With her left hand on the bulge of muscle under the shirt at the top of his left arm, she put her right arm over his other shoulder.

'Take this, Benjy, and don't lose it. You've already got my phone number, but the email address on the other side might come in handy.' She leaned down, her cheek touching his neck, the card dropping into his lap. 'By the way, the food and drink's all on my account. Enjoy the rest of the wine. Ciao.'

At that point, Jennifer Ormiston had raised herself up and moved sinuously towards the door of the bar. Picking up the card from his lap, he noticed Jennifer had written her private email address on the reverse of a business card for The Tollgate Inn. He heard the door squeak, looking up to watch her walk past on the pavement, waving her fingers through the window at him in passing. He'd felt intoxicated then, intoxicated and aroused.

And simultaneously ashamed.

Three

Louise attended church the Sunday after her meeting with Father Davidson, as he had encouraged her to do. She had not been sure about it, and Edward's inevitable sourness over the whole idea had made it much more difficult for her. Nevertheless, part of her wanted desperately the reassurance that only her church could give her. She would see how right it felt to be there, whether the memories of the past would intrude on her worship, keep her from her God.

As she approached the door of the church, the Father let go of the hand of a woman in her late middle age (Mrs Devine, was it?) and came forward enthusiastically to greet her. He said nothing, but simply gripped her right hand firmly in both of his and shook it vigorously, then smiled broadly and indicated with an outstretched arm that she should go in. There were only twenty or so worshippers there, dotted around the church. Inevitably, some turned their heads to look at her, but most had the decency not to stare. She felt like running out of the church at that point, but some source of strength made her stay.

Where to sit? It seemed brazen to sit at the front, and in any case she would feel the eyes of the rest of the congregation on the back of her head. At the rear? There at least she would be able to leave without being noticed, but her reluctance to come further forward would be noticed. Somewhere in the middle, then.

The rituals of music and the censer passed by her, failing to arouse anything remotely spiritual. Edward would be pleased by this, she thought; it was the ritual aspects of her worship he had always disliked most. That she believed in God, that she wanted to worship Him in the company of others, was not something he could really do much about, but what he called the fripperies of her belief, the funny clothes and funny smells, he had never been able to accept.

When the new Father stood to speak, however, she felt her attention sharpen itself and her access to spiritual feeling suddenly open up before her.

'As most of you will know, this is only the second time I have spoken in this church. The first time was important to me, for obvious reasons, but this is perhaps even more so. It's good to see a few more faces here today than was the case last Sunday, most encouraging. Some of you will, of course, think back to times when this whole house of God was full to the rafters. Perhaps then your faith in the Church held a feeling of the reassuringly ordinary about it, something dependable and supportive but as unremarkable as breathing. And that's good, in a way.'

He paused, as though what he had to say next might prove difficult. Louise was dreading the possibility that the difficulty he was having had something to do with her and the recent past. He drew a sharp breath and held it before continuing.

'But faith should be more than that. At its best, it should remind us that Christ's birth, his life and his death, were very far from ordinary and unremarkable.'

He paused again and scanned the faces spread out in front of him, hoping, no doubt, to make eye-contact with as many of them as possible.

'Something happened in this church, in the community in which it sits, in the city as a whole, something which shook us out of all our complacency. A member of our congregation was wronged by this church, and, let it be said, by the Church as a whole.'

There was a cough out there somewhere before him and shuffling noises came from more than one direction. A coat fell to the floor. The exit door at the rear complained on its hinges as a solitary figure slipped out through it. Disturbance. Discomfort. But, she guessed, that was what he wanted.

'Yes, wronged. I'm sorry if that is a shocking thing to say, but we must all be honest and admit the truth; that is the only way forward. The person I am referring to, incidentally, is with us today, and I commend her for her courage in coming, as, I hope, you will all commend her. That courage is all the more remarkable, I believe, when we realise the extraordinary circumstances in which her family has been placed and continues to be placed.'

He looked out at the faces below him again. Not many were now meeting his gaze. Some had found something of interest at one side or other of the church; some were looking down at their feet. One face, however, was looking intently at his and seemed to be waiting for his final words.

'And so, let us pray for all our souls that we may find

spiritual grace, love and forgiveness, of ourselves and others, in this place today and in the days and weeks ahead…'

The rest of Father Davidson's sermon moved away from the subject of Louise and the wrongs done to her, and she could not have told anyone what had taken place in the rest of the service. Father Davidson's earlier words, however, had caused two sharply different reactions in her. As she had sat there and listened to his words, surrounded by those who had doubtless participated in the gossip about herself, Edward, Ben and Sammy, she had been initially shocked, even angry. Her heart had started to beat worryingly fast and, for a moment, the image of the Father swam before her eyes. Yet, very quickly, a restorative warmth had flowed from somewhere, filling her with gratitude for what he had said. He had broken the frozen horror of what the Church had done and opened up a new possibility for her spiritual life.

As she left the church, Mrs Devine was the first to come forward and, after a moment's hesitation, embrace her and tearfully offer an apology. Whether this was for Louise's suffering, or for something in her own thoughts and feelings that the Father's words had caused her to be ashamed of, wasn't clear. Perhaps it was both. Seeing this, several others approached her and, embarrassingly, a queue formed. She began to cry herself, though she really didn't want to, and found herself the last to go.

'I apologise for that.' Father Davidson's voice surprised her, and she turned to him.

'Not at all. I must admit, when you first said those things

I felt quite uncomfortable, but now I feel it's all much more out in the open and I can be part of this congregation again, without fearing what others might say or think. And that's all down to you and your good judgement.'

'Well, I hope it does the trick. I think it might.'

'Yes, I'm sure it will. What you said before, about God's voice being silent and having to deal with the situation yourself…'

'Yes?'

'Well, I think you've risen to that challenge courageously. I hope God is pleased with your efforts.'

And with these words she made a sudden move towards him and put her arms around him, releasing him quickly and moving away from the church without looking at his face, towards the unchanged city street from which she had approached an hour before. It was a face which, had she turned to meet it, she would have seen as startled and strangely moved in almost equal measure.

Four

For several days after Ben's meeting with Jennifer in the tapas bar, he had immersed himself in his work, preferring not to allow his attraction towards her to overwhelm him. He was, he had reminded himself, the husband of a mentally ill woman who had almost died in the marshland of some godforsaken place on the Norfolk coast and who needed his unwavering support. He was also a partner in a highly respected legal business whose reputation, so his boss never failed to tell him, was on the rise. And yet he could not help remembering, also, the open eroticism of the way Jennifer had come on to him, the touch of her cheek on his neck, like a branding. These things he found difficult to shake off, and the more he'd carried on at work as if nothing had happened, the more he'd felt his desire for her grow.

She had not contacted him. Part of him realised this was quite deliberate; sending a blizzard of texts, emails and phone call messages would have seemed desperate. Her silence had said to him: you know I want you, so it's up to you to come to me and say you want me, too. And, of course, he'd known he would ring her, or text or email. The question was, what should he say? That he accepted her apology for her unfortunate words to Leticia, that she couldn't have known what they would lead to, but that this communication between them would be the last? As husband-turned-carer, as sober legal professional, this, he'd realised only too well, was unquestionably the right response.

The trouble was he'd known this would not deal with his lust for her…God, what an awful word that was, lust; yet it described perfectly how he'd felt in her presence. With Leticia, even before her abduction of Sammy and the 'accident' from which she was almost lost to him, it had never been exactly lust. Their sex had been passionate and loving, but always with some restraint. Of course, there was also Louise; sex with her had certainly been about lust, but there had always been the question of the child, the pregnancy. Even as she'd abandoned herself to him during their three-month affair, he'd always known the pregnancy would change everything.

You certainly couldn't accuse Jennifer of restraint; it was a word that barely featured in her lexicon. Would that lack of restraint in her coming on to him lead to lack of restraint in the bedroom? It wasn't, he'd instinctively understood, a question you really had to ask.

Thus, despite the terrible guilt he knew he would feel if he were to have an affair with her, however brief, and despite the considerable risk to his professional reputation, he had made up his mind to send her a text. It would say only that he wanted to meet again to finish their discussion and perhaps for him to get to know her better. He had felt what quite a lot of men feel, he guessed, when a woman they are attracted to comes on to them: arousal and anticipation, but also the kind of intense massaging of the ego that is rarely matched by anything else.

When Bill had popped out for lunch that day, he secreted himself in the safe room and pulled out his mobile. At first he sat there, unsure whether it was a good idea, even intoning to himself that he shouldn't be doing this. Then, dismissing this voice, he hesitated again, going on to try four different versions of the text before settling on:

Hi, Jennifer. Enjoyed our brief drink in town. How about we meet again to talk things over more fully? I'm seeing Leticia today, but I'm generally free after.

He'd left out the bit about 'getting to know her better' and made sure Leticia's name was in there. Nevertheless, pressing to send awoke a quick surge of fear and excitement in him that had taken a whole minute to subside.

Back at his desk and unable to concentrate on some boundary dispute papers he'd been forcing himself to consider, he'd not had to wait long for Jennifer's reply. It was characteristically direct:

People talk too much. Why not just say you want to fuck me? If you do, I suggest the place on the card I gave you. Your place or mine too risky. Let me know a.s.a.p., Jenny.

Christ, he'd thought, Christ…This is getting out of control very quickly, but isn't that what I want?

Yes and no.

But mainly yes.

Five

'Hello, is that the Clergy House?'

'Yes, who's calling?'

'This is Divina, from the office of the Dean. Am I speaking to Miss McLevy?'

'Yes. I'll get the Father for you.'

'No, I think it's you he'd like to speak to, if this is an appropriate moment.'

'Me? Are you sure?'

A shocked Elizabeth McLevy pointlessly smoothed down the thick material of her dress over her thighs. The Dean wanting to speak to her? This was unheard of. As a mere housekeeper, she wasn't at all sure what he could possibly have to say to her, or she to him.

'Absolutely. I'll put him on for you, if that's OK.' There was a short silence, then the sound of garbled organ music from an ill-advised holding device.

'Hello, is that Miss McLevy?'

'Yes, yes indeed, Your Reverence.'

'Good. Would I be right that your day off is Thursday, tomorrow in fact?'

'Yes, that's right. But there must be some mistake. It must be the Father, the new Father, you'll be wanting to speak to.'

'No, Miss McLevy, it's definitely you. Please don't be concerned, though, there's absolutely nothing to be worried about. Would eleven at my office suit you? I assume you know where the Deanery is?'

'Well, Your Reverence, the last time I remember going there would have been when I was appointed to this job. That was a good many years ago.'

'And a good many years of sterling service, Miss McLevy. So, is eleven good for you?'

'Well, yes, that's fine. Should I bring anything with me? How should I dress? Can you tell me what this is about, perhaps?' Had she over-stepped the mark in asking so many questions?

'Just come as you are, as they say, Miss McLevy, and there's no need to bring anything with you. So, I shall speak to you tomorrow at eleven. Oh, and there's no need to mention your visit to Father Davidson. In fact, well, it would be best if you didn't.'

'You'll forgive me, Dean, but I don't understand why that would be.' After recent events with her previous Father, Elizabeth McLevy would rather everything was kept in the open, where the light of day could get at it.

'Well, you'll see, I think, once we've spoken…'

The Deanery was a twenty minute walk from the Clergy House. It was a cold, but bright, January day, one which would ordinarily have filled her heart with the great joy of life and The Lord. Today, however, each step was dogged by her meandering thoughts about what on earth the Dean could want to see her about.

As she turned the corner into a street of tall Georgian houses, one of which housed the Deanery, she had more-or-less exhausted all possibilities without coming to any conclusion, and this had generated the same anxiety she'd felt the previous day on the telephone when the Dean's secretary had rung.

The tinny sound of the voice of this same secretary answered her pressing of the bell-push and the main door of the building clicked open, enabling her to ascend the cold stairs to the first floor where, it seemed, the offices of the Deanery were situated. She was early, and the Dean was on the telephone, Divina informed her. When she was eventually admitted into the Dean's room, she was immediately struck by its airy spaciousness and broad windows overlooking a well-kept garden. The Dean was standing to greet her as she walked in.

'Miss McLevy, how good of you to see me on your day off. Shall we sit over here?'

The Dean's voice was soft but insistent, full of a calm authority that immediately took charge of the situation. He was pointing to two armchairs by the ornate fireplace. Truth be told, she would have preferred to sit at the large mahogany desk in the centre of the room, where things might remain on a more formal footing, but still.

'Can I get you a coffee? Divina makes a very acceptable Americano.'

'No, thank you, Your Reverence. I'm afraid these new-fangled beverages are not kind to my stomach.'

She felt awkward, unsure whether to sit on the edge of the wide, leather-bound chair or to lie back against its well-worn cushions. She quickly decided on the former, but was conscious of being very much on the same level as the Dean, despite his having adopted a more relaxed position opposite her, and this she found unnerving.

'That's fine, Miss McLevy. We'll do without the coffee.' The Dean smiled at her, leaving a strategic pause before continuing and beginning to tap his outstretched fingers together in contemplation. 'So, the first thing I wanted to say to you, Miss McLevy, Elizabeth, is that the Church will always be profoundly sorry for what you had to suffer during the whole of the business with Father Christian and the abduction of the child, and profoundly grateful for the dignity and courage you showed at that time.'

'That's very kind of you, Your Reverence. I'm sure I only did what I thought was right.'

'Of course, of course.' The tapping of the fingers increased momentarily, then stopped, as the Dean leant forward in his chair. 'And the new man, Father Davidson, how are things shaping up with him?'

Elizabeth McLevy, still somewhat taken aback by the Dean's use of her first name, was unsure what "shaping up" meant exactly. She could only give her impression of the new Father from her point of view.

'Well, Your Reverence, he's a much younger man than Father Christian, of course, and no doubt still has a lot to learn. We are getting along fine, and he seems very grateful for what I'm able to do for him. There's one or two coming back now to the congregation, and he speaks well. People seem to like him.'

'That's very gratifying, Elizabeth, thank you. It's clearly

important, after what happened, that we have a smooth transition and a…rejuvenation of what the Church has to offer.' The Dean leaned further forward, now clasping his hands together as though he was reaching some kind of critical point. 'But there is one thing which I feel it's appropriate to mention to you, Elizabeth. It's something which must remain within the four walls of this room.'

'Yes, of course, Your Reverence.' She tried not to show how alarmed she was by this turn in the conversation.

'The fact is, Elizabeth, that the appointment of Father Davidson was unusual. His background is, well, somewhat different from the backgrounds of most of those who undergo training for the priesthood. His life as a young man was a little…chequered. It was, I think, not a happy time for him, a time when he did some things which I'm sure he now regrets.'

'I'm not sure I understand.'

'No, naturally not, Elizabeth, and I am, obviously, unable to share with you the details of that part of his life. Nevertheless, as I'm sure you know, the Church has an inclusive approach to those who have sinned and who have confessed and made reparations for their sins. This has been particularly so in the case of Father Davidson. Not only did he confess and abjure those things in his life that had led him to sin, he also submitted himself fully to the life of the Church, finally becoming one of the most devoted, thoughtful and energetic members of his seminary. It was because of this that we felt he was the right choice for us here, a man full of spiritual life and reforming passion.'

Elizabeth McLevy sat dutifully opposite the Dean, stiff-backed and discomforted by what he had told her. She wasn't sure where this conversation was going, and she wasn't sure she wanted to know. Did he want her to comment on the appointment of Father Davidson? It was very flattering if that was the case, but she couldn't think why he would be interested in what she had to say. Nevertheless, she did have something to say, and decided, since she was there, in his office, sitting opposite him, that she would say it.

'It's very good of you to explain all that, Your Reverence. But, if you're wanting my opinion, I'd say the last thing we really need in this diocese is some sort of controversy. If it had been my decision, Dean – but why on earth would it have been? – I'd have gone for a person of upstanding morality, someone who could navigate the choppy waters we find ourselves in without a whiff of anything scandalous. But then, what do I know, Your Reverence? I cook and clean, that's what I do, and I hope I do it to the satisfaction of the Father. Such decisions are not for me.'

The Dean sat back in his chair, his outstretched fingers now touching the tip of his nose, so that the half-smile he was indulging himself in would be hidden. She was clearly not a woman to be underestimated, this Elizabeth McLevy, and he could not help agreeing with her, which made him hesitate before replying.

'Well spoken, Miss McLevy, Elizabeth, well spoken indeed. You're right, of course, the safe option would have been to bring in someone with greater experience, someone who had taken a more conventional route to the priesthood. But…' He hesitated, aware that he needed to choose his words with great care. 'But, those criteria would have applied in good measure to the appointment of a certain other priest you and I know well, Elizabeth, and we may decide that the outcome of that appointment did not turn out to be wholly successful, despite the many good works achieved by that priest within the diocese in the past.'

These words brought back for Elizabeth the rages of Father Christian, like passing thunderstorms, the belittling comments, the rough fondling after too much whiskey and, of course, the whole affair of the abduction and concealment of little Samuel Bryant, about which she had been silent for too long.

'So, for that reason, we decided, although the decision was not completely, or even mainly, my own, that we needed someone fresh, someone who had been through the mill a little, someone who would understand the lives and sins of ordinary people a little more directly and fully. But you'll be wondering why I asked you here to tell you all this, Elizabeth, and indeed I've probably already said too much. Be that as it may, what I'm going to ask of you is that you keep a careful eye on the new Father. Talk to him, support him, and perhaps watch out for darker moods.'

'Darker moods?'

'Yes. As I said a little while ago, I can't go into the background of Father Davidson in any detail, but it would be surprising if there were not to be some – how shall we put it? – bumps in the road along the way. It's up to us to smooth out those bumps, to make his tenure as open and positive as it can be. It's a matter of trust, Elizabeth, and we'd very much like you to be part of the trust we have placed in him.'

'Well, this is all a bit of a shock, Your Reverence. But

you've put it to me so nicely that I can only say I'll do my best. You can rest assured that, as far as the work of the new Father in the diocesan community goes, I'll help him all I can.'

'And, please, if you become concerned about any aspect of what Father Davidson does, don't hesitate to get in touch with me directly. Divina will tell you exactly how you can do that.' He stood up, signalling very clearly that the interview was over. 'Once again, it's so good of you to spare me some time on your precious day off, and may the Lord be with you, may he watch over you and protect you in all you do…'

He made the sign of the cross, and Elizabeth rose and bowed instinctively in response, following the direction of his broad, outstretched palm, through the door of his office, past a smiling Divina, down the cold, echoing stairs once more, and out into the street.

Six

Neither outstanding nor 'in need of improvement', or whatever the euphemism for 'bad' was at the moment, Edward's school had been very understanding with regard to compassionate leave following Sammy's disappearance and subsequent convalescence. But neither the school's so-so reputation, nor their reasonableness, had made him any more enthusiastic about being there, ramming mathematical theories and methods into reluctant adolescent brains until their, and his, pips squeaked.

In the second week of January, at just about the most inconvenient time for the school, his Head of Department had taken long-term sick leave. Rumours had circulated about allegations of misconduct, but somehow he doubted that Carwen Williams, 52 and early-retirement-bound, would have the energy to carry out any of the rumoured activities. A dour, unbending Welshman, Carwen seemed perfectly happy with his diminutive wife and annual caravan holidays back in God's Own Country.

The Head Teacher had surprised him by telling him that, should Carwen not return to the school, he would consider 'warmly' any application for his job from Edward. He did so in somewhat unsubtle terms, trying, but failing, to suggest that the offer had nothing to do with the shortage of experienced Maths teachers or the time of year. The position came with an additional responsibility for sixth form pastoral care, something which boosted the salary considerably. He was not to think it had anything to do with the school's support for him in the matter of the unfortunate events of Sammy's abduction. Just the opposite, in fact. Quite what the Head had meant by that he wasn't sure and, he guessed, neither was the Head himself.

He hadn't told Louise about any of this. This was because he was sure what she would say. Despite her natural caution, she would tell him to go for it, that it would be so good for his career, just the thing to re-ignite the passion for teaching he had when he started. Actually, he had never had anything remotely like a passion for teaching; teacher training had simply been 'something to do' after his degree. And he knew perfectly well that her encouragement would be mostly to do with the extra money, a new lounge suite, new kitchen units, meals out at stupidly overpriced restaurants. Was he becoming an embittered older husband? When did that kick in? Nevertheless, he had kept it from her.

Of course, the news of Carwen Williams' leave of absence had reached plenty of people at school, many of whom had already accepted it as inevitable that he wouldn't return. Barbara, large, fleshy, bosomy, overbearing Barbara, had leant over him, pawing him and breathing whisky fumes over him, and told him he was made for Carwen's job, that she would work much harder for him than she had for Old Willy, who had always had it in for her.

More disturbingly, one of his sixth formers, a particularly

clever and irritating student called Nathaniel Dixon, with his imposing stature and shock of reddish hair, had said casually as he was leaving his A level Maths class that same day, 'I hear you're taking over from Old Willy, sir?'

'Mr Williams.'

'Yes, of course, Mr Williams. It's about time, wouldn't you say, sir, all things considered?'

'First of all, Nathaniel, the last time I looked Mr Williams was still head of the Mathematics department of this school and, second, I don't think it's appropriate for you to comment on matters of staff deployment, or do you think otherwise?'

'No, of course not, sir, you're absolutely right. I notice you haven't denied that the position might become available, though, sir, or that you might be in line for it.'

And with that, before Edward could say anything further, he had cocked his head on one side and glided from the room in that irritatingly self-absorbed way he had. How the hell had he found out about Carwen's long-term absence? He might have guessed that Edward would be next in line, but it was almost as though he knew more than Edward did about what lay behind it all.

Usually, he could resist Geoff Franklin's invitation to The Partridge for a pint after school, but on days when his lowest-stream GCSE class had been playing up particularly badly, he would sometimes surrender to his blandishments. Geoff was probably his closest friend and ally at the school, a fellow member of the Maths Department and fellow follower of the fortunes of the England rugby team. They had been to Twickenham together on a couple of occasions, something which Louise had done her best to discourage, if only, he realised full well, because he returned loud, full of Guinness and inconveniently horny, particularly if England had won.

Thus, on the evening of the same day as the Head's tentative offer, he found himself in the usual corner of the pub with Geoff and his occasional drinking mate from the History department, Dave Lemon. Their evening sluicing tended to follow a much-repeated pattern; buy a round each, having sworn to have one drink only, flirt with the barmaid, discuss matters rugby- and sex-related, in that order, then revert inevitably to school and their various frustrations with their jobs.

'So, you sly old bugger, you've been buttering up the old man for years and now he's about to offer you the top job, assuming Carwen's gone for good.'

'Head of Maths in a mediocre secondary school in a Home Counties backwater could hardly be described as getting the top job.' Edward knew Geoff would raise his possible promotion sooner or later, and was quick to downplay it; after all, if he accepted the job he'd be Geoff's boss, for God's sake.

'No, no, fair point, but still – a bit more money, eh? Can't be bad. Of course, the way it's all come about is interesting, isn't it?'

There was a sudden silence at this. What was it the French said, an angel passing overhead? He wasn't sure the thoughts of three boozers off the leash from their mundane working lives could possibly count as requiring the attention of angels, but still. Instinctively, all three of them picked up their half-full beer glasses and took a sip of warm, rather sour bitter. It was Dave who responded first to Geoff's question.

'So I hear, but I've only had it from some of the kids, who, as we know, are hardly to be trusted on anything of that kind. What've you heard, Geoffrey, old pal?'

Geoff Franklin looked from one of the faces in front of him to the other, his beer glass still poised half-way between his mouth and the table, as though weighing up the pros and cons of a full revelation. After a few seconds, he put down the glass decisively and wiped his mouth with the back of his hand.

'OK, so this goes no further, right?'

'No.'

'Absolutely not.'

'I wish I completely believed you, but there you are.' Geoff Franklin leaned forward on to his elbows and looked at the two people in front of him with an air of almost comic conspiracy. 'So, I had this from two people separately, OK.'

'One of whom, let me guess, was Angela in the office.' Dave Lemon added a short, dismissive snort of laughter to his suggestion.

'Might be, might be…I'm not at liberty to reveal my sources.'

'I'll take that as a yes, then.'

'Well, anyway, the point is that old Carwen has blotted his copybook big time.' Geoff had lowered his voice to such an extent that the others had to lean forward to hear what he was saying.

'We kind of guessed that, Geoff, but exactly what form did this blotting take?'

'According to my very reliable sources, one of our more nubile Year 12 students, a member of his registration group, broke down in tears in front of him and asked him for help in sorting out some pretty unpleasant bullying on social media.'

'Social media? Carwen? You must be joking.'

'Well, quite. So, anyway, Carwen, knowing nothing about what such a form of bullying might entail, decided to offer, shall we say, a more direct and physical approach to comforting the young lady in question.'

'Jesus, really?' Edward was beginning to sweat. All of the cautious optimism about the money and the status, such as it was, was beginning to unravel. 'You sure you're talking about Old Willy, here? I mean, don't get me wrong, I've been very happy with his leadership in the department…' The others simply looked at him with raised eyebrows, then took another sip from their beer in embarrassed synchrony.

'You're not in interview now, pal. "Very happy" – you sure?' Dave Lemon's tone was light but still carried its point.

'Well, he's always left me alone to get on with doing things my own way, and there's a lot to be said for that. Except when the bloody government steps in and forces us to do things differently, of course.'

'Tell me about it.'

'So, anyway, the point is he's fine as a bloke you want filling in the paperwork, ordering the books and all that, but I can't imagine him, you know, touching up a student; I take it that's what you meant, Geoff?'

'Well, yeah, that's the rumour. Of course, it is only hearsay.'

'On the other hand, Angela's very rarely wrong.'

'Did I say it was Angela? Anyway, there's something else, a double whammy, you might say.'

'Oh?' Edward leaned in further, his face hot. Dave watched him but said nothing.

'It seems one of his GCSE students is claiming Carwen hit him on the back of the head with a Maths book, hit him so hard that he passed out for a few seconds.'

'Bloody hell.'

'If that's true, in a way it's worse for Old Willy – well over twenty witnesses. The other thing, well, just her word against his, actually.'

'Who's the student who was knocked out, allegedly?'

'According to my GCSE class, Rhys Brydon; a bit of Welsh-on-Welsh, you might say.'

'Rhys Brydon? That little toe-rag? I've had a few run-ins with that one myself over the last few years. Trouble from Day One.'

'Yes, Dave, but actual bodily harm and all that, I mean, it's not on, is it?' Edward's tone was measured, cautious.

'If it's all true. So, you taking the side of the students here, Ed? I mean, he's an odd bloke, Carwen, but decent enough, you'd have said.'

'Yes, decent enough,' echoed Geoff.

Edward tipped the remainder of his beer towards his mouth, slammed his glass down on the table, touched both his drinking companions on the shoulder and left without saying another word.

The letter was on the kitchen table when Edward got back from his session with Dave and Geoff at The Partridge.

He'd sent Louise a text telling her he would be a bit late, as he always did now after the events leading up to and after Sammy's abduction. Knowing that this almost certainly meant his giving way to Geoff and downing pints at the pub, she was quite surprised when she heard the turn of his key in the door at around six-thirty.

'You're early.'

She pecked him on the cheek, reciprocating his kiss. This was how they generally greeted each other now. It was a change that had come upon their relationship quite suddenly but inevitably after their revelations to one another about their separate affairs. For Louise, it still seemed to her that something decent, Ben's offering to provide a sperm sample to give them a child, had slipped out of control, whereas Edward's affair with Jennifer Ormiston, the woman who had once been her closest friend, had been totally selfish, a complete, wilful betrayal of their marriage. Of course, she knew Edward would not, did not, see the difference. Hence the peck on the cheek, which, she supposed, suited them both.

'Yes, Geoff and Dave were even more boring than usual. It degenerated into pointless moaning about school, as always, so I came away.'

'Well, that's nice.' She rubbed his arm, as you would to a close friend. 'This came today; I thought I'd wait for you before opening it. It's from the hospital.'

'Oh, really?'

Edward propped his bag against the wall and sat straight down without removing his coat, something Louise could never remember having seen him do before. She sat opposite him. The letter was addressed to both of them, but she let him tear open the envelope and read its contents first. She watched as his eyes scanned the single sheet, his brow furrowing now and again.

'What does it say?'

'Wait.' A further twenty seconds elapsed. 'Here.'

Edward handed the sheet across to Louise who began to scan it, wondering as she did so why its contents could not have been spoken over the phone or sent by email. When she'd finished, she placed the sheet between them on the table and allowed the silence to settle.

'So.' It was Edward who spoke first. 'Sammy's coming home on Tuesday.'

'Yes.'

'I'm not sure I like what they're saying about his recovery.'

'No.' Louise picked up the letter again and re-read the third paragraph:

Sammy is much calmer now, as you saw on your last visit. He is speaking more frequently and crying less. He is not completely recovered, but is asking to come home. The medical professionals treating him believe it is in his best interests that he should return to you as soon as possible to avoid becoming institutionalised. We recommend allowing a representative of the hospital team to visit you a day or two before Sammy's return to provide support and advice.

'I'll ring them tomorrow to say yes to the visit. Agreed?'

'Of course, yes.'

The momentous significance of what would be happening in the next few days stunned them to silence again. All thoughts that Edward might have entertained of telling Louise about his offer from the Head and the rumours swirling around the school were wiped from his consciousness.

Was Sammy ready to come home, and were they ready to receive him?

Seven

When Jennifer awoke from her brief, post-coital sleep, the lights from the long, straight road into the city cast their brittle whiteness from the dark of a January evening on to the body draped across her. She put her hand on its back and allowed her fingers to slide down under the sheet covering it below the waist. It was a beautiful body, she thought, beautiful in its smooth, muscular stillness. Ben seemed to be fully asleep and snoring. She squeezed one buttock and the snoring stopped. Ben woke with a bewildered look on his face, then lowered himself to her face and kissed her, settling back down again between her breasts.

She had been heading home after a so-so interview with a local author when her mobile alerted her to a text from Ben. It was short and to-the-point and might have been an invitation to a business meeting, were it not for the specific mention of the Tollgate Inn. She had virtually burst into the room where he was waiting for her, pushing him down on the bed before his nervous apprehension could get the better of him, just as she'd done the first time they'd had sex a few days after their meeting at the tapas bar in December. He was so damn vulnerable, which made him at least twice as desirable as he already was.

Now, afterwards, she couldn't help reminding herself of those occasions when she had found herself in a very similar position with his brother Edward in a room in the same cheap hotel. They may be siblings, she thought, but they couldn't be more different as lovers. Edward had always seemed at ease with the arrangements they made for their affair and confident, eager even, in their foreplay. In bed, though, he had usually wanted her to take the lead, which had suited her fine. Ben, by contrast, clearly needed coaxing, seducing. Once coaxed, however, it seemed to her that he allowed his full, fleshy body to take over and she could let herself go more completely.

Her attempts to get back together with Edward after the end of their affair now seemed utterly pathetic. How could she have behaved so desperately? Was her behaviour telling her something about her real motives? She fooled herself sometimes, usually when admiring herself in the bathroom mirror after stepping out of the bath, into thinking that her lust was wholly natural, a kind of voracious hunger that needed fulfilling now and again and nothing more. But what if it was really all about power? When she had pushed Ben down on the bed an hour ago, was it desire or power that had turned her on? And had the frequent attempts to claw Edward back again from Louise and the child been more to do with powerlessness, a feeling that he had got away from her and that she was determined to reel him back in to make her feel in control again? Was it control that mattered to her more than anything else?

'That was unbelievably nice. Thank you.' Ben's voice stirred her out of the dark mood she had somehow persuaded herself into. His voice was deep and soft. She could not remember any man, certainly not Edward, thanking her for sex before.

'Well, as they say, thank *you*.' She caressed the smooth fur of the back of his head and lowered her mouth awkwardly to kiss him.

'You know, that first time back in December, I thought I'd feel unbearably guilty while we were, well, doing it. But I'm ashamed to say I didn't. Beforehand, yes, and maybe after. But not then.' As he spoke, he detached himself from her and levered himself up on to the headboard, whilst she remained lying there next to his warm chest.

'I guess you should just hold on to that feeling, then, and forget about the rest. You're too good to waste on that mad wife of yours, anyway, that's for sure.'

Why had she said this? As the words fell from her blundering mouth, she realised she'd pushed it too far. Power again, no doubt. He turned to sit on the edge of the bed, the broad back presented to her. She wanted to run her fingernails down it and press herself against him to begin their lovemaking all over again. But something restrained her; even she realised this would merely make the effect of her stupidly insensitive words worse. She waited for him to respond, but there was only silence.

'That was crass of me, Benjy, I'm sorry. My mouth runs away from me sometimes.'

'Yes.'

It was all he could think to say.

Eight

'It won't be easy, that's the first thing to say, Mr and Mrs Bryant. I'm sure you realise that anyway, but it's as well to know from the start that I'm not going to sugar-coat this or suggest it will be a smooth transition.'

It was a Sunday afternoon, two days before Sammy was due to return to them. The Registrar from the paediatric hospital had driven all the way to their house and was sitting opposite them, alongside the Family Liaison Officer who had been assigned to them when Sammy had gone missing. The FLO was sitting back, legs crossed, with what she hoped would be a reassuring smile. She was clearly there to support and not to speak. By contrast, the Registrar held on nervously to a clipboard and sat well forward on the sofa, her legs pinioned together, her eyes moving from Louise to Edward and back at the end of each completed phrase.

'No, well, good.'

'Yes, good, that's fine. Just tell us what to expect, that's all we need to know.'

'Of course, yes.' The Registrar looked down at her clipboard, flipped over a few sheets, pausing apparently to remind herself of the details of Sammy's case, then returned to the top sheet again. 'From your visits to Sammy, you will be aware that there have been times when he has remained… uncommunicative. The doctors treating him had expected this, indeed they speak of his being a classic case.'

'We're not interested in whether Sammy is or isn't a classic case; we want to know how he is and how he's likely to respond when he returns to us in this house.' Edward's voice had an edge of assertiveness he recognised as very like his father's.

'Of course, I understand. However, the fact that Sammy's behaviour has been in line with what our doctors expected throughout has meant that we have been able confidently to use various techniques to gently take Samuel through the events leading up to the abduction, the abduction itself and the particularly traumatic way in which everything was resolved. These have included reconstructive play, art therapy and symbolic manipulation. Samuel's response to these techniques has been generally encouraging and…'

'Only generally? What does generally mean?' It was Louise this time who sounded a discordant note.

'Simply that your son has become more communicative and, despite his age, shown some understanding of what has happened to him. But he's been through a great deal, Mr and Mrs Bryant, and the path to full recovery has not been, will continue not to be, completely smooth or predictable. What is important now, though, is that he leaves us and returns to his parents. We can supply a good deal of support and expertise, but we can't supply parental love, that's very much where you come in.'

Edward felt Louise's right hand take hold of his left and squeeze. He turned to look at her. She was staring at a point above the Registrar's head and tears were welling up in her eyes. He realised at that moment how much he would have to be there for Louise as much as for Sammy, this child that was his and yet not really his at all. The Registrar was looking directly at him, realising his wife was overcome by her emotions, and expecting a response.

'Yes, that goes without saying, of course. We love Sammy and we know we have a responsibility to give him that love and gradually bring him back to some sort of normality. But, when you think what he's been through…'

'Yes. It will be a slow process, and there will be times when you think you are winning, only to find that certain memories come back to haunt him. When this happens, he may become silent again, or he may vocalise or physicalize his trauma.'

'That's gobbledygook, jargon. What are you saying?'

'That he may shout, cry or kick out.' The Registrar noticed that these last words had stirred Louise from her frozen emotional state. 'But, having seen Samuel on three or four occasions during his treatment, I must say that the physical signs of trauma are much less likely in his case. He's much more likely to go into his shell.'

'But is that a good thing or not?' Louise's voice was cracked, barely audible.

'Not necessarily, but it's less alarming. In any case, any such episodes might well be short-lived, or not occur at all. It's simply something you need to be aware of. Don't forget that, if you need our help at any time, you should contact our specialist team and one of them can be with you quickly.' She pulled something from the back of her clipboard and handed it to Edward. 'This is a leaflet that gives some general advice about children returning to their parents from our care. All our contact details are on there.'

Edward took the leaflet but allowed it to fall lifelessly on his lap. Louise had let go of his hand and folded her arms in front of her, as though protecting herself from the cold. On the sofa, the FLO touched the Registrar lightly on the arm and smiled at her as if to suggest that this would be a good time to stop. They rose simultaneously, holding out their hands to Edward and Louise who got up awkwardly in response.

'So, Mr and Mrs Bryant, according to my notes, someone from our support team will bring Sammy to our reception area at 11.30 am on Tuesday, which is the time agreed for you to pick him up and bring him back here. Therefore, if there are no further questions…' Louise looked at Edward; there must be questions we ought to ask, she thought, but her mind was blank.

The three women in the room moved out to the hall, with Edward tagging along behind. The last thing he saw was the beatific face of the FLO as Louise closed the front door, its Yale lock snapping into place with brutal finality.

Nine

As Edward drove to work the following day, his mind was full of thoughts about the past and fears and uncertainties about the future. This kind of distraction was new to him; normally, he could wipe clean from his consciousness everything that did not relate to the job in hand. Tomorrow, he would be faced with the joint care of a child traumatised by abduction and a serious accident. And how did he feel about this child? He had brought him up as his own, knowing that it was Ben's sperm that had made it possible for Louise to give birth. But when he had found out that Sammy had been the result of a full-blown affair between his wife and his brother, it had changed everything. Sammy had been taken away from them, of course, just at the time when he might have been able to begin to forge a new relationship with him. So, would that process begin on Tuesday?

The whole thing was complicated by his affair with Jennifer. A sour feeling of anger and regret washed over him when he thought of what he'd done to himself, how he had allowed himself to be seduced by his wife's best friend and how she had repeatedly tried to resurrect their affair after it was dead and buried. And yet…he was every bit as angry with his brother and Louise; they had betrayed his trust when he believed they were going about the business of impregnation with dignity and respect. But then, these were not words you could possibly use about his relationship with Jennifer Ormiston, either. The whole thing was a sorry mess, a mess that he, they, had somehow to clear up for the sake of a small, vulnerable three-year-old boy.

The dreary morning briefing overran as usual, leaving a staff room full of professionals with barely time to draw breath before registration. Amidst this chaos, Edward managed to retrieve his post from his pigeonhole. He noticed a plain envelope with his name printed on it and the word "Confidential". Inside was a terse message from the Head: "Please attend my office at the start of Period 2. I have an important matter to discuss with you."

After his first lesson, with a large, silly Year 8 group, Edward pushed his way downstairs against the flow of students moving to their next class and turned into the relative quiet of the reception area and staff corridor. He checked with Angela that the Head was free and knocked on his door with, he hoped, neither timidity nor over-assertiveness. After the usual ten-second pause, he was ushered in and on to one of the two robust wooden chairs on the opposite side of the Head's desk. The Head was leaning forward, hands in the shape of a prayer concealing his nose and mouth, eyes fixed on his computer screen.

'Mr Bryant, Edward, thank you for this. I hope I won't need to detain you too long.' He had quickly changed the focus of his attention and was now looking steadily at Edward. 'You've a big day coming up tomorrow, I'm aware of that. Obviously, I hope all goes well for you.'

'Yes, thanks.'

'However, there's another pressing matter that needs to be dealt with. I don't know what the rumour-mill has been grinding out, but...' He paused and leant back in his chair, hands behind his head. 'There have been certain allegations made about the conduct of your Head of Department, Mr Williams, allegations which it now looks impossible to...gloss over. I'm telling you this, Edward, for reasons that will be clear in a moment, but it goes without saying that none of this goes outside this office.'

'Absolutely, of course not.'

'No, so...' He picked up a piece of paper from the tray to his left and held it up in front of him. 'A parent has written to me to complain that her son temporarily lost consciousness after Mr Williams struck him on the back of the head with a text book. Further, she claims that no action was taken by Mr Williams after the incident to ensure he did not have concussion. Indeed, she claims that Mr Williams went on shouting at her son after he'd come round, showing no concern for his well-being. She goes on to say that the boy was further embarrassed by the fact that the whole incident occurred in front of other students. My own investigation has established that several students are prepared to say that what happened is pretty much as described in the parent's letter.'

The Head paused meaningfully. Was he testing his reactions, or trying to find out, without actually asking, what Edward might know about what had happened?

'Right. That's a very...concerning set of allegations.'

'Indeed it is, yes. Unfortunately, however, the matter

is complicated further by this…' He reached into the tray again, pulling out two stapled sheets from under the first letter he had picked up. 'Another letter, sent a week or so ago, from the parent of a female student in the sixth form, a member of Mr Williams's tutor group.' Edward tried his best to look as though he had no idea what this second letter might contain. 'To begin with I made the decision not to act immediately on the contents of this letter; it contains the kind of allegations that, I regret, we receive more often than you might think, allegations of…' he peered at the top sheet, '"sexually explicit remarks" and "inappropriate touching".'

'You were hoping to speak to the girl first and ascertain the seriousness of what had actually occurred?'

'Very good, Mr Bryant, that's exactly right. However, on Friday, I had three separate visits from other female students, two in his tutor group, one in his Maths class. All three of them cried openly in front of me and spoke of Mr Williams's frequent attempts to create a situation where he would be alone with them. They went on to corroborate what the letter alleges and said that they too had been subjected to suggestive remarks and, in two cases, actual touching.'

'Yes, I can see that puts an entirely different complexion on the situation.'

'Indeed. So much so, in fact, that, after consulting the school's solicitors, I had no choice but to suspend Mr Williams, in absentia, on Friday and call the police, which is why you won't be seeing Carwen again any time soon.'

Edward opened his mouth to speak, but this time could think of nothing to say. His throat was suddenly dry and he felt a tension in his chest. This was serious stuff, and he wondered why he'd been called in at this stage in the proceedings. He guessed that, because he would be taking compassionate leave the following day, the Head had something to say to him that would not wait until his return.

'Rest assured, the police have agreed to carry out their investigations sensitively.' He had obviously noticed Edward's discomfort. 'But, at some stage, I think it not unlikely they will want to interview other students and other members of staff. You might well be one of those yourself, Mr Bryant, your classroom being next door to that of Mr Williams.'

'Well, yes, but…'

'So this is just by way of a heads up, as it were, an opportunity to make sure we're singing from the same hymn sheet.' He leaned forward and smiled in a way that was somehow both reassuring and threatening at the same time.

'Right.'

'Let me be a bit more explicit, Edward. We don't want someone who is clearly demonstrating unprofessional behaviour, whether stress-related or not, to have any chance of remaining as a teacher and in a post of responsibility at this school.'

'Well, no, of course not.'

'The union will play their cards predictably, no doubt; undue provocation, entrapment, the word of a student against that of a senior professional, the effects of stress which the school has done nothing to alleviate, etcetera, etcetera. You a union man, Edward?'

'Yes, I am, but…'

'But you wouldn't want to put your allegiance to the

profession and to an individual within it before upholding our duty to a student or students in our care?'

'Well, no, naturally not.'

'Good. Which brings us to the point of this little chat, I think. You have worked with Mr Williams for, I believe, about six years?'

'Yes, that's about right.'

'And I imagine you had, before all this, a measure of respect for him. But I hope I can rely on you, Edward, not to let that sway you when you give evidence to the police.'

'Evidence?' The dryness in his throat had become painful.

'Well, let's say when you speak to them informally. They'll doubtless ask you about your experience of Mr Williams's leadership, your opinion of him as a colleague. They'll ask you what you know, what students or other colleagues may have said to you, whether you've seen or heard anything from the vantage-point of your classroom next door. Be clear, Mr Bryant, Edward, I'm not asking you to make anything up, absolutely not. However, I am urging you not to hold back with regard to suspicions, however slight, that you might have had in the past that Mr Williams's attitude to and relationship with his students was not…quite right.'

Edward had no idea how to respond to this. He felt as though he were sinking into a mire of equivocation, as though his integrity was being laid bare, his loyalty challenged. Carwen had always seemed a decent enough colleague, if a bit stodgy, a micro-manager without much of an innovative spark. But he wasn't sure he'd go to the wall for him if these allegations were true. On the other hand, the Head seemed to be asking for something more than the ordinary allegiance any member of staff might have towards him and the school; he was asking whose side he was on.

'I can assure you I won't hold anything back. I'll do my best to tell the truth as I see it, I don't think you can ask any more than that.'

'Good, the truth as you see it, that's good.' The Head got up from his desk and looked out at the carefully parked cars in the staff car park, Edward's amongst them. 'I think we're almost done, Mr Bryant. Thank you for popping in for this informal chat. I should say, before you go, though, that for the time being, and this will be the case during your compassionate leave, I shall regard you as the clear front runner for the promotions we've already discussed. Barbara Prentiss will look after things in your absence, but I think we both know that could only ever be a temporary situation. Thank you, Mr Bryant; do close the door on your way out.'

Ten

It was Tuesday morning, and the day they were to drive to the hospital to collect Sammy. Edward had left instructions for his classes during the first few days of his absence and brought back three sets of exercise books to mark. His thoughts, however, remained full of the rather strange challenge to his loyalty implied by the Head's words during their meeting. Things had moved on too fast; he'd had no opportunity to discuss what was going on at school with Louise, and it certainly didn't seem the appropriate time to do it now.

For Louise, the beginning of this day was replete with the emotions stirred up by a chance meeting with Father Davidson the day before. She had gone to the church to pray, kneeling painfully in front of the image of Christ behind the altar. She had prayed for twenty minutes, but her head had been too full of her thoughts and fears to allow the voice of God in. Like the Father, she knew she would have to face this transition in her life on her own.

As she'd risen from her knees, she'd seen the figure of the Father looking at her and smiling. He'd invited her in to his office again and she'd unburdened herself of all her anxieties about Sammy's return. He'd said all the right things, about a mother's special relationship with her son and how this was bound to be different from Edward's as his father. She realised, of course, that her new priest was unaware of the full extent of what had happened between herself, Edward and Ben, but his words had given her comfort, a comfort she'd have found it difficult to find in Edward.

It was a two-hour drive, during which they spoke to each other very little, restricting themselves to comments about the route and the traffic. They instinctively knew the kind of challenges this day would bring and that prolonged discussion of them would not ease their concerns. For Edward, the morning was simply something they needed to get through, something that would be forgotten once normality had been restored and Sammy was used to being at home again. For Louise, there was the feeling that what was about to happen would change her life again forever, a life that had already been knocked wildly out of shape at least three times in the recent past.

When they arrived at the hospital, the wind was high and the place looked even more desolate than when they'd last visited it. Outside, hands folded neatly over her skirt, was the Registrar who had visited them two days ago. As their car pulled around the last bend of the long drive, her expression changed from cold blankness to smiling, corporate goodwill.

'Mr and Mrs Bryant, good morning.' She looked at her watch. 'And two minutes early, very impressive. If you'd like to step inside. I'm sure you know your way to the main reception area by now.'

Edward led the way, Louise walking head-down in his

wake, terrified that she would see Sammy as they came into the impressively wide hall that served as reception and waiting area. But the area was empty; even the receptionist was absent from her post.

'If you'd like to take a seat; it shouldn't take too long to complete the procedures.'

'Where's Sammy?' Whilst Edward took a seat at the side of the wide room, Louise remained standing. Having been anxious about seeing him, Louise was now more concerned that he would, after all, for some reason, be kept from them.

'Well, you are a little early; I expect the nurse is just gathering together his things, making sure he realises what's about to happen. If you'll just take a seat next to your husband, I'll go and see how we're fixed.'

A little early. Husband. How we're fixed. These ordinary, business-like phrases sounded odd when set against the enormity of her inner turmoil. Her breath was coming short now, her heart beating fast. She hoped they would not have to wait more than a couple of minutes. Edward seemed to sense her discomfort, as he could sometimes do, and held her hand, pulling it towards him and placing it on his lap.

In fact, it was less than thirty seconds later when the Registrar returned to the waiting area. She was alone, but had her best reassuring smile on her face.

'Here's Samuel.'

She moved aside, like a compere introducing the next act. Behind her, a nurse of about Louise's own age stepped forward, holding tight to the hand of a small, pale boy whose unblinking eyes looked straight at Louise. They stopped, the nurse bending down to whisper something to Sammy, then moved slowly forward another few steps. The nurse let go of Sammy's hand, so that he stood there awkwardly, not quite knowing where to turn.

In the car on their way to the hospital, Louise had rehearsed how she wanted these first few moments to be; she would remain calm and let Sammy take his time. She would not show too much emotion, but smile as gently as possible and let him come to her.

At first, the actual moment seemed to demand exactly what she had planned for it. Louise let go of Edward's hand and allowed both of hers to rest in her lap. Sammy, though, remained frozen to the spot, unblinking and unsure. And that was when something broke inside her. Painful tears squeezed themselves from her eyes; she stood up and ran forward, knocking over a chair that blocked her path to him.

'Louise, maybe…'

She took no notice of Edward's feeble warning, reaching out her arms and half-walking, half-running towards Sammy. For a moment, he was alarmed and looked in the direction of the nurse, who took half a step forward, but then, as Louise's arms wrapped themselves strongly around him and pulled him in to her, Sammy thrust his head against her womb and cried out.

'Mummy, mummy. Harriet says we're going home. Can we go home now, mummy? Can we go home…?'

During the long journey back in the car, Louise sat with Sammy in the back. Almost immediately, he flopped over and fell asleep, whilst Louise stroked the blond head and smiled. How senseless it seemed to have worried about it all.

Sammy wanted to come home and she wanted him back, wanted it more than anything else in the world, of course she did. Even Edward, occasionally looking in the driver's mirror at the two of them in the back seat, appeared content.

It was only as they reached the outskirts of the city that Sammy woke up, seeming to sense that he was nearly home. Sitting bolt upright in the seat, he noticed Edward for really the first time since they had left the hospital.

'Daddy!'

'Hello, Sammy. Nearly there now. Then it'll be back to your old room.'

'Yes.'

As they pulled into the short front drive, Louise closed the window and noticed the smell for the first time.

'Done wee.'

'Yes, darling, never mind. We'll soon clean it up.'

'It was a long drive, Sammy. Don't worry about it.'

'OK.'

And so they were home. Sammy rushed immediately upstairs to his room; they could hear him playing with his Lego and rearranging his other toys and books. While Louise put the kettle on, Edward filled a bowl with hot water and washing-up liquid and went out to the car to clean the back seat. When he returned, Louise had made the tea and they sat together at the kitchen table, a sense of togetherness beginning to grow between them slowly once more.

The rest of that day seemed to be spent in relentless pursuit of Sammy as he tore around the house and garden, reacquainting himself with his surroundings. It would have been natural to take him to the park, but Edward and Louise both realised it would be a long time before they could venture again to the place of his abduction and, in any case, Sammy made no mention of it.

He ate almost constantly, devouring fruit, cakes, biscuits, pasta as though they hadn't fed him at all at the hospital, but it was not long after it grew dark that he suddenly slowed down and curled up on the sofa in front of the television. They had anticipated that it might be difficult to get him upstairs, bathed and into bed, but the opposite was the case. He was over-boisterous in the bath, spraying water over the bathroom floor, but Louise frowned at Edward when she saw that he was about to chastise him. Edward read him a story in bed, and, when they turned out the main light, leaving only the glow of the stars on the ceiling, Sammy turned over in bed and immediately closed his eyes.

Later, in their own bed, Louise lay closer to Edward than she had done for a while. She could feel his arousal, but when he slid one hand up to her left breast, she gently took hold of it and pushed it back down her body again. She was not ready for sex with him, though she felt the warmth of their shared parental love. Edward accepted this, and did not turn his back on her. They had returned with Sammy, who had slipped back into his old life as though he had never been away, and now there was something between the two of them again that they would have found it hard to express. But it was there, there in the touch of their skin in the dark.

Eleven

'She's a little better today, Mr Bryant. More...coherent. But if you could stick with the half-hour I think that would still be good.'

On the same day that Sammy, his biological child, had been taken home by Louise and Edward, Ben had driven the sixty miles to Leticia's psychiatric hospital in Sussex for his usual meeting with her and her specialist team. Like his brother, he had been given compassionate leave, though as a junior partner he didn't really need to ask for it.

He knew the route well enough by now, but this only encouraged his mind to reflect on what had happened since his last visit. Alongside the uncomfortable feeling that the journey was more like a duty fulfilled than anything else was the sour taste of guilt. He had succumbed to Jennifer Ormiston's open invitation to have an affair, and now, as he clutched the wheel and mechanically negotiated each curve and junction of the journey, he found it hard to understand how his body, his lust, had so overwhelmed his rational judgement. He wondered how he would respond as a lawyer to evidence of similar extra-marital behaviour in a divorce case. He would take the view that the party in his own situation had conducted himself in such a way as to threaten the integrity of the marriage, of course. So why his own aberrant behaviour?

Was he pleased when the specialist informed him that Leticia was more coherent? Of course he was, but he also thought darkly of the awkwardness he might find in smiling at her, telling her he still loved her and would do everything to support her when she was well again. The love that he'd had for her had been thrown out of kilter, changed into sadness rather than joy by the full realisation of her mental illness, her abduction of Sammy, her attempt to kill herself. And now, there was this thing with Jennifer. Christ, what a bloody awful place his life was in at the moment. He couldn't imagine his brother making such a mess of things.

'By the way, she's been talking about leaving the hospital, asking when her treatment will be completed, that sort of thing. Quite a good sign, though of course, as you are only too aware, it's likely she will be released from our care directly into custody.' Ben and the specialist stopped outside Leticia's room, which was windowless on the corridor side, apart from a toughened glass aperture in the door.

'Oh, right. That's quite a new thing, isn't it? I got the impression on my last couple of visits that she was doing her best to avoid talking to me about coming out.'

'Yes. Since Saturday, I'd say. Mind you, she's still sleeping quite a lot during the day, and it's rare for her to sleep through the night without an episode or two. In the old days, we'd have taken these disturbances as evidence of, well, you know, guilt or suppressed violent urges. Now, we tend to take a purely neurological stance – the brain clearing out its painful detritus, purging itself, if you like. Anyway, I'll leave you with her. You know the button to press if…' The specialist moved away, waving a vague arm over his retreating shoulder, taking it for granted that Benjamin Bryant, husband and lawyer, would understand the circumstances under which to call for assistance.

Ben opened the door to her room and stepped inside. An unexpected shaft of winter sun was illuminating the bedside table. She was asleep, on her side and facing away from him, but as he turned and closed the door, she stirred and turned over, letting out a little moan. It took her ten seconds or so to focus and realise it wasn't a nurse or specialist who'd entered.

'Ben…Ben. It's you.' An arm reached out from under the sheet towards him. The room was stiflingly hot and shared the oxygenated narcosis of the rest of the hospital. He wondered if that was why she slept so often.

'Yes, darling, it's me.' At the word 'darling' something tightened inside him and he screwed up his eyes to stop the tears forming. 'The sun's coming in. Do you want me to pull the curtains across a little?'

'No, no, that's fine. I like it. It reminds me there's somewhere outside this room, this hospital, somewhere where the sun shines.'

This was unbearable. He came slowly forward and sat by the bed, taking her outstretched hand and stroking it. The gesture felt wrong somehow, as though he were a priest providing professional succour to the dying, so he raised her hand to his lips and kissed her fingers gently. This time it was impossible to stop the tears from gathering behind his eyelids and, before he could lift his face, they had run down on to her hand.

'Benjamin, I do believe you're crying.'

It was the slightly false, upper-class tone that her mother sometimes used. In the early days of their relationship, he had found it charming and curiously affectionate in its very attempt to be unsentimental. Now, it was a clear sign that she was beginning to behave more normally. He found this comforting and alarming in equal measure. It was obviously good that she was recovering from the physical and mental trauma of what had happened to her, and if they could speak to one another more as they used to, that would perhaps restore the feeling they always had of warm but restrained desire. But then, what about Jennifer? Would he carry on his affair with her? What, in any case, would happen when Leticia was taken into custody? It was absurd, he thought, that six words from his wife could trigger so much anxiety, and yet perhaps really not so surprising at all.

'Sorry, yes. It doesn't help, does it, me crying? I'm sorry, Let.' His voice sounded pathetic to himself, but it was all he could think to say.

'Come here. I need you, Benjamin. I want you to be close to me.'

With surprising strength, she pulled him forward by the hand that he was still holding and, ridiculously, he fell to his knees by the bedside, looking behind him instinctively to make sure no-one could see what he was doing. He remembered kneeling at her bedside on another occasion, in the middle of the night at her ancestral home, before they were married. How long ago that seemed.

'Oh, Benjy, everything's such a mess. I've made such a mess of things.'

She was nuzzling her head into his neck, which was quickly warm and wet with her own tears. He slipped his hand under the sheet and around her body. She had always been slim, but now he could feel how thin she was, how her ribs moved with each caught breath under her hospital gown. Instinctively, he wanted to pull his hand away, but he left it there, squeezing gently. How different from the body of another woman he had squeezed not that long ago, full, fleshy and smooth. He did not quite know what to say to her. That she had made a mess of things was beyond question, but he felt an urgent duty to help her through this, to show her he was there for her.

'But that's all behind you now, Let. That's how you have to look at it. A fresh start.' He pushed her away from him a little so that he could look into her drawn, pleading face. 'You're much better now, the specialist tells me. You've been through hell, physically and emotionally, but you're coming through, getting well.'

'But what use is that when I'm taken in by the police? I took a child, Benjy, your child, as it happens.' They both froze for an instant with the strangeness and horror of the memory. 'And I tried to kill myself. I used to believe that was a sin, the worst of all.'

'But you weren't well when you did these things, Let. We know that now, and the police know that as well. They'll take that into account. In any case, the whole thing was made worse by the actions of that bloody priest. If he'd acted differently…'

'Yes, but he didn't, did he?'

'That's not your fault, Let. None of this is really your

fault, not really. You weren't in control of what you were doing. They're bound to see that. The specialists here. They'll make sure the authorities see that.'

'Bless you, Benjy. I know you're trying to help, but somehow I can't believe what I've done can ever be forgiven. Of course, if only that Ormiston woman hadn't told me about Sammy, none of this would've happened. Not any of it.'

Her voice had become suddenly distant, a cold monotone. She shrugged herself free of his hands and sank back under the sheet. Ben opened his mouth to speak, but he had frozen into silence and something was constricting his throat. A long silence ensued. He was hoping she would drop back into the sleep he had found her in when he arrived, but, as the sun from the window found the edge of the bed, she looked at him again and smiled. Her hand emerged from under the sheet, but this time she put it behind his head and began to stroke his hair rhythmically. Could she see how intolerably painful this was for him? He hoped not.

'Anyway, Benjamin, what have you been doing while I've been stuck in this place?'

'Me?'

'Yes, Benjy, you.'

'Well, work mostly. Several high-profile cases. Good for business, I suppose.'

'And who is fetching and carrying for you while I'm not there?'

'Oh, Bill's got some temp in. Completely useless. It's really best to avoid asking her to do anything. Nothing like you, Let.'

'I should hope not. If she were, your eye might have strayed in her direction.'

'Nonsense.'

'Really? You're more good-looking than ever, Benjy, as you well know. It would just about be the end of everything if some woman made a pass at you while I'm stuck in a madhouse.'

This is unbearable, he thought, please let it stop. He took her hand from his head and squeezed it a little too hard before pushing it back under the sheet.

'You're being silly, Let. I told you, she's some brainless tart who doesn't have the first idea about the job. I'm the last thing you need to worry about.'

'Dear Benjy.' Her eyes grew vacant and began to close. 'I think I need to sleep again now. It comes over me quite suddenly and then I have to…'

The eyes closed and she lay lifeless under the sheet, horribly as he had seen her in the hospital in Norfolk after she had been pulled from the water. He got up painfully from his knees and moved towards the door, opening it carefully and stepping outside into the corridor. He turned to look into the room again, but could see only the top of her platinum blond hair on the pillow. This ordeal was over, but there was a sick feeling in his stomach that would not pass so easily. It was the nausea of shame, and it might, he felt, leave its traces forever.

Twelve

The noise woke Louise first. A high whimpering, followed by silence. Then the whimpering again and the sound of a small voice on the other side of the wall, calling out. She couldn't hear what the voice was saying, but it sounded like the same thing over and over, ostinato, and was getting louder. Edward was snoring, his arm still draped over her. She removed it carefully and got out of bed. She would see what the problem was first, before waking Edward.

The bedroom door creaked as she opened it and Edward stirred and turned over in the bed, reaching out for her. As she put her head around the door, she could see Sammy standing in the doorway of his room. He had stopped the repetitive whimpering, but was breathing hard, as though he couldn't catch his breath. She moved slowly out on to the landing.

'Sammy, Sammy darling. What's the matter? Can't you sleep?'

At this, the shallow breathing stopped. Sammy came out of the room and stood just a couple of feet away from her. He was barefoot and had taken off his pyjama top. His eyes were directed towards his mother, but they were glassy and distant. Louise realised that he was sleepwalking, though he had never done this before the abduction and the accident.

'Stop it. I don't want it. It tastes funny.'

'What does, darling?'

'Don't ask me any more questions. I don't want any more questions.'

'OK, Sammy, I won't ask you any questions.' She knew her words were pointless, but she said them anyway.

'The man in the black skirt. I don't like the man in the black skirt. I want Harriet.'

'Harriet's not here, darling, and there's no man in a black skirt. The man in the black skirt has gone forever now.' She moved a step closer to him. 'Why don't you come in with mummy and daddy now? Come into our room, you'll feel safer there.' As she spoke, she was aware of Edward's presence behind her and felt his hand on her shoulder.

'What's going on? Why's he out of bed?'

'He's sleepwalking, dreaming out loud. We'll get him into our bed.'

'I'm not sure that's a good idea. What if he gets used to it?'

'Now's not the time to think about that, surely?'

Sammy was silent now, but still staring vacantly towards them. Edward stepped out from behind Louise and moved slightly forwards. She held him back, but could not prevent him from slowly reaching out his arms towards Sammy.

'Come on, now, let's take you back to bed. It's cold out here.'

At this, Sammy seemed to wake and focus all his attention on Edward. As his father edged closer, the boy turned his head a little to one side as if in intense fear.

'Leave me alone. I don't want you to take me anywhere.

I hate you. You just want to make me sleep. I don't want to sleep anymore.'

And with that he ran into Edward and shoved him out of the way with surprising force. Louise tried to grab him as he went for the stairs, but could not get to him in time. He negotiated the first two or three steps well enough, but then tripped and fell headlong, rolling over a couple of times before he hit the hard wooden floor of the hallway, where he lay apparently lifeless in the semi-dark, whilst his parents stood at the top of the stairs looking down, momentarily rooted to the spot in shocked disbelief.

'Sammy! Sammy!' As Edward descended the stairs, he was trying not to raise his voice, but his terror overwhelmed him.

'Don't, Ed, don't shout at him. I don't think you should shout. And I don't think you should touch him, either.'

'Because I'm not his father, is that it?' It was a stupid thing to say, and he immediately regretted it.

'No, of course not. It's just not the right thing to do.'

'Yes, of course, sorry. It just came out. I'm sorry.'

She said nothing, but slowly made her way down the stairs towards Edward and her son; this was difficult as her arms and legs were shaking and her head swimming, so she felt, if she went too fast, that she would fall as Sammy had fallen, head over heels, and land on the wooden floor beside him. When she reached the last-but-one step, she sat down. It would have been awkward to manoeuvre herself around Edward and Sammy, but, if she was honest, she was frightened to come any closer. She could see Edward was at a loss what to do.

'Try his pulse. Has he got a pulse?' The words felt brutal, unfeeling as they fell from her.

Edward looked closely at Sammy's neck. It did not seem to be broken, but then he was not sure what a broken neck should look like. He put two fingers against the small, fragile neck. Nothing at first, then, as he pressed harder, he could feel a weak throbbing under his finger ends.

'There's a pulse, I'm pretty sure.'

He looked at Sammy's back and the position of his limbs. The back was twisted a little, one shoulder higher than the other, but he hadn't fallen on either of his arms and the legs were stretched out almost straight in front of him. Louise could see this, too, and Edward's finding a pulse emboldened her to push her way to his side. She knelt over Sammy and began to smooth his hair away from his forehead, aware that she was doing what she had told Edward not to do a moment earlier.

'You're going to be OK, darling, you're going to be OK.'

The ambulance arrived forty minutes later. Louise was relieved when the medics came through the door and moved to where Sammy was still lying, tending to him quickly with practised eyes and hands, looking for serious injury. Edward was furiously angry at the time it had taken them to get there, but realised this was not the time for histrionics. He might have died, he thought, they could have been taking away a corpse. As it happened, Sammy had stirred once or twice, his eyes flickering open for an instant before closing again. And now the medics were trying to wake him up, to speak to him.

'Hello, Sammy. Sammy? Do you know where you are? Can you see Mummy and Daddy?'

Both eyes opened and his head tried to raise itself, but was pushed gently back down by a green-uniformed arm. Louise moved quickly forward and knelt down beside him.

'Hello, darling. You're back with us. Don't try to lift your head up just yet.'

'He'll be fine now, Mr and Mrs Bryant. Everything's going to be fine. But we're going to need to take him in the ambulance to get him checked over. Can't take too many chances with concussion, as I'm sure you realise. But, rest assured we'll have him back as soon as we can. It could have been much worse; he's had a bit of a lucky escape. A strong little chap, obviously.'

'Oh, yes, a strong little chap.'

Thirteen

Following his return from the secure psychiatric hospital, Ben lay on his bed, propped up on pillows. He had been planning to go in to the office, but knew he would not be able to concentrate. The words he had exchanged with Leticia that morning circulated incessantly in his head, stabbing at him in their accusatory irony. He had opened a bottle of beer, intending to sip at it slowly before ordering a takeaway, but had finished it and a second bottle quickly, and was now on his third. Contrary to his expectation, the after-effects of this unaccustomed daytime drinking weren't helping to get things straight in his head. Beside his bed, his mobile glowed blue, telling him he had six missed calls from 'Jenny O'.

After her early afternoon interview slot, Jennifer would normally have stayed on to schmooze her interviewee. Naturally, this always depended on who it was. A wealthy local businessman, a widely-known actor or musician who happened to live locally, an influential blogger – these would be prime targets for her particular brand of networking, which involved showing off to the women and closing down the personal space of the men, as long as they were moderately good-looking. Today, however, the interviewee was deadly dull and devoid of any useful influence in the city, so she had decided to drive straight back to her flat and sit with her legs up on the sofa, a glass of white wine on the table and her mobile open in front of her.

Ben had texted her, she remembered, to say that he would be driving to Sussex again to see his wife today. Jennifer Ormiston, being Jennifer Ormiston, had taken this as a challenge rather than an invitation to leave him alone and so, over the next hour, she fired off a series of texts to him, each shorter but more direct than the last, suggesting he should come over to her flat that evening to shake off the effects of the hospital and his mad, fragile wife by seeing to her own, much more libidinous, needs. She was not surprised that he hadn't replied to any of the messages. Most men worth bothering with needed to be pressed into action, and Ben was especially of this type. It was all part of the delicious prepping that led to the best sex, as far as she was concerned.

She was, however, a little surprised not to have received any kind of reply, even a negative one, after her sixth text and so she closed her mobile; it was time to let him stew, to let him want her so much he couldn't resist.

On the table in the hallway lay four or five envelopes she'd brought home from the studio. She threw two of them straight into the recycling bag, and recognised another as the confirmation of the renewal of her contract with Digital City. The addresses on the two remaining envelopes were handwritten. Her heart sank at the sight of them. What would it be this time? A challenge to something she'd said on her morning show, a plea from some local shop or business to open something-or-other, an elderly gentleman declaring his undying love for her?

She returned to the sofa and tore open the first of the handwritten envelopes. The writer was a great fan of hers, and could not understand why she hadn't been snapped up by a national radio station. Would she dedicate an hour of her programme to the memory of her dog, Jessie, who had just passed on. An hour? For Christ's sake, a whole hour for a goddam pooch? She'd maybe think about a single track. Dogs were useful enough, she thought, when you needed to tug at the heartstrings.

The second envelope was sealed with sellotape. At first, she wondered if she could be bothered to open it; she checked her mobile again to see if there was any reply from Ben. Seeing nothing on the screen, she went to the kitchen to fetch a knife and slit open the envelope. She unfurled the single sheet that had been unhandily stuffed into it and started to read:

Miss Ormiston (but I expect you prefer Ms)
This is by way of an introduction. Not that I'm going to tell you who I am, that would obviously be rather stupid. The fact is, Ms Ormiston, Jennifer, I know something about you that you might not want the rest of the world to know, and especially those of your listeners who think you such a national treasure, isn't that the phrase? Well, a local treasure, at least.
It's what you did in the dim and distant past they might be interested in. I think so, anyway. I'm not going to write any more for the moment. But you will need to pay if you don't want it all to come out. I'm not telling you how much right

now, but it won't break you, I'm sure, you with all that money stashed away.
Look out for my next letter.

Needless to say, this was not the first letter, text or email she had received of this kind, and doubtless it wouldn't be the last. The price of some sort of fame, she supposed. She screwed up the sheet and was about to consign it to the bag with the other junk mail when her hand seemed to decide of its own accord to hover over the raised lid. She smoothed out the paper again and sat on a kitchen stool to take another look.

This one was a bit different, maybe. It appeared to promise another communication of some kind and was very vague as to what she was supposed to have done and how much money he (she instinctively felt it was a he, though you could never be sure) would demand. With no specific threat and no actual demand for money, she couldn't see the police being very interested in the letter, so she refolded it and placed it under a pile of magazines on the hall table, along with the envelope. She had done many things that someone other than herself might have been ashamed of. Take your pick, she said out loud, take your pick.

Of course, there was that. But no-one could have unearthed that, could they? It was such a long time ago.

Back on the sofa, she downed the half-glass of wine that still remained and opened her mobile again. A reply from Ben, at last. It was short, and made no reference at all to the various suggestions she had made about what the two of them might get up to that evening. *We need to talk.* Well, yes, she thought, talk, but not for too long; there were better things you could do than talk. She hesitated over her reply, but couldn't resist it when it came into her head: 'OK, you come round here and we'll give each other a good talking to.' She waited for his response, expecting a delicious counter to her innuendo. It came almost straight away. *Twenty minutes*. Was this the only reply he could muster?

When the doorbell sounded, she was unscrewing a second bottle of Pinot Grigio, intending to let it work its magic on her imminent lover. Setting the bottle and two bulbous glasses on the kitchen top, she debated in her mind whether to go for a full-on assault in the hallway or take her time and let him say whatever it was he so urgently wanted to talk to her about. The problem with the full-on assault was that, if it didn't work, it would make the second approach more difficult. Take your time it is, then.

'Benjamin, baby. Twenty minutes you said and twenty minutes it is.'

As she opened the door, he barely seemed to register her, or what she'd said, brushing past her and searching out the lounge to his right. She followed him slowly, pausing in the doorway like some Hollywood femme fatale. He was sitting on the sofa, leaning forward, arms propping up his head, hands over his nose and mouth, eyes closed.

'Make yourself at home, why don't you.'

'Can you come and sit down, Jenny?'

The voice was faint and muffled as it came from behind his hands. She looked at him. It was obvious she would have to wait before she could have him where she wanted him.

Slowly, all words frozen, on ice, she walked across the room and sat next to him on the sofa.

'I'm here. We can talk, if that's what you want to do. It's what I do for a living, after all.'

And then she remembered where he'd been that day. The texts she'd sent him had been a counter-offensive, but they hadn't worked. Something had been different this time at the hospital, it was the only explanation, and now he 'needed to talk'. This was going to be a whole lot more difficult than she'd thought.

'Look, I've just opened an Italian, as they say, d'you want some?' She pointed out of the room, in the direction of the kitchen.

'No, no thanks, I'm half-pissed already. Beginnings of a headache; shouldn't have driven over here, really.'

'D'you mind if I do?' Not waiting for his reply, she left him where he was sitting, returning fifteen seconds later with a large glass of pale yellow liquid which she set down on the table in front of them.

'The thing is…today, at the hospital, Leticia was more like her old self. It took me by surprise.' He was sitting upright now, his head turned to speak directly to her. 'She needs my support, Jenny, she needs it very badly.'

'OK, sure.'

'I mean, you know, I'm not blind to what she is, what she's done; she's…unstable, maybe even dangerous at some moments, though, God knows, I didn't know that when I married her. And she took my child, the child I gave to Ed and Louise, took him because, I don't know, because she wanted him and he was mine, but then you know all about that, Jenny, whatever you say.' Jennifer listened to this with mounting anger, but thought it best to say nothing. 'And then the attempt to take her own life. I suppose it was that that made the difference for me in the end. She was a disturbed young woman well before I met her; in some ways it was inevitable she should be driven to do what she did, the knife, the water, all that. Someone had to rescue her, and, as her husband, that someone was me, and that someone is still me.'

Her anger had subsided, to be replaced by pity, not an emotion she could honestly say she felt very often. It did not displace her desire for him, however, but transformed it into something warmer and, if anything, more urgent. She still wanted him, but would have to be even more careful what she said, how she looked at him, how she moved her body towards him. She allowed a long pause to open between them before she spoke.

'I'm so sorry, Benjy, sorry you've been put through all this. You don't deserve any of it. I hope your wife appreciates what you've done for her, what you're still doing. It's the lawyer in you. It's a sense of what's right, a sense of duty.'

'Not senses you're all that familiar with, Jenny, I wouldn't say.'

'Well, maybe not. But then we can't all be Mr or Mrs Upright and Sensible, can we. I mean, the world would be a pretty dull place, don't you think?' Shit, she thought, too flip. And, in any case, what she'd implied wasn't true – she didn't think of him as Mr Sensible at all, not when she had him in bed with her.

'Look, Jenny, there's no comfortable way to say this. I don't think I can be there for Leticia and go on with this, with us. Perhaps there was a moment, more than a moment maybe, when I thought I could, but I can't.'

Instead of getting up and making for the front door as she had expected him to, he flung himself backwards on the sofa, both hands behind his head, eyes tight shut. This was her moment. As surreptitiously as was possible under the circumstances, she pushed herself across the sofa towards him, passing her left leg quickly over him so that she was kneeling on both sides of his lap, pressing down.

'Jenny, for God's sake.'

He lifted himself up, but she pushed him back down again, making sure that her breasts were pressing against his face. He could throw me off, she thought, but he doesn't want to.

'One for the road, Benjy. If it's all over, then it's all over, but let's finish with a bang, not a whimper. Or maybe a bang and a whimper, who knows…?'

Fourteen

'Sorry, Mummy.'

'Don't be silly, darling, there's nothing to be sorry about.'

They had gone with Sammy in the ambulance to the local hospital and stayed with him all night. On the following day, he had undergone tests and been monitored for signs of delayed concussion. Now, it was the middle of the afternoon and Sammy had been declared fit and well, apart from the inevitable bruising.

'Not walk around. Stay in bed, like Daddy said.'

'Yes, darling, but you didn't know what you were doing. You were walking around, but you weren't properly awake. It happens sometimes, it's perfectly OK.'

Louise turned to Edward, who was standing back a little, letting her sit by the bed and take Sammy's small hand in hers. She had her other hand up to her mouth, and he could see tears were forming in her eyes. He stepped forward and she instinctively stood up and allowed him to take over. Without a thought, he put his right hand on Sammy's hair and brushed his forehead with his thumb.

'Mummy's right, Sammy, there's nothing to say sorry for. We think you've been a very brave boy, and you need to just take it easy.'

'It hurts. On my leg and on my shoulder. It's hurting.'

'Yes, old chap, that's where you fell on the floor at the bottom of the stairs – you know, like your teddies used to do when they were parachuting.'

'I don't remember that.'

'No, you were much younger then. You're a big boy now, a big boy and a brave boy.'

'Yes, but how long will it hurt for?'

'Oh, not very long, Sammy. Only a day or two.'

'Can we go home now, Daddy? I don't want to go back to the other hospital again.' He looked thoughtful for a moment. 'But I did like Harriet, she was a nice lady.'

'Was she the nurse that looked after you?'

'Yes, but I don't want to see her again now. I just want to go home.'

Not long after they returned to the house, Sammy had something to eat and watched television for a short while. Edward left him cradled against Louise's shoulder whilst he started the washing-up, but when he returned he was asleep. With infinite care, they lifted him from the sofa and carried him upstairs to his room, slipping him under the quilt and kissing him goodnight. He turned once, twice, then was still.

Outside, at the top of the landing, they attached the safety gate he had had when he was much younger; they had been advised to do this by the community nurse who would be there to check on him day by day and keep the paediatric hospital informed of his progress. They moved as noiselessly as they could down the stairs and stood motionless at the exact spot where he'd fallen, looking at each other with wordless understanding: this was how it was when they were full of optimism about their future as parents.

'After he fell, when I said to you not to touch him, why did you think I meant because you're not his father?'

They were at the sink now, finishing the dishes. Edward had been aware that his wife was thinking of something, wondering whether to broach an awkward subject; it was an unmistakeable look she had, unmistakeable to him, anyway.

'I wondered when you'd bring that up.'

'I'm not bringing it up, I just...I don't understand why you would have thought I meant that, that's all.'

'Because...' He put down the glass he was half-way through drying. 'Because it's how I feel about you, and me, and Sammy. I can be Daddy for him, that's not difficult, but it doesn't feel the same as it used to be when he was small. Back then, all I knew was that you'd made a baby with Ben's help and that we had the child that could fill the hole in our lives. That was all there was to it.'

'Except that it wasn't all there was to it, was it? You were still having an affair with my best friend.'

How had they got to this? Since the court case, they had tacitly agreed never to discuss their affairs, his with Jennifer, hers with Ben. It was simply too painful, too difficult to confront. They both hoped that their emotional bruising would come out in time and gradually lose its sting, or change them into some other couple, a different Ed and Louise, who could start afresh, incorporating their moral lapses into their new relationship.

'That's not the point, and you know it. I was already trying to end it with Jennifer, and in any case that had nothing to do with Sammy and how I felt about him. It was your affair with my own brother that really changed things, whether you like to admit that or not.'

Louise let go of the plate she was holding and allowed it to fall in the lukewarm water of the washing-up bowl. How stupid of her to ask him about what he'd said after Sammy had fallen. She could have guessed all this would come to the surface again, why wouldn't it? Perhaps it was best that it did, but she wasn't at all sure. Maybe, at some unconscious level, it *was* very precisely why she didn't want him to touch her child. Perhaps something in her never wanted him to touch Sammy again.

'Look, Ed, and I've never said this before, but…I'm not excusing what happened between me and Ben.' She was leaning forward against the stainless steel of the sink, bracing herself for what she had to say to him and how he might respond.

'Well, good, I'm very glad to hear it.' It was impossible to keep the irony out of his voice.

'But, you know, it was something you and I planned, something positive, that got out of control. Whereas your thing with Jennifer…that was just, well, lust; I'm not sure there's any other way of describing it.'

They had reached an inevitable impasse. For several seconds they were frozen, Louise propped against the sink, Edward gripping the half-dried glass in one hand and the teacloth in the other. Then Edward sat down at the kitchen table, fearful that he might give way to anger and smash the glass on the floor. He could not defend what he had done, but she seemed to want some kind of validation for her own affair. He was surprised when Louise came to the table and sat opposite him, her hands still wet from the sink. He felt it might be some kind of acknowledgement of how brutal and self-serving her words had been and this enabled him to speak, where he would otherwise have remained silent.

'This is no good, Lou. We're never going to resolve what's happened in our marriage.'

'No.'

'But we do have a small boy to look after. He may not be my son biologically, but he's been through hell and he needs a stable home to grow up in. We're all he's got, the two of us.'

'Edward and Louise Bryant, PLC?'

'If you like. A bit more than that, though, hopefully.'

'Yes, a bit more, maybe.'

She reached across the table and put two wet, tentative fingers on his hand and left them there. His hand did not move, but neither did he pull it away from her touch. They sat there for over a minute, aware that nothing they could say would make the situation better and listening out for any noise from the bedroom at the top of the stairs where Sammy was covered in his quilt, the glowing stars still above his head.

Fifteen

Ben arrived later than he'd planned at the offices of Thurgood and Thurgood that morning. He had with him a bundle of legal papers he ought to have read the evening before. He was due to have a meeting at ten with an important client, a meeting for which he would need to be completely up to speed; he hoped in the forty minutes he had beforehand that he wouldn't encounter anything that might trip him up.

As he went through the papers, he found it difficult to concentrate. What had happened the previous night intruded on his thoughts every time he turned a page. With the benefit of hindsight, it had clearly been a bad idea to turn up at Jennifer's flat and expect simply to tell her it was all over. It seemed to make no difference that he was primed to end their relationship, that he had even gone through the words he would use. He was a lawyer, for Christ's sake; why couldn't he use the same skills he used on clients and other solicitors on Jennifer?

Of course, he knew the answer to this – because she had power over him, because whenever he was near her he felt aroused, aroused more than ashamed. And she understood that, instinctively, as even Ben knew some women did. It would not be easy to shake her off, that much was clear, and the first thing he needed to do was to stop fancying her. If he could stop doing that, the rest would fall into place.

But when she'd climbed on top of him last night, when she'd pressed her breasts against him and moved her hips on him, he felt helpless. It was stupid, but that was the word, helpless. With a sense of mounting disgust, he remembered throwing her to the floor and starting to remove her clothing. He had expected her to resist, to tell him to stop, but instead she breathed quickly into his ear and seemed to be enjoying it; the more he pressed himself on her, in her, the more she seemed to want him to carry on. Afterwards, she'd wanted him to stay with her, to 'take her to bed', as she'd put it, but his headache had returned painfully and he knew he'd have to leave, to go home and nurse his disgust.

Half-way through the documents and only twenty minutes to the meeting. The legal text swam before his eyes, and all attempts to concentrate harder merely induced more of a sense of panic. He could ask Old Bill to cover the meeting for him, but he'd want to know why and he couldn't think of any plausible reason. He flicked through the remaining thirty-five pages; nothing that he couldn't cope with, as far as he could see, but there was bound to be something, there always was.

Several hours later, and the morning meeting negotiated with remarkable ease under the circumstances, Ben turned on his mobile again and allowed himself to look at the messages. Seven texts from Jennifer, most written with a mixture of suggestive irony and pleading, and a missed call; he wouldn't bother listening to her voice, he already knew how it would sound. Some of the texts must have been sent during her morning show, he thought. He wondered how she could switch from professional radio host to spurned lover so easily.

That afternoon, after a rushed lunch from the sandwich place on the corner of the street, he dealt with three more clients and gave Old Bill his verdict on the temporary secretary, Alice, at their weekly briefing. At four, he slipped out of the office and headed back to his flat in Bartholomew Road, amongst the psychotherapists and spiritual healers ensconced in their Edwardian villas.

In view of what had happened the day before, he avoided the temptation of a cold beer from the fridge and made himself a mug of tea instead. He sat down on the Chesterfield sofa in the high-ceilinged lounge and brought up his texts with a kind of grim fascination. Three more from her; he wouldn't bother opening them. There was one other, though, from Louise. It was the first time she'd contacted him since the court case, and the contents of the text alarmed him:

Hi Ben. Just to let you know we got Sammy back yesterday. All fine until he fell down the stairs in the night. They kept him in hospital to check for concussion, but he's back with us now. Nothing to worry about, but thought you should know – Louise.

When he read the word 'concussion' his chest contracted. Sammy was not, in any meaningful sense, his son, but the news that he'd been hurt, been taken to hospital to be checked over, seemed to instantly re-establish the biological connection between them. Was Louise glossing over the seriousness of what had happened? Concussion could be delayed for quite a long time, couldn't it?

He considered replying to the text, then decided not to. He'd let Ed and Louise sort themselves out first and then drive round to their house that evening. Yes, that was the right thing to do.

He remembered the house now as the place where terrible things had had to be endured, where the police had asked difficult questions, where all their lives had turned upside down. Outside the front door, he hesitated in the dark, feeling rain coming on. What was he doing here? Maybe a text message would have been better after all. He hadn't seen Louise for some while, but this was not the time to resurrect any feelings he might still have about her. He must also be careful not to show too much concern about Sammy. That wouldn't be appropriate either.

He pressed the doorbell and waited, then saw Louise's distorted form through the glass coming along the hallway. She opened the door cautiously, looking to see who it was at this time of night. When she saw it was him, she opened the door a little more, but looked at him with an odd mixture of affection and alarm; she looked a little worn down, he thought, a little tired and nervous.

'Ben, it's you.'

'Yes. I'm sorry to call like this, out of the blue, but I got your message about Sammy. I wanted to see if he's all right.' He expected her to invite him in, but she remained silent, peering out at him through the space between the door and the frame. 'Could I come in? It's, well, it's raining.'

'Oh.' She half-opened the door and looked out. 'So it is. Yes, of course, sorry, come in.'

She had spoken to him as though he were a stranger. His relationship with his sister-in-law had been an unusual one, certainly, but this coldness was still unexpected. As he entered the hallway, he bent to kiss her on the cheek, but she moved sinuously out of the way and further down the hall towards the lounge.

'Come through.'

'Oh, yes, thanks.'

She ushered him to a chair. It happened to be the same chair in the bay window he'd sat in when she and Edward had first asked him to be a surrogate father. Louise sat opposite him, perched on the edge of the sofa, and looked down at her feet.

'Ed's upstairs.' She paused, thinking of what she should say next. 'One of us stays upstairs now when Sammy's asleep, just in case. He's fine, by the way, absolutely fine. A lucky escape.'

'Good, that's good. I just wanted to pop round to see. Didn't I notice the safety gate on as I came through the hall just now?'

'Yes, that's right. The hospital asked us to put it up again, just until he's settled.'

'OK, yes, I see. So, one of you upstairs…?'

'That's just a precaution. He's a big boy now. He could easily push it out of the way if he wanted to, you know.'

'I suppose he could.'

They had spent long enough together for him to know when she was lying. But why was she? There was still a warmth between them, he could feel it from the safety of his chair across the room, but surely she wasn't worried about showing it in front of Edward? She was far too intelligent, mature, capable for that, wasn't she? Ed must have seen his car arrive and decided for some reason to stay out of the way. At that point, the obvious truth struck him, like a blow to the back of the neck.

'Have you told him?'

'Sammy? Told him what?'

'No, not Sammy, Edward. Told him about us, how Sammy was…finally conceived.'

There was a long pause. Louise closed her eyes and slowly lowered her head towards her hands. She assumed he would have worked it out, would have assumed that something that big couldn't be hidden forever from the man she lived with, ate with, slept with, argued with.

'Yes, I told him.'

She wanted to tell him that her husband had told her something also, something equally devastating, and perhaps even more unforgiveable, but she couldn't. It would have been too much. She couldn't possibly know how ironic such a revelation would have been.

'And what did he say, how did he take it?'

'How d'you think he took it, Ben? It changed our relationship forever. How was it not going to? I think it changed his relationship with Sammy, too. But then, all the horror of what…what was done to Sammy back in December; all that cut across what he felt. So now, now that Sammy's back with us, it's all hands to the deck, as you might say. We're a hundred percent focused on him.' She said this with a kind of offhand cheeriness that almost completely undermined her words.

'Well, that's good, isn't it? I'm glad you're tight, at least as far as Sammy's concerned.' There was another long pause in which it seemed to Ben that she wanted him to say more, say something about the two of them. 'You know, Louise, you and me…' He had begun to lower his voice. 'You know, there's nothing there for me now, I know that. I just wanted you to know.'

She looked at him with a strange mixture of relief and hurt. He wondered whether she missed him, whether she missed his arms around her, missed him telling her everything would be all right, that the baby would come and she and Edward would love it as completely their own.

'OK, thanks.'

He was almost overwhelmed by the thought of how they had been together, how their bodies had interlocked, how she had felt underneath him, on top of him, alongside him. And he thought of Leticia and Jennifer and the whole sorry situation he was in.

'So, anyway, Sammy's OK. That's really good news.' He paused, aware of how artificial this moving on of the conversation was.

'Yes, he's fine. And what about you and Leticia? How is she?'

'Recovering, slowly. It's been very difficult at the hospital. She's been in and out of consciousness during my visits, which hasn't helped.' He stopped, wondering if he should say more. 'But then, actually, if I'm honest, I'm not sure I quite feel the same anyway. You know, when it was just me and her against the world, everything was great, but then, with Sammy being taken, and the suicide attempt, and all that business with the priest...So now, being there for Leticia, it's so different from, well, love and real companionship, all that. It feels like a duty.'

It feels like a duty, Louise thought, it feels like a duty. Yes, that was it. The word hadn't occurred to her before, but it described so painfully well how she felt about her own marriage. She looked up at him again.

'But life is often about duty, isn't it, Ben? Sometimes, that's all we have to cling on to.'

'Yes,' he said.

Numbed by her words, Ben allowed the atmosphere in the room to freeze into almost unbearable silence. Neither of them seemed to know what to say or do next.

'Lou, you OK?'

Edward's voice from upstairs. It electrified Ben into sudden movement. He rose from the chair and moved to the door.

'I'm so pleased Sammy's OK. That's really the most important thing.'

Louise nodded at him as he went through into the hall. He checked that Edward was not at the top of the stairs, then, with absurd caution, opened the front door and passed through. On the drive, he was about to turn when he heard the Yale lock pushed quickly and firmly into place behind him.

Sixteen

One week later, and Ben still carried with him the agonising silence of the end of his meeting with Louise. What she'd said had reinforced his feeling that he should have nothing more to do with Jennifer and that, hard though it was, he should concentrate on helping Leticia in whatever way he could.

The unanswered calls, texts and emails from 'Jenny O' had accumulated all week, but it was on Thursday that the tone of the messages changed. Replacing the suggestively imploring tone or the desperate, heartbroken pleading of her previous attempts to contact him was a growing anger. He had used her, she said, then thrown her away like so much trash. It was nothing short of abuse. That last time in her flat...it had been tantamount to rape the way he'd thrown her to the floor and torn off her clothes. And so it went on.

Then, on Friday, something much more serious. It was a long email that would certainly have attracted his attention in a professional capacity, had he been working for a client. But when it was his own life at stake, his own reputation, it affected him in a wholly different way. He read it twice, the second time more calmly, taking in the audacity of her intentions:

OK, Benjy, the time has come to lay things on the line. You either give me some respect, answer my calls and show me you weren't just abusing me, or I'll use what little power I have to expose you for what you are. At first, I thought the thing to do would be to get a friend of mine to write something in the local rag. She's quite good, and has some contacts in the national press too. That's still an option, I suppose. But then I thought it would be more fun to do it on my morning show. Of course, I'd say that someone had sent me an anonymous letter alleging violent and abusive behaviour on the part of a local lawyer. Details would be kept vague, naturally, but anyone who wanted to would be able to piece together your identity. I hope that's clear, Benjy. I'd really rather not do this, or the other thing with the press, but there we are. Of course, it's perfectly possible I might do something even more extraordinary... Why not pop round and we can discuss this together in a less confrontational way?

The email arrived whilst he was still at work. The panic he felt must have appeared on his face; even Alice, the new temp, asked him if he was OK. When she'd left the office, he copied the email to a secure folder and, making sure there was no-one in the photocopying room, printed two copies, sealing one in an envelope addressed to himself and placing it in the safe, intending to take the other one with him to Bartholomew Road. When he got back to the flat, he would fold the second photocopy and slip it between the pages of a book, writing the name of the book in his diary. She surely wouldn't dare do what she was threatening, would she? But, if she did...

Edward had now returned to work. They had had no recurrences of the sleepwalking of Sammy's first night back at home and nothing other than a couple of tantrums which soon subsided. Louise was confident she could cope with him, but they agreed that she would phone Edward immediately if anything remotely unusual happened. The paediatric hospital and Police Family Liaison Officer also gave their assurance they would be there to help straight away should they be needed.

He expected the Head to call him in the moment he returned, but he had placed an 'Unavailable' sign on his door and directed Angela, his secretary, not to allow anyone past her except under the most urgent of circumstances. Edward guessed that this was the beginning, or the continuation, of the school's decision to involve the police in the accusations made against Carwen Williams. Of course, he was grateful to have the opportunity to get his feet under the table again without any interference after more than a week away from his classes.

He was at home when the call came through. He was unusually tired after his first day back, but that was to be expected. After exhausting himself further playing with Sammy, he tried to get on top of some of the work from students that had accumulated during his time off, but this wasn't going well. He ignored the call, unsure who could be phoning at this time of the evening, but when his mobile sounded again he flipped it open and saw that it was Carwen Williams. Christ, Carwen. He had no desire to talk to him, not after the Head's little chat. When his mobile rang for the third time, though, and Louise called out from the kitchen, asking who it was and why he wasn't picking up, he reluctantly took the call. It would be a simple matter, wouldn't it, to tell him it was inappropriate to speak to him at the moment?

'Hello, Carwen.'

'Ed, I thought you were never going to pick up.' Unmistakeably Carwen's voice; there was only the faintest hint of a Welsh accent, but still something about the lilt of the voice that betrayed him.

'Yes, sorry, couldn't find my mobile – you know how it is.'

'OK, well. I'm in the pub. Not The Partridge, for obvious reasons, the Tollgate. I'd very much like to talk to you, Ed, old mate. I'm sure you can guess what about.'

'Right, I…'

'I fully appreciate that you won't particularly want to talk to me, but it would be, as they say, in your best interests if you did.'

'What d'you mean?'

'Tollgate in half an hour – then you'll find out.'

At this, the phone went dead. Should he ring him back and tell him he was busy? Or come clean and just tell him it wouldn't be appropriate for them to meet?

'Who was that?' Louise again.

'Just Carwen from school.'

'Oh, what did he want?'

'Wants to meet up for a drink, but I'm not so sure.'

'You go if you want, I can cope here. About an hour to dinner. I like Carwen, he's a nice guy.'

'Yes, he's a nice guy.'

The Tollgate Inn held traumatic memories for Edward Bryant. This was where he had met Jennifer, time after time, often in the same dreary room, for sex. It was where he had tried to end it with her, too, around the time he and Louise had asked Ben to be a surrogate father. There was only one entrance and the way to the bar took him right past the same youngish clerk who had been there all those years ago. His fellow Maths teachers had sometimes been here for a drink together, especially at those times when they suspected there might be a significant sixth-form presence at The Partridge, so he wasn't surprised to see Carwen tucked away in the same corner of the long bar room they used to gather in on those occasions.

'All right, Carwen?'

'I've been better.' Carwen was staring at his three-quarters empty beer glass, but Edward could tell it was very far from his first pint of the evening. 'First, I'm off on long-term sick. Not something I thought would ever happen to me. Actually, there's nothing much wrong with me, but my union recommended, as soon as that bloody man made his accusations, that I took leave indefinitely.'

'Right, yes, sound advice. Another drink?'

For answer, Carwen Williams slammed his glass down in front of him. Edward had to wait at the bar behind someone ordering a large round and his mind began to anticipate what Carwen was going to say to him. Buying him a drink was an ice-breaker, of course, but he guessed it would ultimately do nothing to improve his mood. Back at the table, Carwen eyed the fresh pint with renewed delight and immediately poured half of it down his throat.

'Where were we? Oh, yes, second, that young woman in my tutor group. Don't say you haven't heard, because I don't believe you. I don't know what the Head's told you, but there's no way I touched her inappropriately. She was upset, Ed, and I touched her on the arm, that's it. I've touched plenty of students, on the arm or on the shoulder, as encouragement or to get them to toe the line, you know that, Ed. This was no different.' He was trying to keep his voice down, but with limited success.

'Not so loud, Carwen. We don't want half the city knowing.'

'Listen, Ed, I don't give a monkeys who hears this, OK. The more the better. The whole thing's a fucking set-up.' He squeezed Edward's forearm with a powerful left hand, then took two more large mouthfuls of his beer, examining his glass as if mystified by the fact that it was nearly empty again. 'And then there's that little shit in my GCSE class. See, what happened there was completely and utterly trivial, OK? He'd been bugging me all lesson, just trying to wind me up. I noticed he wasn't even on the right page of the text book, so I picked it up, closed it and tapped him on the back of the head with it. He went down on to the desk like a sack of potatoes and let out a series of comical moans, as though he'd passed out. The rest of the class started laughing, and I could see he was laughing too by the twitching of his shoulders. Conniving little bugger.'

Edward had no idea what to say. It certainly put a different complexion on the whole affair, but could he believe him? He'd never known Carwen to lie to him before, but then clearly he hadn't been faced with this situation before. If what he was telling him was true, it would explain the peculiar tone of the Head's conversation before Sammy's return: I want rid of this guy and I'm expecting you to support me, whether or not there's truth in any of it. On the other hand, for himself personally, the whole thing opened up the possibility of promotion, and this might be his only chance of getting it. Carwen was well on the way to being drunk, but Edward needed to know how much of what he'd told him he could trust.

'The Head has spoken to me, Carwen. I don't imagine that's any surprise to you.'

'What do you think?'

'There've been complaints, other students and a parent. Are you saying they're lying?'

'They're doing what you would expect, supporting one of their own who's been invited to tell lies about me and responding to what their beloved child tells them.'

'And what about the delay in getting medical help?'

'Is that what the parent of that little shit says?' Carwen slammed his fist down on the table, sending his beer glass perilously close to the edge. The barman, in the midst of drying a wine glass, looked across.

'Everything OK, gentlemen?'

'Yes. No problem.' Edward's voice sounded pathetically feeble to himself. 'Sorry about that.'

'The thing is…' Carwen continued, as though he hadn't registered the barman's concern. 'The thing is, I didn't need to call for medical assistance, for God's sake, did I? There was nothing wrong with him, nothing that a good leathering wouldn't solve.'

'I wouldn't use that kind of language, Carwen, if the shit hits the fan.'

'No, well, it's this talking, isn't it?' He held up his beer glass by way of illustration, then looked across at Edward's. 'You've barely touched yours.'

'No.'

There was a long pause. Edward looked across at Carwen's face; it was half-turned away from him, but he could see there was something he wanted to say, although the fug of the beer, and maybe something else besides, was making it harder for him.

'So, look. What I suppose I need from you, Ed, is a hundred percent backing. The Head made it fairly clear to me that the police would be involved, so I don't need to tell you that they'll want to speak to you. It doesn't take much working out that you'd be the next in line for my job and I imagine that little arsehole squatting in his office has already told you something of the sort.' He looked across the table, expecting some sort of response, but Edward chose that moment to take a sip of his beer. 'I'll take that as a yes. I know that puts you in a difficult position, but what I'm looking for from you is strong, solid support. We've worked together for years, Ed, and I reckon we can count ourselves mates, more or less, so…' The hand had attached itself to Edward's forearm again.

Edward wanted this whole situation to go away. He was feeling fenced in, and that feeling was gradually making him angry. But the man opposite him was teetering on the edge of rage, and he couldn't rely on him taking a rational approach.

'Listen, Carwen, if somebody asks me, whether it's the police or whoever, what I think of you, I'll tell them you're a good professional, that we get on fine, that you're a great teacher.'

'But?'

'But I can only tell them the truth, Carwen. I said the same to the Head.'

'Oh, so you said the same to the head. You and the Head are like that, I suppose.' Two entwined fingers were thrust in front of his eyes.

'Don't be melodramatic. You know what I'm saying. I wasn't in that room with those kids, so how the hell do I know what went on? The truth, Carwen, as I see it, that's all I can do.'

This was a pivotal moment. He'd said enough to protect himself, and what he'd said was, in any case, exactly what he felt. He wasn't sure it was what Carwen Williams wanted from him, though. He eyed the five empty glasses on a nearby table and realised they were all Carwen's empties.

'The truth? You're going to tell them the truth? OK – let me tell you about truth, Ed. Truth is what the powerful say it is. In this case, truth is what the apology for a human being that runs that school has fabricated. If you're not careful, you'll end up simply parroting the truth as he sees it. I need more from you than that. I need you to say that you know it was all made up, that you're prepared to swear that that's the case.'

'I can't do that, Carwen, you know that. It wouldn't be honest.'

'Oh, right, first it's truth, now it's honesty. What world are you living in, Ed; not the same one as me, that's for sure.' He got unsteadily to his feet. 'I'm going home now, Ed. This conversation's clearly not going anywhere.'

'You're not driving home in that state, surely?'

'First you abandon me, then you want to be my mother, is that it? If I want to drive home, I'll bloody well drive home, OK. And here's another thing for you to think about, Ed.' He turned back towards the table and leant on it, his face within spitting distance. He looked Edward in the eye for a full ten seconds, then continued, lowering his voice. 'If there's some doubt about what you know and what you're prepared to say, you might reflect on what I know and what I might be prepared to say.'

'What d'you mean?' His stomach clenched whilst all sorts of possibilities passed through his head.

'I mean that there are one or two things I know about you that you might not want other people to know, headed as you are up the greasy pole.'

'You know nothing about me, Carwen, so stop bluffing; you know absolutely nothing about my life outside school.'

'Maybe not, but some students seem to. Some students with very loose mouths, shall we say? Some students who are a lot better than I am at ferreting about on the internet.'

'I don't understand, what's this all about?' Edward was on his feet now, so the two of them were staring, absurdly, right into one another's eyes.

'Well, you'll find out, won't you, I guess, if you don't give me the support I need. I guess you'll find out.'

And with that Carwen Williams, not completely sure how to exit the building, turned to leave, passing the clerk at the reception desk on his way out, who looked at him with considerable interest.

Seventeen

When Edward had left for the pub and the casserole she'd been preparing was in the oven, Louise tiptoed softly up the stairs to check on the safety gate and make sure there was no noise from Sammy's room. Much to her relief, there was just the sound of gentle snoring. She returned downstairs, as softly as she had ascended, and sat at the table with the day's post.

A couple of bills, the usual junk mail and two other letters. The more official-looking of these turned out to be an invitation from the head office of the charity for which she had worked before the horror of the abduction. It seemed such a long time ago now, and she remembered, for the first time in a long while, the strange relationship she'd had with Tweedy, her volunteer helper, who had sadly committed suicide. The letter was flattering and said how much her contribution to the work of the charity had been missed in the city, though the writer was aware of how much Sammy's traumatic experiences must have affected her. She put the letter to one side. She would consider going back at some point, but now was not the time. And then, in any case, there was the possibility of doing something different, something more in tune with her degree and teaching qualification.

The remaining letter had a typewritten address and had been posted locally. It was addressed to her alone. She turned it over, but there was no return address on the other side. She opened it and had some difficulty pulling out the single sheet of paper from inside. The letter was word processed and printed, by the look of it, on a printer with very little remaining ink. She had to scan the text twice, unable to believe at first what she was reading:

Hello, Louise

I hope you remember me. But then, you wouldn't, would you, unless I were to tell you who I am, and I'm certainly not going to do that. Nevertheless, I know you. Not intimately, though that would be nice. This letter is about you, your family and what you've all been up to. Maybe you don't care what your nearest and dearest have been up to, and of course you know some of the things already, but some of them might not be too keen, what with their professional status and all that.

The fact is, Louise Bryant, I know what your stupid husband got up to, and I think I can guess what you got up to as well. It's great fun guessing, don't you think? And then there's your brother-in-law – I'm guessing (there I go again) that you don't know everything about him and what he's got himself involved with. You see, the fact is that he's screwing that slut your husband screwed before him, how amusing is that? If you don't believe me, why don't you ask him?

And so there's the small matter of money. This is just a preliminary note from me to let you know what's what. I'll send you another letter in a short while, with details of how much money I need you to pay and how you can pay it.

As I say, you might not particularly care about what your philandering husband and his philandering brother have got up to, but now you know, and that knowledge might well spread like a disease if you let it.

A teacher and a solicitor, the cream of professional life. Who'd have thought it? You're probably wondering how I know all this. But that's all part of the fun, don't you think? There can't possibly be anyone else who knows, can there? Maybe you should work it out for yourself.

Oh, and any attempt to go to the police would be very unfortunate – for you and for all of your cosy family.

She got up from the table, pushed the chair to one side and stood back against the sink, so that the cold surface pressed into her back. She looked across at the sheet lying on the table, next to the half-torn envelope it had arrived in, a terrifying jabber of questions passing through her head – who, how, why? In the midst of this, she could hear, softly and as though from a long way away, a whimpering from upstairs. She backed out of the kitchen, still looking at the letter as though it might simply disappear, and headed for the stairs. Sammy was standing at the safety gate, holding on to the rail with small, tense hands. Her own hands were shaking as she held on to the banisters.

'Mummy, mummy.'

'It's OK, darling, here I am. Don't worry, everything's OK. There's nothing to worry about, just a nasty dream.'

As Edward let himself back into the house following his somewhat alarming conversation with Carwen Williams, it didn't take him long to realise the house was eerily quiet. There was usually the pleasant clatter of pans from the kitchen, the sound of an early evening programme on the radio, perhaps even Louise humming softly to herself. He went through to the kitchen. There was the aromatic smell of their imminent meal, the kitchen table laid out, but no Louise.

He realised she must be in the lounge, perhaps reading whilst waiting for him to get back from the pub. As he passed through the lounge door from the hall, he was surprised to see his wife slumped over on the sofa, her head between her hands, and what looked like an opened letter on the floor in front of her. He went over and perched beside her, placing his hand gently on the back of her hair. The strangeness of his conversation with Carwen that still filled his head was transformed into something more immediate and troubling as Louise remained frozen in her foetal position beside him.

'Lou? What is it?'

Louise raised her head from her hands and shook it two or three times, as if in response to a sudden cold breeze. She reached down and handed the letter to Edward.

'Here, you'd better look at this.'

Edward read each line of the vitriolic text with increasing horror and incredulity. By the end, his anger was fierce and intense. It blotted out all rational responses, and it wasn't until he had calmed down that he felt able to speak.

'This is sick, Louise, there's no other word for it.'

'I know that; I just don't understand how anyone could be nasty enough to send it. As if it isn't bad enough what you and I have done to each other. And the thing about Ben. Where's that come from?'

Edward scrutinised the second half of the letter again, as if, on second reading, it would mean something different. The language in which it was expressed was blunt and offensive; it certainly knew how to press all the right buttons. He had no knowledge of an affair between his brother and Jennifer, but then, he thought, why would he? He hadn't spoken to Ben for some considerable time, for very obvious reasons. There was an awkward half-minute of silence, but he knew he'd have to break it at some point.

'Has Ben spoken to you about this relationship, if we can call it that, with Jennifer?'

'No, of course not.' Her tone was sharp with outrage.

'He was here the other day, didn't he say anything to you that suggested there might be something going on?'

'No, nothing. In any case, that's not really the point, is it? Whether or not he's having an affair with that bitch I once called a friend, someone thinks he is and is prepared to blackmail us about it, along with our own indiscretions from the past. And why me?'

'Well…' Edward allowed himself a moment to think. 'I suppose, if you look at it from his point of view…'

'His?'

'It reads like a man, wouldn't you say?'

'Maybe you underestimate how foul-minded and foul-mouthed a woman can be.'

'Perhaps. At any rate, from their point of view, whoever they are, I guess they see you at the centre of everything, the woman who had an affair with her brother-in-law, who's married to a man who had an affair with the woman who is now seeing that same brother-in-law. They probably felt they could kill three birds with one stone. Perhaps they didn't fancy trying to take on a lawyer or a hardened, promiscuous media personality.'

'Great, so they decided to take on me, us, instead.'

'It makes sense from their point of view, in a warped kind of way.'

'Warped is certainly the word.' Louise snatched back the now crumpled letter from Edward and steeled herself to read it through one more time. 'Do you have any idea who could have written this?'

Edward shook his head, but one thought gradually insinuated itself into his head. The conversation with Carwen in the pub had understandably receded into the background, but now the threats he had made were resurfacing in his mind. What exactly had he said? *There are one or two things I know about you that you might not want other people to know*, wasn't that it? Maybe it was time to fill Louise in with everything that had been going on at school. It wasn't exactly the moment he'd have chosen, but there seemed nothing else for it.

'I'm almost completely at a loss, Lou.'

'Almost? You said "almost".'

'Well…there was something Carwen said to me this evening in the Tollgate…'

'Christ, you went there?' The blasphemy sprang from her before she could hold it back. The Tollgate now held uncomfortable memories for both of them.

'I had no choice; he was already there, and already half-pissed, as it turned out. Anyway, the conversation was all about the situation at school, at least to start with.'

'What situation?' Louise sat up and looked sideways at Edward as though fully acknowledging his presence for the first time.

'I was going to tell you, Lou, of course I was, but with everything else that was happening – Sammy coming back, the accident, the hospital – I never seemed to find the right moment.' This sounded weak, even to himself.

'OK. Then you'd better tell me now.' Louise's voice was cold, hard, the voice of a woman who has passed from shock and disgust into suppressed anger.

'There's a possibility of promotion.' Edward sighed as he began; it would not be easy to rake all this over. 'That's how I first came to be involved with it all. There was a rumour going round that Carwen had behaved inappropriately with two students from different classes. The Head confirmed to me that this inappropriate behaviour was well documented and that he'd asked Carwen to take long-term sick leave. He as good as suggested that I would move smoothly into Carwen's different roles at the school were he to resign or be found guilty of serious misconduct. He said the police might become involved.'

'The police?'

'Yes. I'm afraid the allegations from the two students are, well, not great. Anyway, to cut to the chase, the Head more-or-less told me I'd have to say the right things to make sure the school could get rid of Carwen. It was one of those kinds of conversation.'

'And what did you say?'

'As little as possible – I just said I'd tell the police, and anyone else who asked, the truth as I saw it. That seemed to satisfy him. Well, to some extent, anyway. But then, Carwen…'

'What?'

'In the pub, just now, he denied all the allegations against him. That wasn't so surprising, I suppose, but it was obvious that he'd found out, or worked out, that the Head would be putting pressure on me to make sure he got the boot. He wanted my unequivocal support, as they say, and, if I didn't agree to give it to him, he said he'd reveal something about me that I might not want people to know about. Naturally, sitting there in the pub, I laughed it off; I thought he was making it up to get me to fall into line, and I told him so.'

'But now you think this letter might be from him?'

'Not really. I can't see him sounding me out in the pub if he'd already sent this disgusting thing to you. How does that work? On the other hand…'

'Yes?'

'It could be from the source of Carwen's information, in the unlikely event it actually exists. There's nothing else I can think of.'

'No, right.' The silence between them had returned. 'Should we go to the police? I know the letter warns us about that, but every letter like this does, obviously.'

'It's a big step. On the other hand, I'm not sure I see any other option. In the end, the letter was sent to you, so it's all about how you feel about going through all that.'

'I'm feeling angry, Ed. I just can't see Carwen having anything to do with this, but this shitty piece of paper is going to sit there staring at us unless we do something about it. We can throw it away, but that doesn't really solve the problem, does it?'

'No.'

'Then it has to be the police.'

Eighteen

Earlier that same day, Nurse Zena was singing as she usually did, going about her work on the wards of the hospital. Most of the patients made no comment about this, and some even said they liked it, looked forward to her visits. But Leticia Bryant was different. After Zena had been allocated to her room, Mrs Bryant had specifically asked her not to sing; it made her feel uncomfortable, she said. As far as Zena was concerned, that was just part of the job; you couldn't please all the patients all of the time, but you still went about your job as professionally as you could.

That day, therefore, she had entered the room as quietly as usual, reminding herself again, under her breath, not to hum or sing. There was work to do in the room, but she also needed to wake Leticia to get her to take her tablets. These were fewer than they had been a week ago, and that pleased Zena, who harboured a strong belief that pills were never the answer to anyone's problems in the end.

She noticed immediately that Mrs Bryant had pushed herself right down under the sheets and blanket. She went over to the bed and, as she had done before, pulled back the coverings to see how deeply she was asleep. Her beautiful hair was lying across her face, so Zena brushed back the strands lovingly with her hand and replaced the coverings. She would not wake her, but come back in an hour or so.

Ben had felt trapped by his relationship with Jennifer, if it could be called that, well before her last message, but now there really did seem no way of escape. The email was almost deranged, but it filled him with a constant, obscure fear that never quite left him.

The options were clear enough. He could go round to her flat and try to persuade her not to do what she had threatened, but he was well aware that the last time he'd been there things had not panned out the way he'd expected them to. He could arrange to meet her at the tapas bar again, in the hope that the public space would moderate her behaviour and encourage her to take a more reasonable approach. This was a laughable option; she would never agree to meet there and, even if she did, he knew she was more likely than not to play up to a captive audience. He didn't even consider inviting her to his own flat to talk things through. Any further allegations of rape would simply come across as all the more credible. He could open up to Old Bill at Thurgoods and ask his advice, but broaching the subject would be pretty terrifying, and to do so would be tantamount to professional suicide. He could, of course, simply ignore her, let her do what she wanted and to hell with her. Call her bluff. She'd soon find someone else to seduce, wouldn't she? Women like her always did.

Women like her…

When Zena returned to Leticia's room, the first thing she

noticed was that the window was open. She was sure she had not opened it earlier. There were specific instructions about this room which had been made very clear to her. The window was to be kept closed and locked at all times, except when a member of staff was in continuous attendance in the room. She had a key herself, and checked to see if it was still on her bunch. She went over to the window and locked it tight. There was no-one in the small garden outside, as far as she could see.

Now she noticed a smell of sanitizer in the room and guessed a cleaner had been in and taken it upon themselves to unlock the window, though she had no idea how they had come upon a key for the window of this particular room. It was unprofessional of them to forget to close and lock it afterwards. Though she didn't want to get anyone into trouble, this would have to be reported.

She looked over at the bed. Leticia Bryant was still asleep, down under the sheets where she had left her. She wondered, though, if she mightn't be a bit more awake than before; she should really take her pills now. Sitting on the chair between the bed and the window, she pulled back the sheets, gently as before.

What she saw startled her. There was no patient in the bed, no Mrs Bryant. Only two pillows arranged lengthways to resemble a sleeping body. She went over to the wardrobe. The two spare pillows were missing, and most of the clothes had been removed. She started to shake. How had this happened? How could it have happened on her watch? Her arms felt weak and her body absurdly heavy. It would have to be reported straight away. It would be the end of her job here, and probably the end of her career as a nurse.

She forgot herself and started to sing a hymn she knew from her childhood, gently and quaveringly.

There was no-one in this room now to tell her to stop.

It was four-thirty, and Ben had let himself in through the heavy front door of the Edwardian house in Bartholomew Road. He had negotiated the afternoon satisfactorily, but there was a lead weight constantly pulling down at his head and shoulders now, a weight he had no idea how to remove. A headache was coming on, and he knew he should not indulge in the drink he was already promising himself as he climbed the stairs to the first floor. He had entirely forgotten about the copy of Jennifer's email nestling in the inside pocket of his jacket.

When his mobile sounded, the headache seemed to pulse harder at the back of his skull. It would be her; God knows what she would say next.

When he saw it was the hospital, he instinctively knew something was wrong; he sat straight down on the arm of the sofa in the dark of the living room and took the call.

'Hello, is that Mr Bryant?'

'Yes. What's happened?'

'There's no cause for serious concern, Mr Bryant, but your wife was found to be missing from her room late this afternoon by the nurse who's been looking after her.'

'Missing?'

'Yes. As I say, at this stage, there's no cause for alarm, but some of her clothes were missing from the room, and a window, which should have been fastened and secured, was found to have been left open.'

'I don't understand. How the hell did that happen?'

'We're not absolutely sure at the moment, Mr Bryant. Obviously, we're putting all our effort into finding Mrs Bryant as quickly as we can. We've carried out a preliminary search of the grounds of the hospital, but haven't as yet managed to locate her.'

'But this is ridiculous. Have you contacted the police?'

'Yes, Mr Bryant. Under the arrangements by which your wife was being treated at the hospital, it was necessary to involve the authorities immediately, as I'm sure you can appreciate. A specialist police search team has been dispatched to the hospital and will arrive within the hour.'

'That all sounds pretty serious to me.'

'Hopefully just a precaution, Mr Bryant. I have every confidence our own staff will find her and bring her back safely to the hospital very soon.'

Ben had no idea what to say next. He held the mobile away from his ear, as though this would make the whole thing less real. He was aware of his breath coming in short, shallow bursts and felt the opposite wall of the unlit room moving away from him. He began to think he might pass out if he didn't focus hard on the call.

'Mr Bryant, are you still there?'

'Yes, I'm still here. I'm coming down to you straight away in the car. I want to be there when she's found. If she's found, that is.'

'There's no need for you to travel all that way, Mr Bryant. There won't be anything you can do to help; rest assured we'll keep you informed immediately of any news. As I say, we have everything under control here, the necessary processes have all been put in place.'

'A pity they weren't in place before you allowed my wife to disappear. I'm driving down now, and there's nothing you can say that will persuade me to do otherwise.'

He snapped the mobile shut, replaced it in his jacket pocket and headed back out of the flat. He opened the car door and got in behind the wheel. The interior was still warm. He sat there for a few seconds before starting the engine. His headache had vanished and he was thinking with direct and focused clarity of his route to the Sussex Downs and what he would do when he got to the hospital. He had been due to see his wife tomorrow, and now this…

Suddenly, the threats of an over-sexed, half-demented local radio presenter with some kind of power fixation seemed to fade into silence, like the diminishing segue to another track altogether.

Part Two
Distraction

One

It was that rare event for Detective Sergeant Timothy Laughland, a day off. No doubt he would pay for it when he got back the following day, but it had at least not been cancelled. So here he was, lunchtime at The Forge, a newish drinking hole tucked in behind the high street in what used to be an ironworks. The place was just round the corner from his flat, the flat he'd moved into some while ago from the even smaller and colder premises on the western outskirts in order to be closer to the 'beating heart of the city', as the estate agent put it.

Laughland had opened his laptop and was looking at the latest offerings on his dating website, making sure he was well tucked into the corner where no-one could see what he was up to. He had only been registered on the site for a week or so, and was still embarrassed by the whole idea. Nevertheless, for a busy copper it was, it seemed, the only way to meet someone who was not also a copper.

He was distracted from further swiping of the screen by the loud arrival of four well-dressed individuals in their early thirties, three men and one woman, who burst in through the fashionably stained wood of the entrance door to his left. They were obviously on a lunch break from some kind of training course; each of them was carrying an identical file of papers.

In fact, it was the way she was holding the file that first alerted Laughland. Why, how, did he know that hand, that particular way of holding things up close to the body? As she passed in front of him, he looked up at the back of the hair, taking in also the attractive curves of the smallish body, nicely shaped by the grey woollen coat. The hair had been dyed some kind of copper colour, but there was no mistaking the shape of the head, the slight tilt to the left, the line of the shoulders.

Nicki. Police Constable Nicola Gray, no less.

He shut the lid of his laptop, making rather more noise than he'd intended. All four faces at the bar turned towards him. Three faces turned away again immediately, but one remained looking in his direction. She's lost some weight, he thought, in the cheeks, under the chin. She looks great.

He saw her speak to one of the men in the group, then turn towards his table and begin to walk over, very slowly and with her eyes on everything except his face. What the hell to say? They had been so close at one time, half colleagues, half lovers. She stopped in front of him, her hands not quite knowing what to do with the course programme she was holding, but then managed to push herself up on to the chair opposite him. The tails of her coat opened as she did so, showing a black dress worn well above the knee. Her thighs were still nicely shaped, but more slender than he remembered them. She put the programme down, propped her chin on the palms of both hands and simply looked at him.

'Nicki. It's good to see you again. You're looking…'

'Yes?'

'Well, good.'

'Is that it, good?' She leaned back, arms held out in mock display.

'Good, as in dead sexy, if you want the truth.' He couldn't help himself; she leaned forward again and her features softened.

'Well, that's better. I should think so too, all the money I've spent on this outfit.'

'Trying to impress someone?' His eyes moved from her upturned face to the three men at the bar and back to her face again.

'It's actually none of your business, *Inspector* Timothy Laughland, if I'm honest. Not the way you treated me last year.'

Her eyes were wide and her face was reddening beneath the foundation on her cheeks. She flicked two strands of dyed red hair from her forehead and threw her head back in what she clearly hoped would be a gesture of defiance.

'You're right, Nicki, I'm sorry. Wrong thing to say. And it's still Detective Sergeant at the moment, despite aspiring to better things.'

'Oh, yes, all that aspiring. That was what changed everything, as I remember.'

He said nothing, staring into his pint whilst Nicki flicked the pages of her programme absent-mindedly. He wasn't proud of how he'd treated her after the finding of Samuel Bryant and the lavish praise heaped upon his investigation. There had been talk of promotion to inspector, there still was, and she hadn't fitted his image of what an inspector's significant other should look like.

'You've lost weight.' The words broke the silence, but they'd fallen before he could decide if they were what he really wanted to say.

'Yes. Not all of it's down to diet, sadly.'

She didn't need to go on. Yet he was shocked that what had happened between them had had this physical effect on her. Nevertheless, she looked, he thought, exactly like the Nicki he used to imagine in his mind's eye, except perhaps for the hair – he wasn't at all sure about the hair.

'Look, Nicki, I couldn't be more sorry for what happened, for how I behaved.' What a terrible cliché that sounded, yet it was the simple truth. 'I was, I don't know, intoxicated by the possibility of promotion, I suppose.'

'That's one way of putting it. You know, I only realised weeks later that you'd asked me round that evening because you just wanted to say it right out, to say all that bullshit about your new role, your new responsibilities, the new expectations others had of you. Instead of which, we…'

'We got distracted.' He smiled at the memory of the quick lust that had come upon them in the kitchen of his flat.

'Yes, we got distracted, but that made what happened afterwards, what you said, so much worse.'

He couldn't disagree, nor could he find anything to say. He took a sip of his beer and put it down again on the scrubbed wood of the table, his attention apparently absorbed by the pattern of froth at the top of the glass. Nicki had always been there for him, risking her job for him, even. Yet he had pushed her aside.

After a whole minute, he looked up. Her face was turned away and she was biting her thumb and unsuccessfully trying not to cry. He reached out with his left hand and placed it over her right. She made no move to withdraw it. No words were needed; the touch was painful, but it said everything that had to be said. After a long minute, she slowly brought her other hand across to his shoulder and squeezed gently.

'Look, I need to get back to the others, Tim.' She levered herself with attractive awkwardness off the too-high seat. 'It was nice to see you again, if a bit painful. Perhaps, when we meet next, things might not be so…'

'Raw?'

'Yes, exactly.'

And with that she walked towards the bar again, pulling down her dress and wrapping herself up in her coat once more, not looking round, but saying something to the three men that he couldn't quite hear, their eyes all turned to her. He took another swig from his pint — somehow its undoubted quality was not doing anything for him — and left the table, a third of the pint still in the glass. At the door, he turned in the direction of the bar. She knows I'm leaving, he thought, but she won't look round.

And she didn't.

He walked on automatic pilot to the austere grey- and cream-clad low-rise block, on the second floor of which he lived, usually quite contentedly. He pushed his key into the lock and turned, entering and closing the door behind him, then for some reason stood there, hand on the latch, feeling that peculiar form of desolation experienced only by a man who has behaved badly to a woman and got his just deserts.

Eventually, he walked into the living room, illuminating it only with a single standard lamp. He closed the curtains and slumped down on the sofa, opening up his laptop again and swiping his way through a dozen faces that smiled hopefully at him, each in its own way, but none of them in *that* way.

When the doorbell sounded, he realised he must have fallen asleep. He went to the door and opened it. Outside, one hand propping herself against the door jamb, stood Nicki. Her eyes were blinking very slowly but the smile on her lips was open, without a trace of irony. There was a pale yellow wine stain on her blouse.

'Hello, Detective Sergeant Timothy Laughland.'

'Good afternoon to you, Police Constable Nicola Gray. To what do I owe this pleasure?'

She lurched forward and threw her arms around his neck, whilst her limpet lips all but sucked the life out of him. As she withdrew and looked blearily into his eyes, he could smell the winey sourness of her breath. She turned to close the door, then pushed forward against him again.

'I thought we might…'

'Get distracted?'

'Yes, absolutely, get distracted. Couldn't have put it better myself…'

It was five o'clock when his mobile buzzed and perambulated on the bedside table. As he turned to pick it up, Nicki's body shifted and pressed itself against him. A soft, inarticulate moan told him she'd rather he didn't take the call. He looked at the screen: DI Hargreaves. Nicki or no, day off or no, he had no choice but to press to receive.

'Hello, sir. Something come up?'

'Very definitely, Laughland. Something in which you'll very much want to be involved, I should imagine. As long as I'm not dragging you from the clutches of some young woman, of course.'

'Young woman, sir? At this time of day?'

'OK, good, then get your arse down here as soon as you can…'

Laughland re-trousered with the pleading voice of Nicki Gray still in his ears. It was either pleading or the sound of her sobering up. He told her he didn't know when he'd be back and she should let herself out. At that, she reached over and took a set of keys out of her bag, lying where she'd dumped it two hours ago. She held up one particular key. He had given it to her, didn't he remember? Of course he remembered. She could keep it, he said. Might come in handy.

At the station, DI 'Harry' Hargreaves was waiting for him in reception, chatting to Sally, the robust and immensely patient desk sergeant. They went through to his office, a dark, oppressive, windowless space that Harry himself avoided being in as much as possible. Laughland moved some papers from the only available chair and sat down.

'Thanks for coming in.'

'No problem. I've kind of got used to being called in on my day off. The downside of being a DS, I suppose.'

'You mean there's an upside?'

'Can't think of one off-hand, now you mention it.'

'Anyway, look, we had a call about half an hour ago from the hospital in Sussex where that failed suicide is being kept, awaiting custody and questioning.'

'Leticia Bryant?'

'One and the same. It appears she's escaped.'

'Escaped?'

'Yes, through the window of her room. Seems a nurse, or cleaner, or someone, left it open. Some clothes are missing and an initial search of the grounds hasn't managed to locate her.'

'Isn't it supposed to be a secure environment?'

'Not secure enough, clearly. An unholy row has broken out, as you can probably imagine. East Sussex are blaming hospital security but the hospital itself are saying they've had no officer presence for weeks. The ACC at the Eastbourne nick is apoplectic. Meanwhile, questions are already being raised at this end at ACC level. Not to put too fine a point on it, it's a bloody mess. If she doesn't turn up in the next twenty-four hours, there'll be hell to pay.'

'Has the press got hold of it yet?'

'We don't think so. There's nothing on social media, as far as we can see. Only a question of time, though, I should have thought.'

'So, is it ours or theirs?'

'That's a very good question, Laughland. You'd think they'd be only too keen to wash their hands of it, but apparently the top brass down there are anxious that East Sussex wipes up the mess themselves. Meanwhile, however, the ACC at this end is insisting we get involved. Our investigation in the first place, ultimately our responsibility.'

'So, squabbling on a grand scale, when we should be concentrating on finding a vulnerable woman who's already tried to kill herself and has mental health issues, leaving aside her culpability.'

'That's about the shape of it. Miraculously, though, something seems to have been sorted in terms of the line of command. Our ACC wanted me down there straight away, taking full charge and liaising with East Sussex only where necessary. Their ACC blew a gasket at this, so it's going to be primarily their investigation, at least locally, with someone more junior from here assisting where appropriate.'

'So, not you, Harry?'

'Not me, correct. You, in fact.'

'I had a horrible feeling you were going to say that.'

'Well, I could give it to someone else, but you're the man with the background to the Bryant case etched in your head. You know all the ins and outs. Anyway, I've as good as agreed to it on your behalf, so there you are.'

'There I am indeed. Do they want me down there now?'

'Tomorrow, early as you can. The hospital search has been called off and the East Sussex specialist team have taken over. It's pitch dark, mind you, and the place is in the middle of nowhere. Realistically, they're not going to turn anything up until the morning anyway. Oh, and the husband's been informed.'

'Ben Bryant?'

'Yes. Insisted on driving down there immediately, apparently, so you'll have him to deal with as well. They're still trying to contact the parents. I'll be at this end, taking the flak from the top, so keep me informed of all developments, as they say. This is real egg-on-the-face stuff, Laughland, so a rapid clear-up would be much appreciated.'

'No pressure, then.'

'Oh, I wouldn't say that, Laughland, I definitely wouldn't say that.'

Two

The hospital buildings lay in a fold of the Sussex hills, completely invisible until you turned the final corner of the twisting access road. The main block was a solid, stone-clad edifice, almost overwhelmed by ivy at the front, probably built for the purpose for which it was still used, he guessed. As he parked up and got out of the car into the chill air, it occurred to him that this would not be a particularly easy place to escape from. Undulating hills, largely bare of trees. Typical downland, and affording almost no cover. It was an impression he logged away for future use. He wondered how the search had gone that morning; there had certainly been no call or message on his phone, but he wasn't sure how good the reception was in this remote part of the south coast.

He'd left the flat early that morning. Nicki had tidied up after her, leaving no trace except the smell of her perfume on his pillow, and he wondered when he would see her again. The drive had been pleasant enough; on the way, he'd gone over in his mind all the twists and turns of his investigation into the abduction of Samuel Bryant. This was the second time Leticia Bryant had disappeared, and he hoped the progress of this investigation would be less fraught with danger than the last.

He was met in reception by someone he took to be a fellow detective who stood up and smiled at him as he showed his warrant card. She was young and bore no sign of the kind of resentment he had been expecting, stretching out her hand to him as she came closer.

'Hello, Sergeant Laughland, is it? DC Lucy Templeman, from East Sussex.'

He looked at the fresh-faced, fleshy young woman whose hand he was holding. They had chosen someone who would make the collaboration as stress-free as possible. That was good.

'Hi, Lucy. Should we…?' He indicated that she should lead the way to wherever they could speak in private.

'Oh, yes, of course. There's a room we can use through here.'

The room in question was one set aside for grieving relatives, judging by the calming pale green of the walls and the posters of uplifting homilies. They sat either side of the only table, the DC's notes spread out in front of them.

'So, Lucy, what are the arrangements? Is it you and me against the world?'

'Well, I'm not sure about the world exactly, sir.' She laughed, then froze, unsure whether she should be engaging in humorous exchanges or, for that matter, addressing a superior officer from another force as 'sir'. 'The DI in charge has his hands full at the moment with the search, so…'

'Right, and how is the search going? I take it nothing so far?'

'No, nothing, I'm afraid. Nothing from CCTV, nothing from the psychiatric, nursing or auxiliary staff, no sign of Mrs

Bryant having holed up anywhere overnight. The team's still out there. Of course, at some point they're bound to scale it down. On the other hand, it's pretty high-profile, so I guess they'll have the chopper out soon, if nothing emerges in the next twenty-four hours.'

'OK, good.' He wasn't completely sure he followed her train of thought, but still. 'So what does that leave us with?'

'Entirely up to you, sir, but I presumed you'd want to look at Mrs Bryant's room and the layout of the place, maybe re-interview the nurse who discovered her missing and the cleaner we think was responsible for leaving the window open.'

'Yes, that all sounds good, DC Templeman.' He got up. 'Shall we start with the room?'

Leticia's was the second room down the corridor on the other side of the reception area. It had been locked, but DC Lucy Templeman had a key.

'Was this door into the corridor locked all the time when Mrs Bryant was here?'

'Apparently not. The Registrar told us they regard this as primarily a hospital and not a prison.'

'Right, OK. But I notice there are no windows to speak of looking out into the corridor?'

'No, all the light comes in through the window to the garden.'

They walked into the small, private room, DC Templeman standing to one side whilst Laughland scanned the space. One narrow, single, iron-framed bed, its covers still pulled back from the moment when the nurse had found it full only of pillows. Walls completely bare, painted magnolia. The wardrobe door open; inside, a pair of trainers and a sweater and jeans, nothing else. The window, locked tight now, overlooked a small courtyard garden, neatly if unimaginatively maintained. Beyond lay a tall hedge with seemingly no gaps in its dense growth. Was the access road on the other side of the hedge? He found it difficult to orientate himself, but guessed not.

'So, this is the offending window?'

'Yes, sir. Strict rules in force about keeping it locked unless an authorised member of staff is in the room with the patient.'

'Authorised?'

'Yes, it basically means a key-holder, one of the psychiatric or nursing staff.'

'But, in this case, it seems the window was opened by a cleaner who shouldn't have had a key?'

'That seems to be what happened, though the cleaner in question clammed up when we asked him about it, just kept nodding his head as though he was mystified himself by what had happened.'

'And what's beyond the hedge that skirts the garden, the access road?'

'No, sir, wrong direction. There's a wall, with barbed wire on top. Not easy to scale. I'm pretty fit, but it would be a bit of a challenge for me, I reckon, never mind…'

'Never mind a mentally and physically traumatised member of the aristocracy, you were about to say. And what about the CCTV?'

'There are two cameras in the vicinity of the garden and wall. We've looked at all the footage from just before the moment when we see the window opened by the cleaner to when the nurse returns to the room and finds the bed empty. Zilch, sir, not a sausage.'

'Any gaps in the footage?'

'There don't appear to be, but I gather we're having it looked at again.'

'Right, OK. And what about the nurse and cleaner? Are they still on the premises?'

'Yes, being kept in separate rooms, both co-operating, though I wouldn't say the cleaner's likely to be co-operative for much longer.'

'We'd better not keep him waiting, then. Just one thing, though, what's your feeling about the nurse? Is she telling the truth about not opening the window herself and knowing nothing about the escape?'

'One hundred percent, I'd say, sir. She's terrified of losing her job and worried about Leticia Bryant being found dead, but I don't see any way she'd want to lie about what she's done or what she knows.'

'Good. Then let's see if we can get anything meaningful out of the cleaner. Do we have a name?'

'Of course, sir: Callum, Callum Wicks. He was an inmate in this place a few years ago, one of their success stories, apparently. No problems during his time as a cleaner here, at least until now. But…'

'Yes?'

'He can still lose it on occasions, if put under pressure, apparently, so easy does it, I suppose.'

'Right. But you've already carried out a preliminary interview?'

'Yes, sir. He certainly didn't lose it then; the opposite, in fact, if anything. Said virtually nothing, just kept shaking his head as though the whole situation was unreal.'

'I can't say I disagree too much with him there…'

'Thank you for seeing us, Mr Wicks, Callum. I appreciate that you've spoken to the police already about the disappearance of Mrs Bryant…'

'Leticia. Her name's Leticia.'

'Yes, Leticia, that's right. Would you rather we called her by that name?'

'Yes.'

They were in the room with the soothing walls where he'd first spoken with DC Templeman. She had cleared her notes out of the way and two more chairs had been found from somewhere, one for Callum and one for his responsible adult, a blank-faced woman in her mid-fifties who sat silent alongside Callum, hands folded on her lap, eyes unblinking.

'So, can you tell us when you went to Leticia's room yesterday afternoon and what you saw?'

'Already said.'

'I know, Callum, and you spoke well, I'm sure. But I wasn't there then, so if you could tell us as well, that would be really helpful.' DC Lucy Templeman backed up Laughland's words with her broadest, most encouraging smile.

'OK.' Callum nodded in a way that suggested he now understood exactly how police interviews worked. 'I went in to clean Leticia's room in the afternoon. We have to sanitise every four hours.'

'When was this?'

'14:34.'

'Did you look at your watch, or a clock?'

'No. I always enter Leticia's room at 14:34.'

'I see, OK. And what did you see in the room? Were things as they were normally?'

'Not all the things. Leticia was asleep under the sheets. I wanted to sit on the bed and put my hand on her, but I knew I couldn't do that. I cleaned the room, but it wasn't time for me to leave it, so I...I.'

'Yes, Callum?'

'I got out my pen.'

'Your pen?'

'Yes. I tried to vape earlier in the corridor, but they told me I couldn't.'

'I see, so you started vaping in Leticia's room?'

'Yes. I thought it might wake her up and then we could talk, like we usually do, but it didn't. I opened the window, to let out some of the smoke. When I'd finished, the room still smelled and I knew I'd get into trouble.' Callum's body had started to rock gently backwards and forwards. 'So I opened the window with my key to let out the smell and left the room. I meant to come back at 14:55, but someone shouted at me and I forgot.' The rocking had quickened its insistent rhythm.

'That's OK, Callum, no-one's going to shout at you again now. Everything's going to be fine.' He waited until the rocking had almost completely subsided. 'You said you opened the window with your key, Callum. Can you show the key to us?'

Callum looked doubtful at first, and the gentle rocking started again, but he suddenly stopped, arrested by the woman sitting next to him putting one hand on his arm and nodding to show that he should co-operate. He reached into the side pocket of his overalls and pulled out a bunch of four or five keys, separating one out and leaning forward to show the two police officers in front of him.

'That's good, thanks, Callum. Is it OK if we just check to see that it works?'

Laughland took the keys and handed them to the DC next to him, who promptly left the room. The rocking intensified again, and Callum looked alarmed.

'Don't worry, we shan't keep them long.' The motherly hand was still on his arm, and Laughland waited until Callum had settled again. 'Would you mind telling us where you got the key from, Callum?'

'Always.'

'Do you mean you've always had it?'

'Yes. The same keys as the man who had this job before me. Exactly the same.'

'Are you sure no-one gave you the key so that you could put it on the ring? Or maybe you found the key and kept it because it was useful?'

'No, it was always there, always there.'

The woman by Callum's side shook her head at Laughland as if to suggest she wasn't comfortable with his insistence. At the same time, DC Templeman returned from Leticia's room and gave a quick nod to indicate that she had successfully opened the window with the key.

'OK, that's fine, Callum, the key was always there. Let

me take you back again to when you first entered the room. You said Leticia was asleep. How did you know that?'

'Shape underneath.'

'You could see her shape under the covers of the bed?'

'Yes.'

'I'm going to ask you a very important question now, Callum, so please think as carefully as you can about the answer.' The woman next to Callum leaned forward, concerned. 'Do you think the shape under the covers could have been pillows, and not Leticia at all?'

Callum Wicks froze visibly in front of Laughland. He stopped breathing and his eyes stared down at the table. He opened his mouth as if to speak, then rapidly shut it again. His right fist banged on the table once, twice. The responsible adult beside him tried to calm him again.

'It was Leticia. It *was* her.' He stared furiously at Laughland, but the tone suggested some doubt.

'OK, Callum, let's agree it was Leticia for the moment. Can I ask you about the room itself? Was the wardrobe open or closed when you entered?'

'Not sure.'

'Well, did you have to walk around it when you went to the window?'

'Sat in the corner and smoked.'

Laughland looked across the table. Callum had calmed down, but was not engaging with him, keeping his eyes fixed on his folded hands on the table. Was the confusion he was exhibiting to do with his mental capacity, or was he deliberately avoiding answering his questions? He thought back to Callum's more assured responses to the questions about the timings and the key. His instinct told him there was something not quite right here.

'OK.' Laughland left a pause, but there was only an awkward silence in the room. A brief look towards DC Templeman told him she was not persuaded by any of this. 'Let's go back to what you said about Leticia and the chats you had with her.' A sudden, slight shake of the head. 'You said you wanted to touch her as she lay under the covers. You also said you were used to talking to Leticia, that you hoped she would wake up so that you could chat. It sounds as though you were very close to Leticia. Would that be right?' Another shake of the head, less controlled this time. 'Callum?'

'She's beautiful. I think she is the most beautiful person I've ever met. And I…I felt sorry for her. I knew what it was like to be in this place, so I wanted to help her.'

'To help her?' DC Templeman shifted awkwardly on her chair; they were coming to a critical point.

'Yes. She told me what had happened to her, about her illness and how she'd tried to kill herself. She said the police would take her and lock her up forever. So, you see, I couldn't let that happen to her.'

In the silence that fell in the room at this revelation, Laughland seemed suddenly to see with sharp clarity. It was a clarity distilled from all the things he knew or had been told about in the last two days. Callum Wicks, besotted by Leticia Bryant, had apparently entered her room and, seeing her asleep, tried to wake her by lighting his pen. He had left the window open, even though he had demonstrated a rigid and unchangeable fixation about his routines. The CCTV had picked up no activity from outside the open window of Leticia's room, and then there was the remoteness of the hospital itself. If he couldn't allow the police to take her, what had he done to help her escape?

'OK, Callum. Can you explain to us what you mean when you say you couldn't let that happen to her? What did you do to help her, Callum?'

'Nothing. I didn't do anything to help her.' Callum Wicks pushed himself back from the table and clamped his hands on either side of his chair. He looked away from the three other people in the room, fixing his eyes on the wall to his right. Despite the rigidity of his body, the rocking began again.

'But she was beautiful and you loved her, didn't you, Callum? You wanted to help her? Isn't that what happened?'

'No. I didn't love her. I liked her, that's all. Nothing else happened, only what I told you.'

Callum Wicks turned his head to look at the woman beside him, and across to DC Templeman. His fists were clenched and he had begun to shake. Laughland realised they'd reached a crisis point. Any attempt to question him further could end in their having to restrain him.

'OK, Callum, we'll leave it there. Lucy here will look after you.' Callum Wicks raised himself abruptly from his chair and moved around the table. DC Templeman quickly reached the door before him. 'Oh, just one more thing, Callum, before you go. Did Leticia give you your phone back?'

'Yes, of course. Of course she did.'

'Good, thanks, Callum.'

Three

'What have you done with him?'

'Let him go, sir. Couldn't really detain him. What happened in Mrs Bryant's room was unfortunate, but it's difficult to know what we could charge him with.'

'Perhaps, but you might change your mind in the next few minutes.'

Laughland and DC Lucy Templeman were sitting in the same room as before, darkened by closing the blinds. They were side by side in front of an open laptop. He had inserted a disc and was waiting for its contents to load.

'Despite his denial, I think Callum was deeply infatuated with Leticia, so infatuated that he was prepared to fabricate a whole false narrative to disguise what he did for her. It was the randomness of leaving the window open and failing to return to close it that didn't seem right to me. Callum's whole world revolves around precision and order, so that was never going to happen.'

'So, what did happen?'

'Take a look at this. When you looked at the CCTV before, you were looking in the wrong place and at the wrong time.' He clicked on the screen. 'This is footage of the main entrance, taken at 14:30.'

'That's Callum.'

'Yes, but wait. There, look, something happens over by the desk. A distraction. It looks as though Callum has dropped something all over the desk. Almost immediately…'

'Bloody hell. Leticia Bryant.'

'Grey suit, confident manner, like a visiting consultant. Very clever. Now watch, she reaches the door and walks out towards the road. There.'

'What about outside, have we got any footage of where she went when she left the building?'

'Only this.' DC Templeman leaned in to the screen as Laughland moved the recording forward. 'This footage is much less clear, but, there, you can just see her disappear behind the trees screening the hospital from the road. There's a vehicle there, but no way of telling what type or make, never mind what the registration plate is.'

'Bugger.'

'Bugger indeed, Detective Constable Templeman.'

'Sorry, sir. So Callum's story turns out to be a carefully constructed fiction?'

'Yes. He's obviously given her his phone so she can arrange a rendezvous, then she's waited until the nurse has left the room, dressed in her smartest clothes and packed a few things into a holdall. Callum arrives way before the 14:34 he told us about and they head for reception together. After she's gone, Callum returns to the room, puts two pillows under the covers, opens the window and leaves. In some ways, it was neatly done, and it provided enough of a distraction for Leticia to be miles away before anyone noticed.'

'Too neatly done for Callum Wicks to have organised it?'

'You could be right there. What we need now are the phone records from Callum's mobile. Someone picked her up, and we need to find out who that someone was…'

'I want to know what's going on. I want to know where she is and how she was allowed to escape. That's not too much to ask, surely?'

The apparently sincerely distraught face of Benjamin Bryant was staring directly at that of Detective Sergeant Tim Laughland across the now well-used table of the family room. He had been put up overnight by the hospital, despite their attempts to encourage him to return home, and, unsurprisingly, was not too impressed by the attempts of the hospital staff and East Sussex Police to find his wife over the last eighteen hours or so. Laughland watched him carefully. The very first time he had encountered Ben Bryant, it had struck him that the lawyer was trying to hide something about the situation that had led to the disappearance of Louise Bryant's child, Samuel. Subsequently, he had inevitably seen him more as victim than suspect, but the feeling of that first encounter had never quite gone away.

'No, Mr Bryant, it's not too much to ask. However, we simply don't have enough to go on at the moment to find your wife, though I'm hoping that situation will soon change. You just need to trust me on that one, just as you did when I helped to find Leticia on the Norfolk coast when she might very well have drowned.'

This reminder visibly calmed down the man in front of him, softening his features and allowing him to lean further back, away from the table edge, though Laughland knew he had an important series of questions to ask Ben Bryant that would almost certainly alter his mood again.

'Look, sergeant, I was very appreciative back then for everything you did for me, for us, so I'm sorry if that came across as a bit aggressive. But, after all…'

'I quite understand, Mr Bryant.' He allowed a silence to settle in the room before continuing. 'I wonder if you'd answer one or two questions for me, though, whilst I'm waiting to receive some very important information. They're questions that might clarify what happened during your wife's disappearance yesterday.' Ben said nothing, shrugging as though simultaneously angry and helpless. 'Good, OK. The first is what time you arrived yesterday at the hospital.'

'6:45 in the evening. You can check that with reception.'

'OK. And, to be clear, you didn't take any diversions before your arrival at 6:45?'

'What kind of diversions?'

'Well, anything really that would have lengthened the time it would normally take you to get here. You know the route well, I should imagine?'

'Yes, sergeant, and no, there were no diversions.'

'So you started from your flat when?'

'Around 4:45 in the afternoon.'

'And you received no phone calls earlier in the afternoon from someone at this hospital?'

'Only the one from the Registrar telling me that my wife was missing.'

'And what time did you receive that call, Mr Bryant?'

'Must have been around 4:30. I'd just got back from the office when my mobile sounded.'

'No calls before that?'

'Not from here, no. You can check all this, I imagine.'

'We certainly can, Mr Bryant.'

At this moment, the door opened and DC Lucy Templeman entered with a print-out in her hand. As she handed it to Laughland, Ben found it impossible not to crane slightly forward to see what was on it. Laughland studied the sheet carefully, then removed his pocket-book from his jacket and copied one of the numbers from the print-out, tearing the page from the book and handing it to Benjamin Bryant.

'Are you familiar with this mobile number, Mr Bryant?'

'No, sergeant, I'm afraid not.'

Ben pushed the piece of paper back across the table.

'Please have another look, Mr Bryant. If you do recognise this number, it would save us a good deal of time in our search for your wife. She appears to have made a call to this number yesterday morning. There also seems to have been a return call, about half an hour later.'

'Well, that's impossible, sergeant; my wife's phone was taken away from her when she entered this hospital.'

'You'll need to trust us again on this one, Mr Bryant. We know she had access to a phone yesterday. So, once again, this number?' Laughland pushed the torn-off sheet back to the other side of the table.

Ben looked again at the number on the sheet, praying it was not the number he thought it was. What was it she'd said? *It's perfectly possible I might do something even more extraordinary...* His stomach tightened and his throat was achingly dry. His hand was shaking as he pulled his mobile out of his pocket to check. He hadn't bothered to memorise Jennifer's number, why would he?

'I just need to…' With huge relief, having scrolled down the list on his phone, he quickly realised Jennifer's was not the number he'd been shown. 'No, sergeant, I don't recognise it and it's not in my list of contacts.'

'But I sense you thought it might have been?'

What to say? His wife was missing; this was not the time to tell the police about the wild threats Jennifer Ormiston had made against him, though that time would probably come before too long.

'Well, the first few digits are similar to those of the number of a friend of mine, but that's where the similarity ends.'

'I see. If you're sure?'

'Absolutely.'

At this point, the door opened and the hospital Registrar entered the room. There was the sound of an irate male voice emanating from somewhere close at hand.

'Detective Sergeant Laughland?'

'Yes.'

'There's a Lord and Lady de Tocqueville in reception. I'm afraid they're in none too pleasant a mood, which is, obviously, understandable in the circumstances…'

Ben had asked to stay for Laughland's meeting with Leticia's parents, but had been, with some difficulty, persuaded otherwise. DC Templeman had accompanied him to the visitors' waiting area where she'd hoped to convince him of the pointlessness of staying on any longer at the hospital. She'd told him it would now be unlikely that his wife would be found in the vicinity of the hospital buildings, that the outcome of the interview with Leticia's parents would be completely confidential, but that he would be informed immediately if there was any news. None of this had had any effect on Ben, who resolutely sat tight, his head resting anxiously between his knees.

Back in the family room, faced with Lord and Lady de Tocqueville, Laughland was initially pinned to the back of his chair by the vehemence of Anthony de Tocqueville's rage, despite the fact that Leticia's father had apparently been told that the lack of security at the hospital had been entirely the fault of East Sussex Police and the hospital authorities themselves. During the onslaught, Patricia de Tocqueville remained white-faced in a kind of suppressed, silent fury.

'Look, Sergeant Laughland, we understand your role in all this, and we remain, naturally, very grateful to you for saving our daughter's life when it looked like it was all over for her. Nevertheless, nothing seems to have been achieved yet in the search for Leticia. Your initial response seems to us to have been pathetically slow and limited and the police down here have not done much better. What the hell is going on?'

Laughland knew, in these circumstances, that it was best to leave a space for the temperature to drop a little. Too much space, however, was not a good idea.

'As I think you know now, I was not here when your wife was reported missing. My role has been to investigate fully what happened. I believe I have done that with some success, though there's a long way to go before we find your daughter, and you should be prepared for that.'

'With respect, sergeant, we don't need to know the minute details of your investigation; we simply need to know if you have any notion of how our daughter managed to leave the room in which she was recovering and where she might be now.'

Another pause, shorter this time.

'Might I ask why the authorities here couldn't contact you? Just to establish the facts.'

'It's really none of your business, sergeant, but, as it happens, we were visiting our villa in the South of France, as we generally do at this damp and depressing time of year. It was the usual rule, mobiles off, except to order meals, that kind of thing. Eventually, however, we realised that several messages had been left for us by the police informing us of events here at the hospital and we flew back immediately, on an early morning flight, and drove straight down here. All this can be checked, sergeant, if you're under the misapprehension that we were complicit in our daughter's escape.'

'I'm sure we'll make all necessary checks in due course.' That strategic pause again. 'Meanwhile, I wonder if you'd look at this phone number for me. There was a two-way exchange between someone at this number and your daughter yesterday morning.' He passed the same piece of paper he had shown Ben Bryant across to both the parents. Patricia suddenly looked more animated and began shaking her head vigorously, opening her hands in a dismissive gesture that was very much that of the outraged aristocrat.

'There must be some mistake, sergeant; our daughter has had no access to a phone during her stay at the hospital, sensibly enough.'

'I regret that your daughter used her not inconsiderable charm to persuade the young man who cleans her room to allow her to use his phone. The same man was also involved in what I now believe to have been a carefully planned deception which allowed your daughter to leave the grounds of the hospital without permission. But you don't really need to know all the details. Suffice it to say that this number, which features twice in the phone record of that same young man, was the only number not known to him. I'd like you, if you would be so kind, to tell me if you recognise it.'

Anthony looked at the torn-off sheet and shook his head, then passed it to his wife. At first, her reaction looked as though it would mimic that of her husband, but then she seemed to freeze in the grip of some distant memory. She reached down for the holdall she had brought back with her from France, the airline label still attached, and pulled out a pocket-book not unlike Laughland's own. After some searching, she found what she was looking for and passed the book to her husband.

'You might as well ask the wall as ask my husband about anything from more than a couple of years ago, sergeant.' Patricia prodded with her forefinger to make absolutely sure Anthony saw the relevant entry.

'Christ, no.' Anthony's voice was not much more than a whisper. 'Jesus, Let, what the hell d'you think you're up to?'

'May I see?' Laughland reached out to receive Patricia's

pocket-book from Anthony's shaking hand and scrutinised the fading ink of the entry in the back of the book. 'It's been scribbled down hastily, but it certainly seems to be the same number. May I ask whose it is?'

'It belongs to one Jeremy Halston-Gore, sergeant. You may not remember, but when you ham-fistedly invaded our privacy last year in your pursuit of Leticia and Benjamin, we told you, somewhat reluctantly, that our daughter had been impregnated whilst at Cambridge by a young undergraduate studying Economics. After she fell pregnant, we tried very hard to persuade this same young man to take responsibility for what he'd done and give our daughter some support. None was forthcoming. As a result, and this was probably the most traumatic moment of our married life, Patricia and I were forced to agree with Leticia's decision to have an abortion. The number you have there is, or was, the number on which, time after time, we endeavoured to persuade Halston-Gore to remain alongside our daughter in her hour of need, but, as I say, without success.'

Laughland added the name to the number on the sheet torn from his own pocket-book.

'And does either of you know the current whereabouts of this Jeremy Halston-Gore?'

'I think I can speak for my wife when I say, sergeant, that we don't, and that we would never wish to see or hear from him ever again. To an extent, of course, the distracted behaviour of our daughter in the last few years of her life has been caused by her continued suffering from schizophrenia, but the pregnancy and subsequent abortion contributed in no small measure to her instability. Halston-Gore will carry the weight of that for the rest of his life.'

Laughland left a silence hanging in the air once more as he passed the torn sheet to DC Templeman, accompanying the action with a nod that the ever-resourceful Detective Constable immediately interpreted as meaning that Laughland wanted the name traced.

'I understand that completely, sir. What I find somewhat puzzling, however, is that your daughter should have preferred to contact Mr Halston-Gore rather than appealing to her own husband for help. Do you know of any reason she would have done that?'

'We don't know it wasn't her husband, do we, sergeant?'

'No, that's certainly true, but it's my belief that our investigation will show that Ben Bryant had nothing to do with the incident at this hospital yesterday.'

'In that case, I'm afraid neither of us can help you, sergeant. One can only suppose that Halston-Gore has latterly felt some compunction for how he behaved and has been in touch with our daughter privately. Knowing Leticia, it's perfectly possible she would have wished to keep her newly acquired husband out of any scandal involving an escape from this porous institution and sought help instead from a somewhat dark figure from her past.'

'You could be right, sir. Obviously, it's now our priority to look for Mr Halston-Gore and, hopefully, trace the whereabouts of your daughter. I believe we have your details on file, and you may rest assured that we'll contact you as soon as we have anything to report. Meanwhile, though it must, under the circumstances, be a temptation for you, I would prefer it if neither of you attempted to trace Mr Halston-Gore on your own. You've both been very co-operative and informative, but this is now very firmly a matter for the police, and the police alone.'

Four

As Ben drove home from the hospital in East Sussex, finally persuaded that there was nothing more to be gained by staying there in case Leticia was found, Jennifer's last email began to re-introduce itself into his consciousness. Would she really do what she'd threatened? Would she really want to embroil herself in a rape case, or put her popularity at Digital City at risk by promulgating false stories about a married lover in the local press or on air? As these thoughts were circulating in his head, he missed a turn-off and had to backtrack to pick it up again. He decided to stop at a lay-by and reply to Jennifer's email there and then, to put the whole thing out of his mind. He turned the light on in the car and opened his mobile. There had been no further messages from her. Did that mean she was letting him stew, or that she knew herself she had no intention of exposing him? It was then he remembered he still had the photocopy of the email in the inside pocket of his jacket. He pulled it out and read it again. Somehow, the printed version seemed even more outrageous than the message on screen. There was now no doubt in his mind about how to proceed. He called up the email on his phone and found the words of his reply came easily to him:

If you're wondering why I've taken so long to reply to your message, it's because something that's far more important than your unbalanced ravings has taken over my life. Leticia has gone missing from the secure hospital in which she was being treated. There's no point in going into details, and it'll all, no doubt, be on social media soon anyway. Nevertheless, it puts into perspective your pathetic attempts to threaten me. You would be a very stupid woman to do any of the things you're threatening to do, and the last thing I think you are is stupid. By the way, if you had anything to do with the disappearance of my wife, you might find out just how abusive I can be. It's all over between us, Jennifer. Accept it and move on.

But when the message reached Jennifer Ormiston's phone, she barely noticed the characteristic sound of an incoming email. This was because she had in front of her an envelope whose appearance she instantly recognised. Like the last one, it was sealed with sellotape and addressed in childish handwriting, as though someone had used their wrong hand. She wondered what she should do with it, and found herself uncharacteristically indecisive. Shred it? Burn it? She supposed there would be little point in doing either of these things; another letter would arrive in due course, then another. Better to open it and see what she was confronted with. As she took out the folded sheet, a disc fell from inside it on to the floor. She picked it up; it was a burnable DVD but had nothing written on it. She put it on the table in front of her and read the letter itself:

Ms Ormiston (showing due respect, I hope you're impressed)

In my last letter, you'll remember I said I'd be making a polite request for money, well not that polite, but hey. I also said there was something in your dim and distant you might not want your precious listeners to know about. Who is your average listener, anyway? I'm guessing you get a lot of respectable mums, a few baby boomers, that sort of thing. I don't think they'd be too impressed by the information I have. The evidence is all there on the disc, but suffice it to say that you seem to have been involved in some interesting performances on film, if I can call them that, and without much need for expensive clothes, or any clothes at all. It seems that you conducted several of these performances with the same — what shall we call him? — acting colleague whose need for clothes was similarly non-existent. They're interesting performances, I must say — pretty full-on and not what you might call mainstream. I'm thinking of sending copies of this DVD to Digital City and to the local press. While I'm at it, I might as well send a few to the national tabloids, why not?

Of course, you could avoid all this by paying me some money. Ten thousand, to be precise. That's not too much to ask, is it? However, I'm not unreasonable. I'll give you time to get the money together and think about things. But not too long, obviously. I'll tell you how you can pay the money next time. Meantime, enjoy your performances on the DVD, you slag bitch.

There was no point, she told herself, in playing the DVD that had fallen out of the envelope, being more than aware of what was likely to be on it. How was this stuff still out there? The question was, did she want to go to the police with it?

Ten thousand was nothing, really – why hadn't they asked for more? The problem was, she guessed, that anyone could find the footage if they really wanted to, and was the ten thousand the end of the story? On the other hand, they were right about her demographic. The morning show was upbeat and cheerful, squeaky clean, and she'd built a reputation for responsible local journalism in her interview slot.

It hadn't escaped her that the threats in the letter were not too far removed from her own threats against Ben. This was unfortunate. He was a lawyer, wasn't he? He might have some idea about how she should respond to this sort of stuff and keep the exposure to a minimum. Was there any way she could get their relationship back on to a less confrontational footing? She opened her mobile and saw the reply from Ben to her ill-considered attack on him. His words were strangely forthright and aggressive, but no more than she deserved. It would be a slow and painful process to undo all the vitriol she had poured into that email, full, she now realised, of the obsessive angst of a woman whose power over a man had been thwarted. And now, with that mad wife of his on the run, he would in all probability not even bother to open any text or email she might send him. In any case, she didn't have the time for all that...

Jesus, what a fucking nightmare.

She stared at the disc where it lay on the floor in front of her. Despite telling herself there was no need to see what was on it, she knew she would have to. There might be nothing on the disc at all, though that seemed unlikely, but, if there was, and she ended up going to the police, she would have to know then, wouldn't she?

She slipped the disc into the DVD player and the TV screen fired up immediately in response. Now she'd done it, she wasn't sure she wanted to watch after all. Nevertheless, though the footage was hardly HD, she could see plainly that the female figure in the scenes depicted was her younger self. How old had she been? Nineteen? Twenty? She looked good, she thought, no question about that, but then she recoiled in horror at the idea of passing judgment on her younger, naked, self, especially in the positions in which the camera had caught her. She couldn't remember which shoot this was; she'd done several, some of them with the same guy. For obvious reasons, there were very few clues in the background. From what she could remember, they'd done most of the shoots in the bedrooms of cheap hotels in London and Brighton.

Like most women who got involved with this kind of stuff, she supposed, she'd done it for money. She'd been hard up, and this had been a quick and easy way to accumulate some cash. But maybe there was something else, a glamour, a sense of ripping apart all inhibitions, that appealed to her. She couldn't remember who the guy was. Names were mentioned at the start of each shoot, but these were mostly false. She'd probably used a false name herself. Faces were less important than other parts of the anatomy. But as she watched, fascinated in spite of herself, the camera closed in once or twice on the fake ecstasy of her co-actor's expression. She paused the disc, then went back. Surely, she'd seen the face before, recently, hadn't she? She looked again, bringing her face close to the screen. It couldn't be, could it? Surely that was impossible…

Five

Twickenham, Middlesex. A stone's throw from the stadium.

Sergeant Tim Laughland sat in his car contemplating the frontage of a tall Victorian pile, one of several in the dark, quiet, tree-lined street. It was later than he would have wished, but he'd resisted the temptation to pass the whole thing on to someone from the Met, not knowing how long the request might take to get through the system. He'd driven here, guided by an erratic satnav, the light fading as he went.

"J. Halston-Gore: Financial Consultant." Mr Halston-Gore had had the words imprinted on to the ground-floor window in black-edged gold letters. Redolent of esteemed professional expertise and experience, thought Laughland, even though the business surely couldn't be all that old.

At the hospital, DC Templeman had traced Halston-Gore from his mobile number. She'd told Laughland that it looked as though his address was the same as that of his business – living over the shop – and so it proved. Laughland was on his own now, and it already felt strange without the perky, quick-witted young DC at his side.

He'd come here without support, without calling it in, having made the assumption that Mr Jeremy Halston-Gore, Financial Consultant to the Thameside villa-owners of

Twickenham, would be unlikely to attack him with a meat-cleaver. Now he was actually here, however, he wondered if the decision was entirely wise. It was doubtless the legacy of his lonely, unauthorised and dangerous search for Sammy at the end of last year.

Before getting out of his car, he tried to work out the psychology of what had happened. According to the parents, this was the man who, as an undergraduate at Cambridge, had made Leticia de Tocqueville pregnant. He had resisted all their attempts to get him to stay with their daughter and moved on with his life. He wondered what had made Halston-Gore respond so favourably to Leticia's request for assistance in escaping from the hospital. Was it simple remorse? Perhaps he was very different from the kind of person conjured up in Laughland's mind by the words "Financial Consultant". Perhaps.

He got out of the car and walked across the road under the brittle light of the LED streetlamps, tempered by the branches of trees cutting across them in a gentle breeze. How to play this? Friendly and low-key, of course, at least to start with, though he was aware that he desperately needed to get inside the house.

He lifted the ornate brass knocker, appropriately enough in the shape of a grasping hand, and gave three sharp raps on the door. It was some while before a light came on in the hallway and the door opened, though there was no hesitation in the action. He was confronted by a young man in his late twenties with artfully curled hair, a face that was impressively tanned for an English winter and a broad smile.

'Hello, how can I help?'

Laughland showed his warrant card and the confident young man in front of him bent forward to scrutinise it, the smile turned off as if by flicking a switch.

'You're a long way from home, sergeant.'

'Yes, I am.'

'And it's rather late for this kind of thing, isn't it?'

'I don't know, sir; it depends what you think this kind of thing is. Could I perhaps come in for a chat?'

'That depends what the chat is about, sergeant.'

So much for friendly and low key.

'Well, it's quite an important issue, sir, but nothing to do with your financial dealings. Would I be right in thinking I'm speaking to Jeremy Halston-Gore?'

'You would, sergeant, though I tend to drop the "Gore" these days.'

'OK, Mr Halston, then I could tell you all about this on the doorstep here, but that might be a bit public, really. Much better if we went inside.'

Laughland could see in the stillness of the face and the flickering of the eyes that the man in front of him was already putting together the lateness of the hour, the details on the warrant card and the implied sensitivity of what this policeman wanted to ask him. It seemed to Laughland that a tentative narrative was being constructed at that very moment in Jeremy Halston's head, just as he might construct a narrative about a client's financial arrangements. Then, in an instant, the smile returned. Halston opened the door fully, stepping aside and indicating that Laughland should enter.

He was shepherded into what was obviously the consultation area for the business. There was a large, polished mahogany table in the middle of the room and chairs with smoothly curved mahogany backs. More of these chairs were placed around the periphery of the room.

'Please, have a seat.' Halston had moved to the window and pulled out one of the chairs at the far end of the table, taking a seat himself opposite it. Laughland took the seat offered.

'So, Mr Halston, I'm here in connection with a missing person inquiry. I wondered if you could be of assistance in finding the person concerned.'

'That's somewhat unlikely, sergeant, unless you tell me who it is you're looking for.'

'We're looking for Mrs Leticia Bryant, Mr Halston. Yesterday, Mrs Bryant went missing from the secure psychiatric hospital in which she was being treated. Before her marriage, her name was Leticia de Tocqueville.'

Laughland watched the face in front of him. It was a face feigning ignorance, but without much success. Jeremy Halston-Gore was deciding exactly how to frame his reply.

'The name is vaguely familiar, but I'm afraid I can't put a face to it. I meet many people in the course of my business, sergeant, so…'

'This has nothing to do with your business, Mr Halston. Let me jog your memory. You had a relationship with Leticia de Tocqueville whilst at Cambridge University, she fell pregnant and you abandoned her. Does that narrative sound at all familiar?' The blood had drained from Jeremy Halston's cheeks. He leaned forward, resting his head on his hands. 'I'll take that silence as an acknowledgement that what I've just said is true. You may or may not know that Ms de

Tocqueville went on to have an abortion after the repeated attempts of her parents to get you to take responsibility for your actions failed.'

'Of course I know that, sergeant, they were at pains to let me know, rub my nose in it.' He was angry now, shaking with immoral indignation, the bitterest indignation there is. 'But, look, all that was a long time ago.'

'That's true, Mr Halston, but we have information that links you to Leticia Bryant much more recently. Yesterday, in fact.'

Knowing what was coming, Jeremy Halston raised himself with an effort from the table and went to stand with his back to Laughland in the broad window space, where he was confronted by the reverse image of his own name in gold letters, lit eerily by the LED lights outside.

'We know there was an exchange of calls between you and Mrs Bryant on that day. The first was from her, using a mobile she had borrowed in the hospital, and the second was a reply from you, about half an hour later, to that same mobile. Do you wish to deny receiving a call from or sending a call to that mobile, Mr Halston?'

'I'd like to have my lawyer with me before we go any further, sergeant.' This was an automatic response. Laughland had been expecting it.

'You're perfectly entitled to insist on that, of course, Mr Halston, I wonder, though, if you'll allow me just to make a couple of points before we continue this informal chat at a police station with your legal representative in attendance.'

He waited for a response. Silence. The back still turned, hands in pockets.

'I'll be as brief as I can. Leticia Bryant has periods of serious mental illness; she has, not that long ago, attempted to commit suicide after abducting a child. It's imperative we find her as soon as we can before she, or possibly someone else, comes to harm. Your swift assistance here, now, in our search for her can only stand you in good stead if you're brought to trial.'

At this, the figure in the window turned. Jeremy Halston came forward, spread his arms out on the table and, to Laughland's surprise, began to cry. He fumbled for the chair he had been sitting in a minute before and sat down.

'When she rang me, it was the first time I'd spoken to her for years. She told me the situation she was in, said her husband didn't understand what she was going through and could I help? I'd probably have closed down the call there and then, but all the shame and guilt I felt at how I'd behaved came back to me. She said she'd worked out a way of escaping from the hospital and that, whether I helped her or not, she'd go through with it. I said I'd have to think about it and ended the call. Obviously, at that point, I had no intention of ringing her back, but it didn't take long for me to realise that, if I did nothing, I'd be abandoning her all over again.'

'So you're saying you had nothing to do with the escape itself?'

'No. I simply rang back to say I'd be outside the hospital at the time she said she'd be there and pick her up.'

'And that's what you did?'

'Yes.'

'Didn't you consider what you'd do once she was in your car?'

'I said I'd look after her for a couple of days, make sure she had a bit of money and somewhere to move on to. She said there was somewhere she had a key for, somewhere she could go while she decided what to do next. She said she had something she wanted to do, but she wouldn't tell me what it was.'

'And you didn't press her?'

'No. She was, well, in a bit of a state.'

'OK, so you came back here with her yesterday?'

'Yes. We stopped at a hole in the wall and I let her have a couple of hundred pounds. We got here early in the evening. I gave her something to eat. Afterwards, she said she felt tired and asked me if there was somewhere she could lie down. I showed her up to the attic room. I looked in on her later; she was fast asleep.'

'And now, Mr Halston, where is she now?'

'I wish I knew, sergeant. I went up and knocked on the attic room door at around seven-thirty this morning. There was no reply. When I put my head round the door, there was no sign of her. She'd gone, and taken all her stuff with her. Hadn't even left me a note.'

'I'm surprised you didn't hear her on the stairs, or opening and closing the front door.'

'I'm a sound sleeper, sergeant, and, as a matter of fact, she'd left the front door open.'

Sergeant Timothy Laughland studied carefully the man sitting opposite him. The face looked curiously calm now, as though a weight had been lifted. Did he believe that Jeremy Halston was telling the truth, or should he search the house from top to bottom? He should at least take a look at the room in which she had apparently slept.

Halston led the way up the stairs to the first floor. Here, only one room had its door closed. Laughland stepped aside and opened it – an unmade bed, old furniture, a pile of empty boxes.

'Not in there. The room's up one floor, in the attic, as I said.'

'Of course, Mr Halston, of course.'

A steep wooden staircase at one end of the landing led up to a large open space with a sloping roof. One bed. A ghostly indentation in the pillow from a human head. Some disturbance of the quilt, but this had not been pulled back. Halston anticipated Laughland's question.

'When I came up to see her, she was asleep on top of the bed. I assume that's how she stayed all night.'

'She'd have been a bit cold, maybe. But then, in sweater and jeans…'

'Oh, no, she wasn't dressed like that. A smart suit, grey, two-piece.'

Laughland looked around the rest of the space. Whoever had been in here had certainly removed all trace of themselves when they left. He smiled at Halston and the two of them descended the stairs to the ground floor hallway.

'OK, Mr Halston. I'd like to thank you for being honest with me; I can see it's been very painful for you. It goes without saying that helping an unstable patient to escape from a secure hospital was an extremely ill-considered thing to do, but I'm sure you're only too aware of that yourself. At some point, the Met police will need to question you again about your role in all this, but, when they do, I'll make sure they take full account of how co-operative you've been. I suggest you make no attempt to leave the area; that would work entirely in the other direction.'

'Don't worry, sergeant, I'm not going anywhere. When you do find her, if you do, could you let me know? I'd like to be sure she's OK.'

'Of course, Mr Halston.'

'Good, thanks.' Halston had taken his mobile from a back pocket and was preparing to call Laughland's phone.

'You forget, Mr Halston, I already have your number…'

Back in his car, Laughland sat quietly for a couple of minutes, as he always did after an interview. The first thing he needed to do was contact the Met and get someone down here as soon as possible. As he held his phone in his right hand to make the call, however, he paused. He was struck more than ever by the curious psychology of Leticia Bryant's words and actions. Although she'd had periods of mental instability in her life, she was still a highly intelligent woman who had planned her escape with cool detachment and cunning. She must surely have realised she would be unlikely to get away with her escape for long.

She'd said she had something she wanted to do, but had not elaborated further, at least according to Halston-Gore, but was he holding back information on that score to avoid incriminating himself further? She'd also said there was somewhere she had a key for. Laughland guessed this was a reference to the family cottage on the Norfolk coast. The problem was that this was the place where she'd tried to commit suicide. Did she intend to try again? It was possible, but why go to the trouble of escaping from the hospital and travelling over a hundred and fifty miles to make a second attempt on her life? Was it perhaps out of a sense of completion, finishing off what she'd failed to do properly last time? What had seemed wholly unlikely a moment ago had now taken a more plausible shape in Laughland's mind. Another call would need to be made, this time to Norfolk Police to check out the cottage at Saltham.

But what if the reference to having a key to somewhere where she could hide out was a carefully placed subterfuge? She'd certainly shown herself capable of such deceit in the manipulation of Callum Wicks. What if her intention had been simply to go back home, to Ben Bryant's flat, and do whatever it was she wanted to do there?

And what about Ben Bryant himself? There'd been that moment in the hospital interview when he'd thought he recognised Halston-Gore's number but couldn't find it amongst his contacts. It struck Laughland again that the identity of someone known to him must have entered his head immediately at that moment, someone whose involvement in Leticia's escape might have been a real and disturbing possibility.

Too many assumptions, too many possibilities, but not the moment for inaction. Laughland spent twenty-five minutes getting through to the Met and Norfolk Police, then started the engine and was about to swing the car round to head off in the direction of more familiar territory when it occurred to him that he ought to keep Hargreaves in the loop and at the same time get him to send someone round to Ben Bryant's place to assess what was happening there, if anything.

As far as he knew, Ben Bryant had still been at the hospital in East Sussex when Laughland himself had left to track down Halston-Gore in Twickenham. He had to assume that Bryant had left at some point, probably, he guessed, in the early afternoon, and that he'd now arrived home. Had he found Leticia waiting for him? She'd had a head start, having left Twickenham in the early morning, so he wondered what she'd got up to in the meantime. She'd have travelled by train, of course, changing in London. Was it worth checking at the station? One woman in a grey business suit during early rush hour? This would be a waste of time, in all probability.

He rang Hargreaves, but got no reply. It would have to be a message. He kept it as short and sweet as he could, detailing the extraordinary events at the Sussex hospital and at Halston-Gore's Twickenham address and asking Hargreaves to have Ben Bryant's flat checked out.

The engine was still running. As he paused before driving off, he wondered what the next day or two would bring. Leticia found safe and well? No further news of her whereabouts and a deepening mystery? The worst possible outcome? He couldn't help but think of this last possibility, his mind drifting back to the salt marshes of the Norfolk coast and his part in the saving of Leticia Bryant the last time she'd decided to go missing. Had they reacted quickly enough to the unfolding of events at the hospital? Would the blame fall mainly on the hospital itself or on the police? And then, would the media have a field day with the incompetence of the East Sussex force or with the slow follow-up of Laughland himself and the lack of a senior officer directing things?

He shook himself free of these wholly inappropriate thoughts and drove off to wrestle with the M25 and the route south.

Six

Nicki Gray had popped round to Laughland's flat with a bottle of wine after her shift as he was still driving home from West London. Realising he wasn't there, she decided not to wait for him but to put the wine in the fridge and leave a note.

Now, the following day, she was on her break. She'd just dealt with a particularly unpleasant domestic, but left feeling that calm had been restored, at least temporarily. Nevertheless, it had shaken her up, and she needed a coffee and a moment to herself.

She was also taking time to read over again the report on her performance during the recent course she'd attended. It was a bridge, that's how they'd described it, between uniform and non-uniform, for those judged to 'have potential'. She'd been dead chuffed when they'd said she should go on it, and it had all gone pretty well – in fact, she'd enjoyed it and wanted more. Time was, she'd have been able to share it all with Detective Sergeant Timothy Laughland, and maybe she could again after what had happened during their encounter in his flat.

The report said mostly flattering things about her, which embarrassed her and pleased her in equal measure. She had a 'quick mind' and the ability to 'put evidence together into a coherent hypothesis', whilst her willingness to work hard 'was beyond question'. It was good that she'd not been forgotten about after asking to be moved to a different nick, ten miles from Tim's stomping-ground. Perhaps it hadn't been such a bad move, although now…

Her mobile ringtone interrupted these thoughts. It was DI Harry Hargreaves. Bloody hell. What could this be about? She pressed, put the phone to her ear and pointlessly straightened her back and put on her most professional smile.

'Hello.'

'Hi. Am I speaking to PC Gray? Nicola?'

'Yes, sir, you are.' The "Nicola" was interesting.

'The ACC said I should look at your course report, so I did. Very encouraging stuff. You should be very pleased.'

'I am, sir.'

'Good. Look, we've got something here that might be of interest. It might be your first chance to get some detection under your belt, as you might say.'

'OK, yes, of course, sir. I'll help in any way I can.' She held the phone away from her mouth, so that Harry Hargreaves wouldn't hear how fast her breathing had become. Her heart had also begun to beat alarmingly fast, and she felt a bit faint. They were short-staffed of course, that was the truth of it, but still.

'Good. We've had a call from someone called Edward Bryant about a threatening letter his wife's just received. Pretty nasty, by the sound of it. You'll remember the Bryants, I dare say. Parents of little Sammy, the boy that was abducted. Of course, normally, I'd dispatch Sergeant Laughland to speak to them, but he's off-piste at the moment looking into, funnily enough, the disappearance of the wife of Edward Bryant's brother. Laughland unravelled the whole abduction business last year, so it's pretty much his territory, but, of course, you know all that. It might turn out to be nothing of any great importance, but you never know. Nicki, you still there?'

'Yes, sir.' Now, it was "Nicki".

'What d'you think? You up for it?'

'Yes, sir, quite definitely.'

'Good. House visit, I should have thought; no need to call them in at this stage. I might just text Tim Laughland to keep him in the loop. You comfortable with that?'

'Yes, sir, that sounds very sensible.'

'Right. You can pick up what details we have from Sally on the desk at our nick. Let me know how you get on. Oh, and don't worry, I'll sort everything out at your end.'

With that, DI Harry Hargreaves rang off, no doubt to return to other, weightier matters. She wasn't sure, to be honest, whether she was, genuinely, comfortable with this situation, but it was clearly an opportunity she couldn't turn down. Should she contact Tim and tell him all about it? No, best leave it to Hargreaves and see what happened next.

Seven

That same morning, Jennifer was sitting for a late coffee in the café opposite the Catholic church where, she remembered, she had met with Louise many times. That was before Louise had discovered her affair with Edward. It was a sadness to her that one of the best friendships of her life, perhaps the only true friendship, had foundered on the rocks of her lust.

She had almost finished her coffee, but she kept an eye on the church opposite, attempting without success to repress her impatience. As she was swirling around the dregs in the bottom of the cup and beginning to entertain the possibility that he had put two and two together and decided a no-show was the best policy, she looked up to see him walking quickly down the path from the church door, looking at his watch as he went. She got up and left the café, inexplicably taking a couple of seconds to look at her reflection in the café window. He raised a hand when he saw her and she went over to him.

'Thank you for coming, Father. It's very good of you to meet me.' She shook his hand and looked into his eyes. It was definitely him.

'No problem. I could have come over to the studios; there was no need for you to pick me up from here.'

'Not at all, that's fine. As a matter of fact, I'd like to take a diversion, if that's OK with you. There's something I'd like to chat to you about before your interview. I thought we might go through the gate here into the cathedral and have a seat in that lovely small garden by the memorial. I know it's the enemy, but still…'

'No, not the enemy, Miss Ormiston, not for me anyway. I'm as ecumenical as they come.'

'Good, OK, let's go.'

He was looking at her as they walked. She was used to men looking at her, though they were not usually dressed in a cassock. She flashed her press card at the man in the booth by the south gate and they passed through the barrier, despite his look of mistrust at seeing a Catholic priest and a glamorous, flame-haired local celebrity pass through into the grounds together.

They passed noiselessly alongside an ancient wall, up some stone steps and into the small, square garden she had mentioned. She wondered what he was thinking, whether he was wondering why, after asking him to come for an informal interview about how he'd found his new ministry, she had taken this strange detour for a private chat in a garden cossetted in the foreign surroundings of the Anglican cathedral. On the other hand, perhaps he knew only too well.

For her part, she was wondering herself what her motive was. Altruism was simply not her style, so did she really believe it might be this (presumably) spiritually unimpeachable man of roughly her own age who had sent her the two grotesque threatening letters? It made sense in one way; who else could have known about both her past and her present sufficiently well to realise that she would be a target for blackmail?

There were four alcoves built into the walls of the garden. She chose the one overhung with some kind of ivy, so enclosed as to render anyone sitting on the stone bench inside it virtually invisible. It would be cosy, she thought, but it appeared that they had certainly been more than cosy together in the past, so this really wasn't an issue. As they sat down, she on the right, he on the left, his head appearing against one of the Cathedral towers as it loomed over the garden wall, she reflected ironically that it felt almost like the confessional, a feeling she knew well from her school days. It should at least make him feel at home.

'So, here we are, Father. Before we go any further, I'd very much rather not go on calling you Father. Would Gregory be OK? Maybe even Greg?'

There was a pause, during which he seemed to be furiously thinking to himself and, at the same time, studiously avoiding her eyes.

'Yes, yes, of course. Forgive me, and I know this is something of a cliché, but haven't we met before somewhere? Not in this city, I don't think, and probably at some time in the distant past, but there's something about you I recognise.'

He was still speaking in the measured words of a religious man; it was a practised tone, she assumed. How could she break through this ecclesiastical wall? It came to her, as it usually did, that directness was the best approach.

'I hope this isn't too much of a shock to you, Greg, but in all probability the last time we met we were both completely naked.'

Her words, so oddly out of keeping with this place, stunned him to silence. He slumped forward on to his elbows, forehead supported by the ends of his fingers.

'Oh, yes…that. May Christ forgive me.' The colour had suddenly drained from his cheeks.

'I don't know if Christ forgives you, Greg; that's between you and your God, I suppose. It's a question I left behind me a long time ago.'

'So, you're a good Catholic girl?' The words came faint from behind his hands. Their irony shocked her.

'I was – a Catholic girl that is; I wouldn't say I was ever all that good. But you, I'm guessing you weren't always a good Catholic boy.'

'No. When you and I…did what we did, I was pretty much off the rails.'

'I think that description would fit me as well at that time. I'd been to a Catholic school and suffered the appalling, repressed sapphic passions of the nuns. I'd almost been kicked out several times and when I left I wanted no more to do with God, or the peculiar characterisation of God peddled in that school, at any rate.'

'It's as though our lives are opposing images of one another, as though those photo shoots we submitted ourselves to together marked the crossing-point of our different journeys.'

'What a shame you can't use that in one of your sermons, Greg, it sounded great.'

'Sorry; it shows you how accustomed you get to spouting all this…bullshit.'

The word sounded very odd emerging from the mouth of

this outwardly respectable, cassocked member of the Catholic priesthood. She couldn't imagine any of the priests who had come to her school uttering such a word, though God knows what they'd got up to when they thought no-one was watching.

'A lot's happened since those days, Jenny. If anything, things got a bit worse for a while, drugs, petty theft to pay for my habit, a bit of dealing. Pathetically small beer, really. If it hadn't been for the intervention of Father Donnelly…'

'Father Donnelly?'

'Yes. He did a lot of work with addicts back then. A properly good man, good to his boots, if you know what I mean. He plucked me out burning, as the poet says. A year or two down the line, he saw something in me that was, well, spiritual, I suppose and asked me if I'd be interested in a special scheme the Church was running to train priests from different walks of life. I jumped at the chance, even though my walk had been more different than most, as I think he was aware. The rest is not really all that interesting, I'm afraid. Suffice it to say, I'm here now, and attempting to make up for all the appalling suffering that man unleashed on this community.'

'Father Christian?'

'The same. And then, out of nowhere, you turn up. Darkness visible, and all that.'

'My apologies.' She allowed a silence to settle between them for a moment. 'The thing is, though, another dark thing has just made itself visible. It's why I'm here, sadly. Take a look at this.'

She rummaged in her shoulder-bag and pulled out the second of the two threatening letters. As she passed it to him, she turned away but then realised that she needed to watch him carefully, to see if he betrayed any sign of having sent the letter himself. Judging by the way his face was slowly contorting itself, it seemed to her he was genuinely horrified by what he was reading. On the other hand, this was possibly a man who had been able to fake an orgasm, fake a spiritual leaning, fake a calling in the church...

'It's quite a letter. There's a reference to an earlier letter, too.'

'Yes, equally nasty. From one perspective, you could say it's all cleverly done. There's a drip-drip effect that's quite unnerving. It slowly chips away at you. But then you realise that's exactly what it's meant to do.'

'And what's this disc it's referring to?'

'Can't you guess? It's you and me *in flagrante delicto*. At it. For an impressively long time, actually. You weren't at all bad.'

'Well, maybe not. You were pretty impressive yourself. I don't remember having to try very hard. Perhaps the opposite. But, anyway, all that's a very long time ago.'

'Yes.'

It all came back to her now. This was Greg; she'd liked Greg. A nice, firm body without being pumped up, good hands, professional about the things they were asked to do, the camera angles, all that. Yes, a nice guy, and probably still a nice guy now. The letters couldn't possibly be from him, could they? But, if not him, then who?

'The obvious thing is to take this to the police. I can quite see why you wouldn't want to, of course, especially in your position.'

'Well, yes. But what about yours? Surely you can see they might not stop at this. A letter could be on its way to you as we speak. It's surprising, in fact, that they didn't choose you in the first place. I mean, I'm a fairly archetypal example of a media tart, don't you think? Whereas you, as a priest…'

She was watching him quite carefully now and thinking as she went. It wasn't something that had occurred to her before, but, yes, he had to be a better target, didn't he? Unless, of course…

'Yes, it's certainly a very sobering thought.' There was a pause as he reflected for a moment. 'Listen, I'm still in contact with someone from back then. I don't think you ever worked with him – different outfit – but he's formed his own company since then, making his own stuff for the internet, niche mostly. Apparently that's where the money is. He was a good friend of mine, and I've tried pretty hard to get him to see the light, as it were, and do something socially useful with his life, to no avail. Anyway, the point is, he'd know how someone might get hold of old footage like this, and what the best way of burning it on to a DVD might be. That might narrow down the field a good deal in terms of who sent this to you.'

'I suppose so.'

'And you – I think you need to think about who might have a grudge against you.'

It surprised him when she laughed out loud, the sound reverberating against the walls of the small garden, coiling around the memorial to the dead.

'Take your pick. It's a long list, Greg.'

'Perhaps. Nevertheless, this is a particularly nasty bit of work, isn't it? I mean it's a cut above, or maybe below, your usual nuisance letter. You need to think about who would have gone to this much trouble to blackmail you and might simultaneously hate you enough to use this sort of language. That should narrow things down a little, surely?'

'Maybe.'

In the silence that followed, the question she knew she would have to ask came slowly to the surface and demanded to be spoken.

'Look, Greg, there's no easy way to ask you this, but…'

'But was it me who sent you the letters?'

'Well, yes.' She was shocked that he had anticipated the question.

'No, it wasn't me, Jenny.' He handed the letter back to her. 'I suppose I should be angry with you for suggesting it might be, but I left anger behind me a long time ago. It's the kind of thing I might have done, just possibly, back in the dark days before Father Donnelly when I was desperate for drug money but I hope, even then, I'd have resisted the temptation. In any case, I wonder if I'd be foolish enough to send you a DVD that would be equally compromising in terms of my own position. That doesn't really make much sense, does it?'

'No, you're right, it doesn't.'

Father Davidson suddenly raised himself from the stone seat and stood looking out across the neatly laid-out spaces of the garden. She remained where she was, wondering if he was about to simply walk away.

'You know, it's such a pity to be discussing such things in this place. It's so full of serenity and real beauty, don't you think?'

'Yes, but darkness too. Blood and corruption beneath the stones, all that.'

'There's a sad truth in that. Yet some of us are trying to pretend otherwise.' He turned to her and, absurdly, thrust out his hand for her to shake. 'If I dig anything up about the DVD, I'll get in touch. But if you need to speak to me again, you know where I am.'

He turned away from her and quickly made his way down the steps out of the garden, leaving her with a strange sense of emptiness and confusion, like a good Catholic girl who's just done something unspeakably indecent.

Eight

The offices of Thurgood and Thurgood were ensconced in a pedestrianised part of the city not all that far from Laughland's flat. He had therefore taken the liberty of having a more leisurely breakfast than usual before walking around two corners to what was effectively the legal centre of the city. At reception, he had been told that Mr Bryant was with a client. Did he want to wait? Yes, he did. It would be about forty minutes. That was fine. He followed the bouquet of expensive perfume emanating from the body of the elegant, mature woman whose smile, professionally warm but highly controlled, had greeted him as he'd arrived. A dark corridor led to the waiting area, a meticulously maintained and decorated Georgian chamber that reminded him of Halston-Gore's consultation room.

He took one of the easy chairs in a corner and pulled out his mobile. He checked again the email he'd received from Hargreaves earlier that morning:

Got your message. Dispatched a DC to the Bryant flat last night, around ten. Mr Benjamin Bryant, esteemed lawyer, answered the door in his pyjamas. According to the DC, he was genuinely shocked that his wife had still not been traced and confirmed that he'd not seen her that day. The DC was allowed to search the property without too much fuss. No sign of her. Bryant was told that you'd be talking to him today, so he should be expecting you, though he'll doubtless not be in the best of moods. I told the DC to stay in her car and keep a careful watch on the flat until further notice, so we should pick up any activity whilst Bryant's at work, assuming DC Joyce can stay awake, that is. The time will come when I'll need a full written report on all this, Laughland, as I'm sure you're aware, but for now we need to concentrate all our efforts on finding Leticia Bryant before she tops herself or does something incredibly stupid. I take it you're covering all the possibilities further afield, so I'm about to circulate something to all the hotels and B&Bs here to see if she's washed up at any of them. Good luck with our lawyer and make sure you keep me in the loop.

As he was returning his phone to the inside pocket of his jacket, it sounded loudly for an incoming call. The only other occupant of the waiting room, a severe, balding man in his late fifties, looked disapprovingly at Laughland from behind his copy of *The Daily Telegraph*; it was time to withdraw.

The semifreddo receptionist showed him the door to the small rear garden where, she said, he was more than welcome to take a private call, and he passed through to the cold shade of the tree-lined space and sat on a wrought-iron seat that had seen better days.

'Hello, Laughland here.'

'Ah, good. Norfolk CID here. That woman you're trying to trace.'

'Yes?'

'We sent a car out to Saltham immediately after your phone call yesterday evening. Obviously, considering what happened last time…'

'Yes, of course, thank you. So what did you discover, if anything?'

'Nothing at all. No answer at the door of the cottage, nothing round the back.'

'Right.'

'The guy at the Smoke House opposite hadn't seen anything of her either.'

'Jack Daniels?'

'Yes, that's right. Asked to be remembered to you, though. Said he'd keep an eye out. Mentioned the promise of an eponymous drink sometime, whatever that means.'

'Yes, that sounds like Jack. Good, thanks. I don't anticipate there'll be anything further at your end, but you never know. Thanks again.'

He was narrowing things down, but it was a slow process, and much of it was based on guesswork. There was still over half an hour to wait before he could see Ben Bryant. The garden he was in, though not exactly hospitable, seemed private enough. He scrolled down the names and numbers on his phone and pressed. No reply and the messaging service. He ignored this and tried again, once, twice. Success.

'Hello, Patricia de Tocqueville.'

'Hello, it's Sergeant Laughland here.'

'Please say you've found her.'

'Not yet, I'm afraid. We did trace Mr Halston-Gore. It does seem very likely that it was he who drove your daughter away from the hospital two days ago. The plan was entirely hers, though, we think.'

'Really? Well, I'm sure you know best, sergeant, but Halston-Gore is a thoroughly despicable man and I can't say I'm completely persuaded by what you say.'

Laughland left a pause. It was pointless taking on Lady Patricia de Tocqueville over the degree of complicity of Jeremy Halston-Gore; right now, there were far more important things they needed to be talking about.

'I should also tell you that we're very much of the opinion that your daughter is not in Norfolk. I took the liberty of having your cottage at Saltham checked out, and it doesn't look as though she's taken the option of going there.'

'There's some small relief in that, I suppose, sergeant, given what happened there not that long ago.'

'Indeed. Therefore, what I'd like you to confirm is that your daughter is not with you. That is, not somewhere in Godstone Hall itself and nowhere on the estate, not in any of the outbuildings, farmhouses or cottages on your land.'

'She's certainly not at the house, sergeant, and the reason this call has come through to me is that Anthony is out looking for her right now in those very places you've just referred to. There would seem to be no trace of her at Godstone, sadly.'

'Well, it goes without saying that you should let me know immediately if you find anything that would indicate Leticia has made her way to you.'

'Of course. However, it also goes without saying, sergeant, that our expectation is that every effort is being made at the very highest level at your end to find our daughter. As you know, my husband has been a good friend of the Chief Constable for a number of years…'

'Yes, I remember you saying.' Christ, surely not playing that card at a time like this? 'You have my personal assurance that the attention of two police forces at every level is focused on finding Leticia. It's our highest priority.'

'I very much hope that's the case, sergeant. Goodbye.'

As the final peremptory note of Patricia de Tocqueville's voice cut out, the door to the garden from the legal offices creaked open.

'Mr Bryant has finished his consultation early, sergeant. He's available for you to speak with him now.'

Ben Bryant's office was opposite the room he'd waited in earlier. The door was now wide open and Ben himself was in full view, seated at a solid, broad desk of enormous weight and, by implication, importance. Laughland entered and closed the door behind him.

'It's very good of you to see me again, Mr Bryant, and very good of you to co-operate in the search of your property last night. It wasn't all that long ago we spoke to one another, of course, but things have moved on somewhat.'

'Oh?' Ben sat up, suddenly alert.

'Yes.' Laughland slipped into the chair on the other side of Ben Bryant's desk, ignoring the fact that he'd had no invitation to do so. 'You'll remember I showed you a phone number which you couldn't identify. From my interview with Lord and Lady de Tocqueville, it emerged that this number is that of someone called Jeremy Halston-Gore, now a financial adviser but, some years ago, a fellow student of your wife, Leticia. I tracked him down in Twickenham, where he now has a practice.'

'And is he as much of a creep as he was back then?'

'I'm afraid it would be inappropriate for me to pass comment on that, Mr Bryant. However, he did admit to driving your wife away from the hospital following her escape.'

'Then you've found her, you know where she is?' Involuntarily, Ben began to lift himself up from behind the desk.

'I'm afraid not, at least not yet. I take it you've not had sight of her, or received any calls, texts or emails? Nothing on social media?'

'No, sergeant.' He slowly lowered himself back on to his chair. 'There's been nothing. I fully intended to stay at home this morning to wait for something, but in the end I couldn't bear the silence and came in.'

Sergeant Timothy Laughland looked at the man of roughly his own age sitting in front of him. There was still something about him he didn't quite trust. A prejudice against lawyers, probably. Nevertheless, his instincts told him that the flat she shared with her husband was the most likely bolt-hole for Leticia to aim for after her escape from the hospital and the early exit from Halston-Gore's house. Of course, DC Joyce had apparently found nothing yesterday evening, and now he had to admit that Bryant was showing only the kind of agitation you would expect of a man whose wife has disappeared in bizarre circumstances.

'I see. I'd like to go back to our little chat at the hospital, Mr Bryant, if I may.'

'I don't see what good that would do.'

'Well, perhaps not, but humour me. When I showed you the phone number that, as it transpired, turned out to be Mr Halston-Gore's, you were at first very reluctant to look at it closely. Then, when I showed it to you again, you seemed rather agitated, as though you did actually recognise it.'

'As I told you at the time, sergeant, I thought it resembled the number of a friend of mine, but, when I looked, it turned out not to be that number at all.'

'To be completely honest, Mr Bryant, I can't say I believe you. You looked, admittedly for only a few seconds, more agitated than I would have expected you to look if there was simply some vague resemblance to a friend's contact number.' He paused, watching Bryant's increasing agitation as he sat back in his chair and began running his fingers across his forehead. 'I should have thought, Mr Bryant, you'd want to share with me any information that might help us trace your wife, even if that information might seem to you completely irrelevant.'

The manic rubbing of the forehead stopped, but the eyes had closed, as though blanking out the whole uncomfortable situation. Abruptly, he came forward on to the desk, elbows out in front of him, eyes staring down at the desk-top.

'OK, I suppose this is as good a time as any.'

'Go on, Mr Bryant.'

'It's a personal matter.'

Detective Sergeant Timothy Laughland had only been a police officer for six years, yet he'd heard those words more times than he cared to remember. They usually led to a clamming up and a blood-from-a-stone half-hour of pressing, threatening and cajoling. In this case, though, he sensed the barrier would not be down for very long.

'Nevertheless…'

'Do I need to mention the name of the person concerned?'

'As a lawyer, I'm sure you know all the answers to that question.'

'Yes, well, naturally. The fact is, sergeant, I started an affair a few weeks ago. It's not something I'm proud of, but, as far as I'm concerned, it's now over.'

'What you've just said would imply that the other person in this relationship might not agree with you. Would I be right in assuming that's the case?'

'Yes. It's the case in spades, sergeant. The fact is, this person has threatened me with exposure if I don't continue the relationship.'

'I see. What form did this threatening take?'

'Several phone calls and messages, gradually increasing in intensity, then an email, the contents of which were frankly bizarre.'

'Right, OK. Do you still have the email?'

'Yes, yes I do.' Ben Bryant picked up his mobile and scrolled until he found the message. He turned the screen and handed it across the desk, averting his face as though Laughland's inevitable reaction would be intolerable to watch.

Laughland noted immediately who the message was from, and thus his surprise was muted. He had met Ms Jennifer Ormiston during the investigation into the abduction of Samuel Bryant and she'd struck him then as a woman capable of extremes, extremes of lust, of professional advancement and jealousy, of actual violence, perhaps. Nevertheless, the language of the email was certainly shocking. Any attempt to carry out the list of threats it implied would certainly constitute criminal harassment, at the very least.

'I notice this was sent relatively recently, so I imagine none of these threats has actually been carried out yet?'

'That's correct. By now, of course, she's aware that my wife is missing, and even she wouldn't go ahead with any of those things at the moment. By the way, I copied the email into a different area on my laptop and printed out several copies and squirrelled them away, a practice I've recommended to clients before now.'

'That's very wise, Mr Bryant. Can I ask, did you reply to this email?'

'No, sergeant. I considered doing so – I was angry and wanted to fire off something straight away – but I decided it would be counterproductive.'

Laughland was almost certain he was lying. There was a theatricality about the tone of voice and jutting out of the chin that was grossly overdone.

'Are you sure about that, Mr Bryant?'

'Perfectly.'

'OK. So what made you sit up and take notice when I showed you the phone number during the interview at the hospital?'

'It was that phrase in the email – "it's perfectly possible I might do something even more extraordinary". Jenny's a remarkable woman, sergeant: attractive, manipulative, resourceful. She could do almost anything if she put her mind to it. Naturally, if I'd been thinking straight, I'd have realised the absurdity of Leticia contacting Jennifer, or responding to her contact, at any time during her stay at the hospital. Leticia blamed Jennifer for what happened with Sammy, at least in part.'

'Because Jennifer had told her that Samuel Bryant was your child?'

'Yes.'

A thought occurred to Laughland. He knew that Edward, Ben's brother, had had a long-term affair with Jennifer Ormiston. It would no doubt have seemed deliciously ironic to Jennifer that she was now having an affair with Ben; it might even have been the main reason for conducting such an affair. But was Ben aware of the earlier relationship with his brother?

'Can I ask if your opinion of Jennifer Ormiston's character is shared by anyone else? What would Louise, for example, or Edward make of her?'

'Well, I'm sure you know she's a friend of my sister-in-law; they go back a long way, to the Catholic boarding school they were both incarcerated in. They're pretty much chalk and cheese, but friendships like that between women have a habit of enduring.'

'And your brother?'

'My brother? I'm sure he must have come across her now and then, through Louise. Other than that, I'm not sure Ed would have any opinion about her. He's a mathematician, for God's sake.'

'Yes, well, quite.'

Laughland had his answer, but left a pause anyway in

case there was any more to come from Ben on the subject of Jennifer Ormiston.

'I think we're almost done here, Mr Bryant. Thank you for the information you've given me this morning. I do need to ask you, though, whether you have any idea where your wife is or might be.'

'I'd tell you immediately if I did.'

'I hope that's the case, Mr Bryant.' Laughland got up to leave, thrusting out his hand for Benjamin Bryant to take. 'I'm sure you love your wife very much, but, in her condition and in the circumstances in which she finds herself, it's imperative you don't attempt to shield her, that you keep us in the loop at all times.'

'Naturally, of course.' Ben's hand felt surprisingly clammy and weak.

'Oh, one final thing. Mr Halston-Gore mentioned that, when he was driving her to his flat on the outskirts of London, your wife told him she had something she wanted to do. That was the exact phrase, apparently. Do you know what that something might be?'

'I wouldn't believe anything Halston-Gore tells you.'

'Well, perhaps not, though I can't really see any particular reason he would want to lie about what your wife said to him yesterday.'

'If you say so, sergeant. However, whether or not that's the case, I'm afraid I don't have any idea what Leticia might have meant by it.'

'But if you had to guess?'

'If I had to guess, I'd be making something up, and I'm not sure that would be terribly useful.'

Bryant was on edge, that much was obvious, and there was little point in pursuing the conversation any further.

'OK, Mr Bryant. Don't forget, if there's any call, email, text, anything on social media, you need to let us know immediately.'

'Message received loud and clear, sergeant.'

Out in the busy pedestrianised street, Laughland was still pondering Benjamin Bryant's evasive replies when his mobile alerted him to an incoming call. Hargreaves.

'Laughland?'

'Sir.'

'We've got her. That is, we know where she was last night. A B&B on the Ashfield road. They responded to our social media request for information. Useful for something, I suppose. Anyway, she left early this morning. They asked her if she wanted the room kept, and she said no, apparently. CCTV has her walking into town at six twenty, then we lose her. God knows where she is now, but at least your hunch was right – she's here somewhere. Just a matter of tracking her down…'

Nine

As Laughland was closing his mobile and heading back to his flat to pick up his car, his mind still circulating the possibilities after Hargreaves' call, the landline was sounding in a house in another part of the city.

'Louise Bryant?'

'Yes, who's this?'

'My name's Nicola Gray, Mrs Bryant, I'm a police officer.'

'Oh?'

'I believe your husband rang the police station a couple of days ago to report a menacing letter you'd been sent through the post.'

'Yes, that's right.'

'I've been asked to look into the incident, Mrs Bryant. I'd very much like to speak with you today, you and your husband, if that's OK?'

'I rather thought someone like DS Laughland might be able to help us.'

There was something about the voice Louise was unsure about. It wasn't just that she was expecting a male voice; there was something hesitant in the tone as it came across on the other end of the line.

'Yes, I'm sure he would have done under normal circumstances, but he's tied up elsewhere at the moment.'

'As for my husband, he's at work right now, I'm afraid.'

'That's fine, Mrs Bryant. It's quite usual in these cases to contact the employer to ask for leave to attend. He's a teacher, I believe?'

'Yes.'

'It should be perfectly possible for his Head Teacher to organise cover for his lessons, I should have thought. Shall we say an hour from now…?'

In point of fact, at that moment, Edward had already been pulled out of the first lesson of the morning by the Head. An on-duty Year 8 girl had knocked loudly on his door (make sure the teacher hears you) and handed him the message from Angela, the Head's secretary. Set some work, then wait for the cover and make your way down to my office.

He had been put on hold, as was usual with the Head, then ushered in. Whilst he was waiting, Angela had given him one of her ambiguous looks, a subtle indication, to those who knew the Head's secretary well, that some matter of significance was in the air as far as her boss was concerned. The Head was sitting in his customary position and with his customary air of indifference that marked out a man of practised power and self-preservation.

'Good, you got my message.' He waved Edward to the seat he had sat in not that long ago when the Head had tried to impress upon him the importance of doing the right thing as far as Carwen Williams was concerned. Edward had already made the assumption that this conversation was going to be about the very same matter.

'Shan't keep you a moment.'

Edward had time to reflect on the half-promise he'd been made with regard to promotion. Did he really want it after all? The letter his wife had received was still on his mind, as was the uncomfortable meeting in the Tollgate with Carwen. Then there were his so-called friends and work colleagues; to say that the staff room was a rumour-mill seriously underestimated its power to bolster or destroy reputations overnight. A final, over-dramatic flourish on the keyboard from the Head brought Edward back from his anxious deliberations.

'So, Mr Bryant, how are we?'

'Not too bad, all things considered.'

'Yes, all things considered, that's interesting.' The Head looked down at a piece of paper on his desk, then looked up again and smiled as though something had occurred to him. 'Sammy. The last time we spoke, he was about to return to you. I assume everything went to plan. No problems, I hope?'

'Well…no, no problems we couldn't cope with.'

'Good, good. I called you in this morning because I wanted to give you a further heads-up on the Carwen Williams situation and your own position in light of it.'

'Right, yes, OK.'

'The usual applies, of course, Mr Bryant. Nothing of what passes between us, etc., etc.'

'Of course, I understand.'

The Head nodded, then paused for what felt to Edward

like a very long time, tapping two fingers against his lips as though re-considering how to proceed. This lack of certainty seemed quite genuine, which was unusual for the Head. Quite capable of faking an improvised response, it was normally obvious that, nevertheless, he actually knew exactly what he was going to say.

'So, you may have seen that the police were in yesterday. Put the fear of God into one or two of our Year 11s, but most of the students seemed barely to notice. Anyway, two of the officers came to see me at break. Both from some kind of specialist team. They put on serious faces and spelt out, as if it were necessary, the importance of thoroughly investigating all allegations of abuse by professionals in positions of power and with duties of responsibility and care, all that.'

Edward wasn't sure about the flippant tone, but he had rarely seen the Head looking so tired, looking, in fact, how he imagined he looked himself most of the time.

'Anyway, it turns out they've spoken to Carwen at length and also to the two students concerned and their parents. Their conclusion was that, whilst there was some evidence of inappropriate physical contact in each case, there was also an element of...' He looked down at the sheet of paper in front of him. 'An element of "fantasy and even mischievous manipulation of events". They made it clear to both students that attempting to smear the reputation of a well-respected teacher would, in itself, constitute an offence, despite their age. I gather, from what they were saying, that the parents kicked off a bit, as you might expect, but eventually calmed down.'

'So no action is to be taken against Carwen in either case?'

'That would appear to be so.'

It took Edward a few seconds to realise what the consequences of this might be as far as Carwen Williams' role in the school was concerned, and thus his own promotion. Was it a flood of relief that swept over him? He hoped not.

'So, have you spoken to Carwen since the police came in?'

'Only on the phone. There'll be a follow-up face-to-face at some point, for formalities' sake.'

'But he'll be coming back to take up both roles in middle management?'

'Actually, no. Whilst I haven't spoken to him in person and nothing's been agreed by handshake or signed off on paper, it seems as though the general message is, not to put too fine a point on it, you can stuff your job.'

The directness of these words shocked Edward for a moment. Clearly, the Head had been offended by Carwen's tone but, beyond the minor dent to his self-importance, Edward thought he might actually be well pleased by the way things had fallen out.

'That's quite surprising, Headmaster. Carwen was always one of those you'd have said was married to the job. But, then again, I'm not sure I'd want to come back to a place where a damaging rumour had been rife. It's sometimes hard for colleagues to ignore the idea that there must have been something in the rumours after all.' He hesitated before continuing, partly because the Head was looking at him strangely. 'From a certain point of view, though, Headmaster, I suppose it's not fallen out too badly for the school.'

'Indeed. That's very perceptive of you. We needn't

elaborate too much on that theme, though, I think, and the less said to others the better.'

'Oh, absolutely.'

Edward thought once more of the very peculiar conversation with the inebriated Carwen Williams in the Tollgate. Presumably, the outcome of the police investigation meant the threats Carwen had made would come to nothing, assuming there was anything of substance there in the first place; for the moment, he preferred to ignore the contents of the strange letter addressed to his wife which was lying at home. But he had the definite impression that the Head wasn't done here. Something was continuing to bother him; that same uncharacteristic awkwardness was still there.

'Of course, Mr Bryant, Edward, the other consequence of all this is that it leaves the field open for yourself to take up the roles of Head of Department and Head of Sixth Form, subject, naturally, to your passing through the interview procedures successfully.'

'Well, yes, I suppose it does. I'm a bit loth to take anything for granted, though.'

'Yes, and you might well reflect that such an attitude is a very…appropriate one to take when I show you this.'

The Head bent down to his right and unlocked a drawer in his desk. He pulled out a sheet of paper and slowly handed it across the desk to Edward. He began to tap his fingers on his pursed lips again, as he'd done earlier. It was clear that whatever was on the piece of paper was the source of this unusual discomfort. As Edward focused on the handwritten script in front of him, it was immediately obvious this was not the original.

'This is a photocopy.'

'Yes, and if you read on, you'll see why I've kept the original safely locked away.'

Edward could see from the standard of handwriting, spelling and punctuation that this was an effort from one of their less high-achieving lower school students. It wasn't an easy read, but, as he realised what the content of the letter was, it became an even harder one:

To: The head

Im not going to tell you who I am, Mr Norris. Anyway, that doesn't rely matter. This is about Mr Bryant, the maths teacher. You need to no that he's not quite the person you think he is. I no hes married, because I seen him with his wife after parents evening, but hes also got another women he sees quite often. Not only that, but I no something about her. She's a bit of a hore and has been in porn movies. I dont think you would want someone like Mr Bryant teaching in this school when hes giving it to some tart outside his marridge. What kind of example does that set for students? Not a very good one I dont think. Also I dont think hes actually a very good teacher, so it wouldnt be much of a loss.

He realised that, under different circumstances, the letter might have seemed comical. However, he was naturally well aware of what the writer was referring to, even if the information was out of date. How to handle this? Should he laugh it off? Be appalled? Demand a thorough investigation? Suggest that the whole thing be ignored? He wondered how upset he would really be if the letter meant he could simply carry on with things as they were and be tacitly deemed unfit for higher office. In the end, he decided to buy time by asking some obvious questions.

'Can I ask how you received this?'

'It was in an envelope pushed under my door, believe it or not. I didn't notice it for a while; it had made its way, ironically, under the very chair you're sitting in right now. I asked Angela if she'd seen anyone loitering around my office door with an envelope, but drew a blank there. He or she must have chosen their moment with great care. Oh, and before you ask, I said nothing to Angela or anyone else about the contents of the envelope, though naturally my secretary gave every impression of wanting to know.'

'Right, well, that's something, I suppose. Thank you. And have you investigated the source of this piece of nonsense? Maths is my area, but I'd say the literacy here would tend to suggest a younger student with some communication issues.'

'No, I haven't as yet taken any action, other than to copy the letter and keep it, with the original, locked in my desk drawer. I wanted to speak with you first, Mr Bryant. Obviously, this kind of thing is not unheard of. Students can quite easily develop an irrational hatred of a particular member of staff and give vent to their feelings in a number of ways. However, the lengths to which this student has gone are unusual, I'd say. In addition, I'm about to consider you for two very important positions in the school; from your point of view this couldn't have arrived at a worse time.'

'Surely you don't take this seriously?'

'Well, that rather depends.'

'On what?' Edward felt his anger rising, but was determined to keep control.

'On whether there's anything here to take seriously…'

The Head was now looking straight at him. It was a steady look, not particularly threatening, but not particularly friendly, either. How much should he reveal? He had no idea how his affair with Jennifer had reached the eyes and ears of students at the school, but it seemed as though that was what had happened. The rest of the note was pure fantasy. He could at least say honestly that the affair was over some time ago and that it had never in any way affected his work at the school. He was not sure he could bring off a full denial, in any case.

'I want to be completely honest with you, Mr Norris. It happens to be true that I had an affair with someone, but that affair has been over now for some time. The person concerned has no connection to this school, and my teaching here during that period of my life was not affected in any way. My wife is aware that I had the affair and we have now returned to where we were before it happened. Our son has come back to us and we are committed to looking after him and restoring him to a normal life after the traumatic events of last year.'

'And the other colourful suggestions here?'

'Are nonsense, of course, complete and utter fantasy.'

The Head continued to look at Edward. The interlocking wheels of his brain could almost be heard grinding. Although empathy was not his strong point, Edward tried to imagine what the Head was thinking. Everything had fallen out well. A member of staff he'd regarded as dead wood had resigned and there were no further issues with the police. In front of him was a perfectly adequate replacement for both of Carwen's roles, adequate, but not outstanding. But did he want outstanding? Wouldn't it be better to have someone in place who would fall into line rather than create any kind of turbulence? There were changes to the sixth form in the offing, as every member of staff seemed to know; what better man to have in place than someone who owed a favour, someone whose indiscretions had been overlooked?

'That's very reassuring, Edward.' At last, the Head sat back in his chair and put his hands behind his head. He was back in that mood of relaxed dominance that was his speciality. 'So, I think we understand one another, don't we, Edward? You've been very honest with me, which I appreciate, and we can move forward with the two appointments I mentioned earlier. As I said before, however, that is all subject to the successful completion of the usual processes, obviously.'

'Of course, yes, I understand.'

'But I'm afraid this little note will have to remain filed away for the time being. Like most of my fellow Head Teachers, I've got a special file for such things, so it won't appear in your personal file, you'll be glad to know. Meanwhile, we need to find the little toe-rag that sent this to me.'

'Won't that expose the contents of the letter to other people? I'm not sure I'm comfortable with that.'

'Credit me with some intelligence, Mr Bryant. There are phrases here we can cut out and paste, enough to give a Year Head or English teacher some idea of the script and writing style without revealing any of the unfortunate detail. Naturally, you'll be kept informed about the outcome of my investigation.' The Head stood up and thrust out his hand. 'I think we're done here, Edward. Everything back on track, as they say. I'm sure you'll want to get back to your Year 10 class.'

'Yes, thank you.'

Edward rose from his chair rather more slowly than the man on the other side of the desk. He headed for the door and stepped out into the corridor, only to be met immediately by the Head's secretary, Angela. Had she been listening in?

'Mr Bryant, there's been a message from the police. They'd like you to return home as soon as possible. Nothing to worry about, apparently. I've arranged for your lessons to be covered for the rest of the morning.'

'I see, right, OK. Thanks, Angela.'

He felt like a boxer who's been knocked to the canvas by a punch, only to scramble to his feet again and be knocked against the ropes by another. Not for the first time in his life, he felt the canvas might be the safest place to be.

Ten

When Laughland received the message from Hargreaves about Leticia's appearing on CCTV, he decided to let him do the legwork, or rather manage the legwork of someone else on his behalf. If a further image of Leticia Bryant turned up, he would surely be informed immediately. Meanwhile, now that it appeared she hadn't headed for the marital home, there was one very obvious place to check in terms of a likely bolt-hole.

He drove to one of the gaps in the city wall and turned in to park in front of the cluster of barbers shops, delicatessens and cafes that followed the rise of the wall. From here, he walked a hundred metres to where the Catholic church nestled amongst the spreading retail outlets of the shopping centre. He walked in through the baffled entrance door and stood for a few seconds to accustom himself to the gloom of the interior and to take in the geography of the building. There seemed to be only one other person in the church, kneeling by the central aisle at the front. The figure was female but much older than Leticia Bryant and whoever it was had shown no reaction to his entering from the back of the church.

Laughland's instinct told him the area to the right of the

pews would be worth investigating. He walked slowly past the confessional, from which position he could see more clearly the figure of the woman praying: it was the stout figure of a woman in her fifties or early sixties so deeply engrossed in her dialogue with the Lord as to be oblivious to his presence. He walked on into increasing darkness and discovered an office, the door of which was open, revealing a man of the cloth, the new priest he presumed, bent over a laptop and in deep thought. He knocked on the door.

'Father Davidson?'

'Yes. Can I help you?'

A broad, young-ish face looked up at him with a mixture of warmth and anxiety. Laughland pulled out his warrant card and moved further into the room.

'Sergeant Laughland, Father, from the police.'

'Oh, right, well, have a seat.' Father Davidson closed the lid of the laptop with some haste, his eyes betraying nervousness, trepidation even, above a winning smile.

'Thank you. I should say before I go any further, Father, that I was well acquainted with your predecessor, Father Christian. Given what occurred during and after the abduction of Samuel Bryant, it can't have been easy for you taking over here.'

'No, indeed, sergeant. Nevertheless, here I am. We're beginning to make amends, I think, if slowly. There's a deep hurt here, and I'm aware that the congregation is looking to me to lead the way back to the proper path, as it were.'

'Of course, yes. You have my sympathies. I'm here today, in fact, to ask you about the young woman who carried out that abduction, Leticia Bryant. You may be aware that Mrs

Bryant was deemed unfit to stand trial owing to her mental state and was confined in a secure psychiatric hospital for a period of diagnosis and recovery. Unfortunately, the confinement was, shall we say, less than adequate. Mrs Bryant escaped; we know now that she's in this area because we have CCTV images of her, but we don't know exactly where she is. As a lapsed Catholic, it's possible she might have tried to approach you, Father Davidson, either here or at the Clergy House, especially as it was to the church and Father Christian that she turned after she abducted the child, but of course you know all that.'

'Yes, sergeant. However, I'm afraid I've seen nothing of her. I've been here all morning and I'm sure I would have been aware of her presence. I left the house quite early, at around eight, and I haven't returned since. I suppose she could have found her way there. Should I ring Miss McLevy to check?'

'If you wouldn't mind, Father; that would be helpful.'

Father Davidson picked up his mobile phone from the desk, scrolled and pressed. It didn't take long for the good Elizabeth McLevy to pick up at the other end. Laughland could hear the voice of the woman he remembered well from his visits to the Clergy House. She'd been of enormous assistance to him in solving the Samuel Bryant case. She must surely be happier working for this new Father who, he hoped, didn't have the roving hands of the previous incumbent.

'Miss McLevy? I have Sergeant Laughland here in my office. He wants to know if Leticia Bryant has turned up at the house this morning. Apparently, she's gone missing. Yes, Leticia Bryant.' The sound of McLevy's faltering, angry voice could be heard at the other end. 'No, no, absolutely, Miss McLevy. I appreciate that. But I take it that she hasn't called at the house?' The voice again, louder and less faltering this time. 'Of course, Miss McLevy, we all remember the circumstances. Nevertheless, if she does turn up, you need to let me know immediately. Is that OK?' The call was ended abruptly at the other end. 'As you heard, sergeant, Elizabeth's feelings about what happened at the house are still somewhat raw. However, clearly Mrs Bryant has not been at the Clergy House this morning. Knowing Miss McLevy, I think she'll do the right thing if Leticia Bryant does turn up.'

'I hope so, Father. And you'll let the police know straight away if she appears?'

'Of course.'

Laughland got to his feet. His eye was drawn by the closed laptop on the desk. It was strangely out of keeping with the dark interior of the office and the pervasive smell of incense. He remembered how quickly Father Davidson had closed it down at the beginning of their conversation.

'I suppose you use that to write your sermons, Father. I don't know why, but it seems odd to think of sermons being written on a laptop.'

'I suppose it does. Got to move with the times, sergeant, even in this place.'

'Quite right, absolutely. Don't get up, Father, I can see myself out. And thank you again for your help.'

Laughland retraced his steps to the back of the church. The praying woman had gone. Outside, his eyes were momentarily blinded by the harsh winter light. As he walked back to his car, he wondered what more he could do.

Hargreaves would have put out to all mobiles and PCSOs and someone would be trawling the CCTV output. It was a waiting game, a game no police officer enjoys.

Eleven

At around the same time that Laughland had entered the Catholic church to speak with Father Davidson, PC Nicki Gray was standing on the doorstep of Edward and Louise Bryant's house and pressing the bell. She wasn't wearing her uniform, which made her feel quite uncomfortable. It was Hargreaves' suggestion. He said it would make her feel more confident, more in-role. Instead, she felt more like a fish out of water. Nevertheless, she had her warrant card in her hand, ready to open and hold out in front of her, and she was determined to rise to the occasion.

'Oh, yes, Nicola, is it, about the letter?' Nicki was discomforted by the use of her first name; on the other hand, it was better than Constable Gray. 'Come in. We're through here in the lounge.' Nicki followed Louise, the warrant card still clutched uselessly in her hand.

In the lounge, Edward, who had arrived only a minute or two before Nicki herself, was sitting on the sofa. His eyes flicked towards her as she entered, but then made no contact. In front of him, on a low table, lay a single, unfolded sheet of paper. Louise had moved a chair across so that they could all see the offending message at the same time. This was going to be difficult.

'May I?' Nicki thought her voice sounded higher than usual and oddly constrained.

'Yes, of course.'

She sat down on the chair and Louise moved across to sit alongside Edward on the sofa. Nicki had rehearsed her opening words several times, and she was determined to sound as professional as possible, even though the piece of paper on the table was staring at them and prompting them to simply get on with it.

'Before you show me the letter, Mr and Mrs Bryant, I'd like to commend you for coming forward. It's not an easy thing to do in these circumstances, but you've done absolutely the right thing.'

'Can we just look at the letter? We all know it's a difficult situation, there's no need to remind us of that.' Predictably, it was Edward who felt the need to cut to the chase. Sensing the awkwardness of her husband's response, Louise bent forward, picked up the sheet from the table and handed it to Nicki.

As she read the letter, there was no noise or movement from the other two people in the room. Even their breathing seemed repressed, as though the sharing of the content of the letter was like the inoculation of an anaesthetic. What struck Nicki immediately was the tone of the writing. It was attempting an ironic joviality that was supposed to be menacing, but succeeded only in coming across as pathetically adolescent. The language reminded her of some of the trolling she'd seen on the internet. She wondered what Tim would make of it, then felt instantly guilty for immediately deferring to a man, even if he was a man she had been intimate with.

There were clearly references to marital problems and affairs that, apparently, the Bryants already knew about. She had gleaned something from Tim last year about the nature of these. But there was also a reference to an affair that, according to the writer, the two people in front of her did not know about. Whether it would be appropriate or useful to ask them about these things, and whether they would want to answer, was an interesting question.

A couple of other things attracted her attention. There was a kind of visceral hatred of the professional class underpinning some of the comments, or was she reading too much into it? She was a Sociology graduate, after all. Also, and most relevantly, there was an indication that the writer was known to Louise, or maybe to both of the Bryants. This detecting thing was hard, she realised.

'Thanks for showing me this. As I said before, it's not an easy thing to confront. I can't help noticing that whoever's written this claims to know you. It's there at the start, and they return to it at the end. Can I ask you first, Mrs Bryant, whether you have any idea of who this might be from?'

'No, I'm afraid not. It's an obvious question to ask, I know, and it's been running round in my head ever since I received the letter two days ago. The trouble is, whenever I try to think logically about this, my mind spins out of control and I can't think straight.'

'Of course, Mrs Bryant, I can appreciate how hard this is for you, for both of you.'

'And, before you ask, I don't have any idea who could have sent it either.' This from Edward, spoken, after a moment's hesitation, with terse finality. He had considered, then dismissed, the idea of mentioning the threat Carwen had come out with in the pub. It had been nothing more than a pathetic attempt to dragoon him into supporting him, of course, and now Carwen was gone there seemed no reason to mention it.

'Thank you, Mr Bryant, that's very clear. You'll expect me to say this, but I'm going to say it anyway – if anything occurs to you over the next day or so you must get in touch with us right away.'

'Well, naturally. We're not idiots.' Edward could hear the vitriol in his own voice and instantly regretted his tone.

'I really didn't think that you were, Mr Bryant.' Nicki left a pause to allow the temperature in the room to lower itself a little. 'As to the allegations about the two of you in the letter, unless you want to discuss these, I'm not going to ask you to say anything about them, at least not for the moment.' Day Two of the course: never close down permanently any line of enquiry. 'However, the writer seems to think there's something you don't know about your brother and a relationship he may be having. Would that be an accurate assertion, Mr Bryant?'

Edward's anger rose quickly again at this, and he was about to object strongly to the line of questioning. However, he realised only too well that the information could be relevant to the inquiry.

'Yes. If you must know, it was not something I think either of us knew about and it's not something I've spoken to my brother about either. It's not something I'm ever likely to speak to him about.'

'No, I can see that would be awkward for you, for both

of you.' Nicki felt she shouldn't press harder on this point. 'So, and this is just me thinking out loud, it looks as though this has been written by someone who has information about you, some of which you were not aware of yourselves, and who is, I'm guessing, outside the circle of your immediate family and friends?'

'Yes, that must be right.' Louise broke in before her husband could say anything about this being another bloody obvious point. 'But, the thing is, whatever stupid and ill-considered things we may have done in the past, nothing about them was, to my knowledge, ever shared with anyone else. Except...' Louise stopped, horrible memories resurfacing like magma from the near past. 'Except for Father Christian, of course, and poor Helena.'

'Helena?'

'Yes, Helena Abercrombie. I used to work with her at the charity shop. She found out rather too much, I'm afraid, about my private life. That was partly my fault. God knows how many other people she told about what Edward, Ben and I went through. However, this is certainly not from her, or from Father Christian. Sadly, Helena committed suicide and the Father is in police custody.'

'I see, yes, of course. But Helena, before she died...?'

'It's possible, I suppose.'

'Mmm, OK.' Nicki reached into the pocket of her jacket for her notebook. 'Do you mind if I take notes?'

'No, that's fine.' Louise's voice was distant, her thoughts spiralling out of control at the idea of Helena having spread rumours about their lives to a wide, unknown and unknowable group of people.

'The letter implies blackmail.' Nicki was still writing as she asked the question.

'It does a bit more than imply, I should have thought.' Edward couldn't seem to restrain his reaction to the soft, reasonable tone. He wanted to get hold of whoever had sent this and beat them to the ground with his fists. The note he had just been shown by the Head at school did not raise his anger quite so much but this was different, this was an attack on his family.

'Yes, you're right of course. I think what I meant is that it doesn't go as far as to demand a particular sum of money or issue instructions about how it's to be paid. I take it this is the only letter you've received?'

'Yes, the only one so far.'

'So, what are your thoughts about why they haven't been more specific about the money?'

Edward opened his mouth to speak, but Louise caught hold of his arm to restrain him. She knew instinctively her husband would think they were being asked to do the detecting themselves.

'I can't speak for Edward, but, as far as I'm concerned, not spelling things out at this stage suggests there will be further letters, and that increases the stress, the pressure on us. I think it's a deliberate tactic to unsettle us.'

'That's certainly one possibility.' Nicki had started writing again. 'Another might be that whoever's written this has no idea how to proceed. If we take that view, we might ask two questions. One would be, is this a bluff? Another would be, if the money's less important than the letter itself, what was the original reason for sending it?'

'Your use of the word "bluff" is interesting. It sounds to me as though you're not going to take this seriously, as though you think we're wasting police time.'

'That's not what I meant at all, Mr Bryant. The letter is intimidatory, whether or not the person who sent it follows it up with an actual demand for money. You can rest assured that we'll take it very seriously. It's threatening, and you shouldn't have to put up with something like this arriving through the post.'

'That's very reassuring. Thank you.' Louise offered Nicki a weak but sincere smile and Edward, silenced, looked down at his feet.

'Speaking of the post, do you still have the envelope? We might be able to find some fingerprint or DNA evidence from it, though I should warn you it's not all that likely.'

'Yes, I do still have it.' Louise got up and left the room, returning a few seconds later with the envelope. Edward said nothing, mired in the stupidity of his anger.

'Thank you, Mrs and Mr Bryant, you've been most helpful. I'll need to take both the letter and the envelope with me for analysis, if that's OK. They'll be returned to you in due course.'

Nicki pulled an evidence wallet from her bag, slid the blue zip across and put the two items inside. Somehow, the forensic seriousness of this action stilled both Louise and Edward and their hands automatically came together as they got up to follow Nicki to the door.

'This is in our hands now, Mr and Mrs Bryant. You should try not to be more concerned than is necessary by something like this.' As she stepped over the threshold and turned to give her most professional smile, she saw two people for whom this would be a difficult ask. 'Don't forget, if there is another letter, we need to know about it as soon as possible. However we do it, we'll get to the bottom of this, I give you my word…'

As she returned to her car, Nicki realised her parting shot was not in the textbook. It promised too much and made it too personal.

On the other hand, it felt like exactly the right thing to say.

Twelve

Eleven-thirty.

Laughland was back in his car, waiting. He was unsure what to do, how to support the investigation into Leticia Bryant's disappearance, now that she had been spotted not all that far from where he was sitting. He reflected that he was actually in a pretty good position to launch himself out on to the ring road at a moment's notice, should the need arise.

He decided to pick up a coffee from the wholefood café just inside the city wall, continually examining his mobile to check for incoming messages whilst he was waiting for it to be made. On his way back to the car, he began sipping the coffee thoughtfully. Its aromatic taste and the kick of the freshly ground beans seemed to stimulate him into reviewing his thoughts about the case.

There were so many unanswered questions. What was it that Leticia Bryant was intending to do? Did she even have a plan, or was it all part of the subterfuge she'd employed when she'd spoken to Halston-Gore? In any case, what did her disappearance have to do with the events surrounding Samuel Bryant's abduction? He realised that Harry Hargreaves had sent him down to Sussex in the first place because he had insider knowledge of the Bryant case and, probably, because that would impress the ACC and keep him quiet, still smarting as he was over the whole business of liaising with Sussex over the responsibility for the disappearance.

He reflected, too, on the two most recent women in his life. He wondered how DC Lucy Templeman was coping with the situation that had emerged at the secure hospital in the Sussex Downs. Had they arrested Callum Wicks? He would make a convenient scapegoat for the mismanagement of the Sussex force, certainly, but they'd surely go easy on him, wouldn't they? He also thought of Nicki. She hadn't messaged him for a while, and he knew this meant she was in all probability up to something. He still wasn't sure how he felt about her, but, right now, he would have liked her soft curves and calm matiness in the car beside him.

And what about Father Davidson? He admitted to himself that he was now more than a little biased as far as priests were concerned, but it was still disconcerting to see the new Father close his laptop so suddenly as he'd entered his office. Was he writing his sermon, or doing something else entirely? He certainly looked guilty enough throughout their conversation. Perhaps McLevy had lied on the phone, perhaps Leticia Bryant was at that very moment at the Clergy House. On the other hand, her anger at the memory of what Leticia Bryant had done in abducting the child had been audible on the other end of the line, so this didn't seem to be a viable explanation. Of course, the proper, professional thing to do would be to visit the Clergy House himself. The problem was that the house was right across the other side of the city and he felt he needed to be roughly where he was now, less than a mile from the last CCTV sighting of Leticia.

But then the CCTV itself was ambiguous. She had been captured walking into town on the Ashfield road, but then disappeared from view, despite there being several cameras in that part of the city. Of course, he knew perfectly well that about two cameras in every five were always found to be malfunctioning in some way, but still…

His mobile sounded a few seconds after he had re-entered his car, his coffee cup three-quarters full. He pulled the phone quickly out of his inside pocket and flipped it open. Hargreaves again.

'Sir?'

'You doing anything precarious at the moment, Laughland?'

'Only drinking coffee, sir.'

'Well, you'd better put it down.'

'OK.'

What the hell was this?

'We received a call about twenty minutes ago from a woman saying she'd entered a block of flats and a dwelling in that block, to find the dead body of a woman in the bathroom. She passed out, then re-surfaced about ten minutes later. I'm at the flats now. I think you'd better get over here as soon as.'

'Why, who's the dead woman?'

'One Jennifer Ormiston, spinster of this parish.'

'Jesus, OK.'

Laughland had not done as suggested. The cardboard

cup of coffee crumpled in his hand, flipping off the plastic lid and spraying coffee liberally over the passenger seat.

'What shall we do about the Leticia Bryant search, sir?'

'Oh, you needn't worry about that, Laughland, trust me. You needn't worry about that…'

Part Three

Repercussion

One

When Laughland arrived at the flats and parked in the forecourt there were three people outside, Hargreaves, a female officer and, presumably, the woman who had found the body. Hargreaves was wearing a white overall, blue vinyl gloves and overshoes and had obviously just returned from a first look at the scene in the flat. An officer from the patrol car, abandoned where it had arrived at an acute angle to the block entrance, its lights still flashing, was sitting on the edge of a raised flowerbed, her arm around the shoulder of a smart-suited but strangely shoeless middle-aged female whose body was hunched forward, her hands behind her head. She had clearly vomited into another of the raised beds on the other side of the entrance. As Laughland approached, he couldn't help looking up jealously at the high-spec build in front of him.

'That was impressively quick, Laughland.'

'Yes, I suppose it was, sir. No holdups at the roundabout, a smooth run out.'

'Good. OK.' Hargreaves took his sergeant by the arm and led him behind the patrol car. 'That's the woman who found Jennifer Ormiston. Molly Harrington, station controller, or whatever they call themselves, of Digital City Radio. She keeled over in the bathroom at the sight of the body. Banged her head, but no serious damage, I shouldn't think. Rang it in straight away. Came out of the flat immediately and offered up against the lavender over there.'

'So I see.'

'She's a bit shaken, but I've seen worse. TLC being administered. Anyway, ambulance on its way.'

'Ambulance?'

'Indeed. SOCOs will be about ten minutes, apparently. You want to come up?'

For a few seconds, Laughland was processing the recent events that had led him to this place, a quiet, exclusive development on the fringes of the city, just off the Ashfield road. One woman was dead, a woman he'd interviewed as part of the Samuel Bryant investigation, and another missing, last seen on the Ashfield road, but heading towards town.

'Yes, of course, sir. Sorry.'

'Then you'd better put this clobber on.' Hargreaves returned to his own car and fished out a set of personal protective gear identical to the one he was wearing. 'We don't want the forensic brothers and sisters having a go at us. Naturally, Ms Harrington will have spread her DNA around the place to some extent, including in liquid form on the floor of the bathroom. Still, can't be helped.'

'As you say, sir, can't be helped.' Laughland found himself staggering around on the tarmac, struggling with zips and elasticated fittings.

Suitably clad, the two men wordlessly ascended the stairs to the top floor and the open door to the late Jennifer

Ormiston's flat. They stood outside for a moment, Laughland wondering what he was about to be confronted with. How many dead bodies had he seen as part of his job? Not that many, actually. His mind went back a month or so to a very different block and the sight of Helena Abercrombie's body impaled on the railings underneath her damp, inhospitable flat. This couldn't be worse than that, could it? Hargreaves was clearly musing on something more immediately relevant.

'Molly Harrington says the Ormiston woman had missed two programmes she should have been presenting, which is why she'd come out here to see what the problem was.'

'I take it she'd tried phoning, texting, email, social media, all that?'

'Of course. Anyway, when she got up here, she rang the doorbell twice, but then noticed the door was open, on the latch. If it hadn't been, she'd have left it there and gone back to the studios.'

'A bit odd.'

'My thought exactly. But not nearly as odd as what you're about to see in here. Come on.'

Laughland followed Hargreaves through into the chic, spacious interior of the flat. They passed the lavishly but garishly furnished kitchen on the left and the lounge on the right, its door open to reveal the winter sunlight pouring in through the balcony windows. At the end of the hall, they seemed to be heading into a bedroom, but turned down a corridor to the left, past a second bedroom with a half-opened door, from which, bizarrely, a police boot was protruding, and on towards the bathroom. Here, Hargreaves stopped and turned towards him.

'So, Ms Harrington eventually washed up here, after, as she thought, making sure there was no-one in the flat. To use the loo, she says. Watch where you're treading, obviously.'

Hargreaves stepped aside so that his sergeant could enter first. Laughland's eye was immediately drawn, as Molly Harrington's had been half an hour earlier, towards the fashionable detached bath to his left. A face, only just less white than the bath itself, was looking straight at him, the eyes wide open. The flame-red hair stood out against the enamel surface on which it was resting. An arm outlined its perfectly proportioned shape where it had fallen over the side.

Laughland moved slowly towards the bath, aware of the presence of Hargreaves behind him. There was a good deal of water on the floor, though he could see the level in the bath was lower than might be expected, and he did his best not to tread in any of it. Standing closer, he could see the obscene gash on the wrist of the left arm just under the water. It was hard not to be drawn to the shapeliness of this body, the curves of breasts, abdomen and thighs lying half-in and half-out of the bloodied water, the faint, pale stretch marks from some drastic diet only adding beauty to the line. It produced an odd reaction in him. There was a deep sadness that such loveliness should be lying there devoid of life, but also a strange feeling of looking at something staged, or at the front cover of a lurid paperback. He had once interviewed this woman and driven her to shame. Now, she hardly seemed real.

Dismissing these thoughts, Laughland took in with a more professional eye the rest of the scene. There was blood, he noticed, not merely in the water but seemingly also matted in the hair, as though she had slipped and fallen against the bath at some point. From where he was standing, he thought he could also see some small deposits of blood in the narrow space on the other side of the bath, though he couldn't be sure. To his right, he saw that a knife still lay where it had been jettisoned from the bath. It was a black kitchen knife and its blade and handle were covered in blood. Presumably the weapon that had caused the injury to the left wrist, though it appeared to have landed a long way from the edge of the bath. On the window ledge, there was a pile of stones that had presumably been used to prop up a candle, the candle itself having fallen to the floor just beyond the knife.

'What are your thoughts, Laughland?' Hargreaves was now standing alongside his sergeant, taking in the scene again.

'At first sight, sir, it looks like a classic bleed-out suicide.'

'Agreed. Only at first sight, though?'

'Well, there are some odd things. The water level's quite low. Admittedly, there's a good deal on the floor, but still. There seems to be some blood in the area of the head and maybe on the wall and floor on the other side.' He paused as something else occurred to him. 'Plus, there's no sign of painkillers. There could be something elsewhere in the flat, but there's nothing immediately obvious here. And the knife's gone a long way across the floor.'

'That could be Molly Harrington's doing. She fainted right next to the bath, so the knife could easily have been closer to the edge before she fell.'

A somewhat tentative knock on the door behind them

disturbed their thoughts. It was presumably the other patrol officer whose leg Laughland had seen sticking out from behind the door of the second bedroom.

'I've had a message that the SOCOs are a couple of minutes away, sir. I thought you'd want to know.'

'Yes, thank you.'

'Oh, and the other one's still unconscious. Doesn't look good to me, sir.'

'The other one?' Laughland looked sideways at Hargreaves.

'Yes, Laughland. I'm afraid you need to prepare yourself for another little surprise.'

In the bedroom next to the bathroom, Leticia Bryant was lying at the foot of the single bed, her head nearest the window. There was blood around the back of the head and on the shoulders of her grey suit. Her immaculate platinum blond hair was matted with it. Unlike Jennifer Ormiston, however, her eyes were closed fast. The patrol officer had resumed his position by her side, one hand on her wrist, the other rhythmically stroking her forehead.

'This is utterly bizarre, sir.' Laughland heard his own voice, but it seemed to him to be coming from somewhere, or someone, else.

'Yes, one of the most peculiar crime scenes I've been faced with, that's for sure. She's alive, of course, but only just.' He looked at his watch. 'Six minutes since I called for the paramedics. Bloody ridiculous. You're not telling me there's a higher priority. If she pegs it, there'll be hell to pay.'

As Hargreaves was speaking, they could hear the sound

of an ambulance approaching and suddenly cutting off its siren as it drew in to the forecourt.

'About time. Of course, there'll be a right hullabaloo when the SOCOs arrive and find they can't get as close as they'd like to the entrance door and have to push past the medics on the stairs. Fun and games. I suggest we get out of their way and let them all get on with it.'

Hargreaves directed the paramedics to the bedroom from the safety of the kitchen. He tried to persuade them not to go anywhere near the body of Jennifer Ormiston, pointing out that the SOCOs would be on the scene at any minute and wouldn't be too pleased at their interference. They'd make an assessment, they said, as to signs of life and respond appropriately. Laughland and Hargreaves descended the stairs and met the SOCO vehicle as it entered the forecourt.

'What the fuck's going on, Harry? How're we supposed to get in and out to do our job properly?'

'It's complicated.'

This was clearly not the first time this particular forensic pathologist had worked with DI Hargreaves. Nevertheless, the degree of informality with which she addressed him was surprising. She was a small but formidable-looking woman in her mid-forties with prematurely greying hair and a manner that was simultaneously jovial and threatening. She stepped forward and stretched out her hand to Laughland.

'Helen Arkwright, your friendly local pathologist.'

'Detective Sergeant Tim Laughland.'

She leaned back and took him in with a single glance, then turned to his superior.

'Well, Harry, complicated or not, we need to get in there, so what's what?'

'Top floor, Flat 41. Apparent suicide in the bathroom; through the hall and down the corridor to the left.'

'Apparent?'

'We think there might be some anomalous things in there, but we'll let you be the judge of that. There's also a badly injured female in the smaller of the two bedrooms, but you'll need to wait until she's been stretchered off before you can get in there – protection of life and all that.'

'Some kind of altercation between them that went horribly wrong?'

Hargreaves looked quizzically at Laughland.

'What would you say to that, Laughland?'

'I'm struggling to picture a scenario like that, sir, I must say.'

'Exactly.'

'OK, well, we'll have a little look. If we can get past this big yellow tin can, that is.'

'You want us up there?'

'No, you can keep your size 11s out of the way. I'll come down and we can have a chat as soon as I've got something preliminary to offer.'

Dr Arkwright returned to the anonymous-looking vehicle from which she had emerged and began to suit up with her two colleagues. Laughland wondered how many times she'd done this. Was it something you could ever get used to? What dark dreams would stir you in the middle of the night?

A couple of minutes later, he watched with Hargreaves as the unconscious form of Leticia Bryant was brought out to the ambulance, an oxygen mask strapped to her face and the stretcher on which she was lying covered in a silver wrap. One of the paramedics looked across at them and gestured to suggest that it was touch-and-go.

As the ambulance reversed slowly and quietly out of the forecourt, Hargreaves reassigned one of the patrol officers to speak to the other residents to tell them to remain indoors until further notice, then tape off the entrance to the block. Laughland followed Hargreaves to his car and they both got in, taking off their protective equipment first and sealing it in a large plastic bag in the boot.

In the hermetically-sealed silence, they sat there for almost thirty seconds before either of them could speak. Laughland suddenly felt very odd, as though he wanted Hargreaves to tell him it was all a bizarre joke, that none of it was real. Everything seemed curiously out of shape, yet somehow it would be down to Hargreaves and himself to try to wrench some kind of sense out of it all.

'You OK, Tim?' He couldn't remember Harry Hargreaves ever addressing him by his first name before.

'Not great, sir, if I'm honest.'

'No, well, it's a pretty strange one. Strange and unpleasant.'

'That's something of an understatement.' A thought occurred to him. 'I take it Molly Harrington was completely unaware that Leticia Bryant was in the second bedroom?'

'It appears so, yes. The door to the bedroom was closed as she walked past.'

'So who…?'

'That would be me. The patrol officer, not unreasonably, had concentrated on what he took to be the main incident.

When I got there, I carried out a preliminary search of the whole flat. And there she was. Quite a shock, especially after the scene in the bathroom. I knew who it was straight away, and of course I thought she was dead, but there was a weak pulse at the neck, so…not quite two for the price of one, fortunately.'

Laughland understood that Harry's blunt sense of humour was merely his way of dealing with things, but that didn't stop it wearing thin. The two men sat once again in silence, their thoughts circling obsessively. There would be people to inform, searches to carry out, interviews to conduct. This felt like a dead end, but was merely the beginning for them. Clearly, Leticia's memory of events would be key to understanding what had gone on here, but would she emerge from unconsciousness, and, if so, how long would it take?

After five minutes or so, they could see the white-clad figure of Dr Helen Arkwright shuffling its way from the block entrance across the forecourt towards the car they were sitting in. They both instinctively got out to meet her.

'Well?' Despite his best intentions, Hargreaves found it difficult to contain his impatience on occasions like this.

'Interesting.'

'That's one way of putting it.'

'It could be a suicide. I've seen stranger ones. But…'

'But?'

'But I'd be very surprised if that's what it turned out to be. Of course, until I can have a better look…'

'Yes, yes, we understand that.'

Helen Arkwright pursed her lips and inhaled deeply

through the nose. Like all experts, it went against the grain to give definitive answers without a full set of evidence.

'Some of what I'm about to say is simple common sense, and some not. First of all, if I were going to commit suicide like this, I'd dose myself with painkillers and make sure there was plenty of water in the bath. Neither seems to have happened here. Second, the head wound. It could have occurred as a result of an impact with the edge of the bath, but, if that were the case, it would have to have happened with some considerable force. Therefore, and this is pure guesswork at this stage, I'm suggesting it occurred as a result of blunt weapon trauma.'

'She was attacked?' Laughland broke in, his suspicions having apparently been confirmed.

'Almost certainly. And then there's the wound to the wrist. In all probability carried out with the knife on the floor, but very crudely done and, though I couldn't swear to it at this stage, executed at an unusual angle.'

'An unusual angle?'

'Yes, away from the wrist, south to north, as it were. It's all about the pattern of abrasions. It's also possible, though the water level would suggest otherwise, that drowning may also have occurred in this case. In other words, we could have a combination of factors here. As I say, interesting. Oh, and I take it it's OK for me to have a fish around in the bedroom now that the second victim's been removed?'

'Of course.'

'Good. By the way, someone appears to have recently wiped the wooden flooring of the corridor. We found a rag in the shower cubicle with what is almost certainly blood on it. There's also the suspicion of blood in the wash basin suggesting someone may have cleaned themselves up after an assault on the two women. If you want my opinion, I'd say that both victims were attacked in or just outside the bathroom area and that one was moved to the bedroom, but that will need to be confirmed.'

'Any idea when all this might have happened?'

'Well, you know as well as I do that it's not easy to be very precise about that, but I'd say some time in the last few hours would be a good guess.'

'Thanks, Helen. Much appreciated. We'll let you get on.'

'Now what?'

Hargreaves and Laughland were back in the front of Hargreaves' car. They both knew they needed to work fast but with due deliberation and procedural planning, even if that planning might have to be changed as the investigation unfolded. Hargreaves was leaning forwards and gripping the steering-wheel with both hands, as though this in itself would help him get his thoughts in order.

'Well, obviously there's a lot of tidying up to be done here. After that, we'll need to assign some colleagues so we can reassure local residents and do door-to-doors, all that. No response from number 42 on the same floor, and I don't hold out much hope there. It might be just as productive to ask the residents of the flats behind us on the other side of the road.'

Laughland turned his head round to look at the block Hargreaves was referring to. Perhaps twenty years older and somewhat less chic, the flats nevertheless had balconied windows that would give a clear view of any comings-and-goings from the block opposite.

'There's the CCTV, of course; someone will have to start trawling through the footage from the cameras installed by the block's security firm but, as you know, that can take a while. We'll need to press Helen Arkwright to get the forensic report to us a.s.a.p., though it's almost always counter-productive to rush them too much. That should tell us definitively what we're dealing with, but we can't wait until we've got that in front of us. We have to proceed on the basis of one murder and one attempted murder. Agreed?'

'Yes, sir, absolutely.'

'Right, OK.' Hargreaves looked across the forecourt to where the female patrol officer was still sitting with Molly Harrington on the edge of the raised flower bed. 'Can you try to persuade Ms Harrington to come down to the station and agree to take us through every detail of what happened and maybe provide some background detail? We've got duty of care here, of course, but still.'

'Leave it to me, sir.'

Two

'It's very good of you to agree to help us with our enquiries after what you've been through, Ms Harrington. We do appreciate it.'

'No, that's fine, I want to help.'

When Laughland had left Hargreaves' car and approached Molly Harrington in the forecourt of the block of flats, he could see she'd calmed down a good deal. Nevertheless, he'd taken his time with her and asked the uniformed female officer to remain with them while he spoke to her. In the end, with a tight-lipped smile and a nod of the head, she'd gone with him to the station. Of the rooms that were available, IRG6 was the quietest he could find, and she seemed reasonably comfortable, despite clinging on with both hands to the cup of hot sweet tea on the table in front of her.

'Can you take me through the events of this morning as you experienced them, please, Molly? Take your time, and tell me if you need to stop for a while.'

'OK, yes.' She cleared her throat and took a sip of the tea. 'Jenny hadn't turned up for her morning show and she was due to carry out an interview later the same morning, so I was a bit concerned. I mean, she'd never failed to show up before and there wasn't a text or email or anything on social media. We ran a repeat and I went out to see if I could find her.' She stopped, her bottom lip quivering and water beginning to gather in her eyes.

'Take your time, Molly.'

Molly Harrington ran a single index finger under each of her eyes and sat up straight, raising her chin and widening her eyes in a determined effort to continue.

'When I got to the flats, I spoke to a woman outside who obviously didn't like Jennifer very much but who let me into the block anyway. On the top floor, I rang the chime, but I noticed the door was open, so I went in. I suppose that was wrong of me, but there wasn't much time left before the interview and I needed to get hold of her.'

'That's fine, no-one's going to blame you for that. Tell me what you did, what you saw, once you got inside the flat.'

'Well, I looked into the kitchen and lounge, then went down the hallway into the main bedroom. There was no sign of her, and I realised I ought to leave.'

'But you didn't?'

'No. I needed, well, I needed the loo and I could see the bathroom at the end of the corridor. That's when I went in there, that's when I saw…'

Laughland looked at the woman on the other side of the table; she had frozen, her mouth slightly open, and he thought for a moment she might lose consciousness again and drop on to the table in front of him.

'Molly? Have another sip of tea. You're doing fine. You don't need to tell us what you saw in the bathroom, that's not necessary.'

'Of course, it was then I must have fainted, keeled over and hit my head on the floor. When I came to, it was like waking into a bad dream.'

'But you had the presence of mind to contact us immediately. That was good, Molly, very helpful. Can I ask you about the door to the other bedroom, the one nearest the bathroom? You must have passed it on your way down the corridor.'

She peered at Laughland as though she didn't understand the question, and he realised that, of course, she had no idea about the second victim.

'I suppose I did, I don't really know. Yes, I did pass it. I remember it was closed; it didn't seem likely that Jennifer would have shut herself in the spare bedroom, so I didn't go in. Why, is it important?'

'It could be.' He left a pause before moving on. 'Can I ask what you thought when you saw that Ms Ormiston had apparently committed suicide?'

'I'm not sure I thought anything, really. I was too shocked to think.'

'Of course, I understand. But what about now? Is it something you might have expected her to do?'

'Oh, no, definitely not.' Molly Harrington sat more upright and seemed to find solace in the confidence with which she could answer this question. 'She was just about the last person you'd expect to do anything like that.'

'You seem very sure about that.'

'Yes, I am. I don't want, you know, to speak ill and all that, but Jenny was very sure of her own abilities, I think, a very strong personality. Maybe it's a bit naïve to say so, but it's unusual for a person with such a strong sense of her own importance, with that kind of resilience, to kill herself, don't you think?'

'You could be right, Ms Harrington. If that's the case, we're left with the possibility that someone murdered her. I think we can rule out accidental death. Was she the sort of person who collected enemies rather than friends?'

'Well, if I'm honest, from conversations I've had with her and the other people she worked with, plus the comments she received on social media, I'd say we're looking at Marmite here; she received adulation from some, even proposals of marriage, but some thought she was too outspoken, especially for a provincial little outfit like ours. Then there's the usual trolling that pretty much every female presenter gets. You know, references to her voice, saying she should shut up about things she knew nothing about, and intimate things about her body. You know the kind of thing, I'm sure.'

'Sadly yes. Can you remember any particularly vitriolic texts or tweets, anything she should maybe have brought to the police?'

'She mentioned there was someone who kept contacting her for a while last year, making more-or-less the same comments each time, about her being no better than a prostitute, accusing her of having relationships with all sorts of people. But I think they stopped, at least she stopped telling me about them. I said all the things you'd expect about reporting them, but she said she was only telling me because she thought it was right I should know and that they weren't affecting her. That's what I mean, really, stuff bounced off her. I can't believe she killed herself; it just doesn't fit somehow.'

It just doesn't fit. No, that's right, thought Laughland. Nothing fitted at the moment and it was quite difficult to see how anything would. The Jennifer he'd met at Digital City during his interview about the disappearance of Samuel Bryant had come across as forthright and energetic, even allowing for the drift the interview had taken. She was tall and broad-shouldered, not easy to overpower, unless… unless you took her by surprise.

'So she gave no details of the person who was trolling her? You didn't press her for a name, for example?'

'No, it didn't seem important enough at the time. In any case, I think she said it was anonymous.'

'Right, OK.' Laughland knew it was virtually impossible to track down anonymous online abusers, certainly with the manpower they had at their disposal. 'What about her personal details, Molly? Is there a next-of-kin? Can you remember anything about her background when she applied to join Digital City?'

'She never mentioned anything about her parents. I think we all assumed they'd divorced and re-married, or died. As to a significant other, well, we all knew she picked up different men on a regular basis, but as far as we knew there was no-one serious. That sounds incredibly old-fashioned, doesn't it, but you know what I mean. There was a rumour that she was seeing a married man for some while, but as far as I know it was just a rumour.'

She stopped, tensing her brow and leaning forward on to her hands that had formed the shape of a prayer around her nose and mouth.

'One thing I do remember, now I think about it, was that

there was a gap in her CV. I remember we asked her about it and she just said she was away from it all finding herself, or some such nonsense. From the mouth of anyone else, it would have been suspicious and clichéd, but she could carry off an answer like that without any difficulty and we were all taken in.'

'Do you still have the CV, Molly?'

'I expect so, somewhere.'

'Good, we may need to take a look at some point. What about on air? She must've taken calls from the public, addressed local issues, that sort of thing.'

'Yes, oh, yes, of course.'

'And did she rub anyone up the wrong way?'

'All the time, I'm afraid, but that's why people liked her – she was edgy, if that's the right word. And, anyway, I never knew her not to be able to exit a call without de-fusing the situation. She was very good at that, de-fusing.'

'Yes, I can understand that. OK, Molly, I think that's all for now. You've shown incredible strength in coming here to speak to me, and you've been very helpful in answering the questions. I think you need to go home now and rest. I'll arrange an unmarked police car for you. If you leave your keys, we can get someone to pick up your own car from the flats. Is there someone at home when you get back?'

'Yes, my, well, partner. He knows I'm here, and he'll be there when I get home.'

'OK, good. This is bound to hit you suddenly at some point, probably when you get inside your front door. Look after yourself, and don't hesitate to get in touch if there's anything we can do for you. Naturally, if anything else occurs to you about Jennifer Ormiston or what happened earlier today, I'd appreciate it if you could contact me, DS Tim Laughland, at the station here.'

'Yes, yes, I will. Thank you.'

When Molly Harrington had left the interview room, Laughland reflected on what she'd said. The rumours about Jennifer Ormiston and a married man had been quite accurate, of course, and now he'd been made aware that she'd had affairs with other men. Why was it that his interview with Benjamin Bryant this morning was still uppermost in his mind? He opened his mobile and pressed Hargreaves' number.

'Hello, boss.'

'Laughland; I was just about to ring you. Anything from Molly Harrington?'

'One or two interesting things. The main impression I got, though, and one which confirms my own personal feeling, was that Ms Jennifer Ormiston was a very unlikely candidate for suicide, which kind of backs up what Helen Arkwright told us an hour ago and our own view of the situation.'

'Good. Let's hope the final pathology report backs all that up. Meanwhile, the SOCOs have almost finished their preliminary work on the flat, apparently, so it'll be free for us to trample all over and do a thorough search later today.'

'What about Benjamin Bryant, sir?'

'Oh, yes. DC Joyce went round to his office and gave him the bad news. Apparently, he dropped everything, cancelled a meeting with a client he was due to have in five minutes' time and hared off to the hospital where they've taken his wife. Joyce was unable to describe his reaction very precisely, since he left in such a hurry.'

'It's important one of us speaks to him a.s.a.p.'

'Yes, but not now, Laughland. We've got an officer at the hospital to keep an eye on the situation with the wife, so he can watch over Ben Bryant's movements at the same time.'

'And how is Leticia?'

'Not good. She hasn't yet recovered consciousness, so don't hold your breath on that score.'

'I was more concerned about her health, sir, to be honest.'

'Absolutely, of course. Anyway, you up for that search of the flat?'

'Yes, sir.'

'Good, meet me there at four.'

Three

As he stood once more in the forecourt of the flats, he could take in more completely the façade and grounds of the place, free as it was now of emergency vehicles and marked and unmarked police cars. 'Fieldview Lodge'. He presumed that was a reference to the cricket ground it overlooked. It was a pretentious name, but the solid, inoffensive rise of the building betrayed a high standard of workmanship and the grounds were quite extensive, stretching around the sides of the block and seemingly some way to the rear. Doubtless, these were bought as 'apartments' and not flats, and he wondered fleetingly whether the salary of a provincial radio presenter could have stretched to any of these properties, let alone Number 41 on the top floor, with its suggestion of penthouse exclusivity.

Hargreaves had seen him arrive and was waiting impatiently by the main entrance.

'Stop gawping, Laughland, and let's get on. By the way, before you ask, we've had a look at the Mini over there. It's hers, but it's locked and alarmed. There's a couple of items in there but no-one's attempted to break in. She was obviously expecting it to be business as usual this morning. This is useful, though.' He held up a master key obtained from the freeholder. 'Should enable us to come and go as we please. Come on.'

They gloved up and took the lift to the fourth floor. A breathy debutante voice reminded them of where they were going and signalled the opening and closing of the doors. It was a smooth ride and the doors opened almost noiselessly. This was wholly unlike the rather rougher elevator experience in Laughland's own block, when, that is, the lift was actually working.

Inside Jennifer Ormiston's flat, there was an odd smell of stale perfume and antiseptic and the SOCO team had left sticky labels identifying potential blood spatters and prints in the hall, corridor, bedroom and bathroom. Hargreaves and Laughland knew instinctively that disturbing these would get them into a lot of trouble with the good Doctor Arkwright.

'You take the lounge and I'll have a look in the kitchen.'

'Right, sir.'

The light was fading now, but there was enough for Laughland to take in, through the broad French windows leading on to the balcony, the view of the sweep of the landscaped garden outside and the impressive sward of the cricket ground beyond, on the other side of a sunken road. As he moved back, he noticed a couple of SOCO labels beside the handle of the windows he'd just been looking through.

Inside the room, the furniture was stylish and expensive, probably ordered online from the kind of company you saw advertised in the weekend supplements of serious newspapers. On the coffee table, alongside a set of notes that appeared to be about an interview with someone called Sheila Delaney, there was a half-filled glass of white wine where, presumably, it had been left the night before. He almost tripped over the rest of the bottle, sitting where it had been lowered on to the floor beside the sofa.

'Enjoyed a drink, by the look of it, sir.'

'Yes, I'm getting that impression from the kitchen, too, Laughland. There's a wine cooler here stuffed with about fifteen bottles of Chardonnay and Sauvignon Blanc. A few dishes on the drainer. Fridge full of pricey ready meals. More a drinker than a cook, I'm guessing. Oh, and there was a mobile phone in here. I've bagged it up; should be worth a look if we can get the techies to crack it open.'

Laughland walked out of the lounge into the hall. An empty space, apart from the small table just inside the front door. On this, Jennifer's keys were still lying where she'd thrown them, sad testament to a life lived at a hundred miles an hour. Next to the keys, gathering dust, was a pile of glossy magazines and next to them, precariously balanced, a cactus plant. He noticed the edge of a single folded sheet of paper protruding from underneath one of the magazines and what looked like the torn flap of an envelope underneath that. He pulled out the sheet and started reading. It was immediately obvious what kind of letter it was.

'Sir, I think you should come and have a look at this.'

Hargreaves emerged from the kitchen and took the letter from his sergeant's hand.

'Well, well. This is interesting, wouldn't you say? Not much detail here, though – nothing about what the something is that's going to be revealed, or how much money's involved.'

'No, but it does say another letter's to follow. I wonder if it arrived, and, if it did, where she put it.'

Hargreaves followed the hallway to the main bedroom, whilst Laughland returned to the lounge. There was a bookcase and some fitted shelving built around a desk, but no sign of anything resembling a cupboard. The bookcase had been used almost exclusively for the display of arty pottery and photographs, photographs entirely of Jennifer herself, shaking hands with musicians, mayors and local entrepreneurs, some of whom Laughland recognised. The desk was scrupulously tidy and the drawers, all unlocked, contained only copious amounts of printer paper and items of stationery.

The TV unit, its metal frame matt black with finishing touches in chrome and smoked glass shelves, supported a forty-inch screen with a digital player underneath. Nowhere to hide a letter here. Then a thought occurred to him.

He returned to the lower of the two desk drawers and pulled out the inch-thick stack of printer paper. He fanned it carefully. There, about half-way through the stack, was what he was looking for. A letter in the same font and 14-point text as the other, its envelope flattened out underneath. It was longer than the first, but had the same attempt at a menacing tone. This one mentioned a sum of money – ten thousand – but also, more importantly, a DVD that appeared to be the focus of the blackmail.

He returned to the TV unit and looked along the line of DVDs arranged above the digital player. Had she used the same idea to hide the DVD? He was rehearsing the thoughts of a dead woman, a dead woman he'd met alive only once. Turning the digital player off stand-by, he waited until the drawer slid open. A disc had been left inside, a set of episodes of *Friends*, Disc 5. He closed the drawer and pulled out the box set from the collection. Half-way through, there it was, a plain recordable DVD in place of the disc in the player.

'Boss?' He shouted to make himself heard to Hargreaves, still rummaging in the drawers of the bedroom. 'Boss?'

'You found something, Laughland?'

'Most definitely, sir.'

'Good. You can save me from being corrupted any further by the late Ms Ormiston's kinky underwear, or buried alive under her collection of shoes.'

When Hargreaves had had a chance to read the letter, the two men looked at each other with the same unspoken thought. The temptation was to put the disc on there and then, but they both knew there was an element of voyeurism in the thought. It was pretty clear what would be on the disc from the comments in the letter and they both realised they'd better get forensics to have a look at it first. Hargreaves bagged and zipped before Laughland could suggest anything different.

'OK, so we know what the blackmailer wants and what he wants it for, but you'll notice there's still no mention of how the money's to be paid.'

'No. So, what's your thinking, sir? Subtle turning of the screw or poorly disguised, amateurish lack of forethought?'

'The latter masquerading as the former, probably. They've no idea how to get hold of the money without incriminating themselves, so they've decided to put the frighteners on while they work it out.'

'And is this from our murderer? If it is, why would they kill the very thing that's about to pay out for them?'

'A very good question, sergeant. Perhaps because the money's not the important thing. Perhaps whatever caused them to send the letters in the first place finally overwhelmed them and they decided Ms Jennifer Ormiston would be better off dead. The last two words of this second letter might suggest something of the sort.'

'You mean "slag bitch"?'

'Yes. Of course, how Leticia Bryant fits into all this is another matter. By the way, we cleared up the anomaly of the CCTV footage. She doubled back on herself once she realised she'd been captured by a couple of cameras on the Ashfield road. We have CCTV of her coming back the way she'd just walked and going on towards the flats. It could be she realised she was going the wrong way, or it could be a clever ruse on her part. Either way, I think we can be fairly certain she was planning something by coming here.'

'The thing she told Halston-Gore she had to do?'

'Exactly.'

Hargreaves looked around the lounge, as though checking that his sergeant hadn't missed anything. His eye alighted on the French windows and the two labels the SOCOs had placed near the handle and on the other side of the door.

'Did you notice these, Laughland?'

'Yes, sir. Looks like whoever did this has been all over the flat.'

'Yes. If we're very careful...' Hargreaves pushed down slowly on the handle of the French window, as if it might come away in his hand. It opened outwards on to the balcony. 'Come on, sergeant, don't be shy.'

Outside, it was beginning to get cold and darkness was

just starting to drop down over the garden and sports ground beyond. Laughland looked over the right-hand side of the balcony to the flower beds underneath them, stripped of all colour at this time of year. He thought he saw something below, lying under a half-denuded bush. He leaned over further. Yes, there was definitely something there, something white. A cloth or towel wrapped around something, perhaps.

'I think there's something down there, sir. By one of the bushes on this side.'

Hargreaves, who had been considering the nigh-on impossibility of a safe, unobserved escape from this considerable height, came across and followed Laughland's gaze over the balcony rail.

'My eyesight's not as sharp as yours, sergeant, but even I can see there's something there. Odd that it was missed earlier, though.'

'Not necessarily, sir – you can see it's being illuminated by the light from the ground-floor flat below us.'

'True enough. I suggest we go down and take a look.'

When they arrived at the precise spot under the tiered balconies at the rear of the block, the curtains had been drawn in the ground-floor flat and it was almost too dark to see what was in front of them. Nevertheless, the position of the object and its whiteness allowed it to stand out clearly enough, once you knew it was there. Hargreaves knelt down beside the bush.

'I shouldn't be doing this, and you certainly haven't seen me do it, Laughland. Pass me a stick, will you?'

'A stick?'

'Yes, Laughland, a stick.'

Laughland rummaged around at the base of a tree a few metres away from the flower bed and returned with what he hoped would be an adequately large and robust twig. Hargreaves poked at the folds of what they could now see was a towel. As one fold fell away, they could see the inside of the towel was matted with blood and that wrapped loosely in it was some kind of large, ornamental stone. It too was covered in blood and hair.

'I think we've found our murder weapon, Laughland. No scouring of road verges or woodland, no pulling up of drain covers or going through bins.'

'Too easy.'

'Yes. Which suggests…?'

'Panic, maybe, naivety, carelessness. Or perhaps it's someone who's not really concerned about being found out.'

'Indeed. Then there's the choice of this particular weapon. Was it simply the nearest thing to hand? Was it already in the flat or did our friend bring it with them? One thing's for certain, I need to cover it over with that excellent stick of yours, Laughland, and phone this in pronto, before it gets rained on or covered in dog shit.'

Four

They'd waited outside in the garden at the back of the block where they'd found the stone in its obscene sheath of bloodied towel, freezing their bollocks off, whilst the SOCOs made their way there. With scrupulous care, the team had photographed the site, the flashes of their cameras leaving blotches like bruise-coloured patches of oil on the retina, then removed the towel and its contents from underneath the bush, placing them in a large plastic tube and sealing it with blue tape. Despite Hargreaves' assertive pleading, the SOCOs had been unable to say when they would know for certain whether it was the murder weapon and whether there were any prints on the stone.

Thus, when Laughland opened his front door that same evening, he was in considerable need of warmth. His own flat, however, was freezing cold. He had the heating on demand-only; given the unpredictable hours he worked, it was pointless setting any kind of timer.

He'd visited the chip shop on his way home, but when he unfurled the paper wrappings the smell of fish, batter and frying oil was a lot less appetising than it had seemed in the shop itself. Whilst he waited for the boiler to do its work, he fixed himself a single malt and sat hunched over the coffee table, picking up one chip at a time without much enthusiasm. The whisky was better, though, warming his throat as it went down, though it didn't mix all that well with a deep-fried Maris Piper.

It had been one hell of a day. He knew as he sat there he would be very unlikely to sleep that night. Whether the images of what he'd seen in Jennifer Ormiston's apartment would float under his closed eyelids or whether it would simply be the dull pain of it all that would affect him was immaterial. It was, of course, 'part of the job', but that didn't stop it becoming part of him as well.

After he'd binned most of his takeaway and poured himself a second whisky, his mobile sounded. Hargreaves. Bloody hell, was there no escape?

'Sir?'

'Being the assiduous copper you are, Laughland, I thought you'd like to know that we've just finished going through the CCTV from outside and inside the block.'

'Right, OK.' He hoped he didn't sound too unenthusiastic. 'And...?'

'And it would seem that we have our prime suspect on camera, both entering and leaving the block and riding up in the lift. Unfortunately, though, there's no footage on the landing of the fourth floor.'

'So, please tell me it's a nice clean image, full-face, of someone we know and whose details are all there on our database...'

'I'm afraid I'm going to have to disappoint you there, Laughland. Black Nike trainers, loose-fitting black tracksuit bottoms, grey hoodie pulled completely over the head, with a black scarf around the nose and mouth. No identifying patterns or logos, apart from the Nike tick. Height approximately six foot. Slim, but not especially so. Impossible to make a guess as to age; male and under fifty-five is about as far as we can go, apparently. Pretty bloody useless.'

'Do we have a time of arrival and departure?'

'Our man arrived at just after six a.m., left forty-five minutes later.'

'And what about Leticia?'

'We pick her up at about six thirty, entering the block.'

'An arranged meeting?'

'Could be, but the timings don't seem quite right.'

Laughland was silent for ten seconds, running through his head the various arrivals and departures, entrances and exits. Leticia had doubled back, so the arrival at the flats matched the CCTV evidence from the Ashfield road. There was just one problem with all this, though.

'How did our man, and Leticia for that matter, get in through the main entrance to the block?'

'Ah, that's an interesting one. Something we missed, I'm afraid, though it's easy to see why. We entered by a conventional means if you remember, but, apparently, according to two of the neighbours, more often than not the main entrance door fails to close properly. Something to do with air pressure and prevailing winds. Anyway, both neighbours said they rarely had to use their key and weren't surprised someone had managed to simply walk in. Maybe the landlord would listen to them now, etcetera, etcetera…'

'Fine, but could either Nike Man or Leticia depend on that?'

'No, you're right, of course. My guess is our man staked out the block, watched the comings and goings, maybe over several days and nights. That wasn't an option for Leticia, naturally, but if there was an arranged rendezvous then she could have been let in from the flat, even if the entrance door was shut.'

'Or she might simply not have reckoned on it being a problem.'

'There aren't many other things that seem to have escaped her.'

'That's true. You mentioned the neighbours just now. I take it nothing turned up from the door-to-doors?'

'No, nothing. Nothing from the block across the way, either. Everyone keeps themselves very much to themselves, it seems. Work to live and live to work, not much time for looking out for one another.'

'That's my life in the police force you're describing there.'

'Very good, sergeant, very good. Anyway, I thought you'd want to know all that as soon as.'

'Much appreciated, sir, thank you.' It was going it a bit to say it was much appreciated, but still.

'Oh, and while I'm here some bad news, I'm afraid. The powers-that-be have decreed that we can't have a specialist team on this until the forensics confirm it's a murder, so let's hope Dr Arkwright comes up with the goods sooner rather than later. Until then, it's just you and me, sergeant, and a few A.N. Others, where available.'

At some point during his third whisky, he must have dozed off. He woke up to find an overturned glass on his lap and a stain on his trousers in a very embarrassing place. As he was making his way to the bathroom, yelling all the imprecations he could think of at no-one in particular, the door chime sounded. Jesus, not Harry again, he'd only just spoken to him on the phone.

But it wasn't Hargreaves.

'Hi, Tim. You smell like a brewery.'

'That's because I've just tipped a very expensive single malt over my crotch.'

'Mmm, so I see.'

Nicki stood before him, her eyes looking down at the irregular wet patch on his trousers. She was still in uniform, but he was very glad to see her.

'I hope you haven't come to arrest me, PC Gray?'

'I can't guarantee that. Drunk and disorderly, for a start.' She smiled and stepped over the threshold as he moved aside. It was a choreographed moment they had rehearsed before.

He watched as she entered the lounge, a space which, like most city centre flats in the sort of price range he could afford, but unlike the spaciousness of Jennifer Ormiston's bespoke apartment, incorporated a kitchen and eating area. She took everything in at a glance, but a glance long enough to suggest that she'd like to go through all his mess there and then before she could relax on the sofa. Or, of course, elsewhere.

Because she was wearing her uniform, the whole effect was one of ironic accusation, of punishment even. When he'd first met her, she'd been in uniform, a uniform which she'd filled out very nicely in, as they say, all the right places. She was slimmer now, but the fantasy, the woman-in-a-uniform thing, was still strong. Even stronger tonight, if anything, especially after two and a half single malts.

'It's been a hard day.'

'I know. It's why I'm here.'

'I need you.' One day, he might say something different to her, a different three words, but for now these would have to do.

'I know that too.'

He was standing in front of the sofa, more than ever conscious of the vaporous wetness on his trousers. She came right up to him and undid him. His arousal was quick and urgent as she hitched up her police-issue skirt and began to tug at her black tights. But this wasn't how he wanted her, not tonight.

'No, Nicki. This is too much.'

She looked puzzled, offended, but not for long.

'Bed, then?'

'Yes, bed.'

When the alarm went off as usual at six, Laughland came to slowly, gradually becoming conscious of a throbbing pain in his head. The pitch dark was alleviated by electric light seeping through a narrow slit between the door and the jamb. As he sat up, he could hear the sound of a shower and Nicki's unselfconscious humming. He remembered last night and smiled. He was glad they'd gone to bed; the sex had been long and relaxed and she'd clung to him afterwards, breathing hard. Both of them must have fallen asleep quickly, his fears about staying awake all night dispelled.

The sound of the shower suddenly cut out and, after a

moment or two, the door opened fully, flooding the room with light. Nicki, wrapped in a towel, came over and sat on the bed. She said nothing but simply lay down next to him, whilst his hand extricated itself from the quilt and fell on the beautiful mound of her hip. They lay like this for a few minutes, but he knew there must be a reason why she'd risen before him. She raised herself up and leaned over him, caressing his shoulder.

'Early shift. Got to be in by seven. You?' Her voice was matter-of-fact, but still affectionate. Copper-to-copper, but with an added something that bound them further together.

'Probably ought to show my face soon after that as well.'

'OK. Let me get dressed and I'll make us some coffee and toast. If that's OK with you?'

'Of course. You don't have to, you know…'

'I know, but since I'm up first I might as well. By the way, I brought something for you to look at. When you've showered and suited, you might have a look at it.'

She went over to where her uniform jacket lay over the back of a chair and extricated a folded photocopied sheet from one of its pockets, dropping it on the bed beside him before moving into the kitchen area. Needless to say, he didn't wait until he'd showered and dressed before looking at it.

It was a threatening letter sent to Louise Bryant, demanding money to prevent certain personal information getting out about herself, her husband and his brother. The information was all well-known to Laughland, but he wondered how this person, whoever they were, had got hold of it. It was immediately obvious that the writer was the same as the one whose letters they'd discovered yesterday in a chic apartment on the outskirts of the city. Like the first letter to Jennifer Ormiston, this one was written in a nasty but amateurish tone and made no reference to a specific sum of money, or how it was to be paid. Was there a second letter to Louise Bryant as there had been to Jennifer Ormiston? And how the hell had Nicki come across this? He got out of bed and walked through to the kitchen.

'What's this, Nicki?'

He realised that his tone, in its urgency, might have come across as accusatory. Instead of replying immediately, she smiled and lowered her eyes.

'It's perfectly obvious you've just woken up, I'd say. Sticks out a mile.'

'Oh, God, yes, sorry.'

'Don't apologise – it's a good look. But maybe…?'

He went back into the bedroom, pulled on his trousers with some difficulty then returned to the kitchen and sat at the table whilst Nicki prepared the toast. The kettle clicked off and there was quiet in the room.

'Well, Harry contacted me after I'd returned from the course I'd been on and asked me to help out. He said the Bryants had received some kind of letter and reported it to the police.'

'Short-handed.'

'I prefer to think it was my promise as a potential DC, and so should you.'

'Yes, sorry, I wasn't…'

'Of course, "short-handed" was the first thought that went through my mind as well, but still. I even went round there, to the Bryants' house, in plain clothes.'

'Blimey, OK. And how did that feel?'

'Terrifying. Weird. But I got the job done, despite the husband's constant sarcasm. Anyway, I thought I'd bring the letter to show you, just in case I'm barking up the wrong tree.' She came to sit opposite him. 'I reckon the writer's trying to be threatening, but it comes across as, well, embarrassingly immature, really. That hasn't stopped it having an effect on the Bryants, though. It mentions money, but not the amount and not how it's to be paid. Maybe trying to crank up the pressure, or maybe a sign that the writer hasn't thought the whole thing through yet.'

'You're exactly right, Nicki. But the letter's interesting from another angle. The suspicious death out at the Ashfield road flats Harry and I attended yesterday – we found two threatening letters there, too. Similarly immature, similarly vague. Looks like the same writer to me. What I don't understand is why Harry didn't mention the Bryant letter at the time.'

'That's easy, I haven't told him about it yet. I wanted to be sure of my ground.'

'OK, but he knew of its existence.'

'Well, yes, but I got the feeling it was delegated out of his in-tray and instantly forgotten.'

'Where's the original?'

'Being analysed.'

'Good, OK. Can I keep this copy?'

'Yes, of course.'

'Great. Not sure we've got time for that toast after all.'

Five

When Laughland got to the station, Harry Hargreaves was nowhere to be found. But then it was ten minutes to seven and, apart from the duty sergeant, there was pretty much no-one else about. He knew it was pointless sending Harry a text, but he did it anyway, suggesting they should get together as soon as he arrived.

Meanwhile, he sat at his desk, shivering whilst the heating made up its mind whether it wanted to turn itself on and tapping a pen on his opened notepad. If he'd hoped this would help him to bring into focus the distracting thoughts circulating in his head, it wasn't working.

Nicki had driven in separately, leaving first from his flat, but not before planting a delicious wet kiss on his mouth, a kiss he could swear he could still taste. Did everyone at the nick know about them? No-one had said anything, but that wasn't necessarily conclusive evidence that there weren't rumours spreading around. On the other hand, Nicki was into social media a lot more than he was, and she hadn't said anything about any online traffic of an embarrassing nature. He could hear Nicki's voice now: stop over-thinking it, if it happens it happens.

'Christ, Laughland, you beat me to it. I can't say I remember that happening before.'

Hargreaves had burst into the office and slung his coat on one of the hooks alongside the door. He seemed unsure whether to stand or sit, at first leaning against the wall to Laughland's right, then realising this was a somewhat comical position to take up and pulling out the chair opposite his sergeant to sit down. He felt it necessary, nonetheless, to lean back casually in it, as though re-asserting his authority.

'Did you get my text?'

'I did, Laughland. It came across as rather melodramatic, so this had better be good.'

'Well, I'm not sure good really covers it, but still…' He was about to wade in to the subject of the letter to Louise Bryant when he realised he needed to be careful about telling his boss how he'd come across it. 'The thing is, sir, I had an email from PC Nicola Gray.'

'OK. Isn't that a bit unusual?'

'Yes and no. We go back a long way.' He looked up briefly at Hargreaves' face: no obvious flicker of a smile. 'Anyway, she told me you'd asked her to look into an offensive communication sent to Louise Bryant.'

'Yes, I believe I did. She hasn't come back to me with anything yet, though.' He leaned forward conspiratorially. 'I'll be honest with you, Laughland, I'd been looking for something to give her after that course of hers. Top of the class, flying colours and all that, apparently. The ACC wanted me to give her something to get her teeth into, and the letter seemed just about the right sort of thing.' He leaned back in the chair again and put his hands behind his head.

'And you didn't make any connection between the letters we found at the Ormiston flat and the Bryant letter?'

Hargreaves' face changed from bloke-to-bloke complacency to serious concern in an instant. He came forward again, the legs of the chair scraping on the worn floor-covering.

'Is there a connection?'

'I believe so, sir.'

He pulled out the photocopy of Louise Bryant's letter Nicki had given him, unfolded it and passed it across the table. Hargreaves read quickly, his face becoming increasingly contorted as he scanned each line.

'How did you get this?'

How indeed.

'PC Gray handed it in at the desk this morning. I picked it up from there.'

'It would certainly seem to be the same feeble, degenerate mind at work.' Hargreaves scratched the back of his head. 'Face it, I should have seen the potential connection and I didn't, it's as simple as that. But let's not dwell on my inadequacies; what are your thoughts on this, Laughland? Who is this low-life and what connection do they have to the killing of Jennifer Ormiston and the assault on Leticia Bryant?'

'I'm not sure, sir. As we said with the Ormiston letters, it seems illogical for someone to get rid of the very thing that's hopefully going to pay out, maybe even several times over. But that depends on how serious the demand for money is. If the point of all three letters is to intimidate, to have a psychological effect, rather than to get the victims to pay up, then they might have come from someone with a grudge against them, something that might lead to a more direct, physical attack.'

'OK, I'm buying this so far.'

'To back that idea up, there's a definite feeling of sexual disgust, of misogyny even, hovering behind the pathetic bluster. And why send the letter the Bryants received to Louise? It could have been sent to either of the men on the list.'

'She's the centre of it all – you know, wife, lover, friend?'

'OK, yes, but there's more to it than that. There's a stalker's mentality there, a thinly veiled sexual interest coupled with a bit of class envy. Dangerous stuff, potentially.'

'And yet also feeble, wouldn't you say? The threats seem paper-thin, somehow.'

'Agreed, but if the writer of the letters is our attacker he wouldn't be the first psychologically or emotionally feeble man to commit murder. It's worrying.'

Hargreaves leaned back a little and cocked his head to one side. He seemed to realise at that moment where his sergeant's thoughts were taking him.

'Now, hold on, Laughland. I think I know where you're going with this. I should tell you what you know already, I'm sure. We haven't got the manpower to protect Louise Bryant twenty-four hours a day, certainly not for the rather tenuous reason you've just articulated.'

'I wouldn't call it tenuous, sir.'

'No, but those above my pay grade would see it that way. Look, the best we can do is send someone round there to share our concerns with her and her husband. Ask her to keep doors and windows locked, not to venture out if at all possible. I'll get PC Gray to go round there again, since she's already had contact with them. Meanwhile, we need to do the basics as well; we need to think about how the writer of the letters could know what they seem to know. The threat to Jennifer Ormiston was quite specifically related to her pornographic past, but she features in the letter to Louise Bryant as well, let's not forget. It would appear very unlikely that those referred to in the letters have been randomly chosen. Therefore, we have to assume that whoever's behind the letters has had in some way specific knowledge of, or acquaintance with, the people they're threatening. Agreed?'

'Yes, sir, agreed. In which case, might I suggest that I go round to see Louise Bryant myself? I can give her all the advice you mentioned and also ask her what might link herself, her husband, her brother-in-law and Jennifer Ormiston together, apart from their tendency to get into bed with one another. As you say, she's the centre of it all, it would seem.'

'Good idea, Laughland. By the way, the powers-that-be are considering a press conference, but the decision on that hasn't been made yet. As for forensics, it'll be a while before we get the analysis of the crime scene and the stone we found in the bush. I've done all the usual pressing, but Helen Arkwright tends to move at her own pace. However, the techies should have something later today on the mobile phone. I'm hopeful they'll also have something on the DVD from the second letter to Jennifer Ormiston today or tomorrow. Meanwhile, keep me in the loop on Louise Bryant.'

'Will do, sir, of course.'

'Good. Onward and upward, Laughland.'

Well, onward at least.

Six

An hour or so later, having made up for the missed breakfast at the flat by visiting the station canteen, Laughland drew up outside the Bryants' house, wondering exactly how to play it with Louise Bryant. The last time he'd been there, he'd spoken to both the Bryants individually about their extramarital liaisons, hers with Ben, his with Jennifer. He'd seen them separately, for obvious reasons, but he couldn't remember whether they'd discussed anything that might have linked their affairs together. There was Helena, of course, Helena Abercrombie, Louise's charity worker who'd had her own lustful thoughts about Louise and ended up speared on a railing or two outside the block of flats in which she lived. She'd known pretty much everything, or thought she did, but she was dead now and couldn't possibly be behind the threatening letters.

As he'd left the station, he'd been handed an A4 envelope by Sally on the desk. Molly Harrington at Digital City had dropped it in, apparently. It was important, she'd said, and Sally was to make sure the nice sergeant received it. Sally couldn't resist commenting that she couldn't see what 'all these women' saw in him, but gave him a half-smile that said the opposite.

He'd struck up an immediate rapport with Louise Bryant when he'd worked on the disappearance of her son. As for little Samuel himself, he'd been unconscious when Laughland had fished him out of the back of a wrecked car in a Cambridgeshire lane and watched as they put him in the back of an air ambulance, so he supposed the boy wouldn't know him at all. Perhaps that was for the best.

He'd rung ahead, to make sure Louise would be in. Edward was at work, but Sammy would be there, was that OK? That would be fine. When he arrived, she saw his car outside through the lounge window, and came to the door before he'd reached the end of the short front drive.

'Sergeant Laughland, it's so good to see you again.'

She came forward, into the porch, and made to put her arms around him, but decided in the end to opt for rubbing and squeezing his left arm. She smiled at him, and it brought back in an instant the warm affection of their brief relationship, the strong need he'd had to help her find her son.

'Come in.'

They went into the lounge, illuminated by winter sun, and he sat opposite her on the sofa. Now he could see that she was thinner than he remembered, her cheeks very slightly hollowed out by the suffering she'd gone through. She was soberly dressed in a soft ochre-coloured cardigan and jeans. He had so much to ask her but knew, first of all, that there were things to be said that might upset her, would certainly shock her. There had been no press statement, no conference. She knew, he realised, absolutely nothing about what had happened in the last two or three days.

'Can I get you something to drink? Tea, coffee, perhaps?'

'No, no, that's fine. But you go ahead if…'

'Well…' She got up. 'I'll just get some water, if that's OK.' She was nervous, he thought, and ill-at-ease. Hardly surprising, given the threatening letter and the events of last year. When she returned, she brought a glass of water, unthinking, for him too.

'I believe you had a visit from PC Gray recently?'

'Yes, that's right. I had a nasty letter sent to me, threatening to reveal all sorts of things about my private life and asking for money.'

'But with no details of how much or when or how it was to be paid?'

'That's right. I told PC Gray all that. I think she was going to have the letter examined forensically.'

'Yes. The thing is, Mrs Bryant…'

'Louise, please.'

'The thing is, Louise, we've now discovered two more letters of a very similar kind.'

'Oh, where?'

'In rather unfortunate and harrowing circumstances, I'm afraid.' He was doing his best to ease her into this. 'You won't know this yet because we've so far kept it under wraps, but we're fairly sure someone you know well has been brutally murdered, and someone else you know viciously attacked in the same incident.'

He looked directly at her. Her face had contorted in pain, but it was a pain of bewilderment. The last time this man had come to her house, he had told her that Helena had committed suicide. Now here he was again. Did he make a speciality of this, this pulling of her life out of shape? She was squeezing the glass of water she was holding abnormally hard, as though to break it. She made to drink from it, but then lowered it to the table in front of her.

'Who is it this time?' Did that come across as callous? She hadn't meant it to.

'The murder victim is your friend, Jennifer Ormiston. The other victim is Leticia, your brother-in-law's wife. She's currently unconscious in hospital, but in a stable condition.'

'I see.'

She had no idea how to respond to this news. Jennifer was no longer her friend, for reasons Sergeant Tim Laughland knew only too well. Nevertheless, it was a shocking thing to be confronted with. And Leticia? She couldn't take it in, though she thought immediately of Samuel's natural father and how this would add another weight of suffering to his already painful life. She picked up the glass of water and drank from it copiously. A silence intensified itself in the room.

'If you'd rather I left you alone after such shocking news…'

'No, sergeant. I know it's a dreadful thing to say, but Edward and I have been through so much recently that we're not easily discomforted any more. Perhaps, eventually, that feeling I used to have that life was out there, to be lived and enjoyed, will return. Perhaps Samuel will restore that to me.'

'I hope so, Mrs Bryant, Louise, I hope so.' Despite what she'd said, he left a pause before continuing. 'The thing is, because we found two letters very similar to the one sent to you in Jennifer Ormiston's flat and because she was found dead it's inevitable we're linking the two things together.'

'Right.' She was struggling to see where this was going, but her stomach had clenched in some kind of visceral anticipation.

'Therefore, unfortunately, it's possible that you're also under threat from the same person who sent the letters to Jennifer.'

'Oh, I see.' She picked up the glass of water again and drained it.

'So, the first thing I came here to say to you is that you should be very careful in the next few days not to expose yourself to any kind of risk. It would be my advice not to respond to any calls, texts or emails other than those from members of your family or friends, people you know and trust. Make sure all your doors and windows are secure, even when you're inside the house, and try to limit your time outside the house to a trip to the supermarket.'

'Yes, right, OK.' She bent forward, hands on knees. 'I'm feeling a bit faint, I'm afraid.'

'Here, have my water. Take your time.'

Gradually, she resurfaced, her breath settling once more into its usual rhythm. At that moment, Sammy appeared in the lounge doorway, his eyes flicking from his mother to the man he saw opposite her. He looked as if he might recognise him, but was clearly not sure.

'Mummy.' He came over and buried his platinum blond head in his mother's lap, but then raised it again to look straight across the table. 'Hello.'

'Hello, Samuel. How are you today?'

'OK. D'you want to see what I'm making upstairs?'

'Sergeant Laughland is a policeman, Sammy. He's a very

important man. I'm afraid he doesn't have time to play with you.'

'Oh, OK.' And with that, he scuttled off to re-join the private world of his bedroom.

'He's a lovely boy.'

'Yes. Still with us, but only because of you.'

'Well, I don't know…' It pained and embarrassed him to be the saviour. He would never be able to see himself as one, whether or not it was true. 'Would you mind if I asked you about your friendship with Jennifer? I know things changed between you, but I'd appreciate your telling me what you know about her life. You were at school together, I believe?'

'Yes, that's right. St Benedict's. Not a very positive experience for either of us, I'm afraid, but that was particularly so for her. She felt constrained by all the rules; it was a straitjacket of a place.'

'And you'd known each other ever since?'

'Not quite. There was a gap of, maybe, three or four years when we went off to different universities and she went round the world, all that. We picked up our friendship again when she came to live here and got the job at the radio station.' It hurt her deeply to use the word "friendship" now, but it was no less than the truth of how it was.

'Ah, that's interesting.' Laughland reached into his pocket for the photocopy Molly Harrington had left at the desk for him and unfolded it. 'I've got her CV here, the one she handed in at Digital City when she first applied to work there. The pause in your friendship seems to tally more-or-less exactly with a gap in the CV, at least beyond the university years. Have you any idea what happened during that time, apart from the period you both spent studying?'

'There was the American boyfriend, of course.'

'The American boyfriend?'

'Yes. She'd met him first before going to university, but I think they met up during and after that period. I think it was pretty much a whirlwind sort of thing. A year or two of living wildly. He was a lot older than her.'

'Do you have the name of this boyfriend?'

'Todd Johnson, I think it was. I never met him. He went back to the States and never returned.'

'Do you know why the relationship broke up?'

'No, but I know it was quite a sudden thing.'

'And what's he up to now, this Todd Johnson?'

'I believe he's something big in baseball – a coach or something.'

'But there was still at least a couple of years when you were not in contact with her, even allowing for the time spent with her American?'

'Yes, that's right, definitely. We never talked about that bit of her life, either. She never raised it and I didn't ask. It was kind of understood between us – not something to talk about, to mention, even.'

'I see. Thank you, that's very helpful.' He was speaking as he was scribbling down a sentence or two in his notebook. 'I think I already know the answer to this next question, but I need to ask it anyway. Is there anyone who connects yourself, your husband, your brother-in-law and Jennifer? Anyone who could have found out about what happened between the four of you? Please think carefully, if you would.'

Louise leaned forward, her fingers rubbing at her forehead. Nothing else had occurred to her since PC Gray had asked more-or-less the same question.

'No, I can't think of anyone. Except poor Helena, of course, and she's no longer with us.'

'No, quite.'

Flipping the cover of the book closed, Laughland replaced it, along with the CV, in his inside jacket pocket. He rose and stretched out a hand to Louise, who reciprocated.

'Remember, Louise, take great care over the next week and ring the station the moment you feel threatened in any way. You can reach me on my own private number, if that's easier. I'm only a couple of minutes away.' He fished out a card and handed it to her.

'I still have your number, sergeant. I think I probably still know it by heart.'

She leaned across the table and, unable to resist the need any longer, embraced him. He squeezed her lightly in return, then pushed himself gently away from her.

'You stay there, Mrs Bryant. I can let myself out.'

Seven

On his way back to the station, Laughland had prepared himself for a debrief to Hargreaves about what he'd gleaned from the interview with Louise Bryant. Instead, Harry met him at the front desk, carrying two sealed items that Laughland immediately recognised as evidence bags, and pulled him into the nearest interview room, indicating that he should sit down opposite him.

'I've got something to show you, Laughland.'

Hargreaves pulled out a mobile phone from one of the evidence bags, waved it at his sergeant and set it down on the table in front of them. From a separate, sealed folder he pulled out a single print-out with two distinct pieces of text on it and pushed it front of Laughland's eyes.

'We've managed to crack Jennifer Ormiston's phone. You'll be interested in these two emails.'

Laughland looked at the first of the two pieces of text on the print-out. It was a text he immediately recognised, the poisonous email Ben Bryant had shown him from Jennifer Ormiston threatening exposure if he didn't play ball in their relationship.

'I've seen this before, sir. Ben Bryant showed it to me on his phone during our interview at his office yesterday.'

'And you didn't think to tell me?'

'It kind of got brushed under the carpet, sir, understandably.'

'Fair enough. So you've also seen the reply Bryant sent?'

'He told me he hadn't sent one. He'd thought about it but then decided to let her stew.'

'In that case, I suggest you have a look at the second bit of text you've got there in front of you.'

Laughland looked at the print-out. The first half of Ben Bryant's reply seemed fair enough. It was assertively written, but it made an appeal to Jennifer's intelligence and understandably placed the emphasis on his wife's disappearance. But the end of the email was more direct, and Laughland could see immediately why Bryant had lied to him about sending it. Who knows what he'd actually meant by "if you had anything to do with the disappearance of my wife, you'll find out just how abusive I can be", but it was undeniably a threatening statement.

'Interesting. It looks like we should have another chat with Mr Bryant.'

'Definitely. But maybe, before we do, we need to work out what we think could have happened if Ben Bryant is our man. It would seem that he had the motive to rid himself of Jennifer Ormiston, but what about his wife?'

Contradictory thoughts were racing through Laughland's head. He mistrusted Benjamin Bryant now – perhaps in some ways he always had – yet he couldn't quite see him as their assailant. Apart from anything else, he wondered whether Bryant would have enough cold venom in him to carry out the act. On the other hand, his lying about the reply to the email was unfortunate and might be construed as obstruction. Perhaps they were looking at the events round the wrong way?

'What if it wasn't Ben Bryant at all who attacked Leticia? Suppose the husband arrives first, the mysterious figure caught on CCTV. He enters the block by ringing for Jennifer to let him in. She does so because she's persuaded that he really does want to come back to her and discuss their future relationship together.'

'OK.'

'Ditto at the door to the flat. She lets him in, and they go through to the main bedroom, where she's hoping for a bit of physical reconciliation, if you get my meaning.'

'At that time of the morning?'

'Well, why not?' He thought with mild, fond embarrassment of his own unforeseen arousal in the kitchen of his flat that morning. 'Unfortunately for Jennifer, however, Bryant's come to finish things once and for all, and to tell her to back off from her threats.'

'Fair enough.'

'An argument ensues. Maybe she retreats to the bathroom. At some point, Bryant's wife arrives. She gains access to the block through the open front entrance and walks straight in through the door to the flat on the top floor because her husband has left it open.'

'A bit convenient?'

'Well, yes, agreed. However, let's run with it. She gains access to the flat and hears the row going on in the bathroom. She recognises both voices, but particularly that of her husband. When she gets to the bathroom door, she starts to scream and shout at Jennifer and pushes her husband out of the way to confront her. You know the kind of thing, I'll deal with this, we can sort this out between us…'

'This is pure Hollywood, sergeant.'

'Well, maybe. Anyway, what Leticia Bryant isn't expecting is that Jennifer will turn, grab one of the decorative stones on the bathroom windowsill and come at her.'

'There were decorative stones? Are you making this up?'

'I don't think so, sir. I think there was a scented candle supported by beach stones on the sill. At some point before we got there, the candle had fallen over, because one of the stones had been removed.'

'That's a bit too neat, Laughland, given what we found in the bushes, but I'll take your word for it.'

'Anyway, Leticia turns and makes to run off. Before the husband realises what's happening, Jennifer has struck Leticia on the back of the head, so hard that she collapses.'

'And Ben…'

'Ben loses it, attacks his jilted lover and attempts to cover up what he's done. Then he has a dilemma. His wife is badly injured and needs hospital treatment; on the other hand, he's committed murder and needs to get out of there as soon as he can.'

'So he takes the latter option. But why drag the body of his own wife into the second bedroom and close the door?'

'Maybe he's not thinking completely rationally at that point, maybe he thinks it'll delay things a bit.'

'And all this fits our timings, does it?'

'Well, I interviewed Ben Bryant at around nine-forty yesterday morning at the offices of Thurgood and Thurgood. I was surprised he was at work at all. He told me he'd been planning to stay at home to wait for news, but felt he couldn't bear the silence and came in. I didn't think anything of it at the time, but now it seems a shade suspicious.'

'How?'

'I don't know, as a convenient explanation of his lateness, I suppose. Late or not, though, he'd have had plenty of time to get back to his flat in Bartholomew Road and clean up before seeing his first client.'

Hargreaves said nothing to this at first, leaning on his elbows and pressing his folded knuckles repeatedly against his mouth and nose as if hammering out his thoughts. Eventually, he got up and walked around the room, hands plunged in pockets. Several times he stopped and looked at Laughland as if about to speak, but then carried on walking. When he did speak, it was from a standing position and, disconcertingly, from behind Laughland's back.

'You've created a very plausible narrative here, sergeant, but does it tally with your gut reaction? When you were with Bryant yesterday morning, how did he come across? I know you weren't thinking of him as a murderer at that point, that's fairly obvious, but, looking back, would you say his responses could have been those of someone who'd just pummelled, throttled or drowned the life out of his lover and left his wife to bleed out on a bedroom floor?'

'That's putting it a bit dramatically, sir.'

'Well, you know me, Laughland.'

'You already know what I'm going to say, I think, and that is that he certainly seemed evasive and on edge. At the time, I put that down to the fact that he was probably lying to me about the return email, to the fact that his wife was still missing from a secure hospital where she'd been held under psychiatric care and, well, to a well-practised professional arrogance.'

'And now?'

'Now, I'm not so sure.'

'OK.' Hargreaves came to sit opposite Laughland again, dropping heavily on to the chair. 'So, what about the letters? I take it you'd agree with me that the chances that Ben Bryant wrote them are vanishingly small.'

'Agreed.'

'So we've got two lines of enquiry that are mutually exclusive, three if you include Leticia's unknown motive for being in the flat that morning. By the way, how did you get on with Louise Bryant this morning?'

'I told her about the death of Jennifer Ormiston and the attack on Leticia Bryant. I told her about the similarity between the letters we'd found in the flat and the one sent to her. I warned her to act with extreme caution in the next few days. I also asked her what she knew about Jennifer Ormiston's past. It seems there's a gap of at least a couple of years when Louise lost contact with the person who at that time was her best friend, something that seems to resonate with this.' Laughland took out the copy of the CV Molly Harrington had left at the desk, unfolded it and pushed it towards Hargreaves.

'So, if I read this right, there's a period of her life which Ms Ormiston didn't want close friends or potential employers to know about. This could be useful. It's certainly intriguing. Good work, Laughland. I'll let you hang on to this for the time being. Meanwhile, I think you've persuaded me that we need to have a little chat with our eminent local lawyer. If he won't co-operate, I suggest we pull him in under suspicion, but let's hope it doesn't come to that.' Hargreaves got up from the table and Laughland went to follow him. As he was about to open the door, Hargreaves turned abruptly.

'By the way, the parents of the wife, the de Tocquevilles, or whatever they call themselves, have made an official complaint to the Chief Constable about how things were handled in Sussex and the fact that their daughter is lying in a coma in hospital as a direct result of our failure to track her down quickly enough. I'm quoting directly from the words of the ACC that were yelled down the phone at me half an hour ago. We need to act quickly and professionally, Laughland. If we don't, our illustrious careers, such as they are, will be over.'

Eight

When Hargreaves and Laughland turned up at the hospital, the officer assigned to keep an eye on Leticia Bryant and her husband looked ready to pass out with boredom. No, there hadn't been any change in Mrs Bryant's condition, but neither had it deteriorated. The husband was in with her. He was in there most of the time, except when the specialist came round to examine her. He looked pretty devoted to the cause.

The senior nurse who met them in the corridor outside Leticia's room was not at all sure there should be three people in the room at the same time. Nevertheless, they were allowed in under instruction to undertake any protracted conversation with Leticia's husband outside the room itself.

They slipped through the door, the nurse closing it after them, and stood at the back of the room, hands instinctively clasped in front of them like observers at a funeral. Ben had pulled up a chair so that it was almost touching the bed in which the pale figure of Leticia Bryant was lying, like a waxwork of herself. He was holding her left hand with his right, his other hand resting on top, the thumb gently moving across the prominent bones and veins with what looked like genuine, unforced tenderness. Hargreaves cleared his throat before speaking.

'Mr Bryant?'

This was said almost in a whisper, but it didn't prevent Ben Bryant's head from swivelling round towards the two officers at the back of the room as though it had been shouted out.

'What the hell are you doing here?'

'We'd like to have a little chat with you, Mr Bryant, if that's OK with you?'

Ben stared at them as though he didn't understand, then turned his head slowly to the hospital bed again.

'As you can see, I'm more than a little occupied here trying to bring my wife back to consciousness. Speaking to the police is not top of my list of priorities at the moment.'

'I appreciate that, sir, but we have a number of important questions we need to put to you. As a lawyer, I'm sure you know how these things work.'

Ben said nothing, smoothing down Leticia's forehead with the back of his left hand.

'We wouldn't need to speak to you for long, Ben. You'd simply be helping us with our enquiries.' This from Laughland, who'd decided to soften the approach a little.

'And if I don't co-operate? If I think the best use of my time is to stay with my wife at the moment of her greatest need?'

'Are you saying you're not prepared to talk to us, sir?'

'I suppose that's exactly what I'm saying.'

'Then we might have to consider an alternative approach.'

Ben's head swivelled round again. He already knew what

Hargreaves' words implied, but he wasn't about to make it easy for him.

'An alternative approach?'

'Yes, but I'm sure we can find a more amicable way of dealing with this.'

'It sounds as though you're considering arresting me, but that would be utterly absurd, so that can't be what you mean.'

'We'd rather not go so far as to arrest you at this point in time, Mr Bryant.'

'Arrest me for what?'

'Since you ask, Mr Bryant, for the murder of your lover, Ms Jennifer Ormiston.'

An hour later, Benjamin Bryant was sitting opposite Hargreaves and Laughland in the same room at the station where the two officers had hurriedly convened earlier that day. As a lawyer, Ben had understood immediately that the best thing he could do was co-operate without pushing the police to arrest him under suspicion.

'Thank you for agreeing to speak to us, Mr Bryant. Under agreed protocols, we won't be recording this interview, since it's entirely informal. You're free to leave at any point.'

'I understand all that.' He looked at his watch. 'Can we get on with whatever it is you need to ask me?'

'Of course, Mr Bryant.'

Hargreaves reached down to the floor, keeping his eyes fixed on the eyes of the man opposite him as he did so. He held up a slim smart phone, directing its smooth screen towards his interviewee briefly before placing it very deliberately in front of him.

'Am I supposed to recognise this phone, inspector?'

'I'm not sure. It's certainly possible you might. It belongs, or rather belonged, to Jennifer Ormiston. You might be interested to know that we've managed to extract the recent text messages and emails from this phone. One such was from Ms Ormiston to you, Mr Bryant. It was a threatening email, saying she would embarrass you in a variety of inventive ways if you didn't continue your affair with her.'

'Yes, I showed the email to Sergeant Laughland here, inspector.'

'So you did, Mr Bryant. However, when my sergeant here asked you if you'd replied to the email, you answered in the negative.' He paused, watching the effect of this on Ben Bryant's face. 'We know now, however, that you did reply to it. Perhaps I can read part of your reply to you?' He reached down towards the floor again, but Ben spoke before he could get there.

'I can save you the trouble, inspector. I admit to lying about the reply. It was a stupid thing to have done. The phrase I used is seared into my brain, so there's no need to read it back to me.'

'OK, well, in that case, could you please explain to us what you meant by "you'll find out just how abusive I can be"?'

'As I remember, I was referring to the possibility that Jennifer might have had something to do with the abduction of my wife from the secure hospital in Sussex. It seems ridiculous now that I could have thought that was a serious possibility, but, at the time, I was angry with her, and tired, and, as a result, used a word I shouldn't have used. It was of course a word she'd used in her own email to me, so I was, I suppose, childishly throwing it back to her.'

'Do you not agree it might be taken as a threat to rape her or commit some other assault on her?'

Ben leaned forward, his fingers massaging his forehead. He exhaled deeply.

'I know how it looks. It's why I lied about it. But all I can say is it was a heat-of-the-moment thing. At that moment I hated her more than I've ever hated anyone in my life. It was an expression of that. I had no intention of carrying out any kind of assault on her.'

'Well, that's good to know, Mr Bryant. Unfortunately, though, someone certainly did have such an intention, and did carry it out. Let me take you back to that interview with Sergeant Laughland here. The interview took place at around nine-forty in the morning. Would you agree that that was the case?'

'Yes, I suppose it must have been something like that. I'd just finished with a client earlier than expected.'

'And that meeting with a client, I take it, had been fixed some while before?'

'Yes, of course.'

'And yet you mentioned that you'd contemplated not coming in to the office at all that morning?'

'I may have said that, I can't remember. It wouldn't surprise me. I certainly recall waking up very early in the flat and thinking it would be incredibly difficult to concentrate on work with Leticia still missing.'

'And yet you did come in and meet the client as planned.'

'Yes, by eight-thirty I realised staying at home on my own would be worse than getting on with things as normal.'

'So, let me get this clear, Mr Bryant – you woke very early, shall we say five-thirty, six?'

'I didn't look, but it must have been about that.'

'And you then spent two or three hours wondering whether you should come in to the office or stay at home?'

'Yes, I suppose that's right.'

Hargreaves held Ben's gaze for a few seconds, then looked to one side, engaging with Laughland's suspicious eyes. It was a critical moment, but Hargreaves knew where they had to go next.

'I'm going to put a rather different scenario to you, Mr Bryant. Sergeant Laughland and I think it's entirely possible that you spent that two or three hours doing something very different from contemplating your fitness for professional duties. We think it's very likely you went to see Jennifer Ormiston in an effort to sort out the mess of your relationship with her for good. You had no difficulty seeing her. She gets up early for her morning radio show and doubtless she'd have reckoned on her ability to seduce you once you were inside the flat. What happened next we can only conjecture. Let's say she answered the door of the flat wrapped in a bath towel, let's say it slipped to the floor. But you weren't having any of it. An argument ensued, during which you left her in no doubt that things were quite definitely over between you.'

Hargreaves stopped. He'd spoken quickly, giving Ben no space in which to interrupt, but now he wanted to gauge his reaction.

'This is ridiculous.' Ben looked from Hargreaves to Laughland and back again. He had folded his arms tensely and hunched his shoulders. 'The two of you have obviously cooked up this fantasy between you. It has absolutely no basis in reality.'

'Well, let's move the fantasy on one stage further, shall we? Let's assume that the argument lasted a good while but that, at some point, your wife appeared on the scene. What she'd planned beforehand to say or do we can't know, not at the moment at least, but let's say that, finding you there, the argument widened out to the three of you. Whatever was said to Jennifer, it incensed her so much that she came for Leticia, striking her on the back of the head as your wife was attempting to run away.'

Ben stood up abruptly, leaning on the table and swaying slightly. Laughland made to get up himself, in case their interviewee was about to keel over, but Ben seemed to recover himself quickly and sat down. When he spoke again, there was repressed anger in his voice.

'OK, let me finish this absurd fiction for you, inspector. I imagine the idea is that I reacted to Jennifer's attack on my wife by killing her, is that it? And then, having left my wife wounded and unconscious, I returned to my flat with bloodied clothes, got rid of them somehow and calmed myself down sufficiently to put on a suit and tie, meet a client and then speak to your sergeant here as though I had no idea about any of these events.'

Hargreaves said nothing, simply holding out his hands as if to suggest that the man in front of him might well have described very accurately what had happened. A silence established itself in the room. Laughland looked carefully at Ben Bryant. The anger had been turned off as though by a switch. The lawyer was about to take over.

'It goes without saying that these allegations are nonsense. But they are serious allegations, nonetheless. It's interesting that you haven't arrested me; that tells me you're rather less than confident about your fantasy scenario. I could, of course, withdraw my co-operation, get up from this chair right now, walk out of the police station and return to my wife's bedside, which is where I should be at the moment. I wonder, if I did that, whether it would cause you to arrest me? It might, I suppose, but you might decide the risks are too great.' Ben Bryant sat back in his chair, arms folded. 'There's such a thing, after all, as wrongful arrest.'

He looked at the two officers in front of him. Laughland's face betrayed a mixture of puzzlement and fascination, whilst Hargreaves' face showed only contempt.

'So I propose we cut to the chase.' He reached into the side pocket of his jacket and produced a set of keys which he placed with theatrical care in the middle of the table where they sat like unexploded ordnance in no-man's land. 'These will let you rummage around to your heart's content in my flat and car. You won't find anything, of course, but at least we'll know where we stand. Meanwhile, I suggest you lift me back to the hospital and continue to keep me under surveillance there. How does that sound? That way, I can be with Leticia and you can satisfy yourselves as to my innocence.'

Laughland looked at his superior officer with alarm. Harry had begun to lean slowly forwards as though about to propel himself across the table, and his sergeant was coming to the uncomfortable realisation that he might have to restrain him. Instead, Hargreaves' right arm shot out and grabbed the keys from the table.

'Sergeant, you heard Mr Bryant. I'll get the searches under way, you take our friend here back to the hospital. But, may I suggest, purely as a goodwill gesture on your part, Mr Bryant, that you provide us with a DNA swab before you go? Unless you have any objection, of course.'

'No, I suppose not. Why would I?'

'Oh, and, Sergeant Laughland, make sure they're expecting you at the other end, and don't let Mr Bryant out of your sight until you've handed him over. Understood?'

'Perfectly, sir.'

Nine

The drive back to the hospital took place in complete silence. Laughland somehow managed to concentrate on the route whilst his mind thrashed around trying to make sense of what was going on.

There were, he decided, three Benjamin Bryants. There was the dutiful husband who'd married into money and who'd found himself twice by the bedside of a wife whose mental illness had resulted in the abduction of a child, an attempt at suicide and a probable confrontation with a self-assured local celebrity that had somehow resulted in her own serious injury. Then there was Ben Bryant the lover, the man who'd had an affair with his sister-in-law and fathered a child, the man who'd desperately tried to resurrect that affair and who'd gone on to have a second affair with the woman with whom his own brother had had an extra-marital relationship. Somewhere, under both these, there was Ben Bryant the lawyer, the young partner of one of the oldest law firms in the south-east, a man, like all lawyers, with a shard of ice in his soul.

The question was, which of these could have murdered his lover and left his own wife for dead?

Of course, he knew the answer to the question; the

chances that any version of the man sitting beside him in the passenger seat had committed murder seemed so small as to be negligible. Even though Laughland himself had come up with the possible sequence of events that might have suggested otherwise, it just didn't feel right. And now Ben had voluntarily given them access to his flat and car; if he was the man they were looking for, he was taking an absurd risk.

They pulled up in a bay of the hospital reserved for emergency vehicles. Still silent, Ben went to remove his seatbelt.

'One second, Mr Bryant, Ben, if you wouldn't mind.' Ben's left hand returned to rest on his lap. 'I'd like to ask you a couple of further questions before we go inside. Shouldn't take long.'

'That wasn't the deal.'

'I know, but still, if it's OK with you…'

'I don't really have much choice, do I?'

'During the time you were having a relationship with Jennifer Ormiston, did she ever talk about the anonymous letters she'd received?'

'Anonymous letters?'

'Yes. She received two letters asking for a sum of money, but not specifying how it was to be paid. As a matter of fact, your sister-in-law also received a very similar letter.'

'Oh?'

'Yes. Your brother reported it to the police. The thing is, Mr Bryant, the letters refer to something in Jennifer Ormiston's past, but they also refer to you and the relationships you've had with your sister-in-law and Jennifer Ormiston herself.'

'Right. Well, neither Louise nor Jennifer said anything to me about these letters, and I can't see how anyone could have found out about what happened between me and Louise and me and Jennifer. I mean, none of us is stupid, we kept things pretty discreet. That was why Jennifer's insane, threatening email was so infuriating. She had no right to do that to me.'

'No, of course. So, when you say you were discreet…'

'Well, Louise and I always met at my flat. Except right at the start.'

'Right at the start?'

'Yes. I'd almost forgotten, but Louise and I first met at the Tollgate, that place just outside town. That was before, well, I tried to help her get pregnant by providing her with a sample, but that didn't work, so…'

'So it turned into a full-blown affair?'

'That makes it sound pretty sordid; it was never that.'

'No, OK. And with Jennifer?'

'The same, actually, in terms of where we met at the start.'

'The Tollgate again?'

'Yes. After a while, we met at her flat, but we decided not to at first. How ironic all that discretion seems now.'

'Yes, it must do. Well, I think that's all for the moment.'

Ben reached for the seat belt again, but left his hand on the clip. He looked with rather pathetic eyes directly into Laughland's face.

'You don't think I killed Jennifer, do you, or that I walked away from my wife in that state?'

How to answer?

'I think either you had nothing to do with those things, or

you're the most supremely confident murderer I've ever had dealings with. So, shall we go in?'

Back in the hospital car park, having handed Ben Bryant safely over to the care of the on-duty officer and ward sister, Laughland sat in thought for a minute or so. He gave a silent nod to himself in the front mirror and pulled out his mobile. He realised the number he wanted was still saved from his investigation into the disappearance of Samuel Bryant.

'Hello, yes. I wonder if I could speak to Edward Bryant, please. This is Detective Sergeant Timothy Laughland. There's an ongoing investigation I need to speak to him about.'

It took a while before the Head could be consulted, and then a further wait whilst a teacher not in the classroom could be found to cover. Eventually, the slightly irritated voice of Edward Bryant came through to Laughland's phone.

'Hello, is that Edward Bryant?'

'Yes, of course, who else would it be? Is this about the threatening letter? Have you found out who sent it?'

'Not yet, Mr Bryant, but this call is part of my investigation into that very thing.'

'Right, well, good, OK.'

'So, first of all, Mr Bryant, are you somewhere reasonably out of earshot of students, colleagues and support staff?'

'Yes, I'm in the isolation room.'

'OK. You'll recall that, during my work on the disappearance of your son Samuel, I became aware of your relationship with Jennifer Ormiston. I believe we spoke about it, just the two of us, at your house. Sadly, as I'm sure your wife has told you, Ms Ormiston has died under suspicious circumstances.'

'Yes, it was quite a shock. I mean, our relationship ended messily and I came pretty much to hate her for how she behaved afterwards, but still…'

'Yes, I understand, Mr Bryant. What I need to know, and this might be useful both in my investigation into the source of your wife's threatening letter and in my work on the Ormiston case, is how it might have happened that your relationship with Jennifer Ormiston came to be known to a third party.'

'Well, yes, it's something I've asked myself, over and over. Jennifer and I were very discreet; it's unlikely anyone could have found out about our relationship.'

He stopped, the sound of his breathing indicating he was thinking through what happened between himself and his ex-lover. Laughland, of course, heard the echoes of Ben's words not twenty minutes before.

'So, your, what shall we call them, liaisons happened at places other than Jennifer's flat?'

'Yes, and we were very careful to leave separately, communicate via an email address known only to us, all that.'

'When you say "leave separately", Mr Bryant, what do you mean exactly?'

'Well, leave the hotel. We used to go to the same place and even used the same room wherever possible.' He paused. 'I suppose that wasn't so clever, now I think about it.'

'And that place would be…?'

'The Tollgate, just off the road to the coast going east. I think we knew it had a bit of a reputation, but there were never any questions asked, so it's where we went. Why, d'you think that's relevant?'

'It might be, Mr Bryant, it might be.'

'You'll let me know immediately if you get anywhere, won't you, either with Jennifer's death or the letter?'

'Yes, Mr Bryant, you can rest assured on that score.'

Ten

'And you think it's the Tollgate that's the important connecting factor here?'

'It looks very much like it, sir. My feeling is that's where the letters come from. Whether the person who sent them is also our man on the CCTV at Fieldview Lodge is another question.'

'If it's one and the same, then we're definitely looking for a man. If it isn't, we could be looking for a male or a female and anyone from the manager to one of the room staff.'

'That's true, sir. Either way, I think we should pay a visit soon-ish.'

'Agreed. The awkward thing is, the ACC's decided to hold a press briefing this afternoon. He's worried that stuff will start to seep out on social media and wants the hacks to get the facts right.'

'A press briefing rather than a conference?'

'Yes. I gather a statement will be read out and no questions taken. Of course, that won't stop them trying, and the whole thing could be a shambles and counterproductive.'

'In what way, sir?'

'Well, you know, it's harder for the press to lie about what's happened and what we're doing about it if the questions they want to ask happen in open court, as it were. Plus, and more importantly, when the briefing's percolated through to the local press, radio, TV and the internet, it could precipitate a further attack.'

'On Louise Bryant, you mean?'

'Yes, or another woman altogether. Of course, it all depends on what we're looking at here, a nutter or someone with a specific grievance.'

'Where d'you want me, sir?'

'With me and possibly a few colleagues, Laughland, at the Tollgate.'

'And the briefing?'

'The ACC will have to do that on his own, with a few of his lackeys. I'll make sure he's properly briefed, of course. Plus, thinking about it, it might be a good idea to have a female presence there. Two brutal attacks on females; it'd be good to have a woman with a reassuring smile, don't you think?'

'Yes, sir. I think I know the very person.'

The briefing was crowded. Word had got around that the ACC was going to be there and that there was at least one killing involved. As the senior police officer in question entered the room, he looked nervous, glancing behind him for the reassuring face of DI Harry Hargreaves and then remembering that he was fronting this on his own. When he got to the improvised platform, he indicated that those accompanying him should sit down whilst he himself remained standing. He was wearing his distinguished service medals, but kept tugging at them to make sure they were firmly attached. He looked to the far end of the table and saw that Hargreaves' suggestion as to a female presence looked the part and gave the whole thing a warmer, less bureaucratic feel.

He pulled out a sheet of A4 paper from his pocket and unfolded it. It was as Hargreaves had given it to him, except for one or two small emendations added in pen, largely, he knew, to give him the feeling that he was the one in charge.

'As you've all been informed, I believe, this will be a press briefing and not a conference. For the uninitiated, that means no questions, however much you might want to ask one.' He looked up, expecting some kind of reaction, but there was none. 'Therefore, I'd like to read out this brief statement:

Yesterday morning, the body of a woman was found in a dwelling off the Ashfield road. We are still awaiting confirmation from forensics, but we are treating the death as suspicious…'

'Does that mean murder, sir?'
'As I said, no questions…

I can confirm that another woman was found seriously injured at the same address. This second female is recovering in hospital, and we very much hope that she will eventually be able to help us with our enquiries.'

'Is that code for charged with murder?'

The ACC looked up. This was from a journalist he didn't recognise. It was a sharp question, the sort of question you expected from seasoned journos on national red-tops. He decided to say nothing, hold his hand up and continue reading.

'We have CCTV images from the area which we're working with, but they haven't as yet provided us with any useful information, although we have confirmed that the person we wish to speak to is male and under fifty-five years of age. We believe the death and serious injury occurred at the same time, at around six-thirty to seven o'clock yesterday morning.

I would urge anyone who has any information they feel may be useful to police to come forward and contact us. In particular, if any member of the public was aware of a male person acting suspiciously on the Ashfield road early yesterday morning, they should contact us immediately. My colleague here will give you a contact number after the conclusion of this statement. I cannot stress enough that we need to find whoever was responsible for this attack as soon as possible. Thank you for your co-operation.'

He turned to go, leaving the four other people seated at the table uncertain what to do. As he pushed his way as quickly as he could to the door through which he'd entered five minutes before, a voice could be heard above the fusillade of other questions from journalists ignoring the instruction not to respond.

'Would we be right in thinking the dead woman is Jennifer Ormiston, Assistant Chief Constable?'

That same voice again.

The room fell quickly silent. The ACC, one hand on the

door handle, turned in panic before launching himself out of the room and into the safety of his office.

As Edward Bryant was coming out of the isolation room after speaking to Sergeant Timothy Laughland on the phone, the Head came out of his office opposite and called him in. Had he heard what was being said during the phone call? More to the point, had Angela, his secretary? He couldn't see how that could have been the case, but you never knew.

'Edward, a word if you would.' The Head ushered him into the room and indicated he should sit in the usual chair. 'This shouldn't take too long.'

He had in front of him what looked like the photocopy of the pathetic, defamatory note from a student they had discussed at their last meeting. This was resting on an opened double page of one of the yellow exercise books they used in English.

'I thought you should know we've tracked down the miscreant who sent you this note.' He held it up in front of him by the ends of forefinger and thumb, as though the paper itself was tainted in some way. 'Through some excellent work by the English department, we came to the conclusion it was the work of Charlie Fullan in 8B. To be fair to him, he owned up immediately and apologised. I've suspended him for the moment, pending notification to the governors.'

'The governors?'

'Yes, but you needn't be concerned, your name and the details of the note won't be mentioned. The only slightly odd thing was that he claimed to have been forced into writing the note by someone else. I didn't believe him, naturally, but he stuck to his story. When I asked him whether he'd been threatened, he didn't seem quite so sure, but made up something about feeling 'shit scared', as he put it. The parents have been in, supporting his story, but I've told them that, as far as I'm concerned, the matter is resolved, the only thing left to be decided being whether we convert the suspension to full expulsion.'

'That seems a bit harsh, perhaps.'

'You may be right; I'm certainly recommending to the governing body that we stick at suspension.'

'If you want me to have a word with Charlie myself, or to the parents…?'

'No, I don't think that would be a good idea, Edward. It's drawing a line time, I think, definitely drawing a line.'

Eleven

To say that PC Nicola Gray was chuffed when Laughland asked her to be present at the press briefing would be to seriously underestimate what the opportunity meant for her. It was, she'd said, a win-win situation; no need to worry about actually saying anything, just smile sympathetically and be supportive. Who knows, someone might ask who the nice policewoman was at the end of the table. But did he think it was demeaning to be the token female with no voice? He'd let her sort that one out in her own head, he said.

This conversation with Nicki was still running through Laughland's mind as he sat with Hargreaves in the last of the school-run traffic on the ring road, which was bumper-to-bumper for a while. Once they'd negotiated the two sets of traffic lights, though, Harry opened up to fifty along the straight stretch of the coast-bound road, now and again glancing in the mirror to check that the larger, black vehicle behind them was keeping in touch.

Turning off at the roundabout that marked the outer limits of the city in this direction, they were soon in the forecourt of the Tollgate Inn, though it took them a while to find a parking slot. The van behind them simply came to a halt outside the entrance, waiting for Hargreaves to come across before the four officers disembarked, as per instructions. The sky was darkening now, the Christmas lights that no-one had thought to remove still blinking as a stiff breeze blew them across the cheaply-rendered exterior like ship's rigging.

Without speaking, Laughland and Hargreaves unbelted, got out and locked back. They went over to the rather sinister-looking but anonymous van, its windows dark but allowing some impression of the figures inside. Hargreaves stepped forward to tap on the driver's-side window which came down immediately.

'Sir?'

'Stay there for the moment. I don't think there's any clear and present, as they say, but one of us will let you know if the situation changes.'

'Sir.'

As the window purred shut, Hargreaves and Laughland were already opening the double doors of the side entrance to the building. The reception area was straight ahead of them and they could see the main bar off to the left, with its sprinkling of drinkers, late or early. There seemed to be no-one behind the desk as they approached, but then a heavily made-up woman in her middle years with badly-dyed blond hair emerged from beneath it, as though preternaturally aware of their presence.

'Good evening, gentlemen. A drink in the bar, would it be?'

'Sadly no.' Hargreaves and Laughland simultaneously pulled out their warrant cards and thrust them forward at the somewhat startled woman in front of them. Her genial face collapsed as though punctured.

'Oh, right.'

'We'd like to speak to the manager, if that's possible.'

'Well, that would be me, for my sins.' An attempt at a smile hovered briefly across her mouth before giving up the ghost. 'You'd better come into the office, I suppose. It's only me on at this time of the day, I'm afraid. I'll need to get someone from the bar to cover. Wait one sec.'

She lifted a hatch and passed through from the reception area into the bar, allowing Laughland and Hargreaves to take in the interior. There was probably a much older building hidden somewhere beyond the magnolia-painted extension work, but it was well-hidden.

'You fancy a night here, Laughland?'

'Not really, sir.'

'No, I expect you bring your conquests back to your smart city pad. Would I be right?'

'It's a while since I achieved anything that could be described as a conquest, sir.'

'I believe you, Laughland, I believe you.'

The manager returned with a rather sheepish-looking young man who didn't seem too keen on being left in charge. She lifted the flap of the hatch and gently encouraged him into the reception area.

'Shall we go through to my office, inspector?'

Hargreaves and Laughland walked down a corridor devoid of natural light, past a lift and set of stairs which, they presumed, led to the upstairs rooms of the hotel. Half-way down this corridor, they were invited into the airless, lightless interior of the manager's office. A flick of a switch brought the single bar of strip light on the ceiling humming into life.

'I'm Jeannie, Jeannie O'Rourke.' Her hand shot out from behind the desk and was taken by each of the two officers in turn. 'Not the most salubrious of surroundings, but there you are. Can I get you a drink? Coffee maybe?'

'No, I think the sergeant and I are OK on that score. May we?'

'Oh, of course.'

They sat down on two chairs that looked as if they were rejects from the restaurant, Laughland having to fetch his from the back of the room. There were framed certificates on the wall for hygiene and customer satisfaction, but Laughland noticed none of them was very recent. There was no computer on the desk, but a laptop lurked in one corner, where there was another restaurant chair.

'My sergeant here has a few questions he'd like to ask, don't you, sergeant?'

'Er, yes, yes, I do.'

Laughland already had his notebook out, ready to record the manager's responses rather than carry out the questioning himself, and this deferral took him by surprise. It didn't take him long to realise, however, that his boss wanted to watch the demeanour of the woman across the desk closely as she answered his questions. Laughland slowly shut his notebook and placed it on the edge of the desk.

'It's likely the news won't have reached you yet, Ms O'Rourke, but we're investigating an attack on two women in a flat off the Ashfield road. One of the women has, sadly, died, and the other is in a serious condition.'

'Oh, I'm very sorry to hear that, of course, but I don't see…'

'We believe the woman who died, Jennifer Ormiston, has stayed at this hotel several times in the past couple of years. She used it as a discreet meeting-place for herself and at least two men. We believe she may have used the same room.'

'OK, I see. Is that *the* Jennifer Ormiston?' The colour had completely drained from her face and the heavy make-up now had a clown-like effect. She reached to her left, pulling out from the desk drawer a packet of cigarettes and a lighter. 'It's probably against the rules, but would you mind if I…?'

'No, that's fine. And, yes, I suppose it is *the* Jennifer Ormiston.'

It took her several attempts to get the lighter to ignite, the cigarette having been removed unhandily from the packet and placed between her lips with a shaking left hand. Laughland sensed it would not be particularly productive for Jeannie O'Rourke to be in a state of complete meltdown, even if he needed to be fairly straightforward in his approach. He very much doubted she was the originator of the letters, though he wondered if Hargreaves was of the same mind.

'I think it might be useful for us to agree on a few things before we go any further, Ms O'Rourke. This hotel has something of a reputation for servicing the needs of those wishing to carry out sexual liaisons, if I can put it like that. Indeed, it was, I believe, the subject a few years ago of a minor investigation into the facilitation of sexual encounters with trafficked sex workers.'

'We were completely exonerated. No action was taken.'

She had straightened her back and propped her hands on the table in a gesture of defiance, the coils of cigarette smoke drifting unpleasantly across Laughland's nostrils.

'I believe that was the case, Ms O'Rourke, and we're not here today to pursue any further enquiries in that regard. We'd simply like to confirm that Ms Ormiston stayed here and that you were aware that she entertained men in one of your rooms during the day.'

'Yes, yes, she stayed here. Doubtless there were visitors, but we don't object to that, as long as they don't stay overnight.' She leant back in the creaky, high-backed office chair in which she was sitting and took a long draw on her cigarette, seemingly more relaxed.

'We're not questioning your policy on guests, Ms O'Rourke. The thing is, however, in our search of Ms Ormiston's property and at one other location, we found threatening letters about the private life of Ms Ormiston and that of three other people of her acquaintance. We now believe that this hotel is the thing all these people have in common. It appears Ms Ormiston used it for liaisons mentioned in the letters, and that a third person, also referred to in one of the letters, used it for a similar purpose.'

Laughland was swimming freestyle here, trying as far as possible to maintain anonymity but also provide Jeannie O'Rourke with enough background for her to see the point of their visit. He realised there was another reason why Harry had handed this over to him – it was bloody difficult.

'I see.'

'So, to put it plainly, Ms O'Rourke, what we need to find out is who, amongst the staff at this hotel, would have known in enough detail about what Jennifer Ormiston and the others were up to in order to blackmail them.'

'Blackmail? So what's the connection with the attacks?'

Hargreaves couldn't help butting in at this point.

'Blackmail can turn nasty, Ms O'Rourke, especially, as in this case, when the perpetrator has made a complete mess of it.'

'I see.' Jeannie O'Rourke's eyes flitted between Laughland and Hargreaves, not quite sure where to focus. Laughland took up the thread again.

'So, what we need you to tell us is who had the best chance of finding out what was going on.'

Jeannie took a long, thoughtful drag on her cigarette before stubbing it out, half-finished, on the saucer of an empty coffee cup.

'Well, there's me, of course. I knew that woman had been here, but beyond that I had no knowledge of what went on up in the room. If I started interfering in all that, I'd never get my job done.'

'OK, we'll take your word for that for the moment. Who else?'

'I suppose you might say whoever's prepared the room amongst the room staff. But, actually, they're all under strict instructions not to disturb guests once they've signed in. Of course, if something was left in the room afterwards, there'd maybe be an opportunity to get hold of embarrassing information that way. On the other hand, I make it very clear to staff they need to hand in anything found in the rooms. I've not come across any member of the room staff since I've been in charge here that's not done that.'

'OK, but I should warn you it's certainly something we might need to follow up later. So, who else are we talking about?'

'The obvious, I suppose – the reception staff. They know I trust them to be discreet, but they also know I'm usually around and about and that not much escapes me.'

'I'm sure. Nevertheless, what kind of knowledge or information might someone serving on reception be able to get hold of, assuming they were able to avoid your professional scrutiny?'

'Well, quite a lot, I suppose. Every guest has to fill in a card, and this information is then entered on computer by the receptionist. A bank card number is required for security purposes; all above board. Then there's the room itself. Usually, the receptionist will show the guest up to the room and chat to them in the lift or on the stairs, the landing, that sort of thing. Naturally, they'd be aware of any extra guest who came in, too, and which room they entered. If they showed them to the room as well, they might observe what happened between the guests. It's not unknown for gossip to spread, I'm afraid. That's why I take particular care as to who I appoint in that role.'

'I see, that's very useful. So, you're happy with the staff you've got at the moment in that position? I imagine none of them is full-time?'

'The hotel business is tough, sergeant; we do the best we can for the staff we take on.'

'OK, so you've no concerns about your current reception staff?'

'Not really. Of course, there's Jake.'

'Jake?'

'Jake Armstrong. He's quick and pretty good with the guests, but I've had to speak to him once or twice.'

'About?'

'Inappropriate remarks about the guests, particularly women. But he knows I've got my eye on him. He's pretty good at the online side of things; that's not my forte, sergeant.'

'What kind of remarks are we talking about here, Ms O'Rourke?'

'Nothing very much. The odd disparaging comment, references to the way they look, how they behave. Not usually to their face.'

'And you were happy to keep him on?'

'As I say, he keeps us afloat on the online side of things; he's useful to me, what else can I say?'

Laughland looked across at Hargreaves and exchanged a raising of the eyebrows. They knew each other well enough by now to realise they were sharing the same thought. If the letters were sent by Jake Armstrong, it might not have been the first time he'd used blackmail to his advantage, a previous victim perhaps sitting opposite them right now.

'OK, Ms O'Rourke, I think we need to go and see Mr Armstrong; do you have his home address?'

'Well, I do…' She looked at her watch. 'But it might be simpler for you to stay exactly where you are. He's on duty in about ten minutes. Usually arrives a few minutes early.'

'Right, Jeannie, I want you to go back out to reception, send the young man who's covering back to the bar and, as far as possible, do whatever it is you usually do in the way you usually do it, OK?' Hargreaves had taken over again. 'We'll stay in here and come through to reception when Jake's behind the desk. Keep him chatting for a bit, that might be useful.'

'OK, I'll do my best.'

'Your best would be good, Jeannie. After all, we wouldn't want to probe too deeply into any information Mr Armstrong may have that secures his position here…'

It was twelve minutes later and, from what they could hear, Jake Armstrong had still not turned up. Hargreaves asked Laughland to investigate surreptitiously what was happening in reception, but his silent, questioning gesture to Jeannie was answered by one which suggested she had no idea where Jake was.

In the office, Hargreaves received a call from a DC in the van parked directly outside the entrance. He'd forgotten about the van, or at least where it was parked, and knew he wasn't going to like this.

'Sir?'

'Yes?'

'Thought you'd like to know. About thirty seconds ago, a young-ish male, IC1, approached the entrance to the hotel. As he was about to enter, he turned and looked at the van. It seemed to spook him. He turned to the entrance again, but then walked round the side of the building and across the outdoor drinking area. From there, we lost him in the dark. Did you want us to pursue, sir?'

'Yes. Get a couple of men to follow across the outdoor area and beyond. If you can pick up anything without using torches that would be helpful – we don't want to alarm him any further. If not, it's more important we get hold of him than we put him at his ease. Also, bring up a map of the area and look to cut him off somewhere by road. You know the drill.'

'Yes, sir. Thought you might say that, so we're on it already.'

'Good, keep me informed.'

'What's that, sir?'

'That, Laughland, was news of our man, approaching the building, seeing the hearse parked smack bang in front of the entrance and deciding escape was the best policy. Shit. Shit. Shit.' Each expletive was accompanied by the heavy detonation of a fist on Ms O'Rourke's Formica desktop.

'Unfortunate.' It was all Sergeant Timothy Laughland could think to say.

'I didn't hear you reminding me we needed to move the damn thing.'

'No, sir; I'm afraid it didn't occur to me, either.'

'Come on, sergeant.' Hargreaves was instantly on his feet. 'We need to head him off at the pass.'

Twelve

Guided by Google and by the intermittent reports from the officers in pursuit of Jake Armstrong across the fields to the rear of the hotel, Laughland and Hargreaves had ended up pulling in behind the black police van that had caused all the trouble in the first place. They were on a bridge over the main south-east railway line. The pursuers had informed them that Armstrong was sticking to a footpath that took a more-or-less straight route across three fields and through a small copse. They had used their torches, but mainly to direct their own way on the path, being guided as much by the sound of Armstrong's half-run, half-walk and his contact with branches and undergrowth in the copse. There was general agreement at the bridge that it would be another five minutes or so before Armstrong drew level with their position, but there was an unspoken awareness of the danger. The path dropped down, gently at first then abruptly, towards the railway line.

'I realise we're not shod or equipped for this, Laughland, but we need to get over the barbed wire fence here, across the field that runs parallel to the line, and block off his route at the other end of the path. You up for that?'

'Yes, sir, of course.' He tried to sound as enthusiastic as he could.

'We'll take the remaining colleagues from the hearse with us, just in case. Come on, Laughland. We've got just about enough time to get across there.'

The four officers found no difficulty at first, making good progress to the left of the dark curve that fell downwards towards the line by keeping their torches focused just to the right of their improvised path. Two minutes in, though, Laughland's shoes began to pick up more and more heavy, wet earth from the ploughed field underneath their feet and he could tell from Hargreaves' heavy breathing that the same was happening to him. As a result, the other two officers in their police-issue boots overtook them.

When they'd opened up a gap of fifty metres or so from Laughland and Hargreaves, however, they stopped, angling their torch beams down below where they were standing. At the same time, the pursuers were approaching from the left, emerging from the copse, their own torch beams flickering out in front of them. One of the officers directly ahead turned and dispensed with all protocols to yell at them through cupped hands.

'He's beaten us to it. Gone down the slope towards the line.'

'Christ, Laughland, this could be messy. I needn't tell you how important it is we don't finish by picking up Mr Armstrong in several pieces. Questions will be asked, Laughland, questions will be asked.'

In the distance, they could see the torches of the pursuers moving to their left, further away from where Hargreaves, Laughland and the two officers from the van were standing, and down the slope towards the line where it curved away to the south.

'What the hell are they doing?'

'I think they've realised where we are, sir. They're forcing Armstrong to move towards us along the railway line. Providing the slope on the other side's too steep and slippery to climb, it could work.'

'Only if we get ourselves down that slope and on to the line. Or, better still, send these guys down there and co-ordinate from up here. What d'you think?'

'Sounds good to me, sir.'

Twenty seconds later, Laughland and Hargreaves were illuminating the slope down which the two officers from the van were edging sideways like two monstrous insects. When they reached the bottom, there was at first an eerie silence. They could see the torches of the two insects playing along the line, the metal rails gleaming icily at their touch. Did they have him in sight? Even if they did, they wouldn't risk shouting up the slope. It was a simple question of letting them get on with it.

And then the noise came. A soft, distant humming at first, and a singing in the rails. They looked to their left. The worst possible scenario was about to unfold below them. The lights of the oncoming train at first lit up the bank a hundred metres up the line, then struck them blind as it came round the corner. The engine sounded its horn, a habitual warning that was unlikely to make much of a difference now. Hargreaves and Laughland watched helplessly from the top of the bank whilst the train scythed through, under the bridge and away to the East Station. In a few seconds, the silence had restored itself.

Laughland found it difficult to stop his head filling instantaneously with images of body parts, of a blood-spattered engine casing, of fellow officers torn apart in pursuit of their duty, and of senior officers, grim-faced, shaking their heads in condemnation of two of their own, officers in whom they had placed their trust and who…

'Laughland, it's just possible we may have got away with this one.'

Hargreaves' matter-of-fact tone disguised his own relief. Ahead of them, two torch-beams were moving from side to side up the bank, the officers holding them emerging from the dark with a young man in their grip, a young man who was staring at the ground and whose thin legs were shaking, barely able to hold his own weight.

The insects had caught their prey.

'No comment.'

This was the leitmotiv, or rather the entire extent, of Jake Armstrong's responses to their initial questions back at the station. It wasn't, of course, in the least surprising.

It had taken some while for everyone concerned to clean up and prepare for the interview. The police surgeon had declared Armstrong fit for questioning, and the duty solicitor had been summoned. Though she didn't look too pleased to have been called in at this time of the evening, it didn't take her long, following a brief meeting with her client, to recommend that he should say absolutely nothing at all of any consequence. Armstrong himself, a thin, pale-faced individual with comically brushed-back hair and a permanently cocky demeanour, had immediately folded his arms as he sat down, in an attempt to demonstrate just how uncommunicative he intended to be.

As at the hotel, Hargreaves took a back seat in the interview room, watching and sizing up. Laughland had an ace up his sleeve; it was a question of when to introduce it into the game. Until that point, with no forensics of any kind yet to go on, the first stage of the interview had been somewhat pointless, though you never knew if or when they would crack.

'OK, Jake, so you're not interested in telling us why you decided not to call in for work this evening and take a walk on the wild side instead. That's fine. Of course, you'll know that your non-compliance is something we can raise if this comes to court, and a jury might be a bit puzzled by your behaviour, don't you think?'

'No comment.'

'Fair enough, then let's cut to the chase, as they say, a not inappropriate phrase in your case. A number of threatening letters have been found at two separate addresses. These letters are very unpleasant in tone and make demands for money to be paid. They're to do with the shadowy past of one particular individual and the extra-marital affairs of three others. What can you tell me about these letters?'

'No comment.'

'The letters were written on a computer. We think this might have been your computer, or possibly the computer at the reception desk of the hotel. Accordingly, we've seized the PC from that area and a laptop, which we believe to be yours, from the office of the hotel manager. It won't be too long before we have clear evidence of what was written and stored on those computers. Do you have anything to say that might help us to understand what we find there?'

'You won't find anything.' The words were out of his mouth before he could think about whether he should be departing from the agreed script. The duty solicitor put a hand on his arm and gave a quick shake of the head.

'Is that "you won't find anything", as in "there's nothing there to find", or is it "you won't find anything", as in "there's something there but you're not clever enough to unearth it"?'

'No comment.'

Laughland's eyes were still fixed on the smirking face of Jake Armstrong, but he could hear Hargreaves drawing a deep breath and shifting on his chair as though he was about to explode into some kind of unhelpful tirade. It was time to up the ante and see what happened.

'It might interest you to know, Mr Armstrong, exactly how we came across two of the letters I mentioned a minute ago. It might not, I suppose, but it might. Let's see, shall we?'

The smirk on Jake Armstrong's face disappeared. He leant back in his chair and folded his arms. Laughland wondered if he'd got under his skin. Maybe just a little?

'If it makes you happy.'

'Oh, it does. The letters were discovered in the flat of a well-known media personality. We were there because the dead body of that same media personality had been found a few hours before. Whilst we haven't had final confirmation yet, it's a virtual certainty that the death will be counted as suspicious.'

'What're you saying?'

'I'm saying that this is almost certainly a case of murder

and that, whilst our investigations have led us in a number of different directions, currently our number one suspect would be, well, you, Mr Armstrong.'

'Me? What the fuck…'

The solicitor's hand was on Armstrong's arm again, this time with a firmer grip. Her face was suddenly taut with concentration. This had escalated somewhat rapidly into a different game altogether.

'My client, as you well know sergeant, is entitled to know definitively what charges you might be likely to bring against him. This suggestion of a much more serious offence is a bit of a bolt from the blue, wouldn't you say? Where's your evidence for any of this?'

'Your client fits the image of a man seen on CCTV entering and leaving the block of flats in question at the time the killing was carried out.' Laughland realised that this was stretching things more than a little. 'We believe he became frustrated at his own inability to get hold of the money safely and panicked. We have evidence that your client has been reprimanded before for misogynistic comments to guests at the hotel, a misogyny that also characterises the texts of both letters. We believe it very likely that we'll find the letters stored on one of the computers being analysed at this very moment, however well Mr Armstrong might have hidden them. Who knows, we might find all sorts of other things on there. It can't be all that long, either, certainly less than twenty-four hours, before we have the DNA evidence from the flat which, we contend, will put your client at the scene of the crime. That good enough for you?'

In contrast to his earlier demeanour, Jake Armstrong

now gave the impression of being very agitated. His hands were rubbing the tops of his knees obsessively and his breath was coming in fits and starts. He leant across to his solicitor and whispered in her ear before returning to his obsessive rubbing once more.

'I'd like to speak with my client alone, please.'

'Of course.' Hargreaves stood up and held out a hand to indicate he would show suspect and solicitor to a private area where such a conversation could be carried out immediately. Things were moving, but it wasn't yet clear precisely in which direction.

'My client wishes to make the following written statement.'

They were back in the interview room again. Armstrong's solicitor pushed a piece of paper across the table to Hargreaves, who positioned it to his left so that Laughland could read it at the same time:

I wish to confess to the writing of three threatening letters, two to Ms Jennifer Ormiston and one to Mrs Louise Bryant. I did not intend to cause harm by them and wrote them as a kind of joke. All the people in the letters came to the hotel and that is the only place I met any of them. I further admit to downloading pornography on my laptop. This was for my own personal use, and was not shared with any other individual. I absolutely deny murdering Jennifer Ormiston or anyone else and you will find no evidence that I did so.

Hargreaves retained the piece of paper, folding it and pushing it across to Laughland.

'Thank you, Mr Armstrong. You've done exactly the right thing in telling us about this. I can assure you that your co-operation will be taken into account if and when you're charged with threatening behaviour and blackmail. However, I regret to inform you that we shall be holding you for a further twenty-three hours whilst we gather evidence with regard to the suspicious death of Jennifer Ormiston.'

'You can't do that.'

'Can, and will, Mr Armstrong. Don't worry, we'll make you as comfortable as we can…'

Thirteen

The news that Leticia Bryant had recovered consciousness arrived via the desk sergeant as Laughland and Hargreaves were leaving the interview room. It was late, and they were both looking forward to signing off for the evening, but an early opportunity to speak to Ben's wife couldn't be ignored, assuming, that is, the hospital would allow them anywhere near her, not something, they knew, they could take for granted.

It was the hospital Registrar, no less, who was waiting for them as they arrived. He led them up to the ward in which Leticia Bryant was being treated, though this was, of course, wholly unnecessary, and shepherded them into a scrubs room.

He had been informed, he said, that they wished to speak to Mrs Bryant and was well aware of the context in which she had received her injuries. This context, he made it clear, was the sole reason he had agreed to their interviewing her at all at this stage of her recovery. There would be a senior member of the nursing staff in attendance for the whole interview. It would be up to them as police officers whether Mr Bryant was present, but, he added, he'd shown less than full compliance when it had been suggested to him that he should leave the bedside of his newly conscious wife. Undue pressure was not to be put on the patient, and any attempt to do so would be met with an immediate request to leave the ward. Mrs Bryant would be provided with a marker pen and white board; as far as possible, her responses should be recorded in this way rather than verbally.

'Bloody hell, you'd better watch yourself, Laughland.'

Hargreaves' words were delivered directly into his sergeant's ear as they made their way to the room in which Leticia Bryant was now propped up in bed, the back of her head encased in some sort of protective device and swathed in bandages. She was smiling wanly at her husband, who looked on the verge of tears as he held and squeezed her left hand. The ward sister entered behind them and gave Laughland a pen and small white board, then stood to one side, hands folded against her pristine uniform. Hargreaves could see it was Ben Bryant they'd have to deal with first.

'Mr Bryant, it's great news that your wife has regained consciousness.'

Ben's head swivelled round as though he'd only just become aware of the presence of the two police officers in the room.

'Yes, it is. But it's no thanks to the incompetence of the police, both here and elsewhere, as I'm sure you'll agree.' With these words, Ben turned again to the woman in the bed beside him whose head had fallen to one side, her eyes beginning to close.

'You'll appreciate, I'm sure, Mr Bryant, that we urgently need to ask your wife a number of questions about what happened yesterday morning in Jennifer Ormiston's flat. We'd appreciate the opportunity to speak to her alone, if that's OK.'

'No, it certainly isn't OK.'

'I understand exactly how you feel, Mr Bryant, but I need hardly remind you that you are yourself still helping us with our investigation into what happened at the flat. You kindly allowed us access to your flat and car, but that's an ongoing inquiry. The hospital Registrar has made it very clear that this should be a short, compassionate interview and that the ward sister here should be in attendance throughout.'

Leticia's eyes had opened again, perhaps alerted by Hargreaves' suggestion that her husband had been involved in the police investigation. Aware of this, Ben lowered his wife's hand gently and released it, rising from his chair and walking away from the bed.

'Whether or not I remain, ludicrously, part of your investigation, I can tell you here and now that any attempt to pressurise my wife to answer your questions in her current state will result in action being taken against you for unprofessional conduct.'

The ward sister opened the door and Ben passed through, casting a glance back at the bed as he went and fixing Hargreaves and Laughland with a final look behind him. The sister snapped the door shut again and allowed herself the slightest of smiles; if she had little time for policemen in her ward, she had even less for lawyers and belligerent spouses. Hargreaves brought a chair from the back of the room and positioned himself to Leticia Bryant's right, whilst

Laughland lowered himself on to the chair vacated by her husband.

'Mrs Bryant, Leticia, we'd like to ask you a few questions about what happened in Jennifer Ormiston's flat. We intend to keep the questions to a minimum, and we won't be asking you anything about what happened before you arrived at the flat yesterday morning. Does that seem OK?'

Leticia looked at first as though she'd not understood, but then turned her head to look at the sister by the door and nodded her head once.

'Sergeant Laughland here – you remember Sergeant Laughland, I'm sure – will invite you to respond to our questions using the pen and white board. It's best you speak as little as possible, OK?' Again, the single nod of the head. 'The first thing we'd like to know is how you sustained your injury, Mrs Bryant.'

She reached out slowly for the board and pen and wrote three words on it in a shaky hand.

RUN AWAY STONE

Laughland ran through the scenario he'd outlined previously to Hargreaves and tried to relate it to what Leticia Bryant had written.

'You were running away, and someone hit you with a stone?'

Two nods of the head.

'And what happened before you were attacked? What did you see?'

Leticia leant back in the bed and began moving her head from side to side. Alerted by this, the sister came forward and pushed between Laughland and the bed, picking up her patient's wrist and taking the pulse.

'I'm afraid you need to stop this interview right now; this patient is hyperventilating and the pulse is too high.'

Fortunately for Hargreaves and Laughland, Leticia suddenly sat upright again, pulling her wrist from the sister's grasp and picking up the board and pen. The concentration on writing seemed to calm her, and the sister, somewhat reluctantly, withdrew a couple of paces to stand at the foot of the bed.

HOOD KILL J BLOOD WATER STONE

Leticia's arm fell from the board and the pen scuttered across the floor.

'The man in the hood, Leticia, tell us about the man. Could you see what age he was?' She gave a feeble nod, but then followed this with a shake of the head, as though unsure. Her left hand flapped ineffectually above the bed.

'She wants the board again.' Laughland bent down and retrieved the pen, placing it carefully in her right hand. Leticia hesitated, the board shaking in her left hand, the pen hovering over its surface, then began to write again.

YOUNG BIG

Leticia dropped the pen once more and held out a flat right hand, palm down, raising it painfully as far as she could above the bed, then used both hands to indicate the width of the shoulders.

'Tall and broad-shouldered, is that what you're saying, Leticia?'

She nodded, then slumped back on the bed, exhausted. Her eyes had closed within two seconds and the nurse was by the bed again, feeling her patient's temperature and taking her pulse. Hargreaves and Laughland looked at one another, each wondering what Leticia had meant by 'young'. It was vague, yet she had struggled to put the word down on the board as though it was important, significant.

'That really is it, now, gentlemen. It's time you left the room.'

Fourteen

The following morning, Laughland was woken at six-thirty by his mobile. He turned to take the call, expecting also to feel the warmth of Nicki's body beside him before he remembered she'd felt too tired to come over.

'Laughland, you awake?'

'A somewhat superfluous question, sir, if you don't mind me saying so.'

'Good point. You need to get in as soon as. All sorts of stuff to go over and forensics due in at seven-thirty. Your thoughts about what Mrs Leticia Bryant told us yesterday would also be much appreciated. Half an hour?'

Before Laughland could reply, Hargreaves had rung off, leaving Laughland to push back the quilt and scramble out of bed into a stubbornly cold flat to shower and dress.

Laughland hoped this tendency towards holding early-morning meetings would be short-lived; his brain was reluctant to work properly until after his first cup of decent coffee. This time, the desk sergeant indicated with a nod of the head that Hargreaves had already arrived and was waiting for him in his office.

'Thanks for coming in so early, Laughland. We've got

plenty to think about and some fresh stuff about to hit us, so I thought we'd better start early.'

'Good idea, sir.'

'I don't think you really mean that, but still.' Hargreaves opened a file in front of him and took out the first printed sheet. 'I've been…'

'So I see, sir.' It was well-known that Hargreaves was an off-the-cuff, seat-of-the-pants copper. This degree of organisation was startling.

'Anyway, first off we need to pool our thoughts on the revelations of our aristocratic young hospital patient. What d'you make of her scribblings on the board?'

'I think we need to take them seriously, sir. I mean, I know there are several factors that might suggest otherwise, but, nevertheless…'

'What factors might those be, Laughland?' Hargreaves looked down at his notes to remind himself of his own misgivings.

'Well, straightforwardly, there's the blow on the head and the recovery, all that. But, then, there's the possibility that she's shielding her husband. The CCTV images certainly don't rule out Ben Bryant, so lowering the age of her attacker might certainly be designed to throw us off the track. I think we can rule out Leticia herself as the perpetrator of the attack on Jennifer Ormiston; the blow on the back of the head makes that impossible. My guess is she went there to have it out with Ormiston over her role in the Samuel Bryant business, but when she arrived things were already out of control.'

'Meaning?'

'Meaning our attacker had already killed Jennifer Ormiston or was in the throes of doing so.'

'Good, yes, agreed.'

'OK, then there's the possibility that she seriously underestimated the age of the attacker. We must assume the two attacks happened very quickly, one after the other, and Leticia Bryant wouldn't be the first witness to get the age of her assailant completely wrong.'

'Right, but despite all that you believe her?'

'Yes, yes, I do.'

'Me too, as it happens. On the Ben Bryant front, I deliberately held back any forensic search until I'd sent over a couple of our most trusted colleagues to look into whether one was necessary at all. Anyone who throws you his keys and lets you get on with it is probably fairly confident you're not going to find anything.'

'So, was anything found?'

'Nope. Car clean, but not obsessively so. Nothing unusual in the boot. Running gear was found in the flat, but not the right colour or type. No Nike trainers, damp and blood-spattered or otherwise. No sign of a washing-machine; presumably well-remunerated lawyers have their clothes expensively dry-cleaned. Piles of newspapers on the floor, bundles of legal papers on the kitchen table, but nothing amongst the mess that drew their suspicion. Given what his wife's just told us, I'm not minded to take that particular line of enquiry further. Of course, if something turns up in the path report, we might have to change our tune.'

'You mentioned that might be with us fairly soon?'

'Yes, any moment now, I hope. As I mentioned before,

Helen's pretty good, if you don't press too hard. I'm having it couriered over.'

'Right. And what about Jake Armstrong?'

'Ah, yes, Mr Armstrong. You know, I sometimes wonder if the law shouldn't be changed to allow us to administer just one punch to the face when such an action is entirely justified. Don't you agree, Laughland?'

'I can't honestly say I do, sir, though I understand your point as far as Armstrong is concerned.'

'We're still holding him, of course, whilst we wait for the report. He's a bit of a better fit than Ben Bryant in terms of Leticia Bryant's age profile, but I don't think most people would describe him as particularly young-looking, even though he is pretty slight.'

'And, if the CCTV is showing us our man, he's a good three or four inches too short. What about the computers, sir, has anything come through there?'

'Yes, indeed. We had a team working on them overnight.' Hargreaves went back into his folder and pulled out a second sheet. 'The threatening letters are there all right, saved on the hotel reception PC. Since he's admitted the demanding money with menaces offence, that's pretty conclusive. On the lap-top, we found the porn he'd already alerted us to, nasty stuff, apparently, violent, weird. But also quite a lot of ultra-right-wing material, racist garbage masquerading as valid, outwardly reasonable political opinion. There was a list of names, with contacts.'

Hargreaves turned the sheet of paper round and pushed it across the table. Laughland scanned the names, hoping he would recognise at least one of them.

'I'm afraid none of these means much to me, sir.'

'Not to me either, but we're having them checked. As to whether Jake's our killer, again we'll have to wait on the path report, but my instinct is there's too much riding against it.'

'I agree. Apart from anything else, I can't see him overpowering a woman like Jennifer Ormiston. She'd be taller than him, for a start, and a good deal fitter. He's more feeble little worm than vicious murderer.'

'Yes, indeed.'

They both realised they'd hit an impasse. Leticia Bryant's description of the male in the apartment, odd though it was, seemed to be the only explanation they had that fitted all the logic and evidence of the case. Of course, thought Laughland, this hadn't even been confirmed yet as a case of murder and attempted murder, and their next move might depend heavily on the forensics report. As he held that thought, Hargreaves' phone chirped into life.

'Yes, Hargreaves here. No, don't worry if your hands are full, I'll come out to you straight away.'

He got up and left the room without a word to his sergeant. Laughland guessed this was the forensics report from Dr Arkwright. In all probability, it wouldn't tell them much they didn't already know or couldn't guess, but it would be useful to know they weren't working entirely on guesswork and instinct. When Hargreaves returned he was clutching a Jiffy bag which he'd already torn open.

'Here it is, Laughland. Looks like there are two copies.'

They sat opposite each other and read the summary page of the report carefully, occasionally looking up to see how the other was reacting:

Summary report of Forensic Officer Dr Helen Arkwright
[Case HAR/SUSD/20/01/28]

As a result of extensive examination of the body of the deceased female (Victim 1) and of the premises in which the body, and that of a second female, not deceased at the time of the writing of this report (Victim 2), were discovered, I can confidently offer the following analysis:

Victim 1 died primarily as a result of drowning, as evidenced by the considerable amount of water in the lungs, though there was also a wound inflicted to the cranium which would almost certainly have induced unconsciousness prior to drowning. I can confirm that the wounds to the left wrist were inflicted post mortem by the kitchen knife found on the floor of the bathroom. Therefore the balance of probability is that Victim 1 died as a result of homicide, not suicide.

Analysis of the wounds of both victims, of the floor of the corridor leading to the bathroom and fabrics in the bedroom nearest to the bathroom suggested that the second, non-fatal, attack on Victim 2 was carried out using the same weapon as that used in the assault on Victim 1, this being almost certainly the ornamental stone found wrapped in a towel in a garden area outside the premises. Analysis of the stone and towel elicited DNA matches for Ms Jennifer Ormiston and Mrs Leticia Bryant, the latter being already on the central database, the DNA of Victim 1 having been recovered from the body of the deceased. A further DNA trace was retrieved from the stone, but this has not been identified. From this evidence, it has also been possible to deduce that the unconscious body of Victim 2 was moved from the site of the attack in the corridor into the bedroom in which she was found, and that the stone, wrapped in the towel, was jettisoned from the balcony adjoining the lounge area. Traces found in this area, in many other places on the premises and on the handle of the kitchen knife used to cut Victim 1's left wrist, match the unidentified trace found on the stone.

The recordable DVD disc submitted to us (enclosed) showed traces of DNA identified as that of Victim 1 (Ms Jennifer Ormiston) and DNA identified from the database as that of Mr Jacob Armstrong. No other DNA traces were present on the disc.

This concludes the summary report for Case HAR/SUSD/20/01/28. Further details can be found in the body of the main report.

Hargreaves had finished his reading of the summary well before Laughland, who had been jotting down the main points, and his own thoughts, as he read.

'Come on, Laughland. What d'you make of it?'

'It confirms our conclusions pretty accurately. There's no mention of Ben Bryant's DNA, so everything points to his innocence. It also seems to confirm that Armstrong isn't our man, either. I'm not sure why he's on the database, but clearly it's someone else's DNA all over the stone and the knife, not his.'

'Done for a minor fracas outside a night club a year or so ago, apparently. It means we can rule him out of the murder and attempted murder, but we've got him for the letters. There's not much point in our looking at the DVD now, other than to amuse ourselves, but someone will have to have a look at what's on there and trace the footage back to either the PC or Armstrong's laptop.'

'You're probably right, sir, but are we completely certain there's no connection between the killer and Armstrong? Might it be that what's on the DVD could suggest a link? I'm not sure we can just leave it to the techies.'

'You just want to get off on it, Laughland, be honest.'

'I thought you might say that. Actually, sir, I think it might be a tough watch, after seeing her corpse draped across the bath like that.'

'You may be right.' Hargreaves dug into the Jiffy bag and pulled out a small, sealed plastic sleeve. 'In which case, I propose it should be your tough watch and not mine, sergeant, if that's OK with you?'

Fifteen

For the first week after her meeting with the Dean, Elizabeth McLevy had felt a weight of responsibility on her shoulders. She'd been asked to keep an eye on the Father, but saw only his abundant calmness and good humour, his desire to put things back on a spiritually even keel. He caught her looking at him once or twice, but simply met her smile with one of his own. He was very different from Father Christian and, whatever his past, she had faith in him. She would forget all about her visit to the Deanery and get on with her work in support of the new Father.

Except, of course, that the serious request made of her by the Dean that day had not really gone away at all, but merely been suppressed. Which was why, on that afternoon in the garden, it had resurfaced suddenly and shockingly, taking her breath from her. She had been sweeping in front of the French windows and could see into the study. Father Davidson was sitting with his back to her at his desk in front of his laptop. He would be working at a sermon, she thought, and went back to her sweeping. But a second look told her that this was not the case. Father Davidson appeared to be watching a film, the kind of film that ought to form no part of the religious life. It must be what they called porn, she thought, and she froze, gripping the handle of the brush until her knuckles were white when she realised what was going on in the film. She looked away quickly, but the impression had burnt itself into her mind.

Needless to say, she held on to this dreadful knowledge, hoping that she would be able to reconcile it with her duty and loyalty, but eventually, as the memory of the serious, smiling face of the Dean pressed on her consciousness, she knew she would have to do something about it, especially when, on a further occasion, the Father slammed his laptop shut in front of her as she approached his desk to clean. To tell the Dean would be a betrayal of the Father, but the right thing to do for her Church.

'Hello, Divina here at the Deanery, how can I help?'

Elizabeth McLevy opened her mouth to speak, but nothing came out. It was a good question; how indeed could she help?

'Hello?'

'Oh, yes, my apologies, hello. This is Miss McLevy here from the Clergy House. The Dean asked me to get in contact with him if…should there be…' She had no idea how to put this, and felt that, in any case, she should be saying it to the Dean himself.

'You'd like to speak with The Dean?'

'Yes, very much, yes, thank you.'

There was a pause of perhaps twenty seconds during which, to the accompaniment of the same tremulous organ music she had heard before, Miss Elizabeth McLevy tried to find the right form of words that expressed not only what she had seen but how she felt about it and what she thought should be done about it.

'Good morning, Miss McLevy, how good to hear from you. I don't believe we've spoken since that day we had our little chat in the Deanery office.'

'No, indeed, Your Reverence. It's that very conversation I've had at the forefront of my mind these last few days.'

'Oh?'

'Yes. You see, you asked me to keep an eye on the new Father and I'm very much afraid, well…Father Davidson is so much kinder, so much more energetic and likeable than the old Father and the parishioners love him, but…'

'I think you need simply to tell me what you have to say, Miss McLevy. There's no one in the office and Divina won't be able to overhear what you say.'

'Well, I'm afraid I saw the Father watching what I believe they call extreme pornography, at least it was extreme to me. I believe it is not the only occasion on which he has done so, and I thought you should know.'

'How did you come to see this, Miss McLevy?' She told him, each of her words tightening his stomach like turns of a vice. 'I see. I'm afraid I must ask you, Elizabeth, whether there were any, any…children involved in what you saw.'

'What a dreadful thought, Your Reverence.' She stopped, trying to think clearly about what she'd seen. 'The truth is, as soon as I saw what was happening in the film, I looked away. I was looking through my own reflection in the window, too, so the whole thing was only an impression.'

'I see.'

'But I don't want you to think I was imagining it.' Elizabeth

McLevy's voice rose assertively. 'It was definitely pornography, no doubt about it.'

There was silence at the other end of the phone for ten seconds or so. She wondered if the line had failed, or if the Dean was about to rebuke her.

'Your Reverence?'

'I'm still here, Miss McLevy. The first thing I want to say is that you've done absolutely the right thing in sharing this with me, and you must let me deal with it myself. You must carry on serving the Father in the usual way, remembering that your work is, in however small a way, also the work of The Lord Himself.'

'Yes, Your Reverence, of course. You can rely on me. But I wouldn't want…I mean the Father has been a shot in the arm for us; it must surely be a moment or two of weakness. We're all sinners, Your Reverence.'

'You're right, of course, Miss McLevy. But, as I say, you must leave this to me.'

After the Dean had replaced the receiver, he found himself gravitating towards the well-used walnut sideboard to one side of the window overlooking the garden. Amongst other items, it contained his favourite sherry. He looked at his watch; it was a little early for his pre-lunch drink, but he certainly felt the need for a large glass of something.

As he sat down in the armchair by the open fire, he remembered this was where he had sat facing Elizabeth McLevy after he'd invited her to come and see him. The request to keep an eye on the new Father had come from him, after all, yet here he was sipping at his sherry and wishing she'd kept her confidence to herself. This shocked him, and he shook his head twice to try to rid himself of the thought.

What to do? The obvious thing was to send it upstairs, but he knew the Bishop would be very likely to take as little action as he could get away with; after all, the idea of appointing someone with the background of Father Davidson had been substantially the Bishop's in the first place, so to take a decisive stance would be tantamount to admitting he'd made a serious professional error.

He could deal with the matter entirely by himself, of course, and this appealed to him as the most humane yet efficient means of getting to the root of the problem. However, in the light of recent revelations about the Catholic Church, this might be seen as brushing it under the carpet, in which case the whole thing could get quickly out of control.

Of course, a moment or two's weakness such as this would normally come under the category of 'minor misdemeanour' and be dealt with swiftly and quietly, but, in Gregory Davidson's case, there was his less-than-salubrious past to consider; if only he knew what had actually occurred and whether it was tip-of-the-iceberg territory.

As he drained his sherry glass, a thought occurred to him. It was an elegant solution. He would certainly have to deal with it himself at some point, but it would be useful and appropriate to share it with one of his oldest, most trusted friends and ask for his advice. All bases covered. He got up, walked to the telephone table and found the number in the well-worn address book. He lifted the receiver, then hesitated, inwardly assuring himself that this was what he should do and working out exactly what he should say.

'Hello, yes, I'm calling from the Deanery. Would it be possible to speak with the Assistant Chief Constable? Yes, of course I'll hold…'

Sixteen

Having considered several rooms at the station, Laughland decided, in the end, to drive back to his flat to ensure that he had guaranteed privacy. Leaving his coat on, he turned on the heating, pulled the kitchen table across to a radiator, opened his laptop and inserted the disc.

It was every bit as uncomfortable to watch as he'd thought it would be. Jennifer looked noticeably younger but still recognisably herself. She had certainly thrown herself into the shoots with some enthusiasm. Some of the clips were solo efforts, but there seemed to be one male participant to whom she, or the producer, turned more often than any other. He, too, had demonstrated keenness in his engagement with the role, as you might say. There was no other material on the disc – no commentary from Jake, no mention of his right-wing pals. Just the porn, as far as he could see.

Concentrating on one sequence in particular, he froze the disc at the point at which it was easiest to scrutinise the features of the go-to male actor. It was a fresh, almost innocent, face, despite what was going on beneath it. A face he knew he had seen somewhere. Somewhere recently.

It was that face.

'I can see you're busy, sir, but you need to look at this.'

Laughland had watched the pornographic sequences again and frozen the images at different points to make sure he wasn't imagining things. Deciding that he wasn't, he allowed himself an hour or so to think through the implications and consequences of what was on the disc before driving back to the station and going straight to Hargreaves' office.

'For God's sake, Laughland, you know my rules.'

'Yes, sir, my apologies. However, this won't wait, I'm afraid.'

Hargreaves executed a few clicks with the mouse and turned from his PC to look his sergeant in the eye. Laughland was prone to sudden surges of intuition, only some of which proved to be useful. The Ben Bryant scenario he'd painted, for example, had turned out to be of no consequence in the end, though the narrative had been plausible enough.

'OK, sergeant, you've got my full attention.'

Laughland approached the desk, sat on the chair opposite Hargreaves and opened his laptop. With no further word spoken, he accessed the disc and froze the image that most clearly showed the face of the male actor, turning the screen round so that Hargreaves had a clear view.

'You'll need to tell me what it is I'm supposed to be looking at here.'

'Sorry, sir, of course, yes. This is an image from one of the porn sequences on the disc we found in Jennifer Ormiston's flat. There was nothing else on the disc, by the way, apart from the five or six short videos, no direct appeals from Armstrong or his cronies.'

'OK.'

'So, I've checked the sequences several times…'

'I bet you have.'

'And I'm pretty sure I know who the male is you're looking at there.'

'Right.' Hargreaves leant forward and squinted at the screen. 'You'll need to enlighten me.'

'The sequences were shot a good while ago, of course, so you need to make allowances, but still…that face is the face of Father Davidson, I'm sure of it.'

'The new Catholic priest?'

'Yes.'

Laughland expected his superior to laugh openly at him, perhaps even to slam the laptop shut and hand it back to him. Instead, he leaned back in his chair and covered his mouth with his left hand, his eyes half-closed in contemplation.

'That's really quite odd, Laughland.'

'Yes, I know, sir, it beggars belief.'

'No, not that. In your absence, something came through from the ACC about the very same individual. Apparently, his golfing pal the Dean has been on to him about following up on concerns about inappropriate behaviour at the Clergy House.'

'Not again, sir, surely. Lightning striking twice?'

'Well, I was told it was to be kept quite low-key but that something ought to be done promptly, if only for the record.'

'I see. This inappropriate behaviour, do we know what it consisted of?'

'Funnily enough, Laughland, a penchant for pornography apparently played a part in it. His background's a bit dark, I believe, not what you'd expect. The Church being inclusive, I suppose.'

While Hargreaves continued to squint at the frozen image on the laptop, Laughland tried to get his head around what he'd found out and what he'd just been told. He'd visited Father Davidson, of course, when the hunt for Leticia Bryant was still on. Didn't he remember the Father's behaviour with his laptop then had been a bit odd? So, a professional man with a dark past finds that past exposed in old porn footage touted by a feeble blackmailer. At the same time, his behaviour is causing concern for some reason. Had he brought his dark past with him, and had he made sure that the woman in the footage could not ruin his career in the Church?

'Don't tell me you think Father Davidson is our killer, Laughland.'

'It seems unlikely, sir, but the concerns are there, and the links with Jennifer Ormiston are there. A professional man whose position is threatened can react in ways you wouldn't expect.'

'But would you describe him as young, Laughland?'

'Not young, no. Fresh-faced, perhaps, for someone of his age. Tallish, though, and reasonably broad-shouldered. Had to be, I suppose, for his performances away from the pulpit.' He nodded at the laptop.

'Quite. Anyway, I sent someone round to make discreet enquiries, nothing too heavy, obviously.'

'Oh?'

'Yes. That young PC I sent round to the Bryants. Just the person, I reckoned.'

'You mean Nicola Gray, sir?'
'Yes, the very same.'

Seventeen

A call to the Clergy House had confirmed that Father Davidson was at St Mary's, but not before Elizabeth McLevy had put two and two together and begged Laughland not to be hard on the Father; she had no idea it would be a police matter and she would never be able to look at the Dean in quite the same way again.

Thus, Laughland and Hargreaves were standing, ten minutes later, on the pavement in front of the Catholic church, considering how to broach the matter with the Father. They had no idea whether PC Nicola Gray would be there or not; she hadn't contacted the station after Hargreaves' request to attend. If she was, the presence of three police officers would seem pretty heavy-handed for what was supposed to be a light-touch visit. On the other hand, if there was something more sinister in Father Davidson's unusual connection to Jennifer Ormiston, such niceties would have to be overlooked.

Hargreaves had needed some persuading, in fact, to accompany his sergeant on what he considered largely a waste of time. It was unusual, certainly, for a man of the cloth to have the kind of history indicated by what they'd seen on the disc, but did the fact he'd been caught watching a bit of porn recently really suggest anything other than the fact that priests were also men? Had he murdered Jennifer Ormiston? He hardly qualified as young and surely the Church was already aware of his past? Laughland's request for back-up for their visit had been met with a straight refusal – that really would be a waste of manpower – but Hargreaves had at least conceded that it would be interesting to know a bit more about the shared past of the priest and the media celebrity and how this had come to the attention of that apology for a human being, Jake Armstrong.

Opening the door to the church on the right-hand side, they heard the sound, some distance away, of two male voices raised in anger. As the heavy door shut behind them, sending a muffled echo through the body of the church, the voices were silenced. It seemed to Laughland that they'd come from the direction of Father Davidson's inner sanctum, where, not that long ago, he'd asked him about the whereabouts of Leticia Bryant.

'I'm following you, sergeant. Churches give me the creeps.'

Laughland led the way round the seats at the back of the church and up the side aisle, past the confessional. The male voices were still silent, but, as they approached the priest's office, a soft, measured female voice could be heard distinctly:

'You've got to stop this now. Just put it down and step away.'

The pitch and tone of the voice were unmistakeable; they were Nicki's, and Laughland's throat constricted suddenly in fear.

As they approached the office, they could see the door was open. At the desk stood the figure of PC Gray, her left hand clutching her right. Seeing them out of the corner of her eye, she turned her head for a split second, then immediately turned back again to whatever was happening on the other side of the room.

'You need to calm down for me and put the knife down, Nathaniel, can you do that?'

No reply.

'Other officers may well be on their way, Nathaniel. It's best you stop now.'

Despite the alarmed expression on Nicki's face, Laughland moved slowly forward into the room, whilst Hargreaves stepped back, making a sign to indicate he was going to call for an urgent response.

A bizarre scene met Laughland's eyes as he came to stand alongside Nicki. In the far corner of the room, Father Davidson was sitting in a chair, his head pulled back, exposing his throat. A sharp, broad-bladed kitchen knife was pressed against it, so that you could see the impression on the skin. Behind the chair, gripping the knife, stood a young man in his late teens. He was tall and well-built, easily able to subdue the Father from his position behind him.

Laughland looked at the face. It was sharp and intensely focused, the face of an intelligence turned in upon itself. The hair was reddish-brown and the eyes penetrative. He wondered why the boy's face seemed familiar, then it all slotted into place, like tumblers in a complex lock mechanism. It was the hair, of course, and the eyes. A way of standing, of looking. A name in a list Hargreaves had shown him and a gap in a CV, a line of stretch marks, pale under bloodied bathwater, the empty space in a personal history unfathomed even by a close friend. Nicki had got his first name out of him; that had been nicely done, though he'd obviously had a go at her with the knife. A split-second calculation told him it all made sense.

'Hello, Nathaniel. It is Nathaniel, isn't it? Nathaniel Dixon?'

'Who wants to know?'

'Detective Sergeant Tim Laughland.'

'How come you got here so quickly? Or at all, come to that?'

'I wanted to speak to Father Davidson.'

'Well, as you see, he's otherwise engaged.' He gave a half-repressed laugh, as though vaguely amused by the situation.

Laughland allowed a short hiatus to develop, his eyes meeting those of the young man behind the chair but also flicking down to the throat of the priest in front of him. As he saw the blade press harder against the skin, he knew he would have to break the silence.

'I met your mother once, Nathaniel. That is, I interviewed her. She was full of energy, full of life. And intelligent. It can't have been easy, killing her.'

'She was a slut, that's the only word to describe what she was. And she didn't stop being a slut, either.' He removed the knife from the throat of the priest and began pointing it at Laughland. 'She even seduced that pathetic apology for a Maths teacher. He had to be sorted out, the school had to know. But that didn't work. I fucked up. I shouldn't have relied on that little twat in Year 8, should've just done it myself.'

'But your mother, Nathaniel, did you have to kill her?'

Laughland saw a movement to his left, in the door frame. Hargreaves was holding up five fingers, then nodding towards Nicki. Back-up in five minutes, and they needed to get the wounded PC out of there. He waved a low palm at him, hoping he would understand that everything had to remain exactly as it was at that particular moment.

'You don't understand, I didn't mean to kill her. I explained to her how she'd messed up my life, asked her why she'd had me in the first place; because, she said, you can take the girl out of the Catholic Church, but you can't... and then I asked her why she'd given me away, given me to abusers and cretins. But she wasn't interested in listening to me, and when that other stupid bitch turned up I just lost it. There comes a moment when you know it's all over and has to be finished. I took the nearest thing to hand and brought it down on both their stupid heads.'

'But you made it look like suicide.'

'I wasn't thinking straight. I ought to have realised it wouldn't fool anyone, but I was panicking. And it was so hard, bringing the knife down and across her wrist, the hardest thing I've ever done.'

The memory seemed to weaken him. The arm holding the knife dropped down on to Father Davidson's arm. The priest lowered his chin and looked at Laughland, as if suggesting he might grab the boy's wrist now it was limp in front of him. Laughland shook his head – it was too risky. As if to confirm this, the arm holding the knife was suddenly stiff again, and the other arm pulled back the priest's neck as before, so the blade was once again pressing into it.

'One thing I don't understand, Nathaniel, is the business with the right-wing group and entrusting the pornographic archive stuff to Jake Armstrong. He's hardly in your league, is he?'

'That's the funny thing; it was Jake who came across the footage, not me. Nothing much else to do in that seedy place out there, I suppose. He recognised who the woman was and showed me. Of course, he didn't realise…I encouraged him to set up the blackmail. Anything to punish her. That's when I told Old Willy at school, just to spread it around. At that stage, then, it might have been enough. Of course, Jake went further, tried to be too clever, but still. As for the group, they're pretty much all useful idiots, but there's something behind it, something that needs doing. You see, my mother and this fake priest here, my father, they're just symptomatic really. The whole thing stinks, everything's so degraded. It all needs sorting out.'

The knife was now pressing harder than ever into the flesh of the neck. Any second now, it looked as if it would break the surface of the skin and finish the job.

'I can see how that all makes sense, Nathaniel, I really can. But there's one thing I think you should be aware of.'

'Oh, and what would that be?'

'The man you're pinning to the back of this chair is not your father.'

The hand holding the knife relaxed so that it was no longer touching the skin, but it remained very close to the throat.

'How the hell would you know that?'

'Because I know exactly who your father is.'

The knife moved a little further from the throat and the boy's eyes were moving rapidly in thought. A sudden movement sent a strong left arm under the priest's chin, whilst the knife was pointed once more directly at Laughland.

'You don't know what you're talking about. I worked it all out. She...and him. All the timings are right. It can't possibly be anyone else.'

'Your father's name is Todd Johnson, Nathaniel. He's American. He and your mother had a prolonged, passionate relationship. But they were both young, and Mr Johnson decided, when he found out about the pregnancy, that he didn't want to buy into parenthood at that point in his life, so back to the States he went. The pornography was a side-line for your mother; it, and the man you're threatening here, really played a very small part in her life.'

Slowly, the knife pointing at Laughland was lowered and the grip around Father Davidson's neck loosened. As Laughland had hoped, there was something about the name and the certainty with which he'd fabricated the narrative that seemed to do the trick. He moved a few inches towards the chair in which Father Davidson was wisely remaining completely still, but the boy saw him coming and brought the knife once again to the priest's throat. This time, though, Laughland noticed the blade was shaking.

'What if I just kill him anyway? He's a priest, isn't he? The Church is all part of the stinking hypocrisy of everything. One priest less would be something, wouldn't it?'

'But that wouldn't be logical, would it, Nathaniel? The whole thing wouldn't really make sense, would it? Such a random act is not worthy of your intelligence, surely.'

Laughland had said the right thing, as it turned out, but also, almost, the wrong thing. As though in slow motion, the shaking right hand moved away from the throat and the boy stepped back, leaving Father Davidson feeling at his neck with his left hand. It was Nicki who saw what was about to happen next.

'He's going to cut himself.'

She pushed past Laughland and reached the boy just as he was falling to the floor. The knife had cut into his left wrist, but not deeply enough to cause rapid exsanguination. Nevertheless, he had passed out. For the first time, Hargreaves entered the room, whilst the sound of other officers and a medical team could be heard entering at the back of the church.

'Bloody hell, Laughland, you've made one hell of a mess of the good Father's church.'

'That's one way of looking at it.'

Father Davidson rose from the chair, his left hand still feeling at his throat, and then fell to his knees and vomited copiously into a waste paper basket. At the same time, PC Gray leaned back against the desk and released the grip she had been holding on her right hand. Laughland watched as she saw for the first time how blood from the wound was running down the sleeve of her uniform. She turned towards him and stared wide-eyed into his face, then fell against him. He caught her and led her out to the medics.

'Come on, babe, you're going to be fine. Officer injured here.'

One of the female medics tended to her whilst three others entered the office to deal with the unconscious figure of Nathaniel Dixon, his blood seeping into the Father's Turkish carpet from the wound at his wrist.

'So, you and Ms Gray? I guessed, actually, but…'

'Yes, me and Ms Gray.'

'And why not, eh? She's a brave copper, that's for sure.'

'Yes, yes, she is.'

Laughland slumped into the nearest pew and put his head between his knees. They had reached the end, more by luck than judgement, and now he badly wanted to sleep.

Eighteen

It was one week after the events at the Catholic church. Both Laughland and Nicki had returned from compassionate leave two days ago. Any chance that Harry hadn't disclosed the nature of their relationship was dispelled within five minutes of Laughland's return after he'd breasted a barrage of smirks and innuendoes from colleagues. It would all pass over, he knew; he just hoped Nicki wasn't suffering the same sort of thing in uniform. It was already bad enough for her after the CID course she'd sailed through with flying colours.

He was sitting in Hargreaves' office, the blinds drawn against the slanting late January sun. Harry was behind his desk, hands behind his head, looking reasonably chuffed.

'So, everything's going to plan thus far, Laughland. There's a hundred percent match between Dixon's DNA and the DNA found at the scene of Jennifer Ormiston's murder, so, even without the full confession, we've got a watertight case there. Matricide, though, eh, Laughland? It's the first one of my career and very likely to be the only one of yours, I should think.'

'I certainly hope so, sir.'

'Of course, he's given us plenty of unpleasant details about the various homes and fostering arrangements he's been through. Bullied and interfered with on a regular basis, according to him. It'll all have to be followed up.'

'Are the psychiatrics in?'

'Yes. Perfectly able to stand trial, apparently, which is good news. Trouble is, of course, they'll no doubt plead diminished responsibility. Can't let them get away with that, Laughland. It just won't do.'

'Thing is, sir…the strange thing is that when we had that conversation in the priest's office, with the knife pressing into Father Davidson's neck, I kind of followed what he was saying. I mean, there's no excusing killing your mother and threatening to kill the man you thought was your father, but you couldn't help understanding what drove him to it, you know, the stench of things. I mean, this whole case has been a story of lies, deception, lust, abuse, blackmail. Life pretty much in the raw and not a pleasant smell.'

'You know your trouble, Laughland, you think too much. Always have and, I imagine, always will. It's our job to root out the lies and fumigate the stench, isn't it?'

'You're right, of course, sir, but still…and, speaking of stench, do we know yet what our pornographic priest was up to?'

'Apparently, Father Davidson and Jennifer Ormiston had met up recently. He'd agreed to try to locate the source of the material on the disc. That's his story, anyway. We certainly won't be taking any further action. It's all between him and his Dean now or, of course, him and his God.'

Leticia was now sitting up in the hospital bed. The nurses had removed the bandages and the strange contraption that had protected her skull. She looked, thought Ben, as he sat there next to her holding her limp hand, thinner and older, even thinner and older than she'd looked in the Sussex hospital. She'd always been slim – it was one of the things he'd found attractive in her – but now she looked like her mother, yes, that was it. The slow blink of the eyes, the rather lifeless hair, it was Patricia de Tocqueville sitting there in front of him.

'I've got some really good news, Let. They said I should tell you, that it would be better coming from me.'

'Oh?'

'The police have decided they're not going to press charges against you for the abduction of Sammy any more, and they're not interested in what you were doing at Jennifer Ormiston's flat, given the injuries you sustained and the fact that they're about to prosecute that boy. Isn't that great news?'

He looked at her, and her mouth made a feeble effort to smile. Her hand squeezed his a little harder. Her eyes still looked distant, as though it remained difficult for her to fully take things in.

'Of course, that's partly the influence of your parents. I think your father is in the same Lodge as the Assistant Chief Constable.'

'Yes, well, that wouldn't surprise me. But I expect you're interested, Benjy.'

'Interested in what?'

'Interested in what I was doing in that flat, why I left the hospital.'

'Perhaps, but you can tell me all that when you're out of here; you don't need to go through all that now.'

'But I want to. I want you to know, at least as far as I know myself.'

'OK, I'm here to listen, Let. But none of it will make any difference, either to the police or to me. I'm here for you now, that's all you need to know.' Ben winced inwardly as he said these words; he had said something very similar to her before, some while ago, whilst she was lying in a different hospital bed, and gone on to let her down badly.

'I think I must have been having what the doctors have always referred to as "one of my episodes". It seemed to me I just had to get out of that place and return here to see the woman who had started the whole thing off by telling me about Sammy. The strange thing was, although I wasn't well at that point, I was full of energy and what you might call cunning, I suppose. I worked out exactly what I would do and went ahead and did it. Of course, it was Jeremy who found out Jennifer's address for me and picked me up in his car, but you mustn't blame him, he was a sweetie. I used him, it was as simple as that, just like I used poor Callum who cleaned my room.'

She stopped, pushing back against her pillows to sit up straighter.

'Then, when I ended up standing outside the flats, everything I'd planned seemed to evaporate. I'd been going to hurt her. Not physically, I don't think, but psychologically. It had all been very clear to me. But then…'

'You know you don't have to put yourself through this, Let.' Ben gripped her fingers, so hard that she pulled them back out of his grasp.

'I know. The thing was, of course, I was there, and I'd

gone to a lot of trouble to get there, so in I went. I still find it difficult to remember the exact details of what happened in the flat. I mean, I know what I wrote for the police when they came here to interview me and I feel sick when I begin to think about it, but then the events themselves are shrouded somehow. Sometimes it seems as if the events happened to someone else.'

'But that's good, isn't it? I mean, there are some things it's better not to have a memory of.'

'You're right, of course, Benjy, as you always are.'

It seemed to Ben it was the moment to tell her, though he wasn't sure.

'And there's something, as a matter of fact, that I'd rather not have a memory of myself. Nevertheless, if we're going to have a successful marriage after all this has washed over us, I think you ought to know.'

'Ought to know what?'

'Whilst you were in that dreadful place in the middle of nowhere, I had a brief affair.' He couldn't bring himself to tell her that it was Jennifer Ormiston; that would be too much, at least for now. He felt her hand grip his.

'Of course you did, darling, I knew that.' Her voice sounded with the sang-froid of her mother.

'You knew?'

'Naturally. When you came to see me that time in hospital and cried as you knelt beside me, your face betrayed you, I'm afraid.'

'It did?

'Yes. I think you underestimate your attractiveness to women, Benjy. If a silly little temp at Thurgood's managed to entice you into her bed, I'm not at all surprised. I don't blame you, anyway, Benjy, me being incarcerated, ill or off my head most of the time.' The grip of her hand came even harder. 'But I knew it wouldn't have been anything like what we have, darling, nothing serious.'

'No, darling, you're right, it was nothing like what we have. You're very understanding, sweetie, I don't deserve you.'

'The not-deserving is entirely on the other side, as far as I can see.'

'Well, anyway, it's over now.' A tight silence developed itself in the room. Did she realise more than she was saying? He wasn't sure. 'In any case, speaking of Thurgood's, Old Bill tells me he'll be happy to have you back when you're completely well. I think he's utterly browned off with the brainless fools he gets from the agency.'

'Is that what appealed, her brainlessness?'

'What?'

'Your temp, silly.'

'Oh, probably.' He gave out a guilty and insipid laugh. 'Anyway, I told him I'd be more than happy to have you there, back at the firm.'

'Where you can keep an eye on me?'

'Or where you can keep an eye on me…'

It was a Saturday morning. Detective Sergeant Timothy Laughland was sitting opposite Edward and Louise Bryant as they sat, nervously rigid, on a sofa in their living room. It was exactly where he'd sat when he last visited the house, to ask Louise about the threatening letter and the past she'd shared with Jennifer Ormiston. That time, he'd spoken to Louise alone, but this time he was more than aware of the presence of her husband sitting alongside her, tense and watchful.

'Thank you for agreeing to see me today, Mr and Mrs Bryant. I thought you'd want to know that we've arrested two people in connection with the murder of Ms Ormiston and the sending of the three threatening letters. We're confident that we have the forensic and other evidence to charge both.'

'That's excellent news.' Louise smiled warmly at him, Edward remaining apparently unmoved.

'Yes.' Laughland allowed a pause to fall for a few seconds. 'You may be interested to know that one of those arrested is seventeen years of age and a student at your school, Mr Bryant.'

This stirred Edward Bryant into sudden life, and he leaned forward on the sofa, his head angled in puzzlement, his brow furrowed.

'Oh, really? Which one?'

'Nathaniel Dixon.'

'Nat Dixon? Are you sure? I mean he's a pain in the arse, but…'

'There's no doubt about it, I'm afraid. I'm unable to reveal the finer details of the case at the moment, but he's admitted murder and malicious wounding, and we have the forensics to corroborate his admission.'

'Murder? I thought you meant the letters.'

'Sadly not, Mr Bryant. He mentioned, as part of his confession, that he'd persuaded a younger student to write an offensive note about you and give it to the Head Teacher. Are you aware of such a note?'

Edward looked for a moment as if he would deny all knowledge of Charlie Fullan's illiterate missive slipped under the Head's door, but changed his mind.

'Yes, I am.'

'Edward?' Louise's voice was urgent, alarmed.

'It wasn't particularly relevant to anything outside school at the time, just some little idiot sounding off. I suppose I should have taken it more seriously. It didn't help that the Head seemed eventually quite anxious to sweep it under the carpet, or at least into his covert filing system. Come to think of it, he did mention that the writer of the note claimed to have been forced to do it by someone else, but that sounded like a typical Year 8 fantasy.'

'And what was in the note, if I may ask, Mr Bryant?'

'Just some stuff about the affair I had with Jennifer and some nonsense about her being in porn movies.'

'I see. It's a great shame, of course, that neither your Head Teacher nor you thought to bring all this to the attention of the police. Perhaps if the coercion of the younger boy had been taken more seriously, things might have turned out very differently.'

'Yes, yes, I can see that now, but it's a hindsight sort of thing, isn't it?'

'You could be right, Mr Bryant.' Realising there was little more he could say, Laughland rose from the chair opposite the stiff-looking couple on the other side of the coffee table. 'I take it you've no objection to my asking the Head Teacher for the note? It's another bit of evidence against Nathaniel Dixon.'

'No, if it helps, but…'

'Don't worry, sir, it'll all be handled with great sensitivity, I can assure you. Many thanks once again, I can see myself out.'

A few seconds after the front door had opened and closed, a blond head introduced itself into the room and buried itself into Louise's lap.

'Was that portant police man?'

'Yes, darling, it was.'

'Can Daddy come and play with me upstairs?'

'Of course I can.'

Edward rose from the sofa and held out his hand for Sammy to take, eager to break the claustrophobic atmosphere in the room. Louise hugged her son close for a second and kissed the top of his head before releasing him. As Edward pulled Sammy away from her, she looked up towards her husband, framed for a moment in the lounge door. In the blue flame of her son's eyes, she spoke clearly and slowly, choosing each word with care.

'No more keeping things from one another, Edward, no more evasions, no more lies. There've been too many lies. Here, right now, is where they stop.'

Her husband looked back at her and gave a barely perceptible nod, before moving out of the room and up the stairs, leaving her with an obscure mixture of unconditional love and deep insecurity. She hoped the former would eventually overpower the latter, but she also knew that, just then, this was the painful reality of a life she had to continue to live messily but in some sort of renewed faith. What else, after all, was there to do?

In the car outside the house, Laughland beat a tattoo on the steering wheel, reflecting on the strangeness of the whole thing. In some ways, he thought, it was all about two very different mothers and their children. Sammy had been born out of the desperate need and weakness of Louise Bryant, then abducted, battered and traumatised until finally finding his place in the bruised family he'd just been speaking to. Nathaniel had not had Sammy's luck; his relationship with his mother had been about abandonment and horror, the cold feeling of not being wanted at all. Nothing could excuse murder, but still.

He started up the engine and eased the car out into the quiet suburban road. As he drove, the professional copper in him slowly pushed away the feelings of the son who still had two parents who loved him, whose care had never been compromised, who were proud of what he had chosen to do. As Harry had said, it was their job to go on digging up the roots and making things smell a little less foul, a little less toxic.

The following day, Sunday. An almost pitch-dark early morning.

From somewhere next to him came the sound of a woman sleeping, like the purring of a cat. As he shifted slightly in the bed, she turned and put her right hand on his chest. He squeezed it with his left hand, forgetting.

'Ouch…ouch…ouch.' She was quickly awake and in pain.

'Sorry, darling, I completely forgot.'

'Yes, well.' She sat up in bed, holding her right hand out in front of her until the pain subsided. 'You know you just called me "darling".'

'Did I?'

'Yes. Luckily for you, because of that, you're forgiven.' She leaned across and kissed him on the mouth, holding her hand out of harm's way, before rolling out of bed and moving towards the kitchen area.

'Cup of tea?'

'Yes, great, thanks.'

As she worked, she put on the radio at a low volume. Digital City. She'd need re-educating on that score, he thought. When the kettle had clicked off, he could hear a voice that seemed familiar to him. It was Molly Harrington's:

'Here at DCR, we wanted to pay tribute this Sunday morning to Jenny Ormiston, one of our best-loved presenters, who, as most of you will know, sadly passed recently. "JO", as she liked to call herself, was so much part of us here that the station simply won't be the same without her. That energy, that voice that got us going in the morning is gone.'

'You listening to this?'

'Yes.'

'Jenny will be remembered too by her guests on the programme for her warmth but also for her unflinching ability to ask just the right questions. As a tribute, we wanted to play something by one of her favourite artists, and this seemed the best choice.'

The sound of one of Elton John's most mournful songs, full of abandonment and despair, washed over Laughland as he lay in bed. He'd never really listened to the song before, but at that moment it seemed to fill the cold Sunday air with an all-too-appropriate melancholy.

'Turn it off, Nicki.'

She did as he asked, knowing well enough why it was too painful to listen to, and the Sunday morning silence returned. She came back to the bed and looked at him. In the light from the kitchen, he could see how lovely she was and vulnerable in her nakedness. But he also knew how clever and brave she was, how much he wanted to keep her alongside him whatever happened in the future.

'You cold?'

'Yes, a bit.'

'Then get back into bed and I'll tell you a story.'

'What about the tea?'

'Let it stew. D'you know the one about the prospective Detective Constable and the prospective Detective Inspector?'

She got in and rolled on top of him.

'I can't say I do.'

'Well, it goes roughly like this...'

For exclusive discounts on Matador titles,
sign up to our occasional newsletter at
troubador.co.uk/bookshop